BRÁZIL
RED

Also by Jean-Christophe Rufin

THE ABYSSINIAN
THE SIEGE OF ISFAHAN

BRAZIL RED

Jean-Christophe Rufin

Translated by
Willard Wood

W. W. Norton & Company   New York · London

Copyright © Editions GALLIMARD, Paris, 2001
English translation copyright © 2004 by Willard Wood
Originally published in French as *Rouge Brésil*

Manufacturing by The Maple-Vail Book Manufacturing Group
Book design by Anna Oler

Library of Congress Cataloging-in-Publication Data

Rufin, Jean-Christophe, 1952–
   [Rouge Brésil. English]
   Brazil red / Jean-Christophe Rufin ; translated by Willard Wood.
      p. cm.
   ISBN 0-393-05207-9 (hardcover)
   I. Wood, Willard. II. Title.
   PQ2678.U357R6813 2004
   843'.914—dc22   2004012205

W. W. Norton & Company, Inc., 500 Fifth Avenue, New York, N.Y. 10110
www.wwnorton.com

W. W. Norton & Company Ltd., Castle House, 75/76 Wells Street, London W1T 3QT

1 2 3 4 5 6 7 8 9 0

BRAZIL
RED

I long had a man in my house that lived ten or twelve years in the New World, discovered in these latter days, and in that part of it where Ville-gaignon landed, which he called Antarctic France.

Montaigne
Essays, Book I, Chapter XXXI

I

Children for the Cannibals

CHAPTER 1

"Imagine for a moment what a man must feel, my lord, on seeing the water he'll be cooked in boiling before him."

As he spoke, the sailor cast a morbid look at the embers.

"Liar! Liar!" said the Indian, rising from his seat.

"What? So I am a liar! Perhaps you don't eat your fellow man? Or is it the recipe you dispute, you rogue? It's true, my lord," the sailor went on, once more addressing the officer, "that not all Brazilians proceed in the manner of those who captured me. Certain of them 'buccaneer' the flesh, which is to roast or smoke it. Will you argue with that, gibbet-thief?"

The sailor, with the feeble but resolute strength of a drunkard, seized the Indian by his doublet and thrust his shiny nose at the other's face. The confrontation lasted several seconds, each staring with hatred into the other's eyes. Abruptly the sailor loosed his hold, and they both burst into laughter and noisily shook hands. The bell in the great tower of the Rouen cathedral struck eight, and the cabaret, directly across from the venerable edifice, shuddered at every stroke.

The officer, with his long thin body and bony face, seemed downcast. He was in no way moved by the meeting between these two old friends. He had a mission to accomplish and his impatience was growing. The year 1555 was already half over, and any delay beyond the month of June would see the winds turn unfavorable. He struck the table with the flat of his hand.

"We are aware," he said in an even voice, touched with cold menace, "of the danger of the coasts on which we will land. However, our decision is made: we will sail for Brazil in a week, and there we will found a new France."

The sailor and the Indian straightened on their stools. A remnant of their laughter and the ineffable images summoned by the mention of Brazil gave them a lingering air of irony, though perhaps it was only dreaminess.

"We have no more time to waste," said the officer briskly. "Is it yes or no? Will the two of you agree to join our expedition and interpret for us with the natives?"

The sailor, who enjoyed being stood to drinks and intended to prolong the pleasure, attempted a ruse.

"My lord," he whispered in a drunken voice, "I've said it before: you'll find interpreters aplenty once you are there. We Normans have been going to Brazil for three generations, after the famous red wood that gives its color to the Gobelin brothers' tapestries. Yet the Portuguese have the gall to claim that they discovered the country, when the plain truth is that we have been trading there longer than they."

As no one interrupted him, he grew bolder.

"Within two days of landing on those shores, you'll have twenty fellows from the towns around here come running up to be your go-betweens."

"Must I repeat," said the officer wearily, "that the Chevalier de Villegagnon, who will lead our expedition, wishes to leave nothing to chance. We are bringing everything we will need to found a settlement. We plan to have our own interpreters and be dependent on no one."

All eyes in the inn were fixed on the grotesque couple formed by the frail sailor and the Indian. The sailor recovered his courage first, probably because he was used to sudden changes of tack.

"My lord, you have told us when you sail, which is all well and good. But we are more concerned to know when you will return."

"Never. We will be starting a new province for the king. Those who sail with us will end their days on the far side of the ocean. We will supply them with an abundance of everything, but the word 'return' must lose all meaning for them. They will simply be from France and France will be there."

"Have you ever been to those parts?" asked the sailor, his eyes a malicious slit.

"Not yet," the officer conceded, looking at the sailor defiantly. "But I have visited many other countries, in the East."

The sailor rose, suspending from his narrow rigging of bone the little flesh that life had spared him. Gravely he said:

"I too have sailed in the Orient. A bagatelle! We are almost at home there. The American continent is another matter. Four times I have made the damned voyage. And each time to Brazil, which you now talk of making into a new France. I have seen it all: the fevers, the cannibals, whom I only escaped by miracle, and now these Portuguese dogs, who cut off our hands and feet when they capture our ships. Where do you think I found the strength to come through all this?"

With a broad wave of his arm, a gesture that fortunately carried his mug past his lips, he brushed aside an invisible objection.

"Don't talk to me about riches! Gold, parrots, dye woods—those things fatten the shipowners, who never budge from here. But when it comes to the simple seaman, life is the only thing of value he still has, and even then . . . No, my lord, the one thing that gives us the courage to endure these torments," and so saying he cast a surreptitious glance at the Indian as though that man had been the cause of all his suffering in the New World, "is the hope of returning here."

Resting his two fists on the table, the sailor put all his energy into the last bit of his peroration.

"I am sorry to disappoint you," he said, "but it's as well that you should hear my categorical answer now: I will not go."

The officer bit his lip. In other circumstances, he would have thrashed this stubborn scoundrel. But if he did so, every free man on the crew would pull up stakes tomorrow. That left the Indian, who belatedly realized the fury he would face after his friend's refusal. All eyes now turned toward him.

Despite the heat of the late spring, his shirt was buttoned at the neck and wrists. This precaution derived from considerations neither of comfort nor of vanity. Rather it came from the secret fear of not knowing just how far a man might unbutton himself. In the months that had followed his arrival in France, the poor man had several times been guilty of outrages in this department, unveiling his most private parts in public with the innocent intention of affording them fresh air. Much fun had been had at his expense.

Charitable hearts might have found excuses for him. He had been captured by his enemies while fighting in the forests of Brazil and bought as a slave by French seamen, one of whom was the man now seated beside him. Some Norman merchants, thinking to honor King Henry II, who had announced a pending visit to their province, sent the Indian to France along with fifty others of his kind. On landing in Rouen, he had been asked to dance before the king and queen, clad only in the feathers he had been wearing at the time of his capture. And having appeared naked before the king, he had difficulty understanding why he should cover himself in the presence of ordinary Frenchmen.

"Well?" asked the officer abruptly, breaking a silence in which the Indian's indecisive panting could be heard.

A terrible struggle was going on inside the unfortunate man. The mention of Brazil had flooded him with images of forests, dances, and hunts. The color of the sky in America, of its leafage and its birds, rinsed from his soul the gray of daily life in Rouen. And yet he had fallen in love with this town from the very first day, when he had danced before the sovereigns under a chilly spring rain that mixed voluptuously with his sweat. When he was captured, he thought he would be killed. Yet in France, which prided itself on participating in the Renaissance, he had experienced a renaissance of his own. Freed along with his compatriots on the orders of Catherine de Medici, he had wandered through the streets of Rouen. One afternoon, while lying in the shade of the north tower, he had been noticed by a stout Norman woman whose father was a wealthy barber. She pleaded with her parents until they agreed to take in the Indian, clothe him, and provide him with his daily bread. And one fine day the two were married, along with four other couples of the same composition who had been inspired in part by their example.

The picture of his sweet wife, with her healthy red cheeks, came to the Indian's mind and gave him the courage to push away the seductive idea of a return to his forests.

"No!" he said simply.

This was plain, and his poor command of French hardly allowed him to say more. But the conviction he had put into this one word, and his suddenly fierce countenance, showed clearly that nothing would sway him.

The officer, exhausted from his months of preparations, viewed this final obstacle with despondency. He was not far from despair, as his bowed back, slack arms, and drooping head openly showed.

The entire inn was engrossed in this affair. A great many seamen were gathered there, and all of them had silently followed the conversation. Their muttered discussions now indicated how much each wanted to express his ideas on the subject. Suddenly, from a table near the back, in the darkest and coldest corner of the room, a man who had been sitting alone and unnoticed broke through the sea of murmuring and spoke the four words that would decide everything.

"Why not take children?" he said.

The officer twisted around to see who had spoken. Chairs grated on the floor tiles. Everyone tried to make out the features of the speaker through the gloom. So as to show himself better, the man slid a candle along the table until it rested before him and revealed his face. He was a small, bent man with sparse gray hair, held in place by a taffeta skullcap. Fringing his upper lip was a short mustache, also sparse, that swept up at the ends to exaggerate the small smile on his lips. He waited, still and sanctimonious, for the assembly to take its fill of his inoffensive figure and return to the subject at hand.

"Children, sir? What do you mean?" asked the officer in the over-hearty voice a man might use in addressing a ghost, to convince himself that it exists.

The intruder inclined his head briefly, as an acknowledgment of respect.

"My lord," he said, "it is well known that children have the gift of languages. If an adult is made captive in a foreign land, it will take him ten years to master a few common words. A child will speak the language fluently in so many weeks and without the trace of an accent."

At this remark, his listeners noticed that the stranger himself had a slightly foreign accent. Although he spoke French excellently, a slight hint of the South made him seem at once sympathetic and suspect. It was hard to pinpoint where he came from, whether he had the native pronunciation of a man from Provence or the slight burr that betrayed the otherwise perfect speech of a cultivated Italian.

"And might we know, sir, whence this certitude derives?"

"Why, it seems to me that it is no more than common wisdom and far from anything related to my own person. But as you do me the honor, in effect, of asking my identity, I will tell you that my name is Bartolomeo Cadorim, and that I come from the Republic of Venice."

Some clarifications have a darkening effect. That a Venetian with the look of a priest should be in the port at this time suggested espionage. But the man seemed more amused than troubled by the whispering and muffled hostility of the gathered seamen.

"Captain Le Thoret, Knight of Malta," said the officer in turn. "In the service of the Chevalier de Villegagnon, vice admiral of Brittany."

The Venetian half rose to perform a sort of bow from behind his table, never losing the ironic smile that put everyone so ill at ease. Then he went on:

"We have a great deal of experience in the matter of go-betweens, as the Venetian Republic has long had commercial relations with the farthest corners of the world. When our caravans have taken children along to the Orient, they have made excellent interpreters, the best we have had for China and the Middle East. The Spaniards do the same thing. In Mexico, for example, they could at first speak to the Aztecs only through the native woman known as La Malinche, but by using children they managed to acquire a large supply of go-betweens, so as to suit their every purpose."

"And at what age, according to you, should one send these young students?" asked Le Thoret, interested by the man's proposition.

"The age of five or six is excellent."

"Impossible!" said the officer. "The Chevalier de Villegagnon has given strict orders that no woman is to embark on our ships. It strikes me that at the age you suggest, a child would still need its mother or a nursemaid."

"Older children can also be used," said the Venetian. "In point of fact, the gift of languages seems to be taken from them only when their bodies are fully formed."

He was on the point of making further observations on the

strange correspondence between the organs and the understanding when he noticed the soldier blushing and checked himself.

"And then you have to find children who are able to go and yet are not complete ruffians," said Le Thoret thoughtfully.

Recruiting men for the new colony had not been easy. Hardly any volunteers had stepped forward, despite assurances that they would receive a life-lease on land. With the atrocious rumor of man-eating savages making the rounds, even the poorest beggars looked on the mission with more terror than hope. In their ignorance, they preferred all the forms of certain death to which their poverty condemned them over the uncertain chance of being eaten by one of their own kind. And now Le Thoret would have to go looking for children. Yet it was unquestionably the best recourse, and Villegagnon was sure to adopt it at the first suggestion.

"So what they say is true," said the Venetian casually, "you are setting out for Rio. And you intend to lay this egg in the nest of the Portuguese! Yet the pope himself, apparently, grants them sole sovereignty over Brazil."

"That a Spanish pope once divided the New World between the Iberian nations means little to us," said the officer, rubbing his eyes, weary of a refrain he had been repeating for the last two months. "It is nowhere written in Adam's testament that France is forbidden a share in the American continents."

"Hear! Hear!" shouted the sailor, raising his pint.

The crowd of drinkers, whose high spirits had till then been held in check by the glacial manner of the officer, raucously supported this sentiment. The officer quieted the laughter by raising his bony hand, from which a finger had long ago been torn off by a harquebus volley.

Suddenly recalling that he was addressing a foreigner, he looked suspiciously at the man:

"It would be useless to ask further questions, sir. The king does not wish this affair to become common knowledge. It concerns only France."

Nine strokes of the clock, which set the mugs on the table rattling, opportunely brought this indiscreet conversation to a close. The Venetian paid for his plate of broth and shuffled to the door, where with an eery smile he wished the officer a safe journey. The sailor had fallen asleep. The Indian left to go find his wife. Le Thoret went out into the square and shivered under the fine rain. He had hoped to take a little rest during the short week remaining before the great departure. Instead, he would now have to make the rounds of the orphanages.

CHAPTER 2

An endless line of willows, planted like a row of halberdiers, just stopped the fields' gleeful slide toward the cliffs. The sea below was imperceptible except for the faint sound of unseen waves. An offshore wind had sprung up, tearing holes in the clouds, and a white sun shone coldly on the wet grass.

On a green field, a bay horse grazed peaceably, almost motionlessly. From time to time it swished its tail at the flies swarming in the sunshine after the wet of the storms.

"Look," whispered Just, "there he is!"

"But how can you tell?" asked the girl stretched out beside him.

"Three balzan'd feet, for the king is meet," answered Just impatiently.

"'Balzan'd'?" she queried.

"Yes," said her brother, "the white stockings above his hooves, he has three of them: a horse for a king!"

"Stop pretending you know everything, and don't treat me like a child just because you've picked up a few things tagging along with the ploughmen."

"Keep your voice down, Colombe! He'll notice us."

But the horse continued to graze without seeming to have heard them.

"In any case," the girl muttered, "balzan'd feet or no balzan'd feet, it's not all that hard to recognize Monsieur de Griffes's stallion."

It annoyed Just to hear the name of their rich and detested neighbor on whose lands they had stealthily ventured.

"Don't talk about him, do you mind?"

He continued to look at the horse enviously.

"You're right," said Colombe, "let's call the horse . . . Gringalet!"

"Gringalet, Sir Gawain's steed!" said Just laughing.

But they made no move, both remaining lost in reflection, lying flat on the ground in spite of the wet grass soaking their fronts and the tips of crocuses making hard round indents on their skin through their coarse shirts.

The horse lifted its head and sniffed the salt air, perhaps intrigued by the scent of some dead crab or gull, and looked for a moment as if listening to the distant heaving of the shingle on the beach.

" 'Certain that his master whispered in his ear, he listened,' " Colombe recited.

At this allusion to Gawain, the knight errant, the victorious and valiant nephew of King Arthur, the hero of their readings during the endless Norman days, the boy's black eyes burned with a bright flame. And though he remained lying down, he seemed to spring forward imperceptibly.

"Go on!" said Colombe.

As though waking from a dream, Just looked at her, then at the rope in his right hand. Slowly and silently, he rose to his feet.

"Come, imagine that you are Bel Hardi and that I am your lady fair. Do it for me."

She spoke her command in a strong, authoritative voice. For a moment, the boy thought the horse had heard them and might run off. With the danger imminent, Just dropped all hesitation and moved forward.

Experienced stalkers, the two children had positioned themselves downwind of the animal so as not to alarm it. To get close, Just would have to take the horse by surprise, but with no brusque movements. Once on his feet, he walked slowly and deliberately toward the horse, the rope behind his back. The stallion allowed him to approach without laying back its ears or flaring its eyes. When he was within arm's reach, Just stretched out his hand quietly toward the horse's neck, which was still steaming from the recent rain, and stroked it firmly. The horse was tall at the withers, and Just stood only to its shoulder. He moved closer and put his arms around the horse's neck.

Just felt true kinship toward this animal, not only because it was just possibly Gringalet, Gawain's horse, but also because of its dark and fire-glinting mane, which so closely resembled his own wild mop. With the rope now around the horse's neck, Just lifted one end to its muzzle, where he calmly tied a knot at its mouth to make a simple halter. The stallion showed no impatience. When the boy took the other end of the rope and extended it like a short lead, he had the pleasure of feeling the animal falling in with his own movements. He started walking, and their two dark figures made a large loop across the field. A strip of sea on the horizon separated the green of the ground from the dark sky, where stormclouds were again gathering. Just brought the animal around a little more so as not to leave it facing the glare of the sun on the wet grass. Then he took hold of the horse's mane, put one foot lightly against its leg, and vaulted high onto its back. He spurred it with his heels and the animal obeyed its new master.

"Colombe," the boy called out, "you can come!"

Just held himself very straight, proud but apprehensive. He normally rode only the bony nags on their own estate. His narrow face worked at staying impassive, but his eyes laughed and his mouth twitched from the effort of holding back whoops of pure joy. He held the simple rein lightly at the tips of his long hands. Slight though it was, this link between his will and the horse's strength seemed superfluous, so naturally did the contrasting elegances of the huge animal and its fifteen-year-old rider harmonize.

Colombe ran up, oblivious to her wet dress clinging to her body, radiant at Just's victory.

"Nicely done," she said, "now help me mount."

"You? No, you're a lady and ladies don't ride steeds."

"Stop all that, Just. It's not a steed, just Monsieur de Griffes's horse. Come on, give me a hand up."

Colombe's blond hair, made dark and lank by the rain, was plastered to the sides of her face. But her eyelashes, though also soaking, were still pale, setting a golden nimbus around her eyes, lighting them and filling them with irony and enigma. She had learned from

an early age to put her eyes, with their strong power to provoke interest and disconcertment, to good use. When she fixed them on someone, as she now fixed them on Just, it was with the intention of
breaking down that person's last shreds of resistance.

"All right!" he said. "Grab my arm."

Colombe gripped his elbow, and he pulled her up. Just's junior by
two years, she was almost as tall as he, though narrower and frailer.
She balanced lightly on the horse's croup, which she straddled with
agility. Then she reached her naked arms around Just's waist.

"Bel Hardi," she whispered in his ear, "if this is really Gringalet,
then he will carry us to fabulous countries."

But Just gave the horse a cautious squeeze of his legs and kept him
at a walk. He sensed that the animal's confidence in him had shifted.
Though Just generally looked distracted and lost in his dreams,
almost asleep, he was in fact extremely attuned to animals, plants,
and all the mute creatures of the natural world. He felt the horse tin-
gling with confused anxiety, perhaps because of Colombe's shouts.
She, by contrast, with her darting eyes, knew how to read every
human sign, even to the most imperceptible shadings of the soul, yet
she was quite oblivious to animals or to things said to lack a soul. She
continued laughing and shouting in her high voice.

"Let's go to the fence! Make him go out onto the path."

Just was as eager as she to ride as far as their mount could carry
them, but he was petrified with fear. When they reached the end of
the field, Colombe impatiently lashed out with her foot at the
crudely squared branch that served as a gate. The horse shied away,
almost throwing them.

"Be careful, Colombe!"

All on his own, the horse set off at a walk along the path toward
the wood. They were soon in the midst of a grove of large beeches,
whose high first branches left an open and unthreatening understory.
The horse seemed to calm down. The path climbed, and at the far
end of the wood they reached a rise from which they could look out
over the valley and the fields surrounding them. In a hollow in the
distance they could see Monsieur de Griffes's new manor house, still
bristling with wooden poles. The roofers were putting the final
touches on the roofs of the turrets and the grand staircase.

"Let's not stay here. His men might see us," said Just by way of explanation as he urged on the horse, and perhaps also to hide the feelings always provoked in him by this palace under construction.

All the things they loved about Italy—the tall windows opening onto the light, the spiral columns supporting the balconies, the classical ornament of the facades—were given to the vile de Griffes like so many fat perquisites. A magistrate, a merchant, and a usurer into the bargain, Chancellor de Griffes knew as much about Italy as he had been able to buy of it. Whereas they, who had grown up in that land of the arts, trailing in the bewildering wake of a father who served under arms, lived in a feudal barracks.

These thoughts darkened their mood as they proceeded along the path, and they grew silent. The road kept to the heights, and opened suddenly onto a view of Clamorgan, their ancient estate.

In former times, the castle had been renowned: it had a keep, ramparts, and a drawbridge. Closer approach, however, revealed that the moat was no longer filled with water, and the bridge could not be drawn up. As to the keep, its fate was in the hands of a vast curtain of ivy, which, while preventing the keep from falling, was also strangling it.

From a distance Clamorgan still cut a handsome figure. That was how Just and Colombe preferred to see it. But the estate's vast landholdings were almost entirely neglected, unlike de Griffes's land, which was worked by skillful tenants.

"Faster, prick him with both spurs, Bel Hardi," said Colombe, reminded of the fantastic nature of their cavalcade by the sight of the castle.

But Just was unwilling to rush the horse. The sky had closed the last window through which the sun had momentarily been waving. All of a sudden it was dark and cold. The horse raised and lowered its head jerkily, sensing the oncoming storm.

"Let's head for home," said the boy, turning the horse around.

"No!" said Colombe, "for once we've found a bit of fun here."

More than anything she was miffed at being disobeyed. But Just had his back to her: she could no longer use her eyes on him. She started drumming on his shoulders. Her light-boned fists bounced off the boy's sturdy frame, and he continued to lead the stallion calmly along the path back. Colombe was about to start crying when she suddenly saw a willow branch hanging above the road. As they came up to it, she caught it and noiselessly broke it off. With the leaves stripped off, it made an acceptable riding crop. Holding the branch in one hand and Just's shirt in the other, she reared back and rapped smartly on the stallion's rump. Frightened more than hurt, the animal took off at a gallop. Just managed to keep from falling by grasping its mane with both hands, but he had dropped the rein, which slapped against the animal's face, increasing the horse's terror and the pace of his gallop.

They raced toward the castle, and then, as the track curved back toward the sea, they drew away from it, heading toward a fallow field bordered by a wall. Powerless to do anything, Just applied the part of his mind not gripped by fear toward not falling. A little farther on, the track crossed a stream. They would have to let go just before they reached it, Just thought, and let the muddy streambed break their fall. But the horse didn't give him the luxury of waiting. As they passed a fountain set on a raised plinth, the courser shied sideways, sending both riders tumbling. The boy rolled onto a grassy embankment unscathed. Colombe, being lighter, was flung toward a milestone, which struck her temple. She lay motionless on her back, bleeding lightly from the forehead. Just bent over her and found her unconscious.

He took her head gently in his hands, spoke to her, kissed her, cradled her. As the seconds passed, he heard nothing but the distant galloping of the runaway horse and, all too close, the loud plashing of the fountain. Then Just, the proud heir of the Clamorgans, plain Just whose sister had made him into Bel Hardi, recovered his wits. Colombe was still not waking up. He let out a great wail, a hoarse cry, his voice breaking. He listened to her heart: it was still beating. She was alive. He gathered her in his arms, noticing that she was light, and sopping wet, and missing a shoe. He set off at a run, his tear-filled eyes fixed on his still unconscious burden.

"Love, love," he sobbed, "don't die!"

CHAPTER 3

France was making war in those years but not living it. Since the end of the last century and of Charles VIII's dreams of eastward expansion, France had settled on Italy as a jousting green for its captains. They returned laden with glory, even after defeat. Taking pleasure in conquering realms, only to lose them immediately, they contracted alliances that seemed meant to break down and cause the master cards of this game without rules—kings, queens, and knights—to be constantly reshuffled. This gallant cavalcade of armored popes, of princes in love with the arts, and of conquerors dizzied by intrigues had one great merit for the kingdom of France: it gave the country peace and kept its armies busy far from home. Nothing, not even the great defeat at Pavia, troubled the order that had been restored after the end of the Hundred Years' War. Attics were bursting with the fruits of the harvest, and a steady stream of cloth and wine, of spices and fine artisanal work flowed through every country. Kings roamed their realms, coming forth to meet their subjects and vassals, while the nobles lived on their lands and made them prosper. Castles that showed the influence of the classical world and the colors of Italy were springing up everywhere.

Dom Gonzagues was making these very reflections as he looked out the window of the monastery. The drizzling rain of Normandy

fell silently on the fat fields, so green they hurt his eyes. These peaceful times with their plump oxen, their goats, their cows with distended udders, their apple trees covered in thick clusters of
rain-sheeted blossoms and promising a miraculous harvest to come
wearied the soul of this old soldier despite himself. In the twenty
years since he had first worn the Cross of Malta and followed the
Chevalier de Villegagnon, his life had been nothing but the sword,
forced marches, and an empty belly. He had fought the Turks at
Algiers, won glory but no profit against the Imperials in Hungary,
the English at Boulogne, and finally found defeat at Tripoli. And all
the time that he confronted battles, flames, vermin, and rotten food,
the field in front of him had never varied, in all likelihood, from this
same lush green.

And to think that he could instead have led a peaceful life in his
castlery in the sunny province of Agen. He was the youngest son, but
his brothers would surely have given him a bit of land all his own
where he might have lived simply and happily. Thoughts of this kind
had tormented him almost every day since he arrived in these rainy
lands. Fortunately, the lingering effects of two harquebus wounds,
one to the groin and the other to the shoulder, came to rescue him
from this slack surrender of the spirit and prick him with the memory of past battles toward the delights of battles yet to come. When
all was said and done, he had no use for cows.

The soft voice of a nun calling his name brought an end to this
already half-repressed bout of melancholia.

"Dom Gonzagues de La Druz?"

"The very same, Good Mother."

Short and plump, his eyes lively and his beard so sharp it seemed
to have slashed the long scar at the base of his neck, Dom Gonzagues
was weighted down with swords and daggers, though nowhere near
the front. The clicking of his weapons echoed in the stone-vaulted
chamber as he came to attention with a blush. The mother superior
smiled at the soldier's awkwardness. She sensed that if she caused
him confusion, it was not so much as a nun but as a woman. And
who is to say she did not secretly find this flattering?

"I received your letter yesterday," said the mother superior, standing three steps from Dom Gonzagues and holding him with her

handsome blue eyes. "You are looking for orphans to take to the New World?"

"Yes, Mother," stammered the soldier, cursing himself and railing at God for having taken such a beautiful nun into his service.

"Then I will tell you, Captain, as I would ask you to tell the Chevalier de Villegagnon, that we have the greatest desire to help him in this matter. It is an act of piety to bring the word of Christ to these new lands. If God had not chosen another fate for me, I would have been the first to accompany you there."

This was a speech to make the unhappy Gonzagues wish he were already among the savages: he believed them incapable of any greater perversity. Yet he found the courage to reorient a few of the bristles on his face so as to suggest a smile.

"Now, you have expressed a preference for orphans," said the mother superior. "In former times we had many, as the older members of our order well remember. But the land is now so prosperous that it provides for all. The poor are still among us. We are not yet at the point, fortunately, where a Christian might be kept from paradise for lack of opportunities to exercise his charity. But as to orphans, Captain, we have none."

As she said this, the nun shook her handsome head, saintliness and harmony combining to make her features doubly perfect.

"Are you saying that you have no one to offer us?" asked Dom Gonzagues, who had never retreated long under enemy fire—though he had always shown himself weaker and less resourceful when faced with women's weapons.

He congratulated himself on having so framed the question that the conversation would have to end quickly. But the mother superior was not to be so easily defeated. The boredom that pervaded the heavy silence of these stone walls no doubt made her want to prolong her opportunities to talk and, perchance, laugh. She paced the room slowly and silently, finally stopping in front of the window.

"We do have some children, Captain, you may rest assured," she said, this time letting the lightning of her glance fall on an apple tree.

Dom Gonzagues uttered an exclamation of pleasure, congratulating himself on stifling the "Bedamn!" that first sprang to his lips.

"We have some," she resumed, "because sin is always with us, and carnal disorders still allow children to be conceived outside the holy sacraments. Poor girls who have succumbed to their senses have no alternative but to abandon their children, and the parishes bring them to us. But more and more families have taken to accepting these children who are an insult to God. And do you know," she went on confidentially, "the parish priests encourage them in this. In some villages along the coast where the sailors are away at sea for long periods, the priests have persuaded their flocks that a pregnancy may last a longer or shorter time according to the woman! It was reported to me in all seriousness that a certain child was born after a pregnancy of eighteen months. The whole village was praising nature's wisdom in making the child wait until its father returned. And the poor man naturally came to the conclusion that the baby resembled him . . ."

Silent, his eyes lowered before this allusion by a woman to the horrible mechanism of conception, Dom Gonzagues swelled with indignation. His master, the Chevalier de Villegagnon, was right in saying that the Church of France needed to be reformed, as it had strayed from the strict faith of former times. He never would have imagined that corruption could gain so strong a hold while he, for his part, had been fighting to drive back the infidel and the forces of darkness. And this nun with her half smile! She even seemed to take pleasure in his indignation, though he felt he was managing to conceal it well enough—except for the clanking of his accursed sword, which his hot Gascon blood set to trembling against his leg.

"I am determined, sir, not to hide anything from you," the nun went on. "At this moment we have eight orphans in our institution. Four of them are girls and you have told me in your letter that they are not needed. Of the boys, one is not in his right mind: he was born deformed and is subject to fits of unreason. The other three are very young: they are four and six years old, two of them being twins."

"In that case, Holy Mother," said Dom Gonzagues promptly, his breathing labored as though after long exertion, "I can only thank you in all sincerity and take my leave."

This was his third monastery. Le Thoret, who was assisting him in this business, must have visited as many on his side. Each time, Dom Gonzagues had received the same answers and the same tally of human frailties—though never with such insolent provocation as from this damnable mother superior. All the better reason to break off abruptly and so find time for a further visit that night—there were still two monasteries on his list.

"One moment, Captain," said the nun, placing a slender hand on the soldier's cuff. "You are on the point of departure. But that is no reason not to hear me out."

At the touch of her viperine hand, Dom Gonzagues froze with martyrized revulsion.

"You have asked me if I had orphans or might be able to unearth a few street urchins," said the nun softly, "and I have answered no. But perhaps your question was not complete. You want children to make them into interpreters with the natives of Brazil, yes?"

With the point of his beard, Dom Gonzagues incised a figure eight into the air.

"And you are searching among the poor because you thought your best likelihood of success lay in that quarter?"

The captain assented mutely with another figure eight.

"But you would not be opposed to taking children of better birth if any were offered to you?"

With a further nod, the old soldier signaled his capitulation.

"In that case, sir, follow me."

● ● ●

At a forced pace, behind this she-devil of a mother superior who trotted easily along, Dom Gonzagues crossed the entire length of the convent.

They encountered several novices and probationers. If not all were pretty, they all wore their habits with a freedom that the knight of Malta considered not entirely honest. Too gay a smile fluttered about their lips. Such an amiable countenance in a world devoted to the service of God appeared sinful in his eyes. Added to this was the warm smell of wax rising from the floor tiles and a luxuriance of lighted candles, not all of them in ceremonial use. Through half-open doors he glimpsed voluptuous armoires, bulging like wet nurses, brimming with the very items of comfort these daughters of God had taken a vow to renounce. The whole way, Dom Gonzagues pointed his eyes straight ahead like a man intent on resisting temptation by not seeing it in the first place. Finally they climbed several stone steps into a long gallery bridging a river.

"If you walk right to the end," said the mother superior, showing the far end of the windowed hall, "you come out on the other bank, on the side of the forest and the village. We sometimes take this path to attend Mass."

Dom Gonzagues fulminated silently against this portal, which was all too obviously evil. In his mind's eye he saw all the commerce such an entrance made possible.

They stopped in the center of the gallery where a small chamber had been built out over one of the buttresses of the bridge. The nun opened a door and ushered the soldier in. Two high windows looked out over the water. An open pane allowed the murmur of the current to enter and fill the small space, making it an apt setting for conversations not meant to be overheard. The only furnishings in the room were a triangular table with turned legs and three low stools. The mother superior sat down and motioned to the soldier to do likewise. Dom Gonzagues took his seat with considerable effort, less encumbered by his weapons than stiffened by a sincere spiritual alarm.

"It won't be long," said the nun, giving the same smile she seemed to have communicated to everyone in the monastery, despite her vows of renunciation.

They remained silent, listening to the sound of the current. Birds trilled from the bank, making the old soldier jump in alarm, accustomed as he was to ambushes and soldiers using birdcalls in the woods. They had not sat there two minutes when the door opened. Another woman entered and sat down on the last stool. She gave the mother superior and her guest a simple nod in greeting. Without knowing exactly why, Dom Gonzagues felt that this woman, though not wearing a nun's habit, was more modest and pious than all the joyous, heedless females he had encountered inside the monastery walls. Like himself, the woman seemed to have battled unremittingly until that point in one's fifties when the battle call sounds and one no longer answers it, one's face assuming an expression of weariness and serenity. The fine lines on her visage, which Dom Gonzagues identified with the sword cuts strewn over his own by wars, had been attenuated by the skillful and cautious use of cosmetics, a severe hairstyle that ordered her hair into a double wall of braids, and austere but carefully chosen clothes. Two small diamonds sparkled at her ears and played against the sober expanse of her long-sleeved black dress, which was quietly set off at the neck and cuffs by a line of lace. Dom Gonzagues felt true gratitude well up inside him toward this woman, whose propriety compensated for everything else. The only outward sign of his enthusiasm was the nervous misting over of his right eye, which he kept from degenerating into tears with discreet swipes of his sleeve.

"Madam," said the mother superior, who alas! had not vaporized before this apparition, "I present Dom Gonzagues de La Druz, Knight of Malta."

"Captain," said the lady, whose measured voice harmonized with the rest of her person, "I am honored to meet you. And I thank you, Mother, for your kindness in arranging our interview."

"It was simple enough to do," said the mother superior, laughing in her usual way. "And we certainly could not refuse you the favor, as you have been the benefactress of this convent for so many years . . ."

"Yes," the lady murmured, overtaken by a slight tremor. "We have always given thanks to the Lord for his gifts. We submitted to His decrees when they were favorable to us, knowing that we must submit to them with the same patience if ever they became unfavorable. And that day, alas, has now come."

"Flight" was a word that Dom Gonzagues had banished from his military vocabulary. But in the present circumstance he would gladly have resorted to it had it been honorable.

"Aware as I am of your imminent departure, Captain," said the lady, "I never would trouble you with our paltry misfortunes. But at the time of my last visit, Sister Catherine informed me of your request—that you are looking for children to join you in colonizing the New World."

"Yes, madam," trumpeted Dom Gonzagues, making a wad of humors disappear into his handkerchief.

"In that case, I believe you will not be wasting your time by listening to my proposal. I will try to be brief."

She lowered her eyes momentarily, then raised them toward the little lozenges of colored glass that formed the window.

"Well then," she said, "I will tell you. My husband's younger brother is a soldier. He fought in Italy, first in the service of the king of France, then of various other princes. For three years we have had no news of him. Before he disappeared, he brought two children back from Italy. We know nothing of their mother, or whether they share a single mother, or even whether my brother-in-law sired them. But no matter. It is not my station to judge a soldier's life. Soldiers have their glories and their weaknesses too."

Many were the captains, if truth be told, who had shown proof of weakness in Italy. Some had fallen under the sway of those women for whom even the bravest men are no match. Dom Gonzagues had himself taken part in these follies, yet he had managed to steer clear of any all-consuming passions—or perhaps had failed to evoke any, he sometimes thought unhappily. When spoken of by this lady, these follies seemed abhorrent to him. He didn't dare ask the name of the soldier for fear of knowing him and being held to blame for his turpitudes.

"The Good Lord knows that when my brother-in-law entrusted these two children to our care, they found safety in our house and much indulgence regarding the circumstances of their conception. Unfortunately, providence has not been kind to our estate, which lies a few leagues from here. We have been visited by every imaginable plague that can strike cattle and crops, as though the plagues of Egypt had been aimed at us. If the month of August is stormy, then our fields are the first to be ruined by the rain. We've been overrun by grasshoppers, and hail has cut down our crops. What is more, we have been attacked no fewer than three times by roving Bohemians. They took all the furniture and coin they could find. In short, Captain, however illustrious our family may have been in times past, it now suffers from a misfortune whose plain name is poverty."

Dom Gonzagues felt his anger toward his weapons increase—not only were they useless to him but they clattered horribly when he returned his handkerchief to his pocket.

"And now a further blow has been dealt you," said the mother superior, who had hung back until this point but now joined the front lines for the final assault. "My lady's noble husband, after a life of effort and reversals, suffered a grave attack upon his body and died three months ago."

At the mention of this bereavement, the lady expressed two tears, which, with a shaky hand, she managed not so much to wipe away as to daub across her face.

"Before you stands a woman, Captain," went on the nun, "who, while beset with misfortunes, has assumed a host of responsibilities. Alone and unprovided for, she knows that our monastery will always welcome her, in gratitude for the favors her family so long bestowed on us.

"Notwithstanding, she has refused to neglect the children entrusted to her care. Yet what will become of them? Their father, who never let a month go by without writing, has stopped giving any sign of life—most likely having gone to his reward. This lady's lands will soon be dispersed or sold. Tell me truly—what does the future hold for these two souls? Will they join holy orders? They show no inclination in that direction. The blame is not wholly theirs, given the debauchery that pervaded their early life. Jesus Christ will surely come to them some day, wherever they are. But one cannot bind them to Him without violence unless the desire is already in them."

"Sister Catherine is right," said the lady. "But my concern goes beyond this. I would like these children, whose family is soon to die out—assuming they ever truly belonged to it—to have the chance to found a family of their own. They must start afresh and begin a new life, a life that will make them forget their coarse early circumstances. That is why the words 'New World' so caught my ear. I have come to implore you, Captain, to provide for the future of these unhappy children by taking them with you."

Hope started to rekindle in Dom Gonzagues's breast. Slicing through the dark shadows of these confidences, he glimpsed a breach, perhaps a way out. What they wanted of him was clear and simple. And to do good had always struck him as the supreme virtue and guide: he offered no argument. Had he attempted rebellion, the beautiful eyes of these two women, the one holding back tears and the other renouncing sensuality, would have carried his last defenses.

"How old are they?"

"Without any certain knowledge," said the lady somewhat hesitantly, "I would say . . . eleven and thirteen."

"Excellent," said the captain.

Then, checked momentarily by his sense of modesty, he went on in a lowered voice: "Would not the elder of the two be . . . fully formed?"

"There is down on his upper lip—he is dark-haired, which makes it more visible. But his governess states unequivocally that he is not a man."

"Have they agreed to the voyage?"

These were questions that the two women had rehearsed before-hand, and the answers came readily.

"They are determined to leave the estate. The poor children main-tain the confused hope of finding their father—whom they barely know. One has only to keep this hope alive, and they will go wher-ever one wants."

The proposition was an intricate one for the soldier's rude understanding.

"Madam, are you aware that the children will settle on those dis-tant shores forever and remain there even after their death?"

"I have no greater ambition for them than to attach new lands, just as their ancestors attached those which our family is now about to lose . . ."

"Come, madam," said Dom Gonzagues, rising with a clash of steel and boots, "have no further concern on this score. I will take care of it."

There followed a long moment of emotional outpourings, general thanksgiving, and gratitude, which the knight endured as though it were a final trial. He was still afraid that the nun, particularly, might make some final attempt on his decency.

"Come," he said in a hearty manner, "let's take a look at them. Where are they?"

"Captain," said the mother superior, sidling up to Dom Gon-zagues, apparently having grasped that he could not resist her scent of sweet almonds, "surely you can appreciate that we had to put the matter to you first before we notified the children. They are still on the estate, several leagues from here. Now that you have agreed to take them, they will make themselves ready and join you at the time of your departure."

Dom Gonzagues hesitated for a final moment: he would not see them at all beforehand. His reservations counted for little, however, in the balance with this honest woman whose troubles he was eras-ing. Besides, he had already given his word.

"We sail from Le Havre-de-Grâce in three days."

"A coach will bring them to you before your departure," said the nun.

They went out into the gallery. The lady thanked the captain again and set off in the direction of the woods, where her mount must have been waiting. Dom Gonzagues strode briskly back through the monastery, eager to find himself once more on horseback. He had not been galloping for five minutes before he was furious at himself.

I didn't even ask the lady for her name, he thought.

Then, dismissing this final anxiety, he spoke into the wet wind: "Bah! No matter. The family is surely an honorable one."

CHAPTER 4

Clamorgan, when Just and Colombe lived in Italy, had been a name to conjure with, the fabulous land of their origins. Only when their father was reduced to desperate straits did he take the risk of sending them there and did they learn the sad truth about their cherished dream. Fortunately their soldier father was not on hand for their disappointment: he had earned the displeasure of the king of France and could not accompany his children himself. They traveled by coach to Rouen accompanied by an ensign. Then a cart had taken them to Clamorgan.

Their uncle was already very weak. He lived shut up in the only room that still had wall hangings and could be heated. The poor man had stayed in the Middle Ages: he managed his estate as in feudal times, driving it to ruin. Refusing to sell anything or buy anything, he never replaced a single slate that fell from the roof or left the peasants more than a bare sufficiency. The surplus rotted in the attics, discouraging the tenants from working and prompting their exodus. This reflected not avarice on his part but an excessive sense of honor in an era when commerce had replaced chivalry. Then one day he was dead.

A governess who had been a nursemaid took the two children into her home, a dilapidated thatch-roofed cottage. The walls and ceiling of its smoke-blackened interior were hung haphazardly with pans, rakes, baskets, and other useful implements.

It was to this house that Just carried the inanimate Colombe. He laid her down near the hearth on a big bed with a straw mattress. She moaned and complained that her head hurt. An old shepherd who had a reputation for healing—at least where sheep were concerned— came running up the muddy track out of breath and prescribed a concoction of simples for her.

"She'll live," he said.

Only then did Just understand that she truly could have died. He had the happy augury repeated to him by Emilienne, the governess. She was as happy to say it out loud as he was to hear it, and four times he pretended not to catch her words. Limp and feverish, Colombe made a face and drank the dark, steaming liquid floating with mushroom chips. Then she went back to sleep.

Just kept watch at the end of the bed. He was terrified to see his other half gutter like a candle flame. As far back as he could remember, their earlier life had been nothing but a chaos of sudden night journeys, unheated inns, and long marches, all mixed in pell-mell with bright memories of Italy and battles. Everything had always been in motion around them without their ever understanding why. They knew no other family than their father, whose image had grown dim in their memories after four years at Clamorgan.

But this vast rotation of people and events had had a pivot: to each child the other was what didn't change when everything else changed, what stayed constant when everything fell away. In Just's most distant memories, there was Colombe.

They had shared the same hardships and dreams, had learned from the same authors: Ariosto, Virgil, and Homer, whom they read in the original. They played the same tunes, she on the flute and he on the mandolin. This little armful of verses and melodies made up all their baggage while they bumped along with the common soldiers. Now, however, the dream was gone. As he threw elm logs on the smoking fire, Just thought of all the fanciful names Colombe had given him, the last in particular: Bel Hardi! He wiped his nose on his sleeve and swore once more never to leave her, even in death. He was at an age when such vows come easily, but it seemed to Just that no one had ever spoken so solemn a vow, or been so resolved to carry it out.

In the morning Colombe pushed back her eiderdown comforter. She was dripping with sweat, but the fever seemed to have drained completely into the bag of feathers. Before noon, she opened her eyes and called for the others. There were cries of joy and renewed tears. Here in Normandy, where the weather changed hour by hour, it seemed that souls too experienced sudden sunbreaks.

Although the fever had ebbed, Emilienne ordered her patient to stay in bed, lest the large bump on the side of her forehead change "from an effusion to an aposteme." This pronouncement, as strange as a magician's spell, had the desired effect of keeping the patient in her bed. But Colombe was back to her monkey tricks and made horrible faces at Just.

The afternoon was well along when a sound of creaking axles reached their ears. Emilienne was in her kitchen garden. With so many deserted houses on the property, she had her choice of the best abandoned plots. She fetched her carrots from over by the stubble field where the fattest ones grew. The children held still as the wagon approached, for few ever came that way. When they heard it stop in front of the door, Colombe rose on her elbows and said:

"Just, go see who it is!"

Before he had a chance to move, a man's silhouette blocked the doorway. They recognized Belloy, the one manservant left in the castle. He was a small, thickset fellow with a shifty face, and they were afraid of him. On this estate with no master, he gave orders as he pleased and treated the children roughly, as though to dissuade them from ever laying a claim to what was rightfully theirs.

Their first impulse on seeing him squint into the darkness of the house was to hide. But before they could, he had groped his way to the bed and rooted them to the spot with his loud voice:

"Come out of there, you rotten scamps."

Waving his arms blindly, he touched Just, who allowed himself to be caught without resisting.

"Where is your sister?"

"Here," said Colombe in a surly voice, expecting no better treatment.

"Come on, the two of you, my lady chancelloress, your aunt, wants to see you."

Though Just objected that Colombe was sick, they were made to dress in a hurry and take their seats in the cart outside. Belloy turned the horse around. They were already at the bend in the road when they saw Emilienne in the distance running toward them, waving her arms.

•   •   •

The cart drew up to the castle, and Belloy clucked the horse on over the rickety drawbridge. Looking up, Just and Colombe saw the iron portcullis, blocked open by its rusty mechanism. Two fat bulldogs, attached by a chain, were all the guard the ancient fortress now maintained. Belloy brought the children to the guard room, a high hall with stone walls and ogival vaults. The vast chimney, big enough to devour whole tree trunks, was cold and empty, and the air in the room was dank. The floor was strewn with straw, dust, and wood shavings. The only furniture was an enormous oak chest, pushed back against the wall, and an old armchair. They waited in silence, wondering what punishment they would get for letting the stallion run away.

They heard a jingling of harness as their aunt's horses carried her litter over the drawbridge. Ordinarily dressed in bright colors, she surprised them on this day by appearing in a simple black dress. They did not know that she had chosen it expressly for her meeting with Dom Gonzagues at the monastery that morning.

There was a moment of silence while she eyed them, one and then the other. She seemed to be matching their appearance with a secret plan for which she intended them. Despite their disheveled hair, their paupers' clothes, the dried mud that still flecked their skin, she seemed satisfied with her examination. Belloy brought up an armchair, in which she seated herself delicately, while the children remained standing before her, still waiting for her to bring up the business of the missing horse.

"My dear children!" she said in a tone that belied the affection implied by her words.

Colombe tightened her grip on Just's arm.

"Despite your great attachment to Clamorgan," the chancelloress continued, "I know that your foremost desire is—not unjustifiably—to see your father again."

The children looked at her with impassive faces, their distrust for the woman not easily overcome.

"Well, you may rejoice, as your wish is to be granted."

Pausing to reflect for a moment, she added:

"At least for one of you."

They stiffened. Under the pleasant foliage lurked a viper, and it had just shown its fangs. So they were to be separated.

"Master Just, you will soon be a man. Your father will train you to become a warrior as brave as himself. We will provide you the means to rejoin him. Are you pleased by this?"

"No, madam," said Just, aware of the provocation but guarding himself from responding to it.

"Well?"

"I don't want to leave my sister."

His sister! The chancelloress smiled. So these bastard children, conceived of unknown mothers by the side of the road, mothers who were themselves probably uncertain as to the father, had the pre-sumption and stupidity to think themselves brother and sister. There would have been no point in trying to show them their error. Besides, it worked into her plans.

"Do you think the sort of life your father intends for you would be fitting for an honorable maiden?"

"We have lived that life before," Colombe intercepted, afraid of Just's awkwardness. She had been waiting impatiently for her entrance.

The chancelloress examined her. She saw all the young girl's beauty, which she had no intention of acknowledging. She also saw the passion in her temperament, which would make for a thousand difficulties if she tried to send Colombe to the convent after her brother left. It confirmed her fears. She had been right in telling Dom Gonzagues that she would send him two children. She could now use the threat of separation to get what she wanted. She rose and walked slowly away from them.

"Your stubbornness greatly displeases me," she said at last, approaching them once more. "It stands in the way of the reasonable plans I have made for your benefit."

She resumed her seat and forced an almost tender smile onto her face.

"However, I see that you love each other, and I haven't the heart to separate you. I will keep you together as an act of kindness, though it may cost me dearly. But you have to help me."

The children clung to each other warily, expecting some further entrapment.

"Come closer. What I am going to tell you is secret."

They took two steps forward but kept their distance. The chancelloress, not wishing to be assaulted by their farmyard smell, did not press the point.

"Now your father, as you know, is a great captain. In the Italian wars, where many alliances were forged, he served several princes, and they all disputed the honor of having so valiant a man defend them."

Just's eyes glowed at hearing his father thus spoken of. But Colombe sensed the honey coating of these words and remained on her guard.

"This time," said the lady in black, "he has put himself at the disposal of a more distant power."

"He is no longer in Italy?" asked Just.

"Italy does not exist, my child. It is a checkerboard, as it were, of states and principalities. The new land where your father is extending his fame is one of those, only more distant."

"Is he among the Turks?"

King Francis I's unexpected alliance twenty years before with the Turks—enemies of the Christian world since the Crusades—had made a profound impression on all minds. The Turks were discussed in the deepest reaches of the countryside. Just, who heard little news of the world, was merely echoing common rumor.

"The Turks!" said the chancelloress mockingly. "No, my child. But if I were to say the name of the place where he lives, it would tell you nothing, for I myself had not heard of it before. It is enough to know that one must take a ship to get there and that the cruise is a long one."

"A ship!" said Just. "Oh! When do we leave?"

To his sister's chagrin, Just seemed entirely won over.

"Gently, my child. There are still a few points to be settled. No woman is included on the expedition you are going to join. Your sister can therefore not accompany you."

She pretended to hesitate.

"However," she said, turning to Colombe, "you are not yet provided with those forms by which our sex is distinguished. I might therefore say—though it would be taking a slight liberty, and you must not make me regret it—that you are both 'children.' This inclusive word would mask the difference that exists between you."

"Oh, thank you, madam, thank you!" said Just, thoroughly convinced that in the end his aunt was kinder than he had thought. He was only too glad to set aside the idea of human wickedness.

"And yet," she went on to Colombe, in whom she sensed a more obstinate resistance, "I will only tell this fib if you agree to go along with the story and act it out unremittingly. This very day you both must cut your hair identically to look like pages and wear the same clothes, which we'll provide. In short, although there is hardly any resemblance between you," and here, a horrible smile flitted across the chancelloress's face, "at least there will be a relation in clothing and behavior."

Still looking at Colombe, she went on: "You will have to adopt a boy's name, and it seems to me that 'Colin' would work best. If either of you inadvertently misspeaks, it won't be so obvious. Will you promise me to do this?"

"Yes, madam," Just blurted out, though the question had not been addressed to him.

Colombe thought quietly for a moment, then nodded her assent.

"Very well," said the chancelloress, "but remember that once you have entered this fiction, it would cost you your life to extricate yourself from it. And you must seal off your girl's nature with steadfast resolution for as long as nature does not take the upper hand in denouncing you. Let us hope you are successful."

"Is he well? Did he send you a letter?" asked Just, taking the practical details for granted and thinking only of his father.

"No," snapped the chancelloress. "A messenger brought us word from him. But there is more: you must promise to answer all questions with the greatest cunning, especially when it comes to your age. As far as anyone is concerned, Just is thirteen and Colin eleven, is that clear?"

They nodded, somewhat peeved at losing two years off their ages, with the attendant reduction in dignity.

"And now, children, a final piece of advice."

The two were instantly alarmed, knowing that this woman's venom might easily be saved for last.

"You will meet people of all kinds on this voyage. Some will be looking for your father to take revenge on him and kill him. You must on no account reveal your name—or his, which would be the same thing."

This last showed plainly that she had never accepted the fact that her relative had cast the name "Clamorgan" on a pair of bastards.

"And how will we manage to find our father if we cannot say who we are?"

"He will find you, using the instructions I sent back via the messenger who brought me word of him."

She made them repeat all her injunctions, verifying that they understood them perfectly, then bade them farewell with what almost seemed emotion.

"I commend you to God, and pray that He may keep you."

Ever since they had seen the French armies in Italy brandish crosses before attacking the pope's soldiers, with both sides claiming to serve the same God, Just and Colombe had thought it safest to steer clear of religion. When it came to making wishes for the future, they preferred to look toward each other. They gave their hands, which were still clasped, a squeeze.

Once the chancelloress was gone, they returned to their rooms to bundle up their rags, skipping excitedly at the thought of seeing their father again and resuming the life they loved.

"Did you notice?" said Just, "she didn't even mention Gringalet!"

CHAPTER 5

Buried in their memory somewhere, Colombe and Just had the reassuring impression of having traveled once by boat already. It must have been between Marseilles and Genoa, with a regiment.

But this almost forgotten journey would have been aboard a galley, and the Mediterranean had been calm for the entire crossing. The long flat vessel hardly rose above the surface of the sea. It had small auxiliary sails that weren't scary. Its engine was the shadowy deck at water level that gave off sounds of hoarse breathing and blows. They were still too young to imagine the horrors and curses hidden there. Consequently, they preserved a pleasant memory of this first voyage. This false sense of security left them unprepared for the shock they were to receive.

The cart, driven by Belloy, had been traveling at a fast trot since their departure from Clamorgan. They were crowded together in the back, both wearing new shirts and trousers that their aunt had hastily ordered made for them. Just carried a hunting bag on his lap and sat pressed against Colombe, one arm around her neck. As always when they traveled, they huddled together as one, pooling their small warmth and blending their disheveled mops. This last bit of disorder was no longer even allowed them, since both had had their hair cut.

But each felt the other's close-cropped stubble graze his or her ear whenever the carriage hit a bump.

From where they sat, they looked backward and watched the countryside recede. Objects became smaller and disappeared, until it wasn't certain they'd ever existed. They saw Clamorgan's keep vanish in this way.

"I'm certain she lied to us," said Colombe, thinking back to her aunt's black silhouette on the drawbridge bidding them farewell, "but I don't yet know about what."

As they rounded the beech copse, they saw Emilienne dart out toward them. She broke into a run, breathing hard, trying to pass a basket up to them. They didn't manage to catch hold of the basket, and all its lovingly chosen apples and fresh white bread spilled into a muddy rut. The night before, they had cried their fill with the poor woman. She was disconsolate at losing her last two children, moaning that this time the estate was truly dead. But in their haste to get off, the two hardly remembered their tears of the night before and were almost startled to see the old woman run out of the woods. In the old days, they had made cry many a woman into whose care they'd been placed. It seemed their fate to bring unhappiness to anyone who chanced to love them.

The road followed along the coast and crossed pale moors of salt grass. Le Havre-de-Grâce was too new a town to have outlying villages. One left the countryside to find oneself immediately among carpenters' sawhorses and masons' scaffolds. Just and Colombe hardly had time to register that they had reached town before the cart pulled to a stop at the main wharf. A quarter turn of the horses put them facing the landing jetty, and they both exclaimed at suddenly seeing the ships.

The three monsters looked like so many walls of blackish wood. Their enormous poops, decorated with gods from antiquity in red and gold, towered high above the houses. From the iron-hooped masts hung heavy spars like tightrope walkers' balancing poles, some level and others angled and apparently about to crash on deck. Innumerable ropes encased these apparitions in a net that the restless spars chafed vainly against.

Built for sheltered waters, galleys had a fragile elegance that suited

them to intimate scapes and a brief—if sometimes fatal—embrace
with the sea. The three ships, for their part, were cut out for the
ocean. They contained, on a reduced scale and in an arrested state, all
the violence of that vast space, whose farthest limits they were
designed to reach.

The two children had never felt so tiny nor, paradoxically, so big.
For before such behemoths, they hardly differed in size from those
who so ridiculously called themselves grown-ups.

"Listen," whispered Colombe, gripping the boy's arm.

She hadn't dared to call him Bel Hardi, as this brave name and all
the cockades of chivalry lost their power before such extraordinary
apparitions.

Just lent an ear and in turn perceived what made the scene so star-
tling: a great silence filled the dockside. The mooring lines, as thick
as a horse's neck, tautened as the ships slowly swayed, making the
only sound.

"Come," shouted Belloy, "down you get, the two of you!"

He had actually spoken in a low voice, but in the general quiet his
words rang out like a shout. Just and Colombe jumped to the ground,
their eyes still fixed on the ships. Only on turning around did they
discover that the wharf, for all its silence, was filled with people.
Some were in front of them, standing among large wicker panniers,
arrested cranes, and jute bundles. Others leaned out windows along
the street or against the railings of trading vessels. More still were
perched on bollards, hanging from light posts, or balanced on
unhitched carts, whose shafts swayed dangerously under their
weight. And all were looking away from them.

"Follow me," said Belloy.

He started to push his way through the crowd, which fortunately
was not very closely packed. The two children scampered in his wake
without much trouble. A bystander or two grumbled, their gaze still
in the distance, when the children in their hurry trod on their feet.
As they made their way through the ranks of people clustered
between the row of storefronts and the ships' flanks, Belloy gradually
slowed down. It wasn't that he encountered more obstacles but that
he was now searching the faces of those he passed as though looking
for someone.

Suddenly, as a mysterious sign passed soundlessly through the crowd, everyone kneeled. The movement was a slow one, a swell, mirroring the powerful swell that lifted and set down the ships. Still standing while everyone around them had fallen to their knees, Just and Colombe could now look out over the gathered heads and see what everyone was looking at. In the distance, at the edge of the town square where the flat facade of the cathedral reared up, was a platform under a purple canopy. A priest, his chasuble shining, was celebrating Mass.

"Look, Bel Hardi, they are getting ready for battle."

Just had had the same thought at the same moment. The only times they had ever attended Mass had been in Italy when an army was preparing for an assault. They had seen men with battle-scarred faces shedding floods of tears, and young men with hardly the shadow of a beard ready to offer up their brief but adventure-filled lives. Today, they read on the faces of the silent men around them the same hope and the same awareness of death. The women looked on from windows and balconies, while all those on the wharf were men. Moved by the soundless prayer, Just and Colombe fell to their knees in turn and put their hands together to pray, not really knowing how it was done.

But Belloy came and grabbed them by the collar, lifting them brutally to their feet.

"What are you doing, you scoundrels! Get up!"

A few called for quiet or grumbled, but Belloy, followed by his two acolytes, continued to make his way forward through the kneeling crowd straight toward the altar. They approached as close as they could to a central group of knights who wore the white Cross of Malta and were stationed near the platform. The three waited for the end of the ceremony. The children looked around them avidly, as did Belloy. Though neither said anything, both Just and Colombe felt the scene to be full of their father's memory. They couldn't help looking around them for his face.

When Mass ended, the silence was not immediately broken. First the prelate raised his vermilion cross to bless a man who had followed the Mass from a place beside him on the dais. Alone to receive this distinction, the man had remained the entire time on his knees as if to show that he accepted his elevation humbly. Next, the priest blessed the crowd, gesturing broadly toward the sky, as though releasing birds.

The man on the platform rose to his feet, and the priest, his mission now accomplished, left the stage to him. From where they stood, too close to the dais and hidden from it by the close ranks of the Knights of Malta, the children could hardly see the man. He seemed a colossus, as the priest was entirely hidden by the standing crowd, while he still rose above them. They could hear his powerful bass voice:

"To the greater glory of God, let us take to the ships, brothers! France in America awaits us. Hurrah for Christendom, hurrah for the king!"

A roar greeted his words. It was hard to understand how so great a silence could turn in a moment into so great a noise. The clamor went on, with each man adding his own invocation. The colossus jumped down from the platform and pushed his way through the crowd, surrounded by his Knights of Malta, as shouts of "Hurrah for Villegagnon! Hurrah for the admiral! Brazil is ours!" went up in his path. Belloy tagged along behind this group. Clinging to one of the knights, he finally managed to get the information he was looking for. He made his way with difficulty toward a plump man with a pointed beard.

"Monsieur de La Druz!" he shouted.

The soldier did not hear him, intent as he was on following in Villegagnon's great strides. Finally, Belloy managed to grab one of the man's arms and pull him to a stop. Dom Gonzagues consented to the treatment ill-humoredly.

"Here are the children," said Belloy, while Dom Gonzagues looked at him as though about to ask him to choose his seconds. The business of the interpreters had clearly gone out of his mind. When a glimmer of it returned, he made a great show of ceremony.

"Ah! the nephews of Madame . . ."

This was an invitation. He thought Belloy might enlighten him as to the lady's name, which he had lacked the wit to ask during the interview.

". . . of Madame . . . ?" the old soldier repeated.

But Belloy stubbornly ignored the question, saying only:

"This, the older one, is Just. The other is Colin. They have everything they need in their sack. Good-bye, captain!"

And with the agility that made him so frightening at Clamorgan, where he appeared or disappeared with great unexpectedness, Belloy vanished into the crowd.

"Wait just one moment!" Dom Gonzagues called out, feeling in considerable peril with these two goslings on his hands. What's more, he realized that Villegagnon and his guard were now a long way off. He dragged the children along but was unable to catch up with his master, which made him ill-humored. The dock was as noisy and chaotic as it had earlier been silent and prayerful. Men ran in every direction, calling each other, carrying loads on their shoulders, trundling sea chests. Dom Gonzagues hesitated as to what to do, then considered that he had not yet examined the two future interpreters and pushed them toward an open house. He led them upstairs to an empty gallery hung with majolica medallions showing portraits from antiquity.

"Let's see what you look like," said the captain, scrutinizing them one after another.

Just thought that he was going to run his hands over them and discover his sister's disguise, but this was to attribute more freedom to Dom Gonzagues than he actually had. The idea that one of them might not be male never crossed his mind. He only wanted to ascertain that they were not past the age best suited for their duties. The wide foggy sky of the port above the open gallery finally allowed him to see their faces. Colombe's was smooth, passing his test. It was Just's, on the contrary, that caused him alarm.

"What's this?" cried out the old soldier, rudely poking the boy's overlarge shoulder and turning him around. "Your chin is covered in hairs. How old are you?"

"Thirteen."

"Thirteen! Blazes! You are either very advanced for your age or lying to me. I've led lads into battle who were less lusty than you, and they were fully eighteen years old."

Just was pleased by the compliment. He had a great urge to confess to this old captain his desire to bear arms immediately. Fortunately he was able to restrain himself, for Dom Gonzagues's admiration was replaced by sharp anger.

"I should have suspected it!" he said. "How could I have been so stupid as to take that nun at her word? And what am I going to do with you now?" he went on, looking furiously at Just. "Without your blasted driver, who has disappeared, will you know how to get back to wherever you came from?"

Colombe, seeing that they were once more threatened with separation, intervened. Now that she was a boy, she could turn her pale, troubling gaze on anyone she chose without the risk of being thought immodest or brazen. She held Dom Gonzagues's eyes in hers and said quietly:

"Sir, my brother has always been just two years older than I. As I am eleven, which you can plainly see, he must be only thirteen. He started to grow in earnest only six months ago. Our father is very tall and strongly built. It is his nature that is coming through."

Dom Gonzagues shrugged his shoulders but seemed to grow a little calmer. He remained silent and turned his eyes toward the port. From the balcony, the ships' decks were just visible. They were slowly starting to fill up as hundreds of seamen, like ants carrying twigs, formed long chains on the wooden gangways that rose toward the waists. The decks were already crowded with travelers. The ships would soon be loaded. There was no time to lose.

Dom Gonzagues turned back to the children, avoiding the younger one's gaze, and spoke bitterly, jabbing his beard toward Just.

"All the same, that nun played me for a fool . . . Sister Catherine! A plague upon her. I'll remember that. And the other one, your aunt, what was her name?"

Should they tell him her name? The chancelloress had said nothing on this score.

"Marguerite," said Colombe prudently.

Marguerite what? No one wanted to tell him the woman's name! Dom Gonzagues prepared to object but didn't: the name "Marguerite" filled him with a sense of well-being that he was unwilling to disturb by asking further questions. Despite his awkwardness in front of the lady in black, he retained a clear and not unpleasant memory of her handsome face and perfume. He held this Marguerite in a precious recess of his mind, promising himself to return there one day when the spirit moved him to write poetry.

"Come," he said, "I should have examined you before agreeing to take you. But this is not the time to take back a promise. Are you at least willing to go along on this voyage?"

"Yes," they chimed together.

"Well then," said Dom Gonzagues, pushing them ahead of him, "let's see to it that we don't get left behind."

CHAPTER 6

In the bustle of preparations for the ships' departure, a sailor who looked like all the others was going about his business in the port. He walked barefoot, as dirty and as poorly dressed as you become if you sleep on the floor and clean up only on stormy days. There was one detail that set him apart: two giant Scotsmen, straight from the Highland mists, wearing kilts and carrying pikes, followed closely behind him. The sailor might wander to the left or to the right, but the two Caledonians stayed immediately on his heels. He took them on several detours, darting at a fast run up a street strewn with cordage, passing a seller of sweetmeats without listening to his patter. Finally he led them to a large square house fronted on four sides by roads that served as an inn. When he tried to enter, however, one of the Scotsmen grabbed him by the arm and frowned.

"Me visit old uncle!" explained the sailor in a language that neither of his attendants spoke, the dialect of Venice. "Say good-bye to him. Say good-bye to uncle, poor old uncle."

With smiles and gestures, raising and lowering his arm with his thumb and fingers pinched together as though pulling an invisible bellcord, the sailor—dirty and unshaven as he was—managed to radiate good faith, affection, and innocence. Again he told them that he wanted only to take leave of his uncle, and he mimed the respect-ful kiss one might give an old man. This mysterious pantomime led the Scotsmen to an entirely different understanding. They blushed, looked at the building, and judged that it was not their duty to deny a man on the verge of so long a voyage a last consolation of the flesh. One of the guards walked around the inn to make sure there was no other exit. They then allowed the Italian to enter and mounted watch outside, their pikes crossed.

In the new town of Le Havre-de-Grâce, built by Francis I to give France a portal on the Atlantic within easy reach of Paris and the provinces of Flanders, the houses were still white, their plaster fresh and their beams smelling more of trees than of wood. This hardly created the warm atmosphere of a sailors' inn. In the great room with its white walls and pale fire, four morose topmen waited out the hours till nightfall, drinking from blue earthenware mugs that reminded them uneasily of the sea.

The Italian headed directly for a wooden staircase, which he fol-lowed to the second floor. There he entered one of the rooms on the landing. It was a bedroom with a red tile floor that shone with wax. A bed, its curtains drawn, and a small oak cupboard provided the only furniture. The tall window stood open, looking out onto the port in the white morning sun. Set into the thickness of the wall on either side of the window was a stone bench, which, in the haste of moving in, had not yet been provided with a cushion.

On the bench sat Cadorim, the Venetian merchant, who motioned to his countryman to take the seat opposite him. First, the sailor leaned briefly out the window to verify that the two guards were still downstairs. He caught a glimpse of their woolen pompoms and was satisfied.

"A fine pickle I'm in because of you," said the sailor dejectedly.

"What are you talking about?" said Cadorim, looking surprised. "I had you released from prison."

"Only to place me under the guard of those two harlequins."

"They let you come and go, I believe?"

"Never allowing me out of their sight for a second."

"Do you think," asked Cadorim, lowering his voice, "they are treating you in any special way, that is, do they suspect something?"

"As far as that goes, no! It's the way they treat all the convicts who have been reprieved so that they can sail with these ships. They are terrified that we'll give them the slip before the final departure."

He sighed.

"Had you not realized this beforehand?" asked Cadorim with a thin smile.

The sailor shrugged. The old Venetian wagged his index finger at him as though scolding a child.

"Don't worry, in any case," said the sailor. "We sail very shortly."

Both looked toward the port. The three galleons bound for Brazil towered high above the fishing skiffs and coastal traders, their great masts heavy with spars and rigging.

"All the same," whispered Cadorim, "it truly is beautiful!"

The sailor reacted with some asperity:

"Beautiful to anyone remaining ashore."

He spat on the floor. Cadorim looked disgusted.

"Come, my friend, there's the window for that sort of thing."

"And underneath the window there are Scotsmen," retorted the other, groaning.

"Restrain yourself, Vittorio. By tomorrow you'll have the entire ocean to catch your excretions."

Struck by the tone of authority, the sailor changed his demeanor abruptly, as he knew so well how to do. It was this talent that had made him aspire to become a simple crook on dry land. But it was his fate once again to be sent out over the ocean, which he found enormously frightening.

"Oh, your lordship, I beg of you," he whimpered, "save me from this. For good. You know that I would rather stay in prison than sail with these ships. If it weren't for your promise . . ."

"I haven't forgotten it," Cadorim interrupted, pulling a purse from under his cape. "Five hundred sequins, as agreed."

"Yes, of course," said Vittorio in the same pathetic tones, pretending to take no interest in the purse. "But what will I do with it if I'm forced to remain among the savages? Do you think I will find any use for that metal there—where, as it happens, the metal comes from?"

"Well, if that's the case . . ." said Cadorim, briskly making the little sack disappear.

Vittorio stretched out his arm but too late.

"I was right to take you away from those thieves," said Cadorim laughing. "You're not much in the way of purse-snatching."

"Your lordship!" said the sailor imploringly.

He fell to his knees on the tiles, adroitly avoiding the spot he had soiled earlier.

"Come," said Cadorim with a snicker, "you're better at acting, and that's what I've hired you for. Get up."

He handed him the purse, and this time Vittorio did not let it slip away.

"Why don't you tell me about the company you are traveling with. What kind of people are they?"

"They are all madmen," said the sailor, as he tried to stuff the purse into a little grimy sack that hung from a string at his neck.

"I saw a few of them," Cadorim confirmed, "and they did appear to have little knowledge of what they were undertaking. But I am just a merchant and it was hard for me to approach them without raising suspicions. You have observed them at closer range, so tell me about them."

"I've never seen the likes of them before!" said Vittorio.

"A collection of miscreants sprung from the jails, or so I've heard?" suggested Cadorim with an ironic smile.

"Those are by no means the worst," said the sailor, dismissing the provocation. "At least what *they* want is clear. But when they opened up the jails, they didn't just find honest bandits, believe me. For every ordinary cutpurse, they have freed ten crackpots who have been driven crazy by Brother Luther's injunction to go to the Bible and examine it for themselves."

Cadorim sensed that Vittorio was about to spit and stopped him with a gesture.

"So," said Cadorim, interested, "you're saying that there are many Huguenots among the sailors? Are they organized? Are they carrying out a mission for a church of heretics?"

"I don't think so. Every one of these madmen thinks he knows the best way to serve Christ and is prepared to kill anyone who says differently. These zealots are a scattered lot, there's no common ground between them. The fact is that for the most part they hate each other."

"A good description, Vittorio. You appear to have the right talents for the job I've assigned you."

"Don't forget, your lordship," said the sailor, suddenly assuming an air of dignity, "that I was once a novice, and that if I hadn't been unfairly thrown out . . ."

"I know, Vittorio. Go on. Crackpots freed from prison and what else?"

"Well, there's the troop of Knights of Malta. With their white cross on their stomachs and their haughty airs, they are still living as though we were in the time of the Crusades. I'm sure they confuse Brazil with Jerusalem."

Cadorim roared with laughter.

"And Villegagnon, their leader, have you seen him?"

"From a distance. He's the craziest of them all, from what I hear."

"Who told you that?"

"A Norman merchant who has traded in the Levant and speaks enough of our language so that we could understand each other."

"And what did he say?"

"That the whole idea for the colony came from Villegagnon. The Normans, who have been sailing to Brazil for fifty years, have never wanted anything of the kind. They trade under the nose of the Portuguese and ask only that the king of France protect them. But a few troops and a fort somewhere would suit them fine. Instead, this Villegagnon has hatched the idea of transporting the whole country across the ocean. Consider, your lordship, that he has had one of every species invented by civilization put into the belly of his ships: bakers and ploughmen, carders and cabinetmakers, winegrowers, hatters, bookbinders, roofers—and donkey drivers, though there are no donkeys, and street singers, though there are no streets. I was even shown a poor man who made aglets. As though anyone were going to bother lacing his flies among men who go naked."

The gulls on the town square arced through the sky laughing, echoing Cadorim's mirth as he thwacked his thighs.

"And with all that," he said, "they hadn't even thought to provide themselves with interpreters! They amass great stores of the superfluous but only remember necessities at the last minute."

"When it comes to interpreters, that's not so surprising. Their expedition is not simply Noah's Ark, it's the Tower of Babel. The few Frenchmen you encounter among the Knights of Malta bring with them a whole ragtail they picked up on their campaigns. I've met some who claim to be descended from the Teutonic knights. Others are renegade Turks, or captives wrested from the Barbary Coast pirates. And then there are those damned Scotsmen, apparently because Villegagnon also fought in those parts."

"And how does all this crowd communicate?"

"For every one of them who speaks French, there are five who have to use sign language to make themselves understood."

"Well, my dear Vittorio," said Cadorim, his eyes still moist with laughter, "you must be having a fine time of it, and I'm glad I sent you along."

At this, the sailor's face darkened, becoming black and shriveled, like a cooled and carbonized log.

"Your Lordship, these madmen are setting out never to return. That's their business. But I agreed to trade my prison sentence for this ocean voyage on the express condition that you would bring me back to my country. I am counting on it absolutely."

"And you are quite right to do so, Vittorio. But it all depends on you."

"On me!" said the sailor. "Do you mean that you're abandoning me?"

"No, dear friend, a large force will go to your rescue. Yet whether it succeeds will depend entirely on you."

"How is that?"

His eyes darted to the door, then to the open expanse of the square, where his freedom lay. He suddenly felt doomed and searched for an escape, however desperate.

"Ah, I should have expected it," he said. "You don't have any way of getting me out of there. You just wanted a spy, that's all, and now it's, Onward, you brute! How could I have been so stupid as to believe that Venice could do anything for me in America, when our galleys already have enough trouble getting back from Greece safely!"

"Leave our poor country out of it. If anyone can help you, it's the Portuguese and no one else."

"That's better," said Vittorio, putting a radiant smile on his carbonized face. "I should have suspected as much! That's who you're working for. And that gold . . . I understand now."

"For your happiness, the main thing is to believe the Portuguese will rescue you," said Cadorim shrewdly.

"But tell me," Vittorio asked, "when will the Portuguese stop us? Will they board our ships during the crossing? Oh, what a pleasure it will be to see those swinish Knights of Malta carved into bits."

As Cadorim said nothing, he went on with his hypotheses, speaking more and more rapidly:

"Unless they allow us to reach the New World first and turn all those damn Frenchmen into slaves on the spot! Tell them I'll take ten of the slaves, so that I can work them to death in my gold mines before I return here dressed as a prince."

As he spoke, the sound of raised voices and banging doors reached them from downstairs. Cadorim looked quickly out the window.

"One of your Scotsmen is no longer there!"

"He must have come looking for me," said the sailor, yawning. "We've taken our time. The ships are about to leave."

"In that case," said Cadorim, "I have one last thing to tell you, which is the most important of all. I don't know when or where, but you must believe me absolutely: someone will contact you on my behalf. Speak to him in full confidence, as you have just done with me. That is how you will be saved."

"And how the French will be lost!" added Vittorio gaily, his spirits recovering at his countryman's promise.

As the Scotsman's heavy boots rang in the stairway, a last thought occurred to him:

"But how will I know . . . ?"

Cadorim smiled enigmatically and leaned forward slightly. In a low voice he said, "The man who comes to rescue you will have a password."

"What is it?"

"Ribera."

The sailor blanched. So the man who rescued him would also carry the memory of his crime to the far ends of the earth. "Ribera" was the name of the man he had killed.

But the time for hesitation had passed. The guard was just coming to the landing. Vittorio leapt to the door. He slipped through it like a cat and closed it behind him so quickly that the Scotsman saw nothing of the room.

CHAPTER 7

Of the three ships, the last one, which bore the name *Grande-Roberge*, was to carry Villegagnon, vice admiral of Brittany, along with his court of knights and men of science. Dom Gonzagues had a berth on this ship and would not have relinquished it at any price.

He accompanied Just and Colombe as far as another ship, which was moored in the lead. This was the *Rosée*, a trading vessel to which a few cannons had been added. Smaller than the other two, it was slated to transport mostly equipment and animals. A large Baltic soldier stood guard at the gangplank, denying passage to anyone who did not figure explicitly on his roster. As he had difficulty reading French, a nervous crowd had built up around him. The crew, discharged prisoners, and soldiers had embarked first. Now there remained the artisans, whom the Balt was calling forward according to trade, mangling the words.

"Ivan de putchers!" he bellowed.

The crowd asked him to repeat his words, hesitated for a moment, then offered a correction.

"Oh! He wants the butchers."

A hundred voices would then call for the poor men in question, scattered across the dockside in the arms of their wives and children, making their final good-byes.

Dom Gonzagues, dignified, his beard tapering to a point, pushed a path through the crowd up to the guard and announced in a carrying voice, pointing to the children:

"The go-betweens, is this the place?"

Despite his visible desire to obey, the soldier was unable to put more intelligence into his wide-staring eyes than is to be found in the dawn sky during the Baltic winter. Dom Gonzagues grabbed the list from him and started to look through it himself.

"Let's see, go-betweens . . . go-betweens . . ."

Just, leaning over his shoulder, found the word in the list, though he did not entirely understand its meaning. He pointed out the line where the word was.

"So you know how to read!" said Dom Gonzagues. "That's a point in your favor, and perhaps you will discharge your duties creditably after all. In any case, we have found the right place. Go on aboard. We'll meet again at the first layover."

He pushed them in Indian file onto the two joined boards of the gangplank.

"Introduce yourselves to the first mate once you get up there. He'll show you to your berths. Go, and God keep you!"

So saying, he fled toward the *Grande-Roberge* and Admiral Villegagnon.

Colombe wouldn't let Just hold her hand, and they climbed carefully up to the ship's waist without tripping. Once on deck, they followed Dom Gonzagues's instructions and waited for someone to address them. But no one gave them a moment's notice. All those who had recently boarded were clumped at the ship's rail on the wharf side, shouting and waving their arms.

The sailors, who went barefoot, were tightening the rigging, climbing the shrouds, and busying themselves with the mooring lines. On the upper deck a large man with a beard and a deeply weathered face bellowed orders, cupping his hands to his mouth.

Just and Colombe waited for a time, then did as all those who had arrived after them were doing: they strolled around the deck, following their inclination. As they had no farewells to make to landward, they went and leaned their elbows on the rail to seaward, where there was no one. Looking back at Le Havre-de-Grâce from their floating promontory, it appeared to be a natural pouch in the shore, closed by a double flap of new breakwaters. From the black water and the leaden sky dripped an acid of eternity that would soon dissolve the land. The imminent approach of the unknown should have left them deeply troubled. Instead they felt full of confidence, the confidence they instinctively attributed to their father. He had always wanted them to share his wonder at the beauty of the world, and this sense was almost stronger in them than their actual memory of his person.

Meanwhile, the last stragglers had boarded and the gangplanks were retracted. The *Rosée,* its mooring lines cast off and laboriously drawn in, started to roll more pronouncedly.

Just raised a finger: "Listen!"

He had caught the sound of the ship awakening to life. Every milk cow and mule in the holds and the betweendecks, every fat-tailed sheep, every laying hen, every goat, every crossbred hunting dog started to bawl in unison.

At the same moment, the seamen perched loftily among the gulls let loose the foresail. It unfolded in a whisper of cloth. The wind, a moment before ambling through the spars and rigging, whistling under its breath, slammed brutally into the obstacle. The sail took the charge full on and grunted like a giant struck in the stomach.

Just and Colombe were afraid they might miss the departure from where they stood. The quarterdeck was off limits to them, however, and the whole quayside railing was lined two deep with men who would not have given up their place for anything in the world.

"Come this way," said Colombe, pulling Just by the sleeve.

She had noticed where two cabin boys had climbed onto the bowsprit, steadying themselves with a stay. Before her brother could stop her, she had scampered up to them. Taking advantage of her small size, she had even slipped around them to straddle the narrow beam where it extended out over the water. Just had trouble talking the cabin boys into letting him by, as he was bigger and might plunge them into the drink. He finally managed to get around them and found that Colombe's spot, for all its dangerous appearance, was not uncomfortable. Several ropes came together there and formed a sort of cradle where they could sit, one on the other's lap.

The *Rosée* being the first of the ships to sail, they saw nothing in front of them but the empty expanse of the bay, dotted with tiny fishing boats. Three other sails had now been set, and as the wind pushed at them, the ship started to come fully awake. Like a beast of burden unwillingly returning to work, it slowly stretched its drowsy limbs. The masts and yards creaked under the sudden tension as the ship moved away from shore.

Six hundred men's voices called out their farewells, and were answered from the wharf by the keening of the women and children. The pitiful mass of families churned into motion as the ships did, with people running along the dock and out onto the breakwater to shout their good-byes from the last extremity of dry land.

The *Rosée* now turned its nose toward the ocean, as though it had discovered the smell it was looking for, and set out unhesitatingly on the trail of the Atlantic.

When the ships had passed the lighthouse and were in the open ocean, they regrouped and sailed in a convoy. Shouts no longer went out to the coast but passed from ship to ship, though the gusts carried them away. The flagship stood off in the lead, and the children saw the two Neptunes carved on its stern bob in front of them. From time to time the wind brought them snatches of a bagpipe melody played by Villegagnon's Scots honor guard.

Then there was quiet, and Just and Colombe, wet with spray, believed for a moment that the departure ceremonies were over. But the bronze mouths of the artillery pieces shot twenty balls out through the gunports. The two had forgotten the terrible and delicious vibrato of a cannonade. It was the final flourish to the proclamation of their freedom. Colombe burrowed her head into her brother's shoulder, and the two cried with joy, pressed against each other.

They almost didn't hear, with the whistling of the wind all around, the furious voice of the Balt ordering them back on deck.

• • •

After the seeming chaos of departure, Maître Imbert, the captain, gave orders for all passengers to be led to their berths. Preparations had taken longer than expected. It was already late in the afternoon. A storm front loomed on the horizon like a charging herd of aurochs. Maître Imbert expected no good from it.

The betweendecks during these last moments of calm was filled with noisy agitation. Each man was trying to hang his hammock so as to provide himself the most possible comfort, at least as he understood comfort in this dark space with barely the headroom to stand up in. And it was clear to all that on the outcome of these first, minute battles hung their prospects of greater or lesser comfort on the months-long crossing.

Just and Colombe did not have the opportunity to take part in these conflicts. The soldier who had come looking for them led them down three sets of stairs to where the interpreters were to bunk. As they were supposed to be children and therefore short, a windowless hole had been assigned to them in the hold next to the storeroom and not far from the livestock.

"Out iss forbidden!" the Balt shouted at them, convinced that he could only make himself understood on this ship by raising his voice.

Just stooped to enter the passage first. He felt a rounded pile of barrels on one side, and on the other a pinewood bulkhead—he came away with a splinter. The burrow widened as he entered, becoming widest at the far end where it touched the hull. But before he could get there, Just stumbled over a large mass, and a loud voice rang out in the dark:

"Stop, you lout! Can't you see there are people here?"

The newcomers understood that, narrow as it was, the cubbyhole was already occupied. They would have to make do with the meager space at the entrance. They sat down next to each other, leaning against the barrels, their knees drawn up.

"Excuse me," said Just, "but do you know how long we will have to stay here?"

The question was greeted with nasty laughter.

"Listen to him, the rest of you," guffawed the same voice that had greeted them.

Then the voice began to imitate Just's speech, which was a mixture of coarse Norman accents and the lilting intonations of Italy.

More laughter. Listening carefully, Just thought it came from three people. A faint glow from a lantern hanging in a forward compartment started to pierce the gloom. They waited quietly for the darkness to lift so as to learn more about their neighbors.

"I'm thirsty," whispered Colombe in her brother's ear.

A revolting odor, combining the pitch used for caulking, a whiff of salt meats, and the strong-smelling fleece of the livestock, floated in the confined space. Their mouths felt dry.

"You'll have to get used to it," said the voice, for everything that was said in this cubbyhole was heard by all the others.

"Isn't there a water barrel somewhere?" asked Colombe.

"Ha! Ha! A water barrel! Where do they think they are? Why not a fountain while you're at it?"

As taunting and male as it was made to sound, the voice was somewhat hoarse and unsteady, being in the process of changing. Colombe guessed that the speaker must be about the same age as themselves.

"Then what are we going to do?" she asked, in a voice that was natural and unafraid.

"Wait, that's all!"

"Well, then all the better," said Colombe softly. "It means the crossing will be short."

A barrage of jibes met this remark.

"Short!" said the voice, when the laughter subsided enough for the speaker to catch his breath. "Oh, very short, and I advise you to wait until we arrive to drink anything."

Their eyes had now adjusted somewhat. In the half light they could see two forms huddled in the back and, in front of them, the silhouette of a big boy whose head almost touched the ceiling. He must have been able to see them also and to take satisfaction in their pitiful aspect, for he went on condescendingly, as though to emphasize the favor he conferred by placing them under his authority:

"You'll have to make do with the food and drink that one of the sailors brings here twice a day. And you'd best not lose a crumb, because it's pretty meager."

"When will he come by?" asked Just.

"Not till tomorrow, now. You weren't here earlier when he brought us our evening ration."

This was unwelcome news: they had eaten nothing since their departure from Clamorgan. They longed for Emilienne's basket, and the picture of the beautiful loaves spilled in the road still passed before their eyes. Fortunately, the heaving of the ship was starting to make them feel queasy.

"Are you go-betweens too?" asked Just a little later. He had been mulling over the word, whose meaning he couldn't fathom.

"As much as you are, dolt!" their neighbor sneered. "We'll become go-betweens when they put us in with the savages."

"In that case, we'll certainly disembark before you," said Just, shaking his head. "We aren't going among the savages."

"Then where are you going?" asked the boy, the whites of whose eyes could now be seen.

"To find our father."

Laughter was on the point of erupting, but the ruler of the shadows suppressed it with a wave of his hand.

"Keep still, you lot!" he said, in the tones of a carnival barker announcing a midair somersault. "We have a serious situation."

He raised a finger into the air.

"Given that this ship is going to America among the cannibals; given that it is going there directly and without stopping at any other lands; and given that these two tell us that they are going to rejoin their father; I conclude . . . that their father is a cannibal!"

Loosing his dogs' leash, he joined the chorus of barking.

But Just, as quick as when he bow-hunted thrushes in the woods of Clamorgan, jumped at the speaker and grabbed him by the throat.

"Our father," he spoke into the boy's face, "is a great captain and a man of honor. You have me to answer to for insulting him."

Surprise left the mocker defenseless. But he quickly gathered his strength, pushed Just away, and threw himself upon him. Their two bodies rolled over and over on the floorboards, which were sticky with oils and effluvia. For all his fury, Just couldn't get the better of his adversary, who seemed well versed in gutter fighting and pounded Just with his heavy, square fists. The two other boys, who were smaller, rose to their knees and cheered on their champion noisily. Colombe shrieked and tried to separate the combatants. The noise, combined with the kicks echoing through the barrels, brought a sailor to investigate. He leaned into the opening, and the lantern in his hand lit the squalid fight brightly. Just was wiping his bleeding lip, one sleeve ripped from his shirt. His adversary was gathering his rags composedly and backing away toward the smaller boys. Though probably younger than Just, he had the strength and heft of a country boy. The light shone briefly on his close-cropped head, exposing whitish patches of ringworm and a flattened nose.

"Keep quiet in there!" the seaman bawled. "If you like getting tossed around, only wait a bit. You'll get your fill of it."

He disappeared and the light went with him. There was a long moment of silence while each took stock of his wounds. The calm made them aware of the ship's increased motion. The slow swell they had originally felt was supplemented by the vibration of the hull as it collided against short, choppy waves. The ropes that held the barrels they were leaning against creaked under the strain. A great gurgling of innards rose from the depths of the ship, where sick animals were groaning.

"You'll pay for this," said the boy who had fought.

Just answered that he wasn't scared. The truce looked to be short-lived.

But the nausea brought on by the ship's rolling calmed them in spite of themselves. The strange intoxication of seasickness weakened their limbs and numbed their minds. They felt as though the barrels had already rolled over their chests. The sailor's words finally forced a path through to their enfeebled wits: the storm was upon them, ready to avenge God knew what outrage committed by man.

All night the ships ran before the storm, dropping down into its troughs, riding the bulge of its unfurling waves. The wide, rounded vessels pitched dangerously between the walls of water and listed to the point of lying flat on their sides. Fortunately, the ballast in their filled holds and the water trickling down into their depths kept them from capsizing altogether.

Aboard the *Rosée*, the bellowing and the shrieks subsided, to be replaced by a mournful, nauseous silence, troubled only by the whistling of the wind and the loud reports of broken spars.

But as dangerous as the sea was in a storm, the real peril came from the coast, which still lay too close. All night Maître Imbert remained by the helm, which could no longer be governed, staring into the darkness for the dread sign of a reef or an island.

Dawn rose before either of these dangers had been sighted. The weather calmed, and only at the end of the morning were the hills of the providential shore outlined on the horizon.

CHAPTER 8

Morning came as a lesser tumult. Just woke up first with a sore head, his back imprinted with the rough surface of the deck. The cubby was as dark as ever, but narrow shafts of light pinned confetti specks of white on the dark wood. Just's mouth was dry, gluey with thirst. He watched Colombe sleep, then inspected the mound of cloth near the ship's side. He had the vague memory of a quarrel yet to be settled, without remembering its details.

The night left a confused impression in his mind of rolling, of shocks, of whistles blowing. The seasickness had dropped him into total and painful unconsciousness. He vaguely remembered hearing shouts, the sounds of a chase, even gunshots, but he could put them in no sensible order. At the moment, the ship seemed totally immobile, as though the battle had drained it of its last strength. Warily, Just stuck his head out of the narrow cupboard. The hold was in a complete mess. Torn hammocks hung from the timbers, crates of food had come loose from the stores, and shattered stoneware pitchers exposed their glistening contents to the flies. A wan light from the deck made the scene even more desolate. What was most disturbing was the silence. Just ducked back into the cubby and woke Colombe. The three phantoms lying under their heaps of cloth were also starting to show signs of sentience.

"Water!" croaked Colombe.

Just helped her out of the cubbyhole and led her through the masses of garbage.

"Let's go up and see," he said. "I don't understand what's going on."

She held her head as she walked, and he had to support her as she climbed the ladders. The betweendecks was as disorderly and empty as the hold, except for two sailors lying beside one of the guns, moaning. The light was better, and Colombe was regaining her spirits.

As they reached the top of the companionway, Just had to shade his eyes. The sky was uniformly gray but bright, as though the sun were everywhere at once behind this frosted glass. The *Rosée* lay at anchor in a bay surrounded by soft hills. The two other ships in the convoy were anchored nearby.

Colombe squeezed Just's arm.

"Look," she said, "we've arrived."

Behind them they could hear their companions of the previous night climbing out of the hold. Colombe prepared to give them the news, laughing, but she felt Just tug her sleeve.

"What are they all doing over there?" he asked.

She turned and saw a strange scene. All the civilian passengers of the *Rosée* were gathered at the bow of the ship and crowded on the forecastle.

A row of guards held them at bay with drawn swords. Two harquebuses, their barrels resting on forked supports, were aimed at the small crowd. Several seamen went about their business freely. Two were washing the deck around the mainmast. They were sweeping into a bucket an odd amalgam of broken glass and spar fragments, coated in a red liquid very much like blood.

"Look," said someone, and they felt a strong hand come down out of nowhere and grab them by the neck. "It's the go-betweens! We forgot all about them!"

"Bring them over here!" shouted Maître Imbert, who stood among the soldiers facing the first row of captive passengers.

The sailor dragged his two victims across the deck.

"But there were five of them. You troublemakers, where are the rest of you?" asked Maître Imbert.

With his double chin, his good-humored lips, the captain might at times be harsh, but he did not appear to be mean. In point of fact he was not. He looked on human weakness with the forbearance of one who compares it to the infinite cruelty of the sea.

Colombe felt confident enough as she passed in front of him to fall suddenly to her knees.

"Captain," she said, bringing her hands together, "give us something to drink, for the love of heaven. We are dying of thirst."

"Have they not eaten or drunk?" asked Maître Imbert.

The sailor who was responsible for this task answered with a downcast expression:

"Well, what with the storm . . ."

"Then it's time to feed them and water them. I want them to be ready for their new work. Ah, here are the others."

Two miserable figures hung from a sailor's arms as though from a gibbet, while a third shuffled along behind. His curiosity momentarily getting the better of his thirst, Just raised his head from his goblet to inspect the boys who had insulted his father. Now out in the fresh air and revived by the water, he remembered everything. The two smaller ones, to all appearances, were pitiful urchins. With their oversized heads and swollen limbs, they must have grown up in the street like weeds in the cracks between paving stones. But the bigger one knew what he was doing, and apparently he had not forgotten anything either. Taller than Just, he wore a stained shirt and trousers that were worn through at the knees. In the glare of the nightlamp, his features had been distinctive, with his bulldog aspect and flattened nose. In daylight, his face was no longer so frightening, and had there not been the insult to avenge, Just would have willingly looked with compassion on this creature whom life seemed to have thrown from birth against a wall of violence and poverty.

"Give these scamps water as well," said Maître Imbert.

He appeared very pleased and laughed as he looked at the go-betweens.

"Exactly what I need," he said, nodding.

The distant sound of a cannon, re-echoing off the walls of the bay, put a sudden end to this tender moment. The shot came from the flagship, where a puff of smoke could be seen rising.

"The signal!" said Maître Imbert. "Come, take your bit of bread and join the others. We must hurry."

He stepped back several paces and climbed onto a chest to address the passengers, still held at bay by the soldiers.

"Where are we?" whispered Colombe, squeezed in next to Just, in the middle of the unshaven and malodorous group.

He shrugged to show his ignorance.

"Poor children!" whispered a small sad man standing next to them. "They don't even know where they are . . ."

"Listen to me, all of you," began Maître Imbert, putting as much menace as he could into his kindly voice.

"The coast you see there is England," whispered the little man. "The storm drove us here last night . . ."

"The ship is setting out once more," the captain was shouting, "and this time I hope for good."

"Is it much farther, the place we're going to?" asked Just, a bit disappointed not to have reached their destination.

"Poor children . . . It's shameful that you have been told so little," murmured the little man, looking even sadder than before, if possible.

"But in any case, don't think that the others have been luckier than you," bawled Maître Imbert, both hands hooked in his belt. "Don't believe it for a moment . . . They have fled, that's their affair, but they won't get far. I myself brought down four of them."

Probably thinking this number was not terrifying enough, Maître Imbert corrected himself.

"No, it was six—isn't that so, lads? Six fell by my hand, not counting the ones executed by my men. Add those who were drowned, and those who were captured on land by the English marshals—to be sent to the galleys as slaves. It doesn't leave many, does it?"

"The poor fellows were so frightened by the storm that they preferred to jump in the water rather than continue the voyage," said Just's neighbor gravely, looking as despairing as ever.

"So those of you who are still on board have nothing to regret," went on Maître Imbert. "You know what to expect if the weather should act up again! But I'd be surprised if we met another gale to equal that one. On my oath as a seaman, it's been a long time since I've seen anything as bad."

"We haven't arrived, my poor friends. It's just that we haven't started out yet. And we won't arrive for weeks, for months. If we arrive at all."

As he said this, tears glistened in the little man's eyes. The sight moved Just and Colombe, who suddenly felt much stronger than this unfortunate man who had so taken pity on them. They received the news with more optimism than he did.

"Very well. Now, I must select several among you to replace the scoundrels who took flight. And because my crew was battling the wind while your friends were thinking only of getting to land, eight of my men went overboard."

This time it was Maître Imbert who wiped away a tear.

"So," he bawled out again, "we're going to replace them. Let's start with the ship's boys!"

His eyes, which had been trained high on the line of the horizon so as to embrace all of his audience, suddenly dropped down to the first row.

"I believe our go-betweens will do very well as ship's boys. The three oldest in any case."

He gestured at Colombe to step forward. She planted herself in front of him, and he looked her up and down.

"Not very sturdy yet. You'll see to the rigging on deck. Your name?"

"Colin."

Then he called forth Just and the boy with the squashed nose.

"These two are a little better. You don't look scared of much. You'll climb up to the topsails. Your names?"

"Just."

"Martin."

He gestured to them to take up their posts immediately.

• • •

A happy warmth and luminous skies met them as they sailed southward. When they passed Grand Canary Island, a volley of cannon shot was fired on them from the Spanish fort. One of the balls went through the *Rosée*'s hull in the bow, leaving a perfectly round hole above the waterline, which the ship's carpenter had little trouble mending. Colombe made light of it, saying, "That's all it was, then."

But it was a baptism all the same, and Just felt the pride of a combatant.

The summer nights grew longer, but shortened again as the ship approached the equinoctial line. They were beautiful nights, warm and peaceful, which the two children spent on the sun-heated deck, having received permission to sleep where they liked. During the day, they ran about topsides executing Maître Imbert's orders. Colombe was a little jealous of her brother: he had become perfectly adept at climbing the topmasts. The exercise was making him stronger and gave his handsome face a bronze glow. Their days were very different. Colombe found herself a little bored. She tried talking to the seamen on deck and the passengers who strolled by, but the conversations never went far. She often saw the little man who had spoken to them on the day after the storm and learned that his name was Quintin. He had been condemned to death for his religion and always carried a book with him. Colombe, who missed reading, extracted a promise from him to lend her some books.

Just dreamed a lot in his tightrope walker's world. He sometimes took the watch and let himself be carried off by daydreams—the kind that follow from the horizon when it forms a circle around you.

At night, when they came back together, lying close against each other to sleep, Just and Colombe would recount all they had thought during the day. As the days went by, they found it more and more extraordinary that their father should have made so distant a voyage. At certain moments they believed it and wondered only whether he too had met with storms and seasickness, and whether he had savored the gentle pleasures of the tropics. They imagined him either in command, like Villegagnon, or else a prisoner in the hold. At other times they thought they had been deceived, that their father would never have gone so far from all that he loved. Then they would regret not having fled on the night of the storm with the reprieved convicts and those who had preferred an adventurous escape over the terrors of the voyage. Each time a coastline appeared, they made plans to run away if the ship ever came close enough to shore.

But these dreams fused with other ones, fabulous dreams in which they envisioned the land of monsters and magic they would soon meet on the confines of the known world. As they learned more about the New World, from Quintin in particular, they started to invest it with their curiosity.

The days and weeks passed, but though the water in the barrels turned green and their food grew foul, they felt themselves caught up in a happy routine that they would be sorry to see end.

Their only real source of uneasiness was Martin, who ranged as they did on the decks and through the rigging but without ever relaxing his evil glare with its promise of revenge. Just's thoughts were in fact running along a parallel line to Martin's, and Colombe was disturbed to see her brother making plans for a fight that would wipe his honor clean. At least he favored a public settling of accounts in the form of a fair fight or duel, which would end with the victor showing mercy. Martin was hatching something else entirely. His hostility toward them was sly and unspoken. It would certainly erupt in the shadows and not in broad daylight, at a moment when Just was most vulnerable. Colombe feared nights especially and wrapped her arms around her brother while they slept, as though to act as his shield.

The ships were scudding straight south. Large clouds covered the whole expanse of the sky, keeping the rippling soup of the sea warm, from whose surface a muggy vapor rose. Stores of drinking water were running low. The flagship gave orders to make a course toward land.

They anchored off a hilly coast where they stood a good chance of finding streams to refill their water barrels. The ships' boats came back at nightfall with water that was muddy, almost yellow. And they had only been able to fill half the barrels because a band of hostile black men had interrupted the operation.

News spread among the crew of the *Rosée* that they were on the coast of Africa. The sailors cursed the officers of the flagship who, with all their fancy instruments and supercilious airs, had led the convoy astray, whereas Maître Imbert with his long experience could have piloted them surely and unerringly. Apprised of their error, the pilots of the lead ship changed course and headed west. It was high time.

They started to see sails on the horizon again, a sign that they were back on the right course at last. Each sighting gave cause for great alarm. Villegagnon had forbidden the taking of prizes, and they

therefore allowed several lone Spanish ships to go their way unmolested, though it would have been highly agreeable to loot them. But
one morning, the watch signaled a group of sails to the northeast,
and it was eventually determined to be a Portuguese convoy of six
ships. Though the American coast was still a long way off, it was
obvious that the three French ships were on a course for Brazil. This
was enough to mark them as enemies.

It was hard to know at that distance whether the Portuguese
would seek an engagement. Villegagnon took the precaution of
preparing for a battle. The decks of the *Rosée* bustled with sailors,
soldiers, and civilians, the latter drafted by the captain to load the
cannons. The gunports were opened, the chests full of harquebuses
brought out, and all sail was crowded on to take advantage of the
good breeze.

Colombe was responsible for seeing that the deck was kept clean
and clear, in readiness for boarding. She patrolled energetically from
bow to stern. Passing by the mizzenmast, she saw Quintin standing
straight and motionless, his arms crossed.

"Don't you have a task to do?" she asked him, surprised.

"Yes, I am supposed to clean the guns."

"And you have finished already!"

"No, I'm not going to do it."

Colombe took the opportunity to catch her breath for a bit. Her
feverish efforts had in any case been intended more to calm her
nerves than to clean a deck that was at this point perfectly spotless
and tidy.

"I've heard," said Colombe, "that when the Portuguese make a
capture, they mutilate the crew, then cast them adrift on their ship to
die of thirst."

"I've heard that too," said Quintin, whose pale thin face preserved
the mournful expression it had worn on their first meeting.

"Well, that's a good reason to defend ourselves."

"No," said Quintin, his arms still crossed.

Over the silence of the open ocean, the wind whistled in the giant
sails. The leaning ships, dressed in so many skirts, aprons, and
shawls, resembled three old girls setting out for a ball.

"Then," said Colombe, "we should just let ourselves be flayed
alive."

"My child," interrupted Quintin sharply, turning toward her and taking her hands, "the only license men give themselves is to do evil. It's the only passion on which they impose no limits. For my part, I preached the opposite—and was condemned to death."

"The opposite?"

"I mean, not to put any restraint on goodness, on love, on desire."

As he said this, he squeezed her hands in his. His eyes shone with a light she had never seen before, a mixture of appetite, fever, and despair. She was glad when a commotion, which had started on the quarterdeck, swept the entire length of the ship, putting an end to this incongruous exchange: the Portuguese were turning back to their old course.

Shouts of joy went up all around. Demijohns of wine, kept for special occasions, were passed from hand to hand, and each man took a long pull.

The captain ordered several sails struck, and Colombe tried to find Just as he worked in the rigging. She couldn't and so knelt with the others in a prayer of thanksgiving. There was no chaplain on the *Rosée*—the one priest in the convoy had unsurprisingly taken his place on the flagship near the seat of power. Each therefore prayed in his own way and addressed a God who was held at once in common and individually. The sailors with their rough piratical faces called on tender images of the naked Virgin and Child, while innocent passengers with soft white hands, released from imprisonment on religious grounds, lifted their delicate features toward a God of blood and punishment.

It was during this silence that the first sounds of violence burst out aloft: a cry, the noise of a sail ripping, a fall. With the sun shining through the spars, nothing could be seen from on deck of what was happening above. Colombe was all the less able to guess, as Just had carefully avoided mentioning the threats that were directed against him daily. Martin, ever since their altercation, had never stopped eyeing him when they were both hanging in the ship's upper rigging. He would curse Just, insult him, and promise to get his revenge. Just would answer by challenging him to a one-on-one fight. But Martin clearly did not intend to take that risk.

The acrobatics required of the ship's boys already took considerable care and attention, but Just needed even more to avoid a mishap.

By the end of the day he was generally exhausted. On that day, however, the ship's gentle heeling, the balmy air, and the antics of a pod of killer whales distracted him while he was resting on the foreyard.

The spar's varnished wood supported his stomach, while his arms held him in balance on one side and his legs on the other. He was in this position when the knotted end of a rope hit him hard in the side. Just cried out and lost his balance. Fortunately he fell onto the full side of the sail's belly and had the presence of mind to catch himself with both hands on the thick edge of the cloth. For a long moment he hung there, his side hurting, stunned by his fall and his miraculous survival. The knotted rope that had struck him now hung alongside the mast. Martin was watching him from a shroud slightly above him.

All this part of the incident was unknown to Colombe. She only saw Just as he set out toward his attacker, climbing upward.

"They're fighting!" she yelled.

And when she realized that the others standing around her still did not understand, she went to spread the alarm to other groups, even finding Maître Imbert and tugging on his sleeve.

"Stop them, Captain! Look: they're fighting."

The sounds of the struggle drifted down amplified from the heights, but the combatants could hardly be seen. They were fighting hand to hand on the floor of the crow's nest.

Ten or twelve sailors leapt into the rigging at the same time, and Maître Imbert, taking the course best suited to preserve his authority, shouted out the order for them to do so, though they were already halfway up the ratlines. Martin fought with great strength but without daring or skill. Just, who had these qualities in abundance, was kept from putting them to good use by the cramped quarters of their battlefield. He had taken some heavy blows by the time the sailors separated the two adversaries. Just felt that, in leaving off a duel that could only end in death, he had been forced into an act of cowardice. It was this shame rather than any fear of punishment that made him lower his eyes in front of Maître Imbert.

The captain, for his part, placed more value on peace than on fairness. When it came to brawls on shipboard—and he had seen his share of them—he made it a rule never to look for a culprit.

"Clap them in irons, both of them!" he shouted.

"No!" cried Colombe, ready to throw herself to her knees.

But Maître Imbert looked at her so angrily that she stopped in her tracks. Another word and he would have locked all three of them up. She bit her tongue and saw Just led away, still held by those who had saved him from Martin.

It was one of those days in the tropics when the blues seem intent on proving that they are numerous enough to cover the whole universe: the blue-white of the sky, the blue-green of the horizon, the blue-violet of the ocean, and the blue-gray of the foam. It took the special genius of man to invent captivity in the midst of these vast reaches open to happiness. Colombe, seated in the stern near one of the ship's boats, cried silently.

She thought of Just, wounded and hungry in a dark cellarhole like the one they had first known. Then she thought of her own loneliness in the midst of this strange crew. But her self-pity was brief. With a show of will that constituted all the strength of the Clamorgans, she told herself that she was Colin, a free ship's boy, that she was no fool, and that she would surely find a way to free her brother.

· · ·

In the course of the crossing, small groups had formed among the passengers, soldiers, and crew. The minuscule exchanges between them over food, drinking water, or knowledge as to the ship's course and the admiral's intentions—all of which were in scarce supply— only exacerbated the mistrust of each group toward the others. Colombe had formed a team with her brother. Their closeness had sufficed them, but now she was alone. The groups distrusted outsiders, and none wanted to have anything to do with her. Of course she could approach a shipmate and draw a few words from him. But as soon as he had answered, he would scurry back to his work, if he had any, or else back to his friends, where he would tell them the whole incident in whispers. In the general boredom of the crossing, anything at all became an event.

Colombe was almost discouraged, when she remembered Quintin, who had dropped out of sight for several days. Then, while waiting in line for soup at lunch, she saw him. He didn't approach her. Carrying a bucket and pretending to be cleaning, she searched the betweendecks afterward and finally found him rolled up in a hammock slung above one of the guns. She climbed onto the bronze tube and parted the two lips of the net. Quintin lay on his back with his eyes open, seemingly counting the wood grain of the crossbeams.

"What are you doing here?" asked Colombe, a little frightened.

"I'm praying, as you can plainly see."

"Those other times, it didn't stop you from going on deck."

The little man sat up. He squinted, shook his head, and looked around as though just regaining consciousness.

"I become carried away by meditation," he said, with an apologetic face that looked almost like a smile. "I am wholly in the company of the Holy Ghost."

He seemed to be returning from a long voyage.

"Where is your brother?" he asked, recognizing Colombe.

She told him about Martin's revenge and the resulting punishment. Looking like an insect caught in a spider web, Quintin tried to extract himself from the hammock. He very nearly fell onto the cannon. Once on his feet, he fluffed out the flea-bitten lace of his collar and pulled up his stockings. Thus dignified, he took Colombe by the hand and said to her: "Let's go and get the news."

Perhaps because of his loneliness, or his austerity, or his perpetual sadness, Quintin was accepted by all the groups, though he belonged to none. In his company, Colombe was allowed into these mock families. The clusters were governed not so much by a common sympathy as by a shared dislike of all the other clusters. Once they had expended the energy necessary to protect themselves from the outside, the tribes still had long hours to spare for groaning, sighing, and swearing, which did duty for conversation. Wine was rare, as the last drops were being saved by the captain for their arrival in America, and this contributed to the listlessness of the gatherings. Thanks to knucklebones and dice fashioned from horn, this human silence was filled by the tiny rapping of chance.

First Quintin brought Colombe to a group of artisans, among whom were a baker, two carpenters, and a seller of nostrums, who styled himself an apothecary. At Quintin's request, the group, whose members circulated almost everywhere on board, agreed to look for Just and bring him anything he needed, as well as find out what they could about his condition.

Next they met with a cluster of sailors that Quintin knew because of his Bible. Even before the expedition sailed, Villegagnon had announced that, while each might pray according to his lights, there was to be no preaching on board. But in the absence of priests, the Norman sailors sought nourishment for their crude faith. They were riddled with superstition and firmly believed that a calm ocean and the safe return of their ships depended on pious works, supplication, masses, and rosaries. Quintin did not approve of this idolatry, but he did not feel called upon to oppose it either. For his part, he believed in the simple strength of the scriptures. He therefore read long stretches of the New Testament and the Bible to these rough sailors, whom the roaring of storms left unmoved, though the fear of hell filled them with terror.

Quintin asked them to describe the purpose, length, and destination of the crossing for Colombe's benefit.

"I don't know what you've been told," he said to her before the sailors gave their answer, "but when you speak of your father and Italy, it seems to me that you misunderstand the nature of this voyage."

It was perfectly true that Colombe, like Just himself, had often heard the word "Brazil" spoken on board, but she knew not where this country lay. In Genoa their father had spoken to them of distant voyages accomplished by the mariners of that city which joined East and West by a strange route. But Colombe continued to think that these new lands were just stages toward the only real destination, whatever detours one might take along the way: the Mediterranean, with its Italy, Spain, Greece, and Barbary Coast.

The sailors explained to her as best they could, tracing a map of the world on the dusty floor, what the New World was in general and Brazil in particular, which they were going to colonize.

Hearing this, Colombe no longer doubted that her father had played a heroic role in the conquest of these lands. Only when she saw him would she understand why he had chosen to have his children travel anonymously, outside the aura of his glory. Yet they did not have to stand for the ignominy of being held in irons. Her mind turned painfully back to Just.

She queried the sailors about the punishment he faced. They told Colombe that Maître Imbert generally did not set a long period of incarceration, particularly when the captive was a useful hand.

"He prefers a good session with the cat-o'-nine-tails, and then it's done."

"The cat-o'-nine-tails!" said Colombe.

She thought, To a Clamorgan! But remembering the warnings, she did not mention this name to the sailors.

"Is it one of you," asked Quintin, "who administers the lashes?"

"No, Villegagnon has appointed one person on each ship to deal out physical punishment. Here, it's the Balt."

Quintin frowned. He was acquainted with several of the soldiers, but the Balt kept to himself, and no one knew how to address him.

That night Quintin led Colombe back to his hammock, around which a final group of passengers were seated. They were haggard men with long blond hair, wearing linen blouses. Their lips were twisted into a permanent smile of ecstasy, as though they could hear in the silence some sweet heavenly voice singing canticles for them.

"Don't tell anyone, but those are Dutch Anabaptists," whispered Quintin, careful that no one should overhear him. "They dream of breaking with the world, whose end they believe is near. They have no use for the Bible—they follow their own inclinations."

"They are the blessed," said Colombe, looking askance at the ecstatic faces of these peasants, whom she instinctively distrusted.

"The blessed! Poor men. They are the most persecuted men on earth. They wanted to bring down kings, the Church, and all customs. Some of them want to live as Adam did. The truth is that everyone hates them, and it's a miracle that they were not burnt at the stake."

"Why do you sleep with them? Are you one of their sect?"

"Me?" said Quintin, horrified. "Never! I worship the Bible."

Then he added mysteriously: "We only have certain things in common."

The Anabaptists welcomed Colombe warmly, and using a German dialect understood by Quintin, they passed on their news. What was most surprising was that these enemies of the world were perfectly well informed as to what was happening on the *Rosée* and on the other ships as well. An argument had sprung up on the flagship, according to them, between Villegagnon, the cosmographer, and the pilots over the ships' exact location. Some wanted to continue south and others to start heading north. The ships were still far from their destination and supplies were giving out.

The *Rosée* was the best provisioned of the three ships because so many had run away during the storm. On the lead ship, however, there was hardly enough food for everyone. The water had gone bad, and all stomachs were plagued.

"They claim," Quintin translated, "that part of the crew of the *Grande-Roberge* will be transferred to our ship."

Colombe's face fell. This could make Just and his attacker less needed on deck, so that the captain would leave him in the hold.

Night had now fallen, Just was not there, and she would have to sleep by herself.

Two Anabaptists had already started to prepare their bedding.

"Where are you sleeping, sailor?" Quintin asked her.

Colombe shrugged.

"I don't know. On deck, in some corner."

"Stay with us. Would you like to share my hammock?"

This was not a particularly unusual offer. Tight limits had been placed on personal effects so as to load the ship with as many perishable items as possible. Hammocks were scarce, and many slept two and three together in a single hammock.

It took Colombe a moment to remember that she was a boy and should react to this offer as though it were a matter of course. Truth to tell, the prospect of bundling up against the austere Quintin with his wan face and woebegone expression neither gladdened nor worried her. At least she would not be so cruelly conscious of Just's absence.

Hygiene on shipboard was left to the individual's discretion. Some groups washed noisily, hauling buckets of water out of the sea. Others performed their ablutions discreetly. Still others, particularly the sailors, relied on the damp air to dissolve their humors. The so-called Colin withdrew that evening as usual into the shadow of the quarterdeck to splash himself with water from a barrel as furtively as a mouse.

On her return, Colombe found Quintin already lying down, in the same hieratic position as that afternoon. She hesitated briefly, then climbed into the cloth sack after him, shaking the recumbent figure in all directions.

"Don't you pray, Colin?" asked Quintin.

"Well, I do . . . but silently."

"God loves us, Colin."

"I . . . I know."

Two Anabaptists snored, and Colombe was already regretting that she had not made her bed on deck. She turned her back on Quintin and curled up, glad all the same to feel his warmth beside her. Closing her eyes, she saw Just and smiled at him.

"He blesses each of our desires. That is the secret," said Quintin in a grave voice.

But Colombe did not hear him. She was already sound asleep.

CHAPTER 9

All those who were skeptical that the earth was a ball and kept watch in the bow for the abyss and the monsters that guarded it were now beginning to recover hope. The tropical blue grew darker. Families of tousled clouds, big ones and little ones together, raced across the horizon. In the morning, heavy mists covered the sea, which smelt of dead fish. Later, in the afternoon, the wind freshened up until all sails had to be struck except the foresails. Maître Imbert took the wheel himself, which was never a good sign. He ordered four guns readied for firing: if the fog thickened, they would need to signal the other ships by cannon.

But what came to them finally was rain. It fell from a cloud so black it froze the air. Everything near became dark, while the circle of the distant horizon remained lit with a pale green light.

Colombe went to taste the rain, standing by the mainmast, her arms outcast, shivering and delighted. The raindrops were viscous and cold, but it was fresh water all the same. She opened her mouth wide and took in great packets of wet air.

"Don't drink that in," said a passing sailor whom she had met with Quintin. "The rain is pestilential."

The rain fell all day and continued into the evening. Colombe received orders to sleep on deck, as Maître Imbert wanted his crew at the ready and had doubled the watch. She shivered all night under a tarpaulin. By morning, the weather had cleared, and the sun warmed the crew's clothes. But as a sailor had predicted earlier, sores began to appear on their long-soaked skin.

The apothecary prepared a cauldron of unguent, which the crew, forming a long queue in front of him, daubed on their pustules.

Bad news arrived from the flagship. Sailing abreast, the captains traded shouts and signals back and forth, then hove to. When Colombe saw a boat lowered from the *Grande-Roberge*, she decided that the Anabaptists were truly well informed. Yet she saw them ambling around aimlessly all day, smiling at unseen things but paying no attention to the people around them.

"Let's see who they're sending us," whispered Quintin, whom she had not seen approach.

Ten soldiers, armed from head to toe, the great white Cross of Malta splashed across their fronts, climbed in turn down a rope ladder from the *Grande-Roberge* and carefully took their seats in the pinnace. Behind them came a man of the cloth, wearing his cassock, followed by three men in ordinary clothes.

"My word," said Quintin, "the situation must be serious, they are sending us the elite."

The rowers worked in concert to get the boat unstuck from the caravel's side. They cut easily through the chop and soon reached the *Rosée*. The first to reach the deck was the priest.

Maître Imbert greeted him with ceremony and led him to his own cabin in the stern.

"That was Abbé Thevet," said Quintin, "a Franciscan and the king's cosmographer."

Colombe could not tell from Quintin's tone whether there was admiration or contempt in his listing of these honors.

The scholar had scarcely disappeared when the deck bustled with gentlemen and knights. One of these, caught off guard by a treacherous wave as he was reaching for the ladder, arrived soaked. He loftily rebuffed any concern for his person, requesting only a square of dry cloth in order that he might dry off his sword. Colombe recognized Dom Gonzagues.

After its many days at sea, the ship was suddenly thrown topsy-turvy by the onset of these intruders. The crew and passengers had drawn away instinctively, their backs against the far rail.

The boat meanwhile rowed back to the *Grande-Roberge*. Everyone watched what would happen next in silence.

"It must be Villegagnon!" Quintin predicted in a low voice.

But though the crew of the flagship bustled about on deck, no one climbed down the rope ladder. Suddenly, a square shape, dark and massive, was laboriously raised above the ship's rail. Sounds of grunting effort carried to them through the still air. The black shape, held by ropes, wobbled, then started to descend.

Everyone on the *Rosée* moved closer to see, and the ship listed to port under the sudden shift.

The black shape arrived at the pinnace, and the craft tipped in all directions as it was set down and shouts went up. The rowers took their places again, with caution. Finally, the boat pulled away and made slowly toward the *Rosée*.

Then for a long incredulous moment, Colombe and the silent gathering around her beheld, wobbling on the billow, at this juncture in the Atlantic—its middle, perhaps, unless they had already reached the confines of the world guarded by the Cyclopes—a large bureau of dark wood. The boat, with the dark carbuncle on its back and its six oars, resembled a great beetle crawling over the beige ground of the sea in the evening light.

Once the article of furniture reached the *Rosée*'s side, it still took a long moment for it to be hoisted successfully on board. Finally it sat in the bold middle of the deck. It was a writing cabinet with drawers and secret compartments, a fall-front, and turned legs. The wooden surfaces of the ship, from the poor planks of the salt-bleached deck to the rough spars dripping with varnish, were humbled by the high-born elegance of its ebony marquetry. An ornamental figure on the front, inlaid with ivory, represented a double horn of plenty, surmounted by a crown. The workmanship was of such quality that most of the men on the ship had never seen its like. But to Colombe it brought back a sudden memory of Italy. It was autumn and she had been about seven. A lady was speaking to her, leaning against a similar cabinet. Where had that been? She searched her mind but could find nothing.

Meanwhile, engrossed by the giant insect that had landed on their deck, the occupants of the *Rosée* failed to notice that the boat had returned to the *Grande-Roberge* and come back to them yet again.

A voice boomed out, and everyone jumped:

"By Saint Jack of Jerusalem, it looks well there!"

His two large hands on the waist rails, Villegagnon grinned as he looked at the ebony cabinet.

• • •

A head taller than everyone else, his salt and pepper hair cut short and as upright as the rest of him, Sir Nicolas Durand de Ville-gagnon, Knight Hospitaller, paced his new realm. It took no more than a few strides for him to cross from the prow to the quarterdeck, his hand gripping Maître Imbert's shoulder.

"And I thought the *Grande-Roberge* was already small . . . Bah! We'll get used to it in the end, just as we did over there."

In point of fact, his companions had easily grown accustomed to the ship. His "we" was the generous form of "I," quick to include others.

"That ship is a hecatomb!" the admiral continued, in what he meant for a low voice though it echoed from rail to rail.

He looked across at the *Grande-Roberge* as it hoisted the pinnace on deck.

"Eight of every ten men are afflicted. Two have died already. One of them my barber," he said, ruefully drawing his hand over his chin, which bristled with black hairs. "Let us hope that we haven't brought the plague over with us."

Following this brief access of anxiety, Villegagnon came to himself and looked around at the still motionless crew and passengers. He judged that they expected a harangue from him, a kindness he was never loath to bestow. He went and stood next to the cabinet, on which he placed a deliberate hand.

"My friends! Our voyage is proceeding well. New France is near, I'll warrant you. We'll raise it before long. In the meantime, you have the honor of serving as flagship. And not because I am aboard—in truth, the privilege is conferred on you by this."

He nodded at the cabinet and brought the flat of his hand down on its flank. The commode absorbed the shock by letting its fall-front flap drop noisily, like a wrestler opening his mouth on being grabbed around the stomach. Behind the wooden lid appeared twelve drawers inlaid with tortoise shell and brass filigree.

"All of you," went on Villegagnon, exhaling a breath so powerful that, properly aimed, it might have filled a sail, "behold this wooden piece of work: it contains our expedition's Holy Ghost. Within it are the letters from King Henry II granting us authority to take command of these new American lands. Our notary, Maître Amberi—where is he?—will record every acre that we conquer in a document that will be kept in the drawers you see before you. When this cabinet returns to France, it will bring His Majesty the titles to the new kingdom of Brazil, which we will offer him together."

A general cheer greeted these words.

Such was the effect habitually produced by Villegagnon's speeches. If the passengers aboard the *Grande-Roberge* were sated with his words, to the point that their insides no longer tolerated them, they were still fresh aboard the *Rosée* and were received enthusiastically. The seamen swelled out their chests, and the passengers remembered anew why they had joined the expedition in the first place. Even the Anabaptists, who hated all kingdoms and were constantly trying to overthrow them, seemed happy at the idea of having a new one to attack.

"Steady on, Maître Imbert!" the admiral called out, so that his peroration might conclude with an apotheosis. "Shake out the mainsail and give the entire convoy the signal for departure, as you are now its leader."

The sailors, plagued with sores as they were, ill fed and weak, briskly found their wings and climbed into the rigging.

The giant Villegagnon—so like the ebony commode—with his black eyes and beard set off by a nose as long as an ivory ninepin, had in a few words restored life to the vessel, dispelling the torpor, backbiting, and intrigues. When he left to shut himself in the after-cabin, Colombe's eyes were filled with tears.

Quintin, whom she found in the betweendecks holding a bowl in his hands, did not share her excitement.

"All the same," he observed with a disapproving shrug, "he is a man of war."

After they had supped, they made the rounds of the groups they knew. Everyone was talking about Villegagnon's arrival. But the sailors also had news for Colombe.

"Jacques saw your brother," one of them whispered to her.

The sailor in question had not yet arrived among them. He came a little later, grumbling about Villegagnon's men.

"It's starting off badly!" he muttered. "These gentlemen have hardly come aboard and already we are forced to cater to their every whim. The Franciscan was monkeying with his instruments, measuring the height of the stars or some other such business, and I had to hold his lantern for two whole hours."

"Did you see Just?" asked Colombe.

"Yes," said Jacques, spitting on the ground. "This week, I've been assigned to bring him his grub."

"How is he?"

"As well as you might expect, given that his feet are chained to the wall."

"Oh! Poor Just, he's in pain, he's ill."

"You mean he's putting on lard! No exercise, no tiring chores. He's not out in the weather holding the Franciscan's lantern."

"And the boy who struck him, is he with him?"

"Lord, the two are side by side, and they seem to be getting on like a pair of brothers."

This was good news, but Colombe felt a twinge of annoyance at the news of their intimacy.

"Did he send any message for me?" she asked.

"None."

It suddenly came to her that she was perhaps more to be pitied than he.

"Will you see him again tomorrow?"

"Morning and evening."

"Can I come with you?"

"No, Maître Imbert has made me swear to keep their whereabouts a secret. And with all these new soldiers stalking about . . ."

At Colombe's insistence, he finally promised to take Just a message saying that his brother was well and sent his encouragement. The rest of the evening she spent making plans to free her brother. She finally concluded that her best chance lay in appealing directly to Villegagnon for a judgment. From what she'd seen of him, she was convinced of his fairness. She would have to watch his daily routine and find a way to address him in person when his sidekicks and Maître Imbert would not be on hand to stop her.

That night, the admiral ordered three demijohns brought up from the storeroom and passed around the decks, so that his arrival on board could be properly celebrated. The heat had maderized the wine. Colombe, who liked the sugary taste, did not have to be asked twice to help herself generously when the sailors handed around the large wicker-cased bottle, and Quintin helped her lift it to her lips.

The drink, after the previous fitful night on deck, made her fall into a deep and dream-filled sleep as soon as she settled into Quintin's hammock. The next morning, her memory of the night's doings was confused, and she tried to sort out dream from reality. She was tempted to doubt the whole thing. Yet the fact that she had woken up on the ground and not in the hammock seemed to confirm her memories.

Everything had happened in the bluish glow of the warm, moon-dappled sea. The portholes were now left wide open to air out the damp betweendecks and dissipate the increasingly rancid smell of the cargo.

Colombe had met with an obstacle in trying to shift positions. She felt that she was suffocating and opened her eyes. Quintin was plastered to her, his sad face against hers, smiling. He had taken off his shirt, and his two bare arms were under Colombe's jersey. She felt the man's long hands caressing her back. The hour was so late, and sleep lay so heavily on her, that her instinct was not to be startled.

"What are you doing?" she murmured.

"I am holding you against me," said Quintin throatily.

"But why?"

"Because I desire to."

She felt confusedly that it was her duty to resist, but Quintin was being very gentle and it takes a great deal of strength to be the one to initiate violence.

"Wait," she groaned, "it's bad."

Quintin's hands continued to wander all over her body, which was poorly defended in the tropical heat.

"It cannot be bad," he said, "as I am guided by love. God has placed an infallible sense of the Good in His creatures. Nothing that our desires prompt us to do is bad, as long as love is our guide."

This overlong sermon put Colombe on her guard, where Quintin's caresses had merely lulled her. She recognized his mournful peroration and his interminable exegeses of the Bible. This gave her the strength to push his hands away.

"They may be your desires, but they are not mine."

Quintin did not try to use force. He had no strength in any case, and Colombe, who handled ropes on deck all day, would easily have bested him. But nothing of the kind happened. Yawning, her eyes half closed, Colombe laboriously climbed down from the hammock and went to sleep against a cannon.

The next morning, Quintin's face looked so normal, as sad and serious as ever, that she was at first tempted to dismiss the whole thing as a dream. But at noon, having set her bowl on the rail to eat—thus arranging for the wind to rid her midday pittance of its rotten smell—Colombe felt Quintin brush past as he took his place beside her. Checking to right and left that there was no one to overhear, he addressed her in the anxious and despairing voice he had used during their first meeting:

"How tragic! My poor girl, who ever forced you to come on board, alone of your kind, and seal off your feminine nature?"

Colombe's first reaction was anger. All the confused memories she had set aside as doubtful were now confirmed.

"And who gave you license to pry into my nature?"

She trained her eyes on Quintin with visible fury, and he looked away. She was afraid he might use this against her, blackmail her perhaps. But she revised her thoughts immediately on seeing how readily the poor man buckled. Clearly he was not one of those brutes who are ruled by sensuality, a sensuality they impose on others as violently as they experience it themselves. With Quintin, everything proceeded from his head: he complied methodically, almost regretfully, with the doctrine of love he believed he had discovered in the scriptures; and onto the fire of his observance he threw the little appetite nature had given his parsimonious being.

"What was your crime, Quintin?" asked Colombe gently.

"I was a lens grinder in Rouen," he began dolefully, "and a highly respected citizen—until I tried to teach others the truth. And it was revealed to me only three years ago."

"By whom?"

"A traveler from Germany. He suffered many trials there," sighed Quintin. "I hid him in my house until he was able to board a ship for the St. Lawrence."

Colombe stared out toward the choppy wake that the *Grande-Roberge* dragged carelessly behind her, like a deposed queen.

"That is when my vision suddenly cleared, and I traded in my poor lenses for the great universal lens through which everything is seen to be sharp and beautiful."

So saying, he patted his little Bible tenderly.

"My preaching must have conveyed my enthusiasm successfully: I became a close friend to several ladies in Rouen, who recommended me in turn to others of their friends. And thus my nights and days were spent making the infinite love God has given us echo in these ladies' hearts."

"As you wanted to make it echo in mine last night?"

"Yes."

Colombe turned to look at Quintin, believing that even he would smile at this avowal. There was not the slightest crack in his seriousness.

"Were you denounced?"

"No!" he said. "Only by my works. The holiness of our desires was so well understood by these ladies that they became proselytes in their own right. It reached the point where I thought the entire town would become nothing but caresses and praise."

Looking at Quintin, Colombe decided he was simply mad.

"At times like those, there are always poor reprobates to get alarmed—those who feed on unhappiness and are determined to perpetuate it: the clergy full of impostors who dedicate their false love to God, the narrow-minded judges, the despicable police . . ."

Letting the little man whine on, Colombe was surprised to find she was not worried. Quintin was to be pitied, not feared. It was even a relief to share the secret of her disguise with him. With Just, she played her part effortlessly—they had always acted little plays together. Whenever she let her guard down, he reminded her to be

Colin in front of the others. Without him, she often felt on the verge of betraying herself.

"Swear to me, Quintin, that you will henceforth consider me a convert."

"Really?" he said, taking both her hands.

"I mean, enough of a convert," she said, smiling and withdrawing her hands, "that you will never preach to me again."

"Oh! I swear it, and I'll do everything I can so that no one else will discover who you are."

She didn't know whether his happiness was due to her conversion or to his relief at not having displeased her.

In any case, she would need his friendship for the perilous project she had formed.

CHAPTER 10

The prison cell held only three prisoners. Just and his adversary Martin found an old knife grinder who had tried to escape to England already in residence when they arrived. The man kept up a conversation on his own, as his two young cellmates, wearing iron cuffs and chained to facing walls, rehearsed their grievances in silence.

The old man told and retold the story of why he had joined the ship. He had had an argument with his cousin, who was also his business partner, and had signed up for the voyage on what amounted to an impulse. He told them of his wife as well, whom he had watched grow old. Still lusty and drawn to women, he had started dreaming of alluring savagesses. But no sooner had he confessed as much than he blamed himself for a dreamer and a fool, said how much he missed his old shop, the ale he drank of an evening with his cousin at the inn, and especially his wife and two daughters, whose names he could not mention without spurting tears.

After two days, the new prisoners would have given anything to stop his endless flow of words, in which lubricity invariably gave way to remorse, and remorse to idiocy. Moreover, the knife grinder snored like a hog.

However much they resented the man's intrusive presence, it had the effect of distracting them from their own quarrel, and even of uniting them against him. When the pelting tropical rains came, Maître Imbert decided that the weapons on shipboard—boarding pikes, cutlasses, axes—were threatened by rust. He freed the knife grinder and placed him before a heap of arms, put a sharpening stone in his hand, and ordered him to hone all the edges.

Once alone, Just and Martin found themselves sufficiently relieved not to renew hostilities. One morning they heard a scratching on the wall, and a sausage was pushed through a gap between the planks. Martin grabbed it and started to devour it with a show of delight.

"One of my little brothers works in the storeroom!" he said, his mouth full of food.

Eating in front of someone who is starving is not an unalloyed pleasure. Martin hated nothing so much as being alone: he needed to share his feelings whatever they were. And it was not entirely from selflessness that he tossed half the sausage to his rival.

But Just let it fall to the floor and turned away.

"What?" said Martin. "You'd rather die of hunger?"

"You sullied my honor!"

"His honor!" said the young beggar indignantly. "Where do you think you are?"

"I am a gentleman," said Just with dignity, his eyes drawn to the sausage in spite of himself.

"And that's what's taking your appetite away! Do you think gentlemen eat their honor? Look at yourself, friend: you're chained like a veal calf in a stinking hole, you're being taken to the savages, and your teeth are going to start falling out at any moment. It's not by fighting with me that you're going to get out of it, you or your brother."

Just was at that very moment thinking of Colombe, who was all alone on the ship and exposed to every danger. He had to admit that his intransigence, though it would have been legitimate were he alone, was putting his sister in danger—a sister who, as he thought, depended on him.

"I'm going to tell you a secret," said Martin, voluptuously skinning the end piece of his sausage. "I am the son of a prince."

"You!" said Just.

"Yes, me," said Martin, striking the pose of a man who has just eaten his fill of a copious meal.

Just shrugged.

"What, you don't believe me?" said the other, imitating his companion's look of righteous anger. "Ah, no! You're insulting me. My honor is at stake. I'll have to ask you for satisfaction."

"Fine," said Just, repressing a smile, "tell me your story."

"You first, friend. I generally like to know who I'm dealing with. How does it happen that I am in jail with another gentleman?"

Just told his story, reluctantly at first but with growing animation as he warmed to his hearer. While speaking, he even picked up his portion of the sausage as though unconsciously and bit into it, while Martin smiled with pleasure to see him take his share of the greasy salt meat.

"Your turn now!" said Just finally, as he finished telling the story of his life.

"Oh, my story," said Martin, "there isn't much to it. I was found in swaddling clothes in front of a church on the Feast of the Kings. So it follows that I'm a prince."

He said this with a feigned gaiety made all the funnier by his big broken nose. Just and he broke into laughter. It was as though first blood had been drawn between them and their duel could now come to an end.

Born in Rouen and reared in an orphanage, Martin had run away at the age of ten and gone to live in Honfleur with other urchins. At night he stole goods from the warehouses along the wharves. While still a child he had learned to shinny onto ships by their mooring lines and ferret around in their holds. Now that he was older, he had joined forces with the two little ones, who performed this task for him. He knew everything there was to know about ships, ports, and cargoes. And he was very well informed about Brazil, as some twenty French ships made the crossing there each year.

"If I hadn't made the mistake of leaving Honfleur, I'd still be leading the good life," he complained.

Attracted by the new fame of Le Havre-de-Grâce, Martin had gone there. But in the new town, people of his kind were soon brought in for questioning. The provosts had taken him and his so-called brothers to an orphanage by force. By misfortune, Le Thoret had found them there on the very eve of their planned escape.

Just steered him onto the topic of Brazil. Martin expatiated on dye woods, cannibals, and, with much winking, on the good times they might expect with the naked, lascivious Indian women described to him by sailors. Having frequented the wharves, he intimated that he knew a great deal about these matters, and Just watched with revulsion as Martin scratched his crotch, excited by these memories.

Cautiously, now that their differences were settled, Martin invited his companion to talk about the father he was going to meet.

With all the tact his coarseness had allowed him to preserve, Martin put forward several reasonable doubts concerning Just's story. Up till now, only expeditions of French merchants had visited Brazil. It was therefore unlikely that Just's father had taken part in them, unless he had become a corsair. True, some gentlemen had become sea rovers, rediscovering on shipboard the thrill and glory of the great era of the Crusades. The two boys constructed so many hypotheses that in the end they were both uncertain. Martin said that in fact anything was possible and that a captain might have gone off to seek his fortune there. Just, on the other hand, learning that the country had no palaces, no courtesans, no Sistine Chapel, no green countryside dotted with cypresses and Roman ruins—nothing of what had always been his father's passion—doubted more and more that his parent could have strayed in that direction.

"In any case," Martin concluded, "there are merchant ships that return to France every month."

Thus, reaching Brazil no longer filled Just's horizons entirely. The sadness he felt at the possibility of not finding his father there was lightened by the hope of continuing to look for him elsewhere.

The days passed in the floating prison cell, brightened by a few further sausage incidents. In the sweltering heat of their cubby, the hours passed slowly, and they whiled the time away with their stories. Martin remembered a thousand tales, gathered from the lips of beggars, thieves, and girls. He introduced Just to a world he had glimpsed in Italy without ever entering it, one that the long years at Clamorgan had separated him from. When it came his turn to tell stories, Just told of the endless adventures of Amadis of Gaul.

Their hair might fester with lice, their gums bleed, their bellies cry out against being empty, but the two had the bursting health of dreamers.

• • •

Villegagnon's arrival on the supply ship forced a revolution on that vessel. Mind took possession of matter. The volatile grace of the arts, the sciences, abstract thought, defended by the knight's full vigor, easily pushed back the heavy barrels, the remnants of the livestock, and all the stinking chaos of the sutlery. The quarterdeck cabins, formerly turned into a storehouse where Maître Imbert and his mate slept without ceremony, became a light-filled suite of rooms once more, where the sun, reverberating off the sea, streamed in through the broad openings of the stern ports.

Colombe and another ship's boy were put to waxing the cabin floors. Furnishings were then introduced, ferried over in chests on two further trips by the pinnace. Turkish hangings, brought back from Hungary by Villegagnon, were spread out on the side walls to hide the ship's timbers and planking. The ebony cabinet took up residence against this sunlit scarlet backdrop. On the free wall next to the door, Villegagnon himself hung an Italian painting of the Madonna and Child in a frame of varnished black wood. Except with regard to this sanctuary, the knight did not prove difficult: he stretched out his hammock in an adjacent cubby, and those who accompanied him did likewise in no special order. Only the Franciscan insisted on sleeping on the ground in a sort of open coffin, whose model he had seen while traveling in the Levant.

Colombe feared at first that the group of newcomers would stay shut away in the roundhouse and not allow other passengers to approach them. This might very well have been the natural inclination of the more courtier-like among them, who made a haughty show of their difference. But Villegagnon, with his usual energy, lanced these boils of vanity. As soon as he awoke, he strode across the deck, climbed down to the betweendecks, and visited the artillery pieces. He needed space, and in its absence performed circumgyrations at full charge. He needed work, effort, and adversity, and touching the culverins' bronze seemed to communicate to him echoes of the great struggles that shape the world: volcanic eruptions, human conquests, battles. Afterward, he would climb the foremast shrouds and take the watch for an hour. His deep voice, declaiming virelays and Latin odes, drifted down onto the deck. Then, after saluting the four cardinal points, the celestial zenith, and the dark and metallic nadir in the depths, he resumed his place among men. The room where the cabinet held pride of place was kept for secret conversations, and for the ordinary of the mass on days when the weather was foul. But these were growing more and more infrequent. A regular breeze, warm and moist, propelled the ships, which deployed full sail. The masts with their full freight of canvas cast a cooling shadow on deck, like poplars in springtime. Villegagnon had ordered one of the doors taken off his cabin and set outside on barrels to make a desk. He took up his station there on a stool and spent his days in the manner of a king, under everyone's gaze. He was seen dressing and washing. Some days he would plunge his whole hairy body into a barrel of seawater and rub himself with ash. He was seen eating, and the dignity he put into chewing, or rather, manducating his food, owed more to the purifying virtues of the grace than to the increasingly sour smell of the ship's food. He was seen reading large tomes brought over from the *Grande-Roberge*, his back straight and motionless. He was even seen writing, and given the impossibility of engaging in a correspondence with anyone, it was clear that the distiches he loudly declaimed were addressed to the mysterious personages—men, gods, and women—who peopled his empyrean.

Colombe spied on all this, and when her duties kept her from keeping watch, Quintin stood in for her.

Other than these solitary activities performed in public, Villegagnon inquired into matters on shipboard, generally from Maître Imbert but sometimes also, according to his whim, from a passenger or sailor. Colombe tried using the mysterious properties of her gaze on him but was never able to catch the admiral's eye. She wondered in fact whether his eyesight might not be defective, as he held his reading matter very close and did not always recognize his interlocutors.

As Villegagnon's days settled into a regular pattern, it quickly became apparent that the most important time was in the early afternoon. When the day's heat was at its height and the sun had rolled into a ball at the very top of the mast in the topgallant sails, Villegagnon—admiral of the outdoors, of broad daylight, and of scorching heat—was in full command of his powers to hold debates with his officers on essential questions.

The great subject of the moment was to know the convoy's exact location. Ever since October 10 when they had raised the Saint Thomas Islands, near the land of Manicongo, off Africa, they had seen nothing but the deep sea around them. Their latitude was decreasing. Although they were still in the Southern Hemisphere, they were once again approaching the equinoctial line, which they had first crossed as they descended the African coast. But not having a chronometer, they could not determine their longitude. They were reduced to dead reckoning, multiplying the number of days they had sailed by their estimated speed of travel.

The man in charge of this affair was Abbé Thevet. In himself, he was simple and unimpressive. Slightly smaller than average, with a sickly countenance, lusterless eyes, and some unseen obstruction in his nose that forced him always to keep his mouth half-open, he hardly attracted much notice. Yet nothing was so unbearable to him as the obscurity to which his conformation seemed to destine him. He found a way out of his obscurity by becoming a man of science. It allowed him to teach others of his kind, even the great among them, a thing or two about the mysteries of Nature, though he himself had not been favored overmuch by it. Thevet, who was the king's cosmographer and famous for his published account of his travels in the Orient, had acquired a reputation for knowing everything. This earned him many admirers, and still more enemies. But he gloried as much in the attacks as in the praise. For him, the main thing was not to be overlooked.

"Monsieur l'abbé," Villegagnon asked him each day when, after the daily sighting had been taken, the serious hour was at hand for debating the ships' proximity to land, "show me where we are sailing today."

The Franciscan would shuffle to the table, put down his astrolabe, pick up a feather pen, and immerse himself in painful calculations. The assembly kept a pious silence while this sacrament was consummated. Finally, Thevet would straighten up, extend his hand toward the terraqueous globe that rested on the table in its cradle of meridians, and indicate with the close-bitten nail of his index finger a point somewhere on the shore of the western Indies.

"Land!" Villegagnon exclaimed one day.

His restrained energy, his almost soft voice, showed how much the admiral liked to efface himself before the eternal truths. The verities he encountered in poetry, from the pen of Hesiod or Du Bellay, drew tears from him. But when it came to the genius of a man of science, he offered him his bared breast in advance, so as to be pierced by admiration.

"Yes," said the geographer with the authoritarian modesty that caused him to be heard by the great and hated by the ordinary run of men, "according to my calculations, we should already be on *terra firma*."

"Yet we are upon the water," objected Dom Gonzagues, who was present at the interview.

"Do you think the fact has escaped me?" retorted the Franciscan, as harsh with the underling as he was simple with the master.

"Let Monsieur l'abbé develop his thought," Villegagnon cut in.

"Well, admiral, it's perfectly simple," said Thevet unctuously. "Since we should be on land, then it follows that we are there, or very nearly. Our methods place us with respect to these phenomena in the very position of God, and when my finger runs over the globe, it covers the width of an island the size of Sardinia. Give or take an error of this magnitude, we have reached land."

It was just like Thevet's cunning to take human error and present it as myopia on the part of God.

"Did you follow that, Maître Imbert? Are you prepared to make land?"

Standing before Thevet, the sailor felt the double bite of contempt and fear: he knew that it would cost him to contradict the geographer. Yet all his experience led him to discard these laughable predictions. From his long years of sailing, Maître Imbert instinctively recognized the seascape. He rarely got lost and had learned to distinguish the particular taste of each of the ocean provinces in the vast Atlantic. But it was beyond him to explain it. The height at which the birds flew, the quality of light at dawn and dusk, certain colors in the water, drawn from the infinite register of dark blues and blacks, which reflected the relief of the sea floor—nothing of all this could stand up to Thevet's antics.

"Perhaps we still have a little time left," Maître Imbert suggested.

"Time for what? For being dashed onto rocks that we failed to notice? Make your course westward and dismiss all doubts."

Thevet's rejoinder took care of all objections. It was useless to argue.

"Right then, I'll double the watch and order my men to sleep on deck," the captain capitulated, inwardly vowing to keep heading south as his instinct told him to do. "But I warn you, if we have to make rapid sail changes, I'll need a full gang to climb into the rigging."

"Your crew is too small?" asked Villegagnon.

"We lost many men in England, as you know. Most of the passengers are good for nothing at sea: too old, too fearful, and they get dizzy the moment they set foot on the shrouds."

Villegagnon pricked up his ears at these complaints. He sensed that a decision would be called for and his authority needed.

Quintin, following the conversation as he did every day from his position against the rail, ran off to find Colombe.

"This is the moment," he said, tugging her sleeve.

When they reached the table, Maître Imbert was handing a document to Villegagnon, who held it up to his long nose to examine it.

"According to this roster, you have seventeen men."

"Minus the men who ran away, that leaves thirteen. Minus the ones who've been made ill by the food: eight. And subtract the helmsman, the watch, and myself: that leaves five men to work on deck and in the rigging. Considering that you need three men to bring in one of the main sails . . . "

"What should we do?" asked Villegagnon. "If necessary, I can climb up there to lend a hand."

Feeling a sudden scruple, and to avoid any accusation of deliberately reducing the admiral's dignity, Maître Imbert added a final detail.

"To be perfectly precise, I should mention that I still have two ship's boys in irons."

Quintin squeezed Colombe's arm.

"In irons! And for what reason?"

"They fought in the rigging and almost threw each other overboard. Rather than sort out who started it, I clapped them both in the hole."

"Good," said Villegagnon gravely. "But maybe you can let them out. Is there no other punishment, shorter in duration, that you might give them?"

"Actually, before your arrival I was planning to have them flogged."

"Excellent. How many strokes?"

"I'd say . . . twenty each," said Maître Imbert, who had been thinking ten but didn't want to appear soft in front of Villegagnon.

"Perfect, that will remind them of their duties. And after a good night's sleep, you can send them on deck to dry out their scabs."

This cavalier cruelty surprised Colombe, who was counting on Villegagnon's basic humanity. But it was no time to back down. Taking the grave assembly by surprise, Colombe forced a path through to the admiral and fell at his feet. Mindful that she should keep her eyes trained on him, she implored, "My lord, at least spare one of these poor boys, who is innocent!"

The knight was quite ready to address even the humblest person, but it had to be his decision. Nothing so displeased him as this breach of the rules, subjecting him as it did to an unwelcome intercessor. Furious, he wrenched his head away, growling, "Who is this?"

"A ship's boy," said Maître Imbert.

Meanwhile, two soldiers had seized Colombe and were dragging her off.

"My brother was only trying to defend his life! Justice, my lord, justice!"

She yelled for the honor of not giving in, and perhaps also to share Just's punishment, because it was clear that she had failed in her object. The admiral could hardly contain his terrible anger.

"Twenty lashes will not be enough," he said, "make it forty, Maître Imbert. Nothing less will do for rascals of that stripe."

Colombe continued to shout. One of the soldiers tried to gag her with his hand. She was less furious at having failed than at having misjudged Villegagnon. When it came to it, he was simply a man of caste. Compassion—if he ever felt it—was ranked by him below the requirements of order. It was in the grip of these thoughts that Colombe, hardly thinking, said, "Beware, my lord! You will be flogging a nobleman."

The soldier redoubled his efforts to quiet her. Struggling, she managed only to yell, "A Clamorgan!"

Intent on resisting, she did not at first notice that something had changed. Villegagnon, rigid, had turned toward her and signaled that she be released.

"What did you say?" he asked, searching her face.

He stood two paces from Colombe while she, bruised by the soldier's rough handling, rubbed her chafed arms.

"What name did you say?" Villegagnon repeated, in a voice so loud it could be heard in the hold.

Then, like a disarmed combatant who finds a fallen sword within his reach, she hardened her glance and raised it toward Villegagnon.

Colombe's blond eyelashes, shining brilliantly in the equatorial light, made her eyes appear as two half-open suns, shot through with an angry flame that blazed hotter still.

At the same time, she smiled and repeated evenly, "I said that you were going to flog a nobleman."

"You spoke a name?" the admiral insisted, but no longer harshly.

"Clamorgan," said Colombe, a bit reluctantly.

Without thinking, at a moment of extremity, she had used this magic spell. Her aunt's warning came back to her. She was afraid that in warding off one evil she had summoned a worse.

She strengthened the grip of her gaze. Villegagnon advanced his myopic face, the better to see the small character addressing him. Under the grime of the voyage, he recognized the pure and androgynous juvenile beauty celebrated by the Greeks. And, when made to take notice of it, Villegagnon was incapable of despising beauty, as it represented far more to him than an appearance.

"Clamorgan," he repeated thoughtfully. "Where did you find that name?"

"I didn't find it, my lord, it is my own. My father gave it to me, as well as to my brother Just, whom you ordered to have flogged."

Now that a connection had been established, Colombe was no longer afraid. She put a smile of pleasure and insolence on her face. She held the giant in her hands.

Villegagnon straightened up and looked around at the petrified assembly. The wind and the waves whispered, the languorous heat

deadening the sound. The knight's nose wrinkled, like a blood-
hound's at the scent of game. On this accursed ship where nothing
ever happened but the expected and where land was still not showing itself, here finally was something interesting. He motioned to
Colombe to get up and pushed her before him to his rooms on the
quarterdeck.

CHÁPTER 11

Seeing Villegagnon shut himself up with one of the young interpreters he had brought on board, Dom Gonzagues foresaw
complications.

A little earlier, at the time, for instance, when he was striding
through the monastery with Sister Catherine, the poor man would
have swelled with Gascon energy at the idea of having to justify himself. But the weeks on shipboard had changed him unrecognizably.
He had lost weight from dysentery and turned pink from the sun,
which he tolerated poorly; all the trials of his valiant career had
leagued together for a final assault on him. He stared dully at his
bowl, as did his companions at theirs. The meals in this interminable
final phase of the voyage were more dreaded than the hunger they
were meant to assuage. To make up the meager fare, the cook scraped
at the sticky bottoms of the brine barrels. All the meat animals had
been slaughtered. That left only the mules, but they were so thin as
to be beyond any expectation of use. The greatest concern was fresh
water. Dom Gonzagues, normally drawn to stronger drink, had never
imagined he would one day dream such violent dreams in which he
fought to the death to capture a fountain.

No one accorded any weight to Thevet's predictions, and there
was nothing to offer hope that land was near. The youngest and those

spared by fever endured the long spell of privation fairly well. But
Dom Gonzagues felt that he would be among the first to go. His
worry over the interpreters was actually something of a lucky diversion, taking his mind from thoughts of his own death. Though he
expected nothing good to come of it, he felt a shiver of happiness on
hearing that Villegagnon had summoned him aft.

When he entered the state-room where Villegagnon had been
talking with Colombe for the past two hours, Dom Gonzagues was
surprised by the calm and relaxed atmosphere that met him. The
admiral was standing near the windows looking at the wake that
foamed at the ship's stern. The young interpreter was seated on a
stool next to the ebony cabinet. Remnants of an etiquette he would
clearly abandon only at his death made Dom Gonzagues judge that
the young rogue was behaving badly. Colombe leaned an elbow on
the open drop front of the secretary and cupped her head in her
palm.

"Was it you who conscripted these two ship's boys?" asked Villegagnon, not looking at Dom Gonzagues.

"It was I."

"Then let's discuss it. Go back on deck, Colin, and wait there until
you are called."

"My brother . . . ?"

"Later."

Colombe made a show of her displeasure and went out.

Villegagnon grabbed the stool she had left vacant and waved Dom
Gonzagues toward another. They sat under the great Oriental
draperies, the silk of their pomegranate motif glowing richly in the
orange dusk.

"I gather that you've once again given in to a woman . . . ," whispered Villegagnon, a mischievous smile in his black beard.

Dom Gonzagues, terse as ever, nodded.

"And I'll wager," went on the admiral "that you've made verses for
her."

Whether from hunger or shame, Dom Gonzagues felt his head
spinning. He assented again with his chin.

"In French or in Latin?"

"In French," he confessed, his mouth as dry as if he had been
chewing parchment.

"You're right," burst out Villegagnon, who had turned his back to the tapestry and was now leaning against it. "I am starting to believe that that bandit Du Bellay is correct. Masterpieces *can* be written in French."

He sighed.

In a stronger frame of mind, Dom Gonzagues would have asked him to leave off these odious preliminaries and come to the matter at hand. Instead, he had to suffer through a long disquisition on the sonnet, an Italian invention, but perhaps also the point of juncture between Latin and the Romance languages.

"Let's get to the subject," said Dom Gonzagues finally, panting with weariness. "I am at fault. They are too old to be interpreters, I grant you. I never saw them beforehand, and in that I am greatly at fault."

"What did the lady tell you her name was?"

"Who? Oh! . . . Marguerite."

"Marguerite what?"

Dom Gonzagues lowered his gaze.

"I didn't ask. She was the boys' aunt."

"Their cousin," Villegagnon asserted in a loud voice, rising to his feet. "She called herself their aunt, but in fact she is their cousin."

He paced the state-room, then, deciding it was time, stood squarely in front of the old soldier.

"She is the daughter of a deceased elder sister of their father and their uncle. Given the difference in their ages, they called her 'Aunt.' She told you she was their guardian: that was false. Since you don't know the name of this Marguerite, I'll tell you: she's known as Madame de Griffes because she married a certain chancellor de Griffes who owns a property neighboring the estate of these children."

The admiral made another circuit of the room, his hands at his back.

"Her husband and she," he went on, "did everything in their power to destroy the old uncle who was the children's guardian. It wasn't difficult, as he knew nothing about business. De Griffes succeeded so well that he ruined him, and the poor man died. By sending the children off to America, de Griffes and your beloved Marguerite got rid of the last claimants to the late uncle's inheritance. Do you follow me?"

Dom Gonzagues's chin trembled, and his pointed beard seemed to skirmish with the air.

"Thanks to you," said Villegagnon, "de Griffes will come into possession of the lands that were deeded to these children. The lands of Clamorgan."

"Clamorgan!" said Dom Gonzagues.

"Yes," said the admiral, "that is the name the lady made every effort to hide from you, and that she advised the children never to speak. But the fact of it is, their father is François de Clamorgan."

"That's impossible!" said Dom Gonzagues, struggling to his feet, but a sudden dizziness forced him to sit down again.

Dom Gonzagues searched his memory for Clamorgan's face. He tried to compare it to the greatly different appearance of the two go-betweens, and he felt a twinge of doubt.

"Did that rogue tell you this story?" he asked, frowning.

But the admiral was categoric.

"I reconstructed it from what he told me, and I went over it all carefully. He is not lying."

"In that case, I was played for a fool!" said Dom Gonzagues angrily. "Those children must receive justice. They must be returned to France to claim their birthright . . ."

"Not so fast," said Villegagnon, his back turned, his two outspread arms holding the ebony secretary, so as to feel its rough and delicate surface vibrating with powers and secrets against his entire body.

He was fond of standing in this way while meditating.

"Do you know what happened to François de Clamorgan?"

"Of course," said Dom Gonzagues.

"Well, why not look on this voyage as an opportunity for the children? They were vilely used, there is no doubt of that. But if they return to France, what will become of them? Their lands will no longer belong to them. It will take years to have the property restored. Meanwhile, who will take them in? Who will keep them alive? Who will bring legal proceedings against this cunning de Griffes, who is rich enough to buy every parliament in France? The king, you think, might possibly intercede? But that will never happen with the sons of Clamorgan . . ."

"True enough," said Dom Gonzagues, still strongly indignant. "For that matter, what will they do in Brazil? The poor children think they are going to find their father there."

His nose twisted in embarrassment, Dom Gonzagues added:

"And I was weak enough not to puncture that hope."

"You did well," the admiral cut in. "I've thought about it. The best is to let them continue for the moment believing that story. I'll keep them with me: they know Latin, Italian, and a little Spanish. I'll make them my secretaries, and having a little staff will be of great use to me in the colony. They will forget their father. Gradually, New France will offer them destinies of their own, and they will make their life there. When they are rich, they can always return to Rouen and claim their rights. The authorities will be all the readier to grant their suit if they are able to pay."

This was clearly the best plan, and Dom Gonzagues felt toward his leader the deep gratitude a soldier feels when his chief shows yet again that he deserves his position.

"Send the younger one in, and go set his brother free."

Relieved of his guilt, Dom Gonzagues suffered less keenly from hunger. Other than some bright flies dancing in front of his eyes, he rose to his feet without incident and went out, silently uttering terrible and tender curses against Marguerite.

Colombe entered the state-room and stood near the painting of the Madonna.

"Did your father ever take you to this painter's house in Venice?" asked Villegagnon.

She scrutinized the deep pink backgrounds, the rubbed colors, the expression of surprise on the subjects' faces as though the painting had flung open a window on their intimacy.

"It will be the first Titian, I'll wager, ever to enter the New World," said Villegagnon.

Colombe looked at the Madonna, her lowered eyes, her taut skin, her air of gentleness and secret knowledge such as could hold at bay the coarse ignorance of men. She told herself that at least there were two women on this crossing, and she felt a strong pleasure in the other's company.

At that moment, three knocks sounded on the door. Dom Gonzagues was back. Colombe stepped aside, and Just came in without seeing her.

He had been imprisoned a fairly brief time. Yet those few days were enough, by undoing their long familiarity with each other, to make them feel when they met again that they had changed.

Just had grown thinner and, in proportion, taller. His gauntness made the strength and breadth of his frame all the more visible. He stood with his legs slightly apart, like someone just starting to walk again after being bedridden, so that his weakness paradoxically gave his stance an air of assurance. His beard, no longer bleached by salt, further shadowed his hollow cheeks.

"Ah!" said Villegagnon, "but this one is a full-fledged man. Your brother tells me you are only fifteen, but I'd have thought you were at least two years older."

As he said "your brother," Villegagnon motioned toward Colombe with his chin. Just turned and, seeing her, ran toward her.

As long as they had seen themselves as children, they had been prodigal with kisses and caresses. But perhaps because of Quintin's indiscreet exploration, or simply because their separation made them look at each other differently, their embrace demonstrated a new reserve. It was not that their emotion was less—on the contrary—but that their joyful relief was tinged with the new feeling of being different. Villegagnon took it as the natural and virile reserve between two boys, and he exchanged a tender glance with Dom Gonzagues.

"Children," said the admiral when they had drawn apart, "we knew your father well. He was at Ceresole with us."

"We were there too," said Colombe joyfully. "Anyway, that's what he told us. He told us of the battle any number of times. Apparently he laid us in the straw a few leagues away, and some peasants looked after us."

You cannot mention a victory, even if you experienced it lying in the straw, without deeply touching the soldiers who fought in it. Dom Gonzagues, his eyes lowered, his mustache vibrating, was discovering the only advantage of suffering from thirst: that of not being able to cry. But Just lowered his eyes as Colombe told her story and showed an angry embarrassment that she could not understand.

"Will our father be waiting for us where we intend to land?" he asked, his voice hard and cold.

"No . . ." mumbled Villegagnon, not expecting so sudden a challenge. "You will probably have to wait some time before finding him."

"Are there many Frenchmen there?" Just pursued.

"Not yet, but . . . the American continent is vast. Your father, in the performance of his duties, may be traveling as far from the site of our landing as Constantinople is from Madrid."

Watching Just listen to these answers with a closed, hostile expression, Colombe understood that his anger was not due to what she had said earlier, or to anything having to do with their father. He simply showed Villegagnon a persistent distrust that his release from confinement had not erased.

"Am I free?" he asked Villegagnon insolently.

"Better yet: I am taking you both into my service. You will be my secretaries and aides-de-camp."

"On one condition," said Just.

Villegagnon showed some surprise but was not otherwise angered at the firmness of Just's tone, so indulgent had he become toward the children.

"I don't want to be treated any differently than the apprentice with whom I fought," said Just, "nor win a victory over him unfairly. His name is Martin, and he is still in chains."

Villegagnon was familiar with these points of honor and he understood them. In fact, he was delighted to find a resemblance between father and son, which their appearance did not provide.

"Well then, so be it. I'll free the rascal, and if he still wants a fight with you, you'll have to defend yourself as best you can."

While they debated, time had drawn on. The ship's wake took on violet and indigo tones, as a stationary star brightened in the eastern sky. In this last hour of the day, the wind often marked a lull, the sails hung slack, and the ship, enveloped in silence, seemed to be collecting itself for an invisible evensong. But on the contrary, it was at that moment that a great tumult in the bow, somewhat muffled by the tapestries, traveled back to the quarterdeck.

Villegagnon rushed outside and the others followed. The whole crew and many of the passengers were standing in the bow with their noses in the air. Still others came running, erupting from the between-decks and the hold. Villegagnon pushed through to the bowsprit. The horizon ahead of them was red where the last of the sun was disappearing. There was no land to be seen, nor, when the sky darkened, were there any signs of fires. The watch, in fact, had not signaled. The truth was that there was nothing except a strange smell, which was at once faint and gigantic: faint because one had to concentrate all one's attention to find its note in the warm air, and gigantic because it invaded them from all directions, surrounded the ship, and seemed to lie over the entire surface of the sea.

Yet it did not belong to the sea. The sense of smell, whose knowledge is as certain as that derived from sight or hearing, plainly indicated that the odor came from land.

Some lands exhale the smell of grass, livestock, rot, plowed earth. This odor suggested nothing of the kind. It was an acidulous, juicy, ripe, springlike smell. With eyes closed, one might have said it had a color: red, perhaps tinged with orange.

Suddenly, someone found the right word for it and shouted that it smelled like fruit.

It was, in fact, a subtle essence of fruit pulp that spread its vapor over the expanse of the sea, an enormous odor of ripe fruit. An island can be seen but it does not have the same powerful and far-reaching perfume. Only a continent can cast its vegetal fragrances out over the sea, just as the ocean sends its salt spray and smell of kelp deep inland.

Villegagnon cried with joy into his closed fist, and all those around him embraced.

They sailed for two more days before the coast hove into view.

Three and a half months had passed since their departure from Le Havre.

II

Guanabara

CHAPTER 12

Can a land have hidden from the Bible and been unknown to Alexander and Jesus, to Virgil and Attila, unless its banishment was caused by a grave curse?

On the decks of the caravels, the question haunted men's minds. And when the black mass of land, tinted with the cold blues of the morning, appeared in the west, even those who were most eager to see land again felt a surprising horror. The sea that had so frightened them at first had gradually become a protective envelope. The finger of mountains that was slowly parting the smooth valves of the sea and sky heralded a titanic encounter whose outcome was uncertain. For some, it offered hope: the Anabaptists, always hungry for cataclysms, danced on deck at the prospect of coming eruptions, on whose fires the abhorred old world would roast. The simple soldiers, fed on popular beliefs descended from Ptolemy, groaned to think that they would now have to pay for their audacity in venturing to the edge of the world. The still-indistinct silhouettes of giant monks or warriors in chasubles coming into view as they approached the coast were undoubtedly those of executioners sent by God to dash them into the abyss.

Others, armed with more religion, believed they had reached hell—or heaven—according to their deserts and their degree of optimism. Thevet, for his part, was feverishly fussing with the Jacob's staff to measure the declination of the sun. But his trembling hands kept him from making an accurate sighting, and he was thus unable to assign a regular place on his parchment planisphere to this unknown location.

As to Colombe and Just, they didn't know what to think. One on the heels of the other, they excitedly recalled the fabulous discoveries made in King Arthur's time of islands inhabited by faceless knights. But they had trouble believing in them. The long crossing, which had left them physically intact, or almost so, had weakened the invisible spiritual muscle that allows one to leap beyond the sensible world. They no longer believed in faceless knights, only in Villegagnon's brothers-in-arms, with their pirates' mugs, their salt-bitten swords at their sides, and the Cross of Malta on their stomachs. If the two idealized the coast, it was only to spare each other the cruel certainty that it belonged wholly to the ordinary world.

The day passed in beating slowly toward land. That night they still saw no fires and advanced cautiously. But Maître Imbert knew the general area well enough so that when they awoke the next morning, they lay at the mouth of the bay.

The customary afternoon consultation around the map was moved earlier, by reason of circumstances. Thevet arrived in majesty, proud of having predicted landfall. In fact, had Maître Imbert not sailed south instead of following the course set by Thevet, they would still have been on the high seas.

"The Bay of Guanabara," Thevet announced, as though he had created it overnight with his own hands. "That is the natives' name for it. The Portuguese sailed into it fifty years ago on a January day, and as the ignoramuses thought it was a river they called it 'January River,' or 'Rio de Janeiro.' In France we altered that name to 'Genèbre.' Note that the name 'Genèbre' also seems to derive from 'Guanabara.' It is all so very fascinating!"

His pudgy fingers smoothed the three hairs that had come to decorate his chin during the long crossing.

"Genèbre," said Villegagnon, his eyes gladdened by the sight of land. "It sounds a bit like 'Geneva' as well."

"In point of fact," said Thevet, "a person might well believe that we lay in the middle of the Alpine lake of that name, though the mountains that surround it are more rugged."

"Yes, I once sailed across it, returning from Italy," said Villegagnon, nodding.

But Thevet meant to have the last word in these erudite skirmishes.

"And I have crossed it four times!" he said.

Then, as though to show that no guardrail ever held him to the borders of pedantry, he went on:

"It is marvelous how many secrets lie hidden in etymology! A single name brings together the calendarian happenstance of the Portuguese, the bestial vocable of the savages, and the relationship between two countries that fall to France: one of them already speaks our language, and the other will soon submit to our rule."

On the continuous line of the coast, hemmed as it was with capes and inlets, the Bay of Genèbre formed a giant buttonhole. Several leagues in width, it had every aspect of a river's mouth, except that the water was salt. The austral autumn was hot and cloudless. When the sun had risen fully, it painted the sky in dense blues. No bottom could be seen through the clear violet waters, though the ships' hulls could be viewed distinctly to the tip of the keel.

Once inside the mouth of the bay, Villegagnon gave orders to follow the southern shore. Maître Imbert cautiously pointed out that French merchant ships generally did the opposite.

"All the more reason!" said Villegagnon ill-temperedly.

The winds in the bay were regular, and the ships maneuvered well. They drew in near the coast and passed almost at the foot of the enormous silhouette they had seen from out at sea.

Neither a stone Capuchin nor a knight from hell, the rock with its smooth and rounded surface struck the Norman sailors as looking more like a butter crock, while the richer on board saw it as a loaf of sugar. At its foot, a great tumult of trees climbed upward to escape the close fighting among the plants of the lowlands. Along the coast was an unruly mass of twisting branches, aerial roots, and lianas, with never a clearing or a meadow. Other rocks, as big as the Butter Crock, emerged from the dense forest, shining gray in the sun. The ships seemed so small in passing them that these stone teeth assumed a supernatural aura. The whole coast seemed the result of a violent battle, of fierce resistance on the earth's part at the hour of creation. The Great Workman had broken his tools on this work, and a remnant of this grandiose defeat could still be read in the land's violence.

Yet for all its monstrousness, the chaos was not entirely without harmony. The caressing work of the sea calmed these rebellious lands by drawing over their jumble the regular features of beaches. At times the solid land plunged—in mangrove thickets, swamps, and steep cliffs—directly into the water. But for long stretches, serried ranks of coconut trees intervened to preserve the sea's serenity and let the young waves play along vast esplanades of sand.

"What the devil is he doing?" grumbled Martin in the bow, biting his knuckles as he followed the convoy's maneuvers. "He won't find the French on that side."

And in truth, along the whole visible expanse of land, there was no dwelling to be seen or any column of blue smoke that might indicate a hearth. A faint crackling could be heard from time to time coming from land, sounding like footsteps on straw, but it was the momentary stirring of the wind in the tracery of palms and foliage. The cries of birds and monkeys fell from the heights through the silent and unresisting air as though the ships were being pelted with stones.

"Ready the starboard guns," shouted Villegagnon, standing on the quarterdeck.

He ordered a large pavilion bearing the royal fleur-de-lys on a white background to be raised on the aft flagstaff. If the Portuguese were prowling in the area, it was as well for them to know who they were dealing with. But there were no sails in the bay. Unless armed men were hiding along the shore, the way seemed clear.

"I'll bet you anything he's going to make a full circuit of the bay, then head up toward the Norman* establishments," said Martin, greatly agitated.

---

*Around Guanabara Bay lived a number of Frenchmen, mostly from Normandy. Some became renegades and apostates, integrating to a greater or lesser degree with Indian tribal life. Others maintained ties with France, gathering valuable raw materials at their depots, dyewoods especially, and shipping them regularly back to their home ports. —Trans.

Just looked at him, not yet understanding fully. Colombe, for her part, went from one group to another, gleaning tidbits of information, only to conclude that no one knew very much.

The *Rosée*, at the head of the convoy, made toward a small, flat island near the shore. On this stomping ground of the titans, size was hard to tell. They ghosted forward in the lee of the Butter Crock. The ship sucked in every puff of wind like an exhausted runner. It took two full hours to draw up to the island. It proved to be tiny. From close up, they could even see that it was most likely submerged during storms: its entire surface was strewn with bits of bark and debris from coconut trees.

Villegagnon ordered the ships to sail past the island, but he held them in close to the coast.

Soon after rounding the rock, they sighted a larger and higher bulge on the shore. Colombe finally decided to push her way back to the quarterdeck to learn from Villegagnon himself what he planned to do, if he was willing to explain it.

Since Just's release, it had become tacitly understood that the two so-called brothers reported solely to the admiral. They came and went on the ship as they pleased. Officially they had been elevated to the rank of secretaries, but at a time when every effort was directed at sailing and making landfall, their new dignities imparted more freedom than they imposed constraints. Colombe took advantage of this more readily than her brother, who continued to hold Villegagnon in extreme distrust.

Seated on a stool, his elbows resting on a little wooden writing desk, Thevet held court on the quarterdeck. His glance shuttled between the coast they were sailing toward and the torn, blackened, ink-spotted notebook he held in his hands.

"Let's see . . . Viegas mentions three islands over here. This bit of shore must be the island that lies between the two others, between the Ratcatcher, which we've just passed, and the other, more hilly one behind it . . ."

Colombe in the meantime had slipped around his back to look at the pilot book over his shoulder.

"Get away!" said Thevet as soon as he realized it.

Covering the precious pages with both hands, he appealed to Villegagnon:

"These Portuguese documents are state secrets. Are you quite sure of your men, Admiral?"

The Franciscan glared at Colombe as though she were a venomous snake. Villegagnon motioned to her to come stand by him.

"Does your breviary make any mention of submerged reefs in these waters?" suddenly asked Maître Imbert, who was still at the helm.

Approaching this coast from the south struck him as highly ill-advised.

"The rule among volcanic formations of this sort," said Thevet with learned scorn, "is for the projecting rocks to be extremely pointed. They rise solitarily from the water, just as this Butter Crock would do were its summit close to sea level. Hence there are no reefs in the vicinity. You have nothing to worry about."

Maître Imbert scowled and continued to scan the foam.

"Once we get in close to land, guide the ship around in a circle," Villegagnon ordered. "We'll make certain that the sea surrounds the island fully on all sides."

"Why not land directly on the mainland?" asked Colombe, looking at Villegagnon.

The others quailed, expecting the quick-tempered knight to take umbrage at this question. But Colombe smiled, neither showing any fear nor lowering her gaze. During their free exchange on the first day, Colombe had sensed that Villegagnon's roaring exterior hid fault lines by which he might be easily managed. He intended to make her his page, but she understood that what he needed was a fool.

"In all likelihood, there are dangers along this coast that we know nothing of," he answered calmly, with a father's kindly tones. "An island is the safest place to build fortifications, as my order has proven over the past two centuries, first on Rhodes, then on Malta."

"But what if the Indians welcome us with open arms?"

"They'll be all the more inclined to do so if they find us strong and well protected. We are not looking to make them our allies but our subjects."

These political words sounded strange against the backdrop of opaque jungles and deserted beaches.

"Rocks to starboard!" called the watch suddenly.

Maître Imbert put the helm hard over to avoid a reef that barely broke the surface of the water.

The cosmographer, whose science had been thus plainly contradicted, appeared undismayed. He scribbled something in a small notebook that he always carried with him.

"We'll make corrections to Viegas," he said with a smug smile.

In fact Thevet was continually shuttling back and forth between the scientists and the travelers, between the cartographers and the mariners. He would take one group to task using the evidence of the other, and vice versa. The ridicule he had earned for his statement to Maître Imbert was already avenged by the humiliation he would inflict on his learned opponents when he proved to them that reefs might surround volcanic islands.

Because of the dangers in close to shore, Villegagnon decided to strike the sails and send out the pinnace to explore the coast. It returned at the end of two hours. Maître Imbert, who had gone on the scouting party, returned to the ship in a happy frame of mind.

"It's definitely an island, Admiral. There are reefs all the way around it. But on the mainland side, there is a little cove that would make a good port for the ships' boats."

"Perfect," said Villegagnon, with satisfaction. "Drop anchor here, and make sure it holds securely. Tomorrow morning we will start to land."

Night was falling as the orders were carried out. It was already pitch dark when Villegagnon assembled the men on the forecastle and climbed onto a shroud to deliver a final harangue before supper.

"Companions! We are now at the end of our voyage," he bellowed. "The land that you see here is ours."

Gaunt, their gums bleeding, their mouths pasty with thirst, the passengers of the *Rosée* followed Villegagnon's imperious index finger and turned their faces toward the desolate shore of the island, where black waves expired against the blue sand. A fat moon whitened the foremost rustling line of vegetation, leaving the island's depths in threatening darkness.

Most of the cabinetmakers, bakers, hatmakers, and carders who had joined the expedition—some as fugitives, others of their own free will—had believed, despite their fears and doubts, in the promise of a new world. But none had imagined it would be so deserted.

Looking at the island, they abruptly realized that the crossing was not yet their full punishment. They were condemned in fact to the most unimaginable penalty: that of being hurled down from the pyramid laboriously built by civilization, just as Adam and Eve were evicted from earthly paradise. They saw themselves cast out into the savage world, unhappier even than the animals because they had consciousness to make them suffer for having been stripped bare, made vulnerable, and placed beyond the reach of all pity.

"Curb your impatience," trumpeted Villegagnon, who was filled with his own enthusiasm. "Tomorrow you will take possession of your new realm. The fort that you will build there will be the first monument raised to the glory of our king Henry II."

He checked himself for a moment, and his audience thought that he had noticed its distress.

"It was indeed my first thought to call our settlement Henriville," he went on, with the air of a modest courtier preparing a flattery, "but it is not enough for our sovereign. When we are masters of the entire country we will construct a capital between these breakwaters, and it will then be time to christen it with the royal name. What we are going to build now is a stronghold. Let us call it Fort Coligny, in honor of Monsieur Gaspard de Coligny, first admiral of France, who looked on our endeavor with favor."

His hearers sensed that he spoke that name with the same respect as the other, though with less affection.

"Long live Fort Coligny!" he shouted, raising his arms high.

A two-note caw from the dark palms on the island sounded lugubriously over the crew's silence.

"Come now," scolded Villegagnon, "would you have me voice this sentiment alone? All together: Long live Fort Coligny!"

They pronounced these words with all the enthusiasm of men roused from deep sleep by a booted foot. Villegagnon judged it prudent to be satisfied.

Alone of the crew not to share in the general despair, Colombe felt strangely happy. Perhaps it was the warmth of the night, its caressing stillness, or the moist and peppery breath of the forest, but Colombe took pleasure in following the slow rocking of the boat from her seat at the foot of the mast. She smiled at Just, who came to join her, but he looked in an even darker mood than he had that afternoon. Martin, looking furious, came after him.

"Now do you believe it?" asked Just, sitting beside her against the mast.

She looked at him uncomprehendingly.

"Do you think," he said, holding his arm out toward the coast, "that there is the slightest chance of finding Father among the geese and wild ducks?"

It was as plain as anything. Yet she did not know how to answer. In fact, she had stopped thinking some time before about what was inarguably the main purpose of their trip. She was surprised at herself, and a little ashamed.

"Oh yes, Father!" she said.

Then she was silent.

"I swear to you," said Martin, "even if I have to swim across this damn bay to do it, that before three weeks have passed, I'll be on a boat going back the other way."

CHAPTER 13

The moment Cadorim's foot touched the landing at St. Mark's Place, he felt a horrible melancholy. He loved his city passionately: the brick lacework of the Palace of the Doges, the square tower of the piazza, the gold of the basilica—they brought tears to his eyes. Alas, fate had ordained that he was never to live in the city he served. The Republic had at once honored him and plunged him into despair by naming him to the ranks of that invisible army of diplomats and spies it sent throughout the known world. Of itself weak, Venice found strength in the vast knowledge it drew from this array of distant men—men whose loyalty lay in felonious acts, and who were sworn to betray everything so that Venice might remain true to itself.

When Cadorim returned home, it was to bring information to the doge and the great council. It could take a month, perhaps two, to tell everything he had seen, heard, and guessed.

In the meantime he strolled about his city, which, for all that he loved it, he always had difficulty recognizing. His children had grown and looked different; his wife was ever more foreign to him. And his palazzo seemed constantly to be on the move, so many were the construction sites around it. New houses, unexpected bridges, and surprising new church projects were always unsettling his expectations. From his window, Cadorim could now see the brand new facades of Santa Maria

Formosa and the Palazzo Vendramin emerging from a forest of stakes. Thus were architectural jewels born in this branching lagoon, one day piercing through the burr of their scaffolding and exposing virginal pinks, immaculate whites, and ochres—colors that, though delicate, were destined for eternity. Cadorim adored this city of silt and gems, but hardly would he become enthralled by it anew than it would be time for him to leave once more. The ghosts of dusty roads, bad inns, lies, and poor company would drift up the Grand Canal to encircle him at night, until he would finally decide to leave just to escape them.

He had reached that point on this August morning. And in all the city, lit already by a huge summer sun, his mind was the only place that remained obstinately dark. To get to his last meeting he had to cross a score of canals and innumerable small squares. Yet by a terrible backlash of his emotions, the more delight he took in the gondolas, the open-air markets, and the thousand small scenes of Venice's morning life, the more pain he suffered at the realization that he would soon be losing these pleasures for a long time. Finally he arrived at the brand new palace of the man he was to meet that day. As he entered it, Cadorim had the impression of being on the road once more: the building's interior, which was still under construction and exhaled the smell of fresh plaster, was already furnished in a manner that was not at all Venetian. Chests of dark tropical wood, absurd armchairs with ornate carving, and a wall of brilliant glazed tiles demonstrated a strong intention to stamp Portugal's mark on this small enclave. This laughable pretense, far from suggesting greatness, smelled of freshly acquired riches and usurped nobility. Cadorim was accustomed to this sort of barbarousness, which was rampant the moment one stepped beyond the territory of Milan. He sighed as he took his seat in an enormous magistrate's chair, as uncomfortable as it was ridiculous, and rickety despite its apparent stoutness.

He was left to wait for a long moment. Then a door opened, and a chapel, gilded from floor to ceiling, was briefly revealed as the bishop entered.

"My most humble respects, Your Saintliness!" said Cadorim, latching on to the prelate's ring.

One never goes wrong in ascribing a rank to someone that he does not hold. The beneficiary of the error is all too ready to forgive it, believing his flatterer to be simply in advance of the times.

"Come," said the Portuguese, feigning embarrassment, "you may rise. And please, no more 'Your Saintliness.' I am not yet pope."

The greedy modesty of this remark showed clearly enough that, a bishop at forty-five, Joaquim Coimbra imagined all futures still to be possible.

There followed some words of welcome, the inevitable procession of ceremonial plate—a display to which all the barbarians felt bound to subject their Venetian visitors—before they settled face to face in stone armchairs of flagrantly bad taste on the palace balcony, and Cadorim was finally led to the threshold of his topic.

"Thus," said the nuncio, crossing his fingers on his stomach, "you have visited this new port from which the French are mounting hostile enterprises against my country?"

"Yes, I have been to Le Havre-de-Grâce, Your Saintliness."

A gentle tut-tut reminded him that the title was still premature.

"Our king" said the bishop, "is highly grateful to Venice for having acceded to his request. We knew that we could nowhere obtain better information than through you. What then have you learned of French intentions in the New World?"

Cadorim could have given the prelate his report the moment he arrived in Venice more than three weeks earlier. But the Republic had had to negotiate the price of this service first. The Portuguese were not allies of Venice, and by their absurd obstinacy in opening a route to the Indies of their own, they had contributed to breaking the monopoly that the City of the Doges had for so long enjoyed in the Orient. Nonetheless, every event had to be kept in perspective. For all that it was troublesome, Portugal still provided a counterweight to Spain, that is, to one of the pillars of the empire of Charles V, whom Venice distrusted. The Portuguese bumpkins could therefore not be ignored. And if one could possibly do them a service, it was only charitable to perform it for them, on condition that they pay handsomely. This preliminary business, he'd learned the day before, had been settled after much bargaining, and Cadorim was now free to tell everything he'd seen in Le Havre-de-Grâce.

"Three ships, you say," the bishop pondered, after hearing the report. He frowned. "And armed for war, what's more. That is highly troubling."

A red awning over the balcony brought them shade, while the

sunlit surface of the Grand Canal reflected the flash of a thousand tiny duels.

"When my countrymen meet ships that are traveling alone or in small unarmed convoys," went on the bishop, "they can easily persuade them not to proceed to Brazil, which is ours."

The prelate sighed with emotion at the picture of his compatriots reprimanding those who had wandered off course. That they also hacked off their arms and legs and left them to die of hunger was a detail that needed no mention. Besides, one cannot love well if one does not punish proportionately.

"But we have no force on those seas capable of opposing three resolute warships."

A small country and short of manpower, Portugal assigned its representatives multiple duties. Dom Joaquim had come to Italy in an ecclesiastical capacity, but he also held the post of ambassador. He now sank into a political reverie, while a pout of greed stole over his face. Cadorim was delighted by the silence and took advantage of it to let his thoughts drift. Torn by nostalgia at the sight of the barques on the Grand Canal, he wondered where the devil he would be sent off to this time.

"Their destination, you say, is Rio de Janeiro?" asked the bishop loudly, so as to rouse the spy from his daydream.

"Rio, yes," muttered Cadorim.

And to show that he was fully present, he added, "And do you have a garrison there?"

"Alas," moaned Dom Joaquim, "Brazil is so big and our Portugal is so small . . . We have men in São Salvador de la Bahia, but it's as far from the Bay of Rio as Lisbon is from Britain. And then we have a small post in the south at São Vicente, but it doesn't have the strength to mount an attack."

He pondered and raised his glass of Madeira to his lips. He drank slowly, then suddenly set it down with a bang.

"But we will find a way to have our authority respected!" he said, his priestly unction gone. "However difficult, we will mount an expedition from Bahia, Cape Verde, or even Lisbon if we have to."

Then he calmed down.

"Well, the king will decide."

Cadorim had adopted a protective expression, screwing up his eyes to avoid the blinding reverberations of the sun off the lagoon. And behind this grimace, he was dreaming.

"But we will need to draw His Majesty an accurate picture of the present situation in Europe," said the prelate, his eyes cold and distant, as though fixed on an apparition. "The moment for action is upon us. France has been exhausting herself in resisting the emperor, and her gaze is to the east. The battlefield on which she is expending all her might is Picardy, Hainaut. If we contest a miserable trading post of hers in America at this time, there is every likelihood that France will not respond. There is no time to lose."

He chimed his ring three times against the vermilion goblet, as after the Elevation.

"I was not meant to return to Lisbon before next month," he said feverishly, "but I am going to move my departure forward. I must convince His Majesty at the earliest possible moment. God will come to my aid, I am certain of it!"

Cadorim was looking at the horizon toward Murano and the mainland.

Roused by the prelate's exclamation, he recovered his wits. The Portuguese . . . yes, yes. It all came back to him.

"By the way, Your Saintliness," he interposed as the bishop was poised to end their interview, "if you should decide to attack this colony of Frenchmen, I've taken the precaution of putting a man among them who will work for you."

His genial tone implied: "All this is included for the same price."

"Excellent," said the bishop, and this time it was he who screwed up his eyes, but in the role of a conspirator.

Cadorim described Vittorio to him in the most flattering terms.

"Ribera," snickered the bishop, with evident pleasure. "Ribera! My God, how ingenious! What an extraordinary nation of schemers you are!"

Smiling a superior smile, the two men showed clearly enough that they both took this as a compliment. Yet Cadorim's pride was slightly wounded. He was not about to take offense at Venice being less admired for its civility than its corruption. But respect was due all the same.

CHAPTER 14

The idea was Quintin's. He had spread it from group to group in his modest and insinuating way. According to him, the world where they were going to land was not new in any way. It was ridiculous to think that men had not known about it up till now. On the contrary, it was a continent of death, one of those accursed lands that triumph over all life, human in particular. And he quoted twenty obscure passages from the Bible that, he said, supported it.

When the first boats arrived on the island in the morning, the men hardly dared to jump out. Full of Quintin's prophecies, they were certain that the fine white powder stretched out in long beaches was nothing less than powdered bone. What they had thought were tree trunks turned out on closer approach to be the spindly necks of skeletons, stacks of vertebrae dried by the wind. From the leaves, which were as stiff as the ribs of hanged men, came sinister cracking sounds, while clusters of skulls hung from the trees' crowns.

When the men finally worked up the resolve, under the sailors' yells, to jump into the warm, clear water and tread at last on the shore, the illusion dissolved. But an inexplicable terror remained in their minds while they gathered, astonished and shivering, in the meager shade of the first coconut trees. By noon almost three hundred of them, ferried over on the six ships' boats, stood there in a close cluster, rolling their mad eyes.

"Damn me, I'd give my soul for a pair of boots," said Martin.

He had walked barefoot all his life. Yet the slimy touch of the seaweed made him yelp, and even worse were the large fibrous balls scattered about on the sand.

"They're dead field mice, I swear!" he groaned, taking care not to step on the vegetable debris.

Just, who leapt out of another boat, never had the chance to be distracted by his feet. He couldn't turn his eyes from the mountainous circle of the bay, with its dark walls and the dazzling green of its wild vegetation hedging them around. Unlike those who found the emptiness of the island terrifying, he was riveted by the unmistakable signs of life swarming there unseen. Numberless creatures silently held them encircled, which was more menacing by far than solitude. And though overcome with fear, Just couldn't help seeing this mysterious presence as a sumptuous challenge to his courage.

"Stop gaping like a fool," shouted one of the sailors, pulling him from his reverie. "Here, give us a hand unloading these chests."

In addition to the boats landing with their complement of passengers, a raft arrived made of wooden beams and piled high with baggage. Just, wading into the water up to his waist, was glad to help with the unloading, which limbered his muscles and provided a distraction from his thoughts.

"Don't let go of the raft," the sailor shouted.

Irregular waves occasionally rolled in to shore, lifting the boats. Hanging on to the floating load with all his weight, Just couldn't overcome the suction of the waves. Twice already the sailors had failed to haul the raft onto the sand when the waves were at their highest. This time again it broke from their hold and was caught up violently in the breaking wave. The baggage was suddenly spilled out onto the surface of the water.

"Gather all that up!" the sailors yelled.

Just didn't know where to start. There was a confusion of stoles, knee breeches, and notebooks strewn in every direction. The bottom sloped outward gently, but Just was soon in the water up to his neck, and he was afraid of being swept away. Some objects sank, while others drifted irrevocably off.

At that moment, a longboat arrived carrying Villegagnon and Thevet, who had preferred to wait comfortably on board and disembark last. Colombe was with them. Their late arrival was intended to have the effect of an apotheosis. Villegagnon was no sooner on land than he picked up a handful of sand and, letting it sift to the ground, declared, "The soil of France!"

Le Thoret stood behind him with the flag. He held out the pole to his leader, who brandished the silky fleur-de-lys panel in the warm breeze. Protocol next required that Villegagnon carry the flag to the highest point of the island and plant it there. This plan was regrettably interrupted by the piercing shrieks of Thevet. The Franciscan had recognized his chest floating like a cork at some distance from shore.

"My books!" he screeched. "My collections!"

Running to the water's edge, he picked up the sandy mass of cloth and paper that Just had laboriously rescued from the waves and bawled like an animal in distress.

"My clothes! My chasubles!"

All the officers had rushed forward, and in view of the situation's gravity, Villegagnon dropped the flag and took command of the little group. They were now six, counting Just, fishing everything they could out of the water.

"The vermilion chalice!" moaned Thevet, who had fallen to his knees.

What he was losing distressed him, but what was brought back put him into even greater despair: his notebooks were sodden to the core, the ink running in streams. All his notes along with the documents he had assembled for the voyage and his measuring instruments sank into the depths or were destroyed.

Villegagnon, who had wanted to honor the cosmographer by bringing his possessions to land at the same time as himself, was overcome with remorse.

When it was clear that nothing further could be saved, they returned to shore, streaming with water.

"Father, I don't know what amends I can make," said Villegagnon on the brink of tears, "for your sacramental vestments!"

"And all my scientific documents!" added Thevet, who seemed particularly devastated over that loss.

They rallied round to console and support him. The procession re-formed—the one man wet with tears, the others soaked by their swim—but the ceremony had lost some of its splendor. Colombe now carried the flag. At first she kept it rolled up, but when Just joined her, she allowed it to float playfully in the breeze.

Still following Villegagnon and his group, they climbed toward the crest of the island, while the silent crowd of passengers fell into step behind them.

It was now almost noon and the heat was oppressive. The air became drier as they moved farther from the sea. The ground was harder and crustier, rising gently. The coconut trees were replaced by an airy scattering of big cedars. Colombe could see the horrified faces of the arriving men and feel how tense and serious Just was beside her. Yet nothing could shake the sense of voluptuous pleasure she felt in this place. Everything, the burning heat of the sun and the cool-ness of the shade, the rushing of the wind in the branches of the cedars, and the emerald green of the sea all around the island, brought her unexpected pleasure. Except for the surprise of being the only one to feel it, nothing, neither fear nor regret, troubled her pure sensation of ease and happiness.

"Where's that flag!" said Villegagnon impatiently as he reached the plateau that rose in the center of the island.

Colombe ran to hand it to him. Cutting the ceremony short, the admiral propped up the fluttering banner between a few rocks, but not without its flopping over several times, the wind being strong. At the admiral's request, Thevet mumbled out a prayer. Villegagnon brayed his "amens," inviting the crowd to join the chorus. Despite his efforts, the new arrivals could barely endure the silence crushing them.

After this brief celebration, the admiral set aside his prepared speech and dispersed the crowd. They needed to finish unloading the ship quickly and begin exploring the island. Just, out of curiosity, tagged along with the knights who joined behind Villegagnon to survey their realm. As Martin had joined Just, Colombe preferred not to accompany them. She found less and less to like about the young beggar, who spoke too loudly for her taste. She thought that she still held his unpleasant reception of them against him, but the real reason for her antipathy lay elsewhere.

She walked into the shade of some large trees that grew facing the bay. Their tiny, light green leaves cast a thin shadow on the ground. She fell asleep, rocked by the motion imparted to the land by the absence of the ship's constant rolling.

An hour later, Just returned and sat down beside her.

"No water," he announced lugubriously. "No spring, no stream, nothing."

"What are we going to do?" asked Colombe anxiously.

"We're staying. Villegagnon says we just have to dig cisterns and fill barrels with water on the mainland."

Colombe felt relieved to learn they wouldn't be leaving right away.

"Other than the plateau where we are now," Just went on, "there are two small rises at either end of the island. Villegagnon wants to fortify them."

As the sun turned, they watched the colors of the bay change. The darkening blue of the sea refreshed their eyes. From the three ships at anchor came the confused sound of shouts and creaking hoists. The unloading was in full swing.

Martin came and joined them, still as careful as ever about where he set his feet down. In each hand he held a coconut with its top sliced off.

"I had to fight to get these, I can tell you," he said, holding them out to Just and Colombe.

The two drank great draughts of the sweet liquid. They had almost forgotten what a pure drink was like.

"We'll have to watch tonight," said Martin, looking intensely toward the far end of the bay, which was veiled by haze. "If we see fires, that's the right direction."

"The direction for what?" asked Colombe, holding the white, fresh meat of the nut against her lower lip.

Martin shrugged:

"The trading stations of the Normans, by God!"

That night, Martin and Just stood looking out across the darkness of the bay, but they saw no fires. Colombe fell happily asleep.

• • •

"The cannibals! The cannibals!"

The shouts that woke them in the dawn hours came from the little port where the ships' boats were tethered. Dispersed over the island to sleep, the passengers rushed down to the beach. Martin was the first to his feet, his training as a beggar having taught him to sleep lightly. Just and Colombe followed after him, yawning.

The island's entire beach front on the mainland side was filled with travelers. Soldiers, sailors, and civilians stood on the sand at the water's edge and looked steadily at the coast. The arm of the sea separating them from the mainland was narrow enough so that they could clearly see, arrayed in a line on the opposite shore, a band of naturals counting perhaps two hundred warriors.

The cannibal monstrosity had prowled gigantically through more than one mind during this first night in the land of the anthropophagi. It burst like a pierced bladder now that the Indians were there.

"Have you unloaded the pieces of cloth and the paternosters?" Villegagnon asked Le Thoret.

"Yes, Admiral."

"Then send for a roll of red cloth and a bucket of the trinkets. And you," he said, turning to the sailors, "prepare the longboat."

"Shall we get out the harquebuses?" asked Dom Gonzagues.

"Yes, but set them in place here, loaded and aimed. The abbé says that these savages are friends of the French, but you can never tell. The gunners must wait strictly on my signal."

Meanwhile, the oarsmen took their places in the longboat. Villegagnon glanced around to pick his delegation. Thevet was willing to go, though he was still grieving over the loss of his effects. The admiral next chose five Scotsmen from his guard and Le Thoret. Then he called for Just, as he meant to appear with a page in attendance and preferred to bring the stouter of the two in case they needed to resort to force.

The entire group climbed into the longboat. Villegagnon stood in the bow, straight as a rod, his nose as menacing as the battering ram on a galley.

The longboat quickly reached the mainland. The Indians watched it approach without moving. Villegagnon ordered the craft to be brought in sideways, ready to turn back quickly in case of an incident. This had the disadvantage of making the passengers jump out into fairly deep water. Their contortions and discomfort at being wet up to the doublet were scotched by Villegagnon, who walked straight and tall over the sand, like a king advancing toward the seat of judgment. The Indians let him come closer without flinching. They were all more or less the same at first sight: of medium height, and human in their conformation with no more than the requisite number of arms, legs, and heads. In fact, it was their normalcy that made their total nudity embarrassing. Nothing about their appearance permitted a comparison to animals, which one is used to seeing clad in nothing but their fur. Only the thought of classical antiquity could make this license seem comprehensible, even admirable. The comparison was all the more apt as the savages showed no fear or embarrassment, instead striking haughty and noble poses, rivaling Villegagnon in male self-confidence.

"French!" shouted Villegagnon, putting much sincerity into this protestation.

"*Mair!*" said Thevet, offering the word he had read was its Tupi-language equivalent.

Remembering this filled him more with nostalgia than with pride, as it reminded him of his lost papers and all the knowledge that had been swallowed up with them.

On hearing this word the naturals conferred among themselves in their language. One of them, young and vigorous, his hair shaved back from his forehead and a large flat stone in his lower lip, stepped forward. He delivered a speech that was incomprehensible, though amiable in tone.

"They don't look hostile," whispered Villegagnon to Le Thoret.

But Le Thoret, a veteran of the Italian campaigns who had been wounded at Mirandola, remained on his guard, ready to draw his sword instantly. He knew from experience that the enemy often has a pleasant countenance and is none the less cruel for that.

His speech concluded, the young Indian set off toward the jungle, and the other savages enveloped Villegagnon and his little escort and swept them in the same direction. It was dangerous to move away from the water's edge. They would no longer be under the protection of the harquebuses. Yet the admiral never wavered. To resist would have been to behave as captives, to show that they could be vanquished. But as the new and legitimate lord by virtue of his royal patents, Villegagnon could not allow himself to be afraid of anything or feel himself in any way foreign to this land, which henceforth belonged to him.

On this part of the coast, the beach was narrow. They immediately came under the thick canopy of the forest with its many tiers of trees. The dense shade kept the understory unexpectedly cool. Before they had gone a hundred steps, they saw a gap among the larger trees and a long palm-leaf house with children running in front of it naked.

As soon as Villegagnon and his guard appeared, piercing cries rang out all across the clearing. The new arrivals jumped, startled, but Villegagnon saw that it was not an ambush. He thought the Scotsmen, with their cutlasses in their stockings and their air of red-haired devils, had probably terrified the mob of children. But it was not the Scotsmen at all. It was he, Villegagnon, who elicited these moans of pain from all the women in the longhouse.

Having identified him as the leader from his air of authority and guessed that Thevet with his long robe must be another important dignitary, the Indians led them both toward a hammock, where they made them sit down. Uncomfortably installed side by side on this swing seat, Villegagnon and the Franciscan continued for several minutes to receive the tearful and piercing tribute of the Indian women. Some fifteen of them came and squatted before their guests, holding their heads in their hands, moaning and crying as though ravished by their most dearly beloved. Entirely naked, spouting a fountain of tears, the women brandished an array of breasts, thighs, and pudenda before the terrified gaze of the Knight of Malta and the cleric, who were sorely tempted to flee. The male Indians stood grave and motionless on the margins of this scene with a serene expression on their faces, showing clearly enough that this strange greeting passed for normal civility among them.

Villegagnon grew alarmed only when he saw the donkey Thevet, caught up in the general grief and still not fully consoled for the loss of his effects, dissolve in tears beside him. This show of emotion caused the women to shriek all the more lustily.

Finally the racket died down. A tall Indian, older than the ones who had first welcomed them and covered at the hips and back with a fine down of feathers stuck to him with pitch, advanced toward Villegagnon and greeted him. His lip weighted down with the same stone that all the men wore, he embarked on a long speech of welcome.

The admiral rose to his feet, leaving Thevet sniffling like a calf in his hammock, and made a sign to Just.

"Did you bring the presents?" he whispered.

Just ran back to the longboat and, with the help of a sailor, carried back the bolt of cloth and the bucket of beads. He deposited them at Villegagnon's feet, just as his leader intoned his peroration:

". . . And that is why the king of France rejoices to have such vigorous warriors as yourselves for his new subjects. I would add that having exhibited before us the instruments by which your virility may be judged, in the future it will be unsuitable to impose the sight on strangers. This piece of fine cloth, which I am happy to offer you, may serve to cover you. And these jewels will enhance the elegance of your wives, if they will only consent to dress themselves."

The admiral took the bolt and placed it on a stump, where the children, laughing, started to unroll it in the dust. He set out the bucket of glass beads on the ground, and it became surrounded by women, who plunged their hands into it. No one was crying any longer, and all faces now smiled fraternally. The warriors held the new arrivals by the hand, embraced them, offered them gifts of feathers and carved bone. So as not to disrupt the general good humor, the French allowed themselves laughingly to be stripped of their caps, their swords, their belts, which the naturals laughingly draped over themselves.

The authority that Villegagnon had hoped to preserve had been perilously threatened since the embarrassing landing from the longboat, but he had never so despaired of recovering it as in the midst of this joyous tumult during which not a single soul any longer paid attention to him.

And so, though surprised, he was also relieved at the sight of a man whose arrival caused the Indians suddenly to grow quiet. Judging from his costume, Villegagnon thought it must be one of their chiefs, but when the man approached, he realized otherwise.

"Welcome, my lord," said the man in accentless French.

With horror they all realized that he was a white man.

CHAPTER 15

With the light at his back, the man who had just burst into the Indian village looked in all respects like a gentleman. Helmeted, wearing a doublet with slashed sleeves and well-tailored breeches, he carried a long sword at his side. But when Villegagnon moved slightly to avoid the sun streaming into the clearing, he was surprised to discover that these familiar clothes had a strange appearance. The man's headpiece, though cylindrical in shape with the fore and aft peaks of the helmets of the day, was made of poorly tanned cowhide. Black and white hairs still stuck to it. His doublet, which at first glance seemed to be made of gray velvet, was in fact made of tiny feathers artfully stitched together with cotton thread. As for his sword, it needed no protection from a scabbard, being simply made of wood.

Despite his singular attire, the man had the graces of a courtier. Villegagnon, who in his haste had disembarked in a shirt, and a dirty one at that, reflected that the naked men in these parts, like those who wore feathers, displayed a great nobility of manner. He promised himself that in the future he would take greater pains over his public appearance.

The man addressed a few words to the Indians in their own language. They stepped back, and those who had taken belongings from the visitors returned them in silence.

"Gaultier, known as 'Le Freux,' " said the man, bowing before Villegagnon.

His face was clean-shaven, but so obstinately scraped that his skin was a mass of red scales. Between his feathers and his hair, they seemed to represent the aquatic order.

"Are you French, then?" asked Villegagnon, with the perplexity of a man trying to find the right place for a leaf in his herbarium.

"Were I not, Excellency, you would have found me in the stomach of one of these scoundrels. Our people are the only ones they spare, as they hold us to be friends."

Villegagnon, reassured by the naturals' welcome, had somewhat forgotten their detestable habit. He now looked at them askance.

"In truth, we did not expect you to land over here," went on Le Freux, "and that explains my tardiness. When we saw your ships enter the bay, we thought they were heading toward the opposite shore, as all other ships have done. Are you here to replenish your supplies, and do you plan to visit the settlements?"

"No," said Villegagnon, deciding to engage in conversation. "We will stay on the island directly off the shore here."

"You couldn't have made a better choice," said Le Freux suavely. "It is deserted."

The admiral continued to look at the Indians with distrust.

"Now, as to these Indians, you say they are tame?"

"They no longer eat Frenchmen, that much is certain. But they are insolent and thievish. You will quickly get to know them. Although they are far behind all other civilizations, and as weak-minded as children, they have the gall to consider themselves our equals. One has to obtain their respect."

As he spoke, Le Freux glanced down at the bolt of cloth the children had partly unrolled across the ground. He stooped and took hold of it.

"Superb fabric," he said, feeling it between his fingers. "You don't intend it for these savages?"

Villegagnon hesitated.

"I was told . . ."

"Quite, Your Excellency," said Le Freux, cutting short the admiral's embarrassment. "You are entirely right: they will derive great benefit from it. But on condition that they are shown its proper use.

This side of the bay is somewhat isolated, and the naturals here are less familiar with our works. They are capable of learning anything, if one knows how to teach them. As to this piece of cloth, you may rest assured: I'll take care of it."

The admiral thanked him warmly. Having peered closely at the featherwork doublet on the man's back, he no longer doubted that Le Freux could bring the cannibals to do anything.

"Have you been here long?" asked the admiral, while the man busied himself rolling up the fabric properly.

"Almost ten years." And to head off any more probing question, he added, "I was shipwrecked."

"Do you live in this area?"

"A bit here and a bit there," said Le Freux evasively, "wherever my business takes me."

"Do you have a wife and children?"

Villegagnon felt concern for the poor man.

"Well, I have women, as there's no shortage around here. As to children, it's hard to say . . ."

Le Freux gave this answer with bravado, darting lewd looks around him. Several of the soldiers laughed. But Villegagnon and Thevet reacted with such visible indignation that Le Freux quickly changed the subject.

"But how may I be of service to you? You will certainly need many things brought over from the mainland . . ."

"Fresh water," said Villegagnon. "Can you show us a convenient place to fill our water barrels?"

"Nothing could be simpler."

"And food. There are six hundred of us."

The eyes of the castaway sparkled with excitement.

"Well," he said breathlessly, "we'll provide you with supplies of dried fish, flour, fruit—everything you need, in fact. Anything can be obtained here . . . as long as you're willing to pay."

"Pay?" said the admiral. "But this land is now French. Everything in it belongs to us."

"Ah, I understand that perfectly," said Le Freux, with a false grimace. "But these savages are thickskulled. If you're not in a position to crack that skull for them, you can count on their ill will. They're greedy, the villains!"

Villegagnon looked at the naked warriors, the three scattered earthen jars, the palm-leaf house, and wondered where the devil these naturals could be hiding the riches that, according to Le Freux, they so coveted.

"Our ships are laden with objects of value, which we can offer them in exchange," Villegagnon conceded, temporarily admitting to the disparity in forces.

"Count on me to get everything for you at the very best price."

A flight of parrots passed over the village cackling, and this sudden movement in the sky reminded the admiral of the wild forest around them. The pyramid of the Butter Crock stuck up out of the trees. Seen from that vantage, with its cap of greenery sitting askew on its summit, the mountain easily seemed to be sentient. It looked like a gigantic and curious watchman peering down at the emissaries of the king of France.

"Are the Portuguese a long way off?" asked Villegagnon.

Le Freux made a gesture toward the south.

"The nearest are in São Vicente, in Crablice Land. It's ten days' march from here. But their largest post is to the north, in Salvador, in All Saints Bay."

"Do they sometimes come in this direction?"

"Rarely. Sailors go astray from time to time. In fact, only last year there were six of them on your island, and these Indians ate them."

It took all the deference due to a fellow countryman to believe such an assertion. The supposed culprits, standing among their huts, looked nothing if not genial.

"It is our intention to begin immediately erecting a fort on the island," said Villegagnon, trying to appear composed. "Can you send us one hundred of these Indians to help us with the hardest work? Many of our number are skilled artisans and are not as robust as these primitives."

"Work! Don't count on it. No Indian will ever agree to it."

"And why not?"

"It insults their honor."

"Saint Jack of Jerusalem!" shouted Villegagnon, this time provoked beyond endurance. "Their honor from now on belongs to the king of France. And he cannot bestow a greater honor than to command them to build the first monument of his new kingdom."

Le Freux lowered his eyes and let Villegagnon stare challengingly around him at the Indians. Instinctively, Thevet took two steps back and stood among the Scotsmen.

The native warriors, though they had not understood Villegagnon's words, grew tense and stretched their hands toward their wooden clubs, as a wary silence settled over the village. From the fringe of palm trees, other Indians walked menacingly forward into the open. The cry of a macaw from near the Butter Crock sounded a mournful knell, as old as time.

Le Freux allowed the threat to hang in the air long enough for Villegagnon to realize the limits of his authority.

"But never fear, Excellency," he said, "there are other solutions."

The savages relaxed, and the Scots guard, clenching their spears, breathed once more.

"They are constantly at war with each other," went on the go-between. "They'll gladly sell you their prisoners as slaves. And the prisoners have no honor that would keep them from breaking their backs at work."

These words brought welcome news, and Villegagnon, little relishing a further alarm, started back along the path to the beach. They agreed that Le Freux and his "associates," as Villegagnon gravely called them, should come the following day to visit the ships and discuss what they might be willing to provide in return for the goods on board.

The admiral, followed by Thevet and his guard, walked with dignity to the water's edge. From the longboat they watched the little island draw near, alone and vulnerable, in the midst of the immense bay and its dangers.

"Are you absolutely sure that the site is a good one?" asked Thevet, whom the morning on the mainland had thoroughly terrified.

"This island?" smirked Villegagnon, looking at the gentle line of its center ridge. "In six months you'll hardly recognize it."

• • •

Amberi, the notary, had had so much time on his hands during the crossing that he had recorded in a ledger the number of teeth lost by each passenger on the *Grande-Roberge*. Perhaps he imagined that the victims would some day receive compensation commensurate to their sacrifice, that is, proportional to the number of molars they had let fall along the way. He himself had paid the tribute of his incisors, on which he might found considerable hopes.

A month had passed since their arrival in the bay. The coconut water and the fruit brought over from the mainland had soothed the notary's gums, and he cheered up, as did all his companions. Alas, he could not luxuriate in his convalescence as Villegagnon kept him working without a moment's rest. He had been ordered to make verbatim transcripts of everything, from the visit to the cannibals— where he had scrupulously recorded the Indians' mute acknowledgment of the king of France—to the agreements made with Le Freux during his frequent visits to the ships to inspect their holds.

To this the admiral added a titanic task: the establishment of a land registry for the island. Colombe was chosen, along with Quintin, to help him with this job, which required the utmost trust. Surveyor's chain in hand, they ran about measuring bosks and palm groves, taking bearings on reefs, floundering among the reeds of the little marsh. Amberi followed, carrying his writing case and setting everything down as seriously as if it concerned lost teeth.

Before long Colombe knew every corner of the island, and her liking for it only grew. It was similar to a garden, where the species that intertwined so riotously on the mainland were here laid out in order. When the colonizers disembarked, they had instinctively grouped themselves in areas hardly bigger than the ships. As a result, the island still had wild and empty spaces where one might sleep in the shade during the heat of the day and neither see nor hear anyone. Yet every day it grew harder to be alone on the island. Even the most cowardly and the sickliest were emboldened to make a tour of this welcoming land.

Colombe, like many of the others, now looked toward the coast hungrily, as the island had aroused in her an appetite for exploration it was unable to satisfy. But she regretfully noted that Just did not share her curiosity. More and more he was falling in with Martin's views and looking for a way to escape. Colombe was not accustomed to making plans without her brother, and she thought she would follow him if he found a means of returning to France. But in this unknown and isolated place difficulties mounted up, and the likelihood of getting away seemed distant and improbable. Colombe was determined to put the time they stayed in Brazil to good use by discovering its charms. She continued to wait for the time when she might explore a vaster area than this tiny and suddenly overpopulated island.

But Villegagnon obstinately refused to let anyone go about freely on the mainland. He maintained tight control over relations between the island and the continent. Aside from the oarsmen of the boats and a few seamen responsible for transporting Le Freux's goods, no one was allowed to leave the island. Colombe was not discouraged. After all, she had been brought along as an interpreter, and the admiral might at some point remember that. Or some other occasion might present itself. On the day Amberi decided that his land registry was finished, for instance, Colombe insisted on being present when he delivered it to Villegagnon, in case the admiral decided to enlarge the project to a survey of the coastal region.

Halfway up the hill in the center of the island, the admiral had ordered a large terrace to be leveled. Wooden piles supported an array of handsome palm-thatch roofs. Given its height and the natural setting, it made an acceptable government house. It was the dry season, and Villegagnon didn't hesitate to have his ebony cabinet brought there, as well as the hangings from his cabin and an assortment of chests and pieces of furniture from the other ships. The most impressive of these was a four-poster bed complete with curtains. It was so hot at night that the admiral preferred to sleep in a hammock. But combining this comfort with the privacy afforded him by the curtains, he ordered his hammock to be slung diagonally between two of the posts supporting the bed's canopy.

When Amberi paid his formal visit to the admiral, carrying his rolled-up land registry as carefully as a monstrance—and with Colombe following submissively at his heels—a noisy group was gathered in the part of the straw hut the admiral reserved for audiences.

"At least bring back the boat," the admiral said, concluding his speech. "I'll make arrangements for the rest."

At these words, the group quieted and filed out in silence, led by two Scotsmen. Meanwhile, two other guards announced the notary and his assistant. All this was carried on in the breezy shelter of the open straw hut, but with an attention to protocol worthy of the most hushed offices. Villegagnon appeared to be in a rage, but he mastered himself and greeted the notary politely. Amberi, as though unswaddling an infant, laid out the map on the great table that stood facing the little port and the Sugarloaf.

The sight of the island's contours, neatly drawn on paper, brought relaxation to the admiral's face. Since the ships had been unloaded, Villegagnon had had the services of a barber equipped with fine tools. He kept his beard trimmed evenly short, giving him a kempt appearance more in harmony with the four-poster bed than the virgin forest. Colombe noticed that he wore a topaz ring she hadn't seen during the crossing. But all these attentions, and even his gillyflower perfume, in no way detracted from the colossal disorder of his person, with its profusion of bone, of impatience, and of nose.

"Ah!" said the admiral. "The Idea of the island!"

True enough, on this map the savage beauty of the island's hills and coves took the form of a little penciled snake biting its tail on the sheet of paper. Unmoved by a vast expanse of sea or forest, Villegagnon waxed immediately enthusiastic at the sight of a work of man: a book, a painting, or a map.

"Look," he said, his eyes glittering, "the first wall of the fort will be built here."

His hand glided over the blank parts of the land registry.

"Here, a redoubt, there, the storerooms. Here, a jetty. Do you see them? Ah! Amberi, the Idea, the Idea. That is beauty, power. The divine."

This flight of enthusiasm maintained him in an elevated state for a few instants. Then he fell back to earth and, muttering, refolded the map, which he went and placed in the great secretary.

"Excellent, Amberi. I'll examine it carefully. You may go. And you," he said to Colombe, "stay!"

Surprised but unafraid, Colombe looked at the admiral. He sat down at the table, but Colombe, perhaps because of her recent promotion, did not quite dare follow suit.

"Sit down! What are you waiting for? You haven't always been such an oaf."

Colombe smiled and sat nearby on a straight, leather-covered chair.

"I never see you anymore."

"I was with Maître Amberi."

"And your brother?"

"I haven't seen much of him myself since I started running around the island."

"Send him to me. Now that I am parceling out responsibilities, I want to set him to work. And believe me, I have a few good ideas for the eldest of the Clamorgans."

Colombe thought that was all. She was rising to her feet when Villegagnon said to her, "And for you too."

The admiral looked at her as he spoke, all the while avoiding her gaze, which he disliked.

"You're the youngest person here, that is certain. And though the bumbling Gonzagues had no idea of what he was doing, he did well in taking you on as a go-between. I believe we should stay with our plan: that is how you will be most useful to us."

Colombe couldn't believe her ears.

"You're going to send me among the Indians!" she exclaimed.

He misread her enthusiasm for fear: "You have nothing to be afraid of: they don't eat Frenchmen. They are simple people, beautiful and good, like the gods of antiquity. All our ancestors' humanity is there: they are akin to the shepherds of Homer, setting aside one or two little excesses."

He coughed. Colombe relieved him of his embarrassment by giving him a big smile.

"Good," grunted the admiral. "It looks like you're getting used to the idea."

Then he added in genial tones, "You know perfectly well that I would never put you in danger. You won't be going alone. I want you to accompany a force setting off to the mainland in search of six rascals who just fled in one of the boats."

From Villegagnon's description, Colombe gathered that the fugitives were Anabaptists.

"It will provide a good opportunity," he went on, "to visit other villages than the ones we have been shown by the interpreter Le Freux. When you find an Indian camp where they are willing to welcome you, stay there for a bit and learn the rudiments of the language. Try to learn everything you can about the tribes, then come back and tell me. We are far too dependent on those damned go-betweens, and we need to find another way. I'm convinced they are robbing us. You should see what Le Freux makes us pay for their bad flour and stinking fish."

Colombe would be able to return any time she liked. Boats now came and went several times a day between the mainland and the island. The hardest part was preventing her from setting off immediately.

CHAPTER 16

Vittorio jumped up, startled. Ever since the colonists' arrival on the island more than a month before, he had been eagerly awaiting this moment. He was starting to believe it would never come.

"Aren't you the Venetian?" the man asked in a readily understandable Paduan dialect.

"The very same," Vittorio answered, his voice quavering.

He had almost dropped his pickax from the shock. Hard as it was to believe, Villegagnon and his cronies had taken no account of his talents as a miscreant and forcibly assigned him to humiliating work. It was high time that someone rescued him.

"Your health, countryman!" said the newcomer, offering Vittorio a leather gourd.

The good news was that this providential figure had not come to join the long line of laborers but was free in his movements and highly independent in his manner.

"I'm one of Le Freux's partners," he said proudly.

The go-between had become a well-known figure on the island. He could often be seen with Villegagnon, whom he dealt with on an equal footing. He arrived from the mainland in his own boat, an Indian canoe made from a gigantic hollowed-out tree trunk, propelled by ten standing paddlers. And he always left heavily loaded with merchandise from the ships, though what he did with it was a mystery.

"My name is Egidio," said the trader.

Like his partner and master, though more simply, he was dressed in the European style but using materials drawn from savage nature. A pointed cap, fashioned from the skin of an unknown animal and worn cocked forward, gave him the hearty appearance of a mountain peasant.

Vittorio, all aquiver, waited for what was to follow. He invited his visitor to step away from the group of laborers, so that he could speak the password more comfortably. They went and sat at the foot of a palm tree that was patiently awaiting the ax.

"What a project!" said Egidio, looking at the line of laborers hacking at the crusted sand of the hillside.

Every artisan, whatever his skill, be it stitching shoes or baking bread, had been enlisted in this primitive employment of his arms, which consisted of lifting a pickax and letting it fall. From the vantage point of the palm tree, it looked like a row of peasants absurdly engaged in harvesting rock.

"This Villegagnon is mad," said Vittorio, showing that he had caught all the hidden irony of his compatriot's expressed admiration.

"I hope he pays you well, at least."

"Pays us!" said Vittorio, who hadn't lost his habit of spitting at every turn. "There has never been the slightest question of it. We are his slaves, period. You've seen the ten Indians that Le Freux brought, those prisoners? You can pick them out easily because Villegagnon had red tunics made for them so they wouldn't show their backsides. They are prisoners that the native tribes have sold us as slaves. Well, I can tell you that we are on the same footing with them in every respect."

"But all the same," said Egidio, trying to elicit confidences, "Villegagnon gives you everything you need. Your food is provided. And you have drink and lodging."

"Food? Flour made from ground-up roots and smoked fish. You call that food?"

Between Italians, who know the meaning of cooking, this description was a metaphor for hell. To calm his rage, Vittorio took a long pull on the gourd. His head was already spinning from the drink, which tasted mild but whose power he could feel coursing in his veins.

"This is a remarkable alcohol," he said, looking at the gourd. "Where does it come from?"

"It's a brew that the Indians make for their ceremonies, they call it *cahuin*. I can get you some if you like."

"Unfortunately," said Vittorio, suddenly wary and not wanting this stranger to know that he had gold, "I haven't any money to pay for it."

"For you, countryman, it's free."

"You are too kind. Do you know, if we didn't stink so much, I'd kiss you."

Egidio appeared both flattered at the impulse and relieved at the obstacle to its being carried out. They raised their gourds to each other.

"But the others, in your opinion," said the trader, motioning with his chin toward the laborers, "do they have the wherewithal to buy any?"

"You can be sure of it. Every man you see has a small sum hidden about him or his effects, which he guards day and night. They haven't touched a drop of anything resembling alcohol for months, and I'm quite sure they would pay their eye teeth to get some."

Working under the midday sun, the men would stop after every dozen swings of the pickax and mop their foreheads as though to soothe their anger and exhaustion.

"I'll leave you two flasks of *cahuin*," said Egidio, "and you let them have a taste of it. I can get you a barrelful for four silver testoons. And for every barrel you sell, you'll receive two copper deniers."

"Three," said Vittorio, who knew something about buying and selling.

"Done."

They shook hands. The gentle consolation of the *cahuin* further heightened the moment and made the Sugarloaf and all the mountains around the bay dance.

"What about women?" asked Vittorio, who always thought in large terms when it came to business.

"But after the hardships of the crossing, do you think they would be interested?" asked Egidio craftily.

"You should hear the conversations at night around the fire."

"Would Indian women appeal to them?"

"Appeal to them? When they see the Indian women paddle right by the island in their damned canoes, tits to the wind, on purpose to taunt us, the men can hardly keep from jumping into the water—though not one knows how to swim."

Egidio shook his head, as though indulgently reproving human folly.

"It seems to me," said Vittorio, "that unless things change, even the female parrots will become objects of lust."

He went on in lower tones: "I happen to know that some of the oarsmen are planning to take interested parties—for money, of course—over to the mainland at night to chase after the savagesses."

"The fools! Don't let them try anything of the kind! We think the Indian women are free because they put on public view what we take care to keep hidden, but it's false. We don't understand a thing about their familial relations. One woman will bring a virgin to her husband to take into his bed, and another will unleash the wrath of all her kinfolk on her mate because he has cheated on her. There's no rhyme or reason to it. I'm telling you, it's dangerous to be friendly with the tribal women unless you know them."

Vittorio was disappointed and showed it.

"But luckily," went on Egidio smoothly, "we who have been here for some time have access to good and fetching slave girls who will not make trouble for anyone. As many as they want, we can provide them."

Vittorio swallowed with difficulty. After stating his terms, namely, that he be on the first trip and have two girls to himself alone, he agreed to fall in with Egidio's plan and oversee the trade with his companions.

"Tell me, Vittorio," said the go-between reflectively, "this admiral of yours must be rich all the same to run an enterprise like this. Does he have gold?"

"He undoubtedly does," said Vittorio, feeling the sap running in his veins again.

"You don't know for certain? He brought you along on this adventure and his only currency of exchange is that cloth and those gewgaws for savages that he showed us in the hold? Come, he must have something else."

"I saw the men carrying a locked chest that looked very heavy. He had them put it under his bed."

"Under his bed," said Egidio, interested. "That's not a very secure place, with all the convicts roaming this island."

Vittorio sat up. "Convicts" suggested prison; prison suggested crime; and crime, to Vittorio, suggested Ribera. Momentarily he expected to hear the long-awaited signal. But nothing came.

"What have I said that is so extraordinary?" said Egidio. "You're sitting there with your mouth open."

"No . . . I was just thinking . . . what were we talking about? Oh yes, the chest under his bed. Well, it's actually quite a safe place. The four Scotsmen in the admiral's guard, whose vigilance I have some knowledge of, take turns keeping watch over that room day and night."

Egidio, without seeming to pay too much interest, took inward note of these details. Vittorio gave up on hearing any talk of Ribera and, noticing that he had been missed on the worksite, made arrangements to rendezvous with Egidio that same night and returned to digging at the ground, his hopes renewed.

•   •   •

Three boats left the island in the dawn hours of that January day, carrying men Villegagnon had charged with a mission on the mainland. He hadn't wanted to deprive himself of his Scots guard or of any Knights of Malta, who acted as foremen on the island's worksites. So he had gathered a small squadron of some twenty disparate soldiers. Among them were the Balt who had traveled on the *Rosée*, two renegades discovered living among the Ottomans, and a frighteningly thin Hungarian, all cheekbones, who was only half his former self now that he had been amputated of his horse. The troop, though hardly very martial, had the advantage of being silent—no one in it understood any of the others—and of being hardened to manhunts, ambushes, and survival in inhospitable places. They had orders to find the Anabaptists and bring them back to the island in chains. Villegagnon divided them into two groups.

The first would go toward the head of the bay. In the group were eight soldiers and Martin, who had managed by his intrigue to be appointed an apprentice go-between. He hoped—either with the soldiers or without them, depending on whether they fell in with his views—to push forward as far as possible and find a way to the trading posts on the far shore. Before leaving, he swore an oath to Just that he would come back for him. The other group would head in the opposite direction, toward the mouth of the bay. They would make land at the site where the runaways had abandoned their boat, then climb into the forest in the direction of the Sugarloaf, trying to reach the ridge and pass behind it.

Colombe accompanied this second group. She had full freedom to choose an Indian lodge to stay in, one that would welcome her and that had not been too sullied, if possible, by contact with Le Freux and his cronies. Carrying a notebook and a supply of ink, she was to collect as many words of the native dialect as possible so as to learn to communicate with the Indians.

Just had done everything he could to dissuade her from leaving, but there was no getting Villegagnon to change his orders once they had been formally given. Colombe devoted her efforts to reassuring her brother until the moment she climbed into the pinnace. Looking back to see him small on the beach, his long dark hair tossed by the wind, she was touched by his tenderness and anxiety. He was still the one person in the world who meant the most to her. But whereas Just's love for her required her to be present, she by contrast had reached that level of certainty where one can maintain one's love intact and even strengthen it in the midst of comings and goings. Suddenly, there in the pinnace, she had a clear sense of herself as bigger and stronger than he with regard to her passions.

But the crossing was brief, and no sooner did her feet touch the water than she turned to the discovery of this land she had so dreamed of.

The troop set off in single file through a gap in the mangroves at the place where the Anabaptists had landed. It was cool and quiet in the early morning. Colombe felt as though they were intruding on nature just as it was waking up. In the gigantic room under the canopy, the breath of obliviously sleeping plants and animals saturated the air with bitter perfumes. The moist skin of the ebony trees, the rounded arms of the euphorbias, the broad heads of the calabashes sprawled unconsciously and without reserve on folds of humus and giant ferns. Far above them, the widely branching jacarandas drew their shade over this scene of abandon.

The company walked for several hours through the dense forest without seeing a village. The sun was now high. It strewed the underbrush with luminous darts whose tips made garish spots of green erupt in the foliage and bright red wounds appear on the trunks. Walking quietly, the group became aware of the slithering of snakes in the lianas, the startled bolting of wild pigs, and the zigzag flight of small, brightly colored birds. As they gained altitude, they could see behind them through the leaves the pale expanse of the bay under the midday sun and the barque-shaped island near which the boats were moored.

The Anabaptists had evaporated into the jungle, and it seemed less and less likely that they would ever be found. The searchers ate some dried fish carried by the Balt in his sack and drank water from their gourds, then rested under a cedar. Colombe fell asleep, her head on a creeping branch. The forest was so thick and quiet that they did not take the trouble to post a guard. When they awoke to find themselves surrounded by a score of Indians armed with clubs and bows as tall as themselves, there was nothing they could do.

Colombe had not yet seen one of the naturals up close. She knew from the bawdy conversations on the island that they went naked, but she had thought this simply a picturesque detail. On finding before her these silent men uncovered by any cloth, she was not in the least shocked. The winkle necklaces and seashell bracelets that were their only ornaments decorated their wrists and chests without in any way hiding the organs that European modesty consigns to darkness. Like trees that offer their fruits forthrightly, these men, who had been born in the forest and had adopted its fertile simplicity, restored to the human form its familiar fullness. When the Balt rose to his feet trembling, covered in his stinking rags, it was he who appeared awkward and ridiculous to Colombe. And she suddenly felt herself to be as absurdly costumed as he.

"*Mair*," mumbled the Balt, in his terror executing the meager orders Villegagnon had given him.

"*Mair, mair*," repeated the other soldiers, leaving their weapons where they lay on the ground.

One of the Indians uttered a long sentence in reply. An unknown language is more seen than heard: this one was colored by innumerable vowels intermingling like the flora of the virgin forest against a rugged relief of consonants that dominated the melody with their abrupt hardness.

"*Mair*," said the Balt again, in the pretense that he had understood something.

At this, the Indians burst out laughing. The foreigners clearly had no inkling of what they had tried to tell them.

The Indians' hilarity, along with the fact that they had once more slung their bows over their shoulders, quieted the soldiers' fears. The group fell in step behind their new guides, following a narrow track through the grasses.

Colombe walked behind an Indian hardly taller than herself, unable to take her eyes off his moving musculature. She had never imagined that a human being could be made of tight ropes and muscles that bellied like sails. Suddenly she became aware of the mystery of her own movements, of the emergence at the body's surface of forces common to the universe of minerals and animals. And she felt how risible was man's obstinacy in expressing his intelligence only through the tiny muscles of his face, when the superb and ample movements of his body reflected it so perfectly.

They reached the saddle from which one can see Guanabara Bay on one side and the open expanse of the Atlantic on the other. A moist wind gusted up from the ocean side, replacing the close smell of vegetation with the sharp acidity of ocean salts and kelps. Now the flora was changing. It was no longer as tall and consisted of fragrant copses of something resembling rhododendron or holly.

At one point, the narrow path widened reassuringly, but the Indians warned them with signs not to walk in the middle. One of their number, using a long arrow he carried at his side, showed the soldiers that the ground here actually consisted of a bamboo lattice covered with grass. Had they stepped onto it, they would have fallen into a trench bristling with stakes.

They followed the Indians along a track around this obstacle and, before five minutes had passed, found themselves entering a village. Like the one visited by the admiral, this village consisted of a single longhouse, large enough for a hundred people to live in.

The same tearful ceremony awaited them, but as one of the soldiers had already experienced it when Villegagnon landed, they all took part in it with good grace. Everything about the Indians' wel-

come seemed reassuring to Colombe: the children's gaiety as they
played naked on the ground, the men's attention in seating the newcomers on hammocks and offering them calabashes full of food, and
the aromatic smell of the fires on which earthenware pots had been
set to heat.

At the very moment when she felt herself pervaded by the warmth
of their reception, an unexpected danger obtruded on Colombe. The
women, naked as the others, came and surrounded her with laughter
and tender expressions. Caressing her hair and taking her hands, they
gaily drew her off to the side. The dumbfounded soldiers, the scales
abruptly fallen from their eyes, realized that the women had recognized Colombe as one of their own.

CHAPTER 17

As Just went down to the beach that morning, his bare feet shuffling through the dust that had accumulated on the abandoned land, he realized that Colombe had been gone for two whole weeks and he had had no news of her. His mood was dark as he stood in line to get his breakfast. A cook with dirty hands offered him an overcooked sea bream, which he took to the foot of a coconut tree to chew on.

The only alternative to his dark thoughts was the drab green of the bay. In Normandy Just had passionately loved the sea. When his dreams did not carry him off on knightly quests or campaigns in Italy, he would imagine sailing over the sea. A noble heart could feed to satiety on its stormy winds, its swells, and its tides, which sounded the call to battle as implacably as a joust. But could one give the name "sea" to this inert tropical soup? Just watched the frizzling foam that fringed the beach like the meager lace of a chambermaid. For several cable lengths, the water was so shallow and so calm it looked like a rough pane of glass laid on the wrinkled skin of a monster. Everything in this desolate place showed plainly that human life was not welcome here. The effort, energy, and grim determination that cold climates inspire had no place in this steam room where snakes, hairy insects, and brightly-colored birds proliferated.

Like the castaway he felt himself to be, Just held fast to a single idea: returning home. It was not an accomplishment but a precondition. He had no idea what he would do once back in France. His only thought was to ensure his return as soon as possible. This was what had motivated his friendship with Martin. The young brigand had hardly anything else in common with him. If he had captured Just's interest with his tales of heists and low taverns, it was because of his talent as a storyteller, his gaiety. Just never imagined himself signing on to the criminal life, though the other had suggested it to him. He loved the light, honor, and beauty of combat too much to ever practice the dark art of setting traps. But in the extreme circumstances in which they found themselves, Martin was a valuable ally.

The mainland made him think of Colombe. And by a troubling coincidence, it happened just at the moment when, finishing the meager flesh of the fish, he pricked his gums on its bones. His love for his sister was still as sharp as ever, and the idea of returning to France was for him just another way of making plans with her. Yet he felt strangely divided. It reassured him to see her finding happiness in little things and facing the stifling climate and the savage land head on. She was still child enough to take it all in fun: only this could explain her enthusiasm for the landscape and her desire to visit the mainland. At the same time, he wondered whether this exile she had too readily accepted, this dressing as a boy, this life of lies and reduced circumstances, might not strip her forever of what, with no clear understanding on his part, he took to be the mix of modesty, innocence, virtue, and sweetness that makes a woman. Especially, he couldn't stand the idea that she was surrounded by savages who openly exposed their attributes to her.

Just flung the fishbone away and wiped his mouth. Sending Colombe to the mainland had been yet another of Villegagnon's ideas! The suffering Just felt was soothed by the balm of his resentment against the admiral. Ruminating more peaceably, he slowly climbed up to the worksite.

The island had grown unrecognizable in the two months since they had landed. Their axes might bite ineffectively into the fibrous wood of the coconut trees, yet several hundred lay felled. Their stumps poked up out of the beach, providing as many stools for the men to sit on off the sand. Slender logs littered the surface of the island, and from all sides came the sound of hoes, of saws, and of grunting as beams were hauled toward what was clearly developing into a fort. Valuable woods were sawed and loaded onto the *Grande-Roberge*, which Villegagnon planned to send back to France soon to bring its cargo to market. Brazilwood was the most highly valued species, but little of it grew on the island. Le Freux, however, had agreed to log some brazilwood groves along the coast—at an exorbitant price. The tree, which is used for dyeing, has very green leaves and grows to about the size of an oak. Its trunk is so hard that it seems to be dead. A score of slaves, equipped with French axes, hoes, hooks, and other ironmongery, had the terrible commission of felling these trees in the steep and dangerous sites where they grew and then cutting them up. The remains of these noble plants, ferried over in pirogues, lay in twisted heaps on the island's beach, waiting to be loaded onto the ship. Beside this massacre, tall baskets filled with sand stood in rows like barrels. These, set at the island's weakest points, would provide a first rampart against a possible Portuguese attack while the fort was under construction.

Just returned to his work: he was assigned to the quarry. It was on a rocky escarpment facing out to the bay, and it supplied a building stone that was solid though rather poor in appearance. Stonecutters in leather aprons fractured the rock face and tried to give the blocks they extracted some semblance of form. A human chain then passed the blocks along to the first redoubt. Indian slaves provided by Le Freux filled the role of porters. They were made to wear tunics hastily sewn by two of the expedition's tailors. Just's task was to pry away the blocks of stone from the face with a long iron bar and supervise the workers in the quarry. But he also had explicit orders to see that the natives kept their tunics on no matter what. In the evening, drenched with sweat, the poor Indians tried to find rest, and their instinct was to uncover the most overheated parts of their body, never conceiving that these were also the most shameful. Among the slaves were several women, and though they were worn and ugly, Just sensed that their nudity made the eyes of the European workers gleam, almost to the point of danger. He didn't relish his role as a prison guard.

Given his plans for escape, however, it mattered to him that the island remain free of violence and maintain its current level of easygoing supervision.

That morning, as he walked up to the quarry, Just saw Dom Gonzagues coming toward him.

"I've found you at last!" said the old soldier, laying a paw on Just's collar.

Just resented the man's familiarity. He couldn't forget that Dom Gonzagues was responsible for his and Colombe's exile. True, he had meant no evil by it and now showed them a great deal of affection. But Just could not quite bring himself to return it.

"I've written a poem," said Dom Gonzagues. He pulled a wrinkled scrap of paper from his pocket and, holding it at arm's length, began: "'Marguerite . . .'—just a name chosen at random . . ."

"I have work to do, Gonzagues . . ."

"No, please listen, it's very short:

> *Marguerite, on my island like unto a nest,*
> *I hold your name close under my vest.*
> *Thus the bird keeps warm under its wing*
> *A memory of the world's most beautiful thing.*

Just, appalled, nodded his head. It seemed merciful to say nothing.

"But isn't it beautiful?" asked Dom Gonzagues.

"There are some feet missing."

"Feet! What does this have to do with feet, you donkey! Oh, by the way, the admiral wants to see you. You'd better stop by this morning."

This was bad news. Just stayed as far away from Villegagnon as possible. When an urgent call had gone out to all able-bodied men to help with building the fort, Just had readily volunteered. This had spared him from acting as the admiral's page.

When he arrived at the government house, as it was now called, the Scots guard instantly led him in to see Villegagnon, who was indeed waiting for him. He rose to his feet when he saw Just, took his hands, and looked at him for a moment. With his head of thick and luxuriant black hair, his untended but finely drawn beard, which traced a distinct bracket under his lower lip, Just was undoubtedly the finest-looking boy on the island. His nobility, which had nothing to occupy it, took the time to visit each of his gestures and seemed to defy the world—though without arrogance—to offer him a challenge commensurate to his abilities.

Villegagnon appeared entirely satisfied with his examination. He let go of Just and made him sit next to him.

"Clamorgan," he started, with tender gruffness, "I let you play about on that construction site where they needed you. But now I would fail in my duty if I didn't undertake your education as a nobleman."

"But . . . what about the fort?" Just stammered.

The idea of having regular contact with Villegagnon revolted Just despite himself. He was convinced that the admiral had played him for a fool. Though he didn't understand the mechanism, he believed there had been a conspiracy between the chancelloress, the nuns, and Villegagnon to make him and Colombe believe that they were going to find their father again and in this way separate them from Clamorgan forever.

"You can work at the fort every afternoon if you like. But from now on you'll come here first thing in the morning to take lessons with me. Where are you sleeping now?"

"On the site."

"In a hut?"

"No, in the open."

"In that case I'll tell the Scotsmen to find you a corner here. It will be the rainy season soon, and I don't want you to leave the books I lend you lying about."

The prospect of reading gave Just a sharp pang of pleasure, and he thought Colombe would be even happier about it than he was. After all, even though he didn't like Villegagnon, he might as well take advantage of the admiral's solicitude before giving him the slip. It would neither hasten nor retard his departure.

"What have you read up to this point?" the admiral asked abruptly.

Just dredged from his memory a miscellaneous list of Latin and Greek poets. He mentioned having read Hesiod, Virgil, and Dante. Then, having given these proofs of his seriousness, he confessed to the romances of Perceval and Amadis of Gaul.

"That should do for the classics and for chivalry," said Villegagnon. "It seems to me you know enough about them. But we live in a time of new ideas. They come to us through great spirits who love God as much as they love the human race. Have you read Erasmus?"

"No," admitted Just, neither remorseful nor proud.

"Well then, here is the *Enchiridion*, which I believe to be his finest work," said Villegagnon, pulling a small book from an upright chest that served as a library. "Read this in the coming week and try to absorb it, because I plan to question you on its contents. It is written in a Latin that is very easy for anyone who has read Virgil."

Just took an unexpected pleasure in pressing the small volume with its worn beige morocco cover to his side.

"Another thing," said Villegagnon, rising to his feet. "On the ship you showed your courage at fist fighting. That's good, but in the future you'll need to know how to handle nobler weapons. We'll go down to the beach every morning after dawn, and you'll trade sword cuts with me."

Learning to fence was one of the things Just most wanted to do, but he had never imagined it would happen under such strange circumstances. Villegagnon had turned his back at the end of his sentence, as he did whenever his words were likely to provoke an emotional reaction.

Just knew that he should take his leave, but he was too worried about Colombe.

"Admiral, have you any news of my brother?" he asked.

"Not yet, but the detail left only two weeks ago, and besides, the soldiers have not come back yet either."

The words were meant to be reassuring, yet the admiral's tone of voice was anything but. Just rose, hesitating to go out as though he believed Villegagnon might have saved his real thoughts for last. His wait was interrupted by a sudden uproar from the hut next to them, which was used as a waiting room. From behind the palm lattice came the harsh voices of the Scotsmen, followed by loud and threatening shrieks, which could have only come from Thevet.

"Go take a look!" Villegagnon ordered.

Just opened a doorlike panel, and the Franciscan swept in. In his right hand he held a cutlass, and in the left a large yellowish brown fruit, crowned with a tuft of pointy leaves.

"Quick, Admiral," he said, "a plate!"

Seeing a pewter plate on the table, he set the fruit down and sliced it with a quick thrust. The flesh of the fruit was bright yellow and interspersed with fibers.

"Taste this delicious food, if you please."

He had deftly cut a section of pulp, which he held out to Ville-gagnon on the tip of his knife. Surprised, the tall man hardly dared to object. He took the proffered food between his teeth, chewed it, swallowed it, and pronounced his sentence on it: "Good."

"Ah! Ah!" the Franciscan giggled. "At a minimum! 'Excellent' would be more accurate, if I may suggest, Admiral. The go-betweens brought this fruit to me from the mainland. I need to make sure, but I believe it as yet has no scientific name. The natives call it 'ananas.' "

From the excitement in his voice, it was clear that his greed was provoked not so much by the taste of the plant as by the prospect of enriching it with his name, duly latinized to make it universal.

"Monsieur l'abbé," said Villegagnon with a weariness so penetrat-ing as to puncture the friar's complacency, "do please sit down, I entreat you."

He had forgotten Just, who was still standing by the door, afraid to move. The Franciscan sat down and laid aside his blade regretfully.

"No one rejoices more than I at discoveries that advance science," started the admiral. "But must I remind you that you alone of our company are able to celebrate the sacrament? Briefly, I would ask you this: when do you intend finally to say Mass?"

The Franciscan grew sullen.

"I no longer have any ornaments."

"Christ Our Lord, if I remember, set us an example of poverty. The humblest place may be consecrated by prayer."

Villegagnon, who had fought the pope's armies, frequented humanists, and even rubbed elbows in Italy with bold spirits who declared themselves for the Reformation, was made indignant to the core at anything that smacked of pomp. He believed in a free and invisible Church, uniting men who had been touched by divine grace whatever their works or their deeds.

"Don't count on me," said Thevet, "to proselytize to the savages before they have gained an elementary knowledge of our languages and our ways."

"I am not thinking of the savages!" thundered Villegagnon. "Who has said anything about them? Their turn will come. But it is our own subjects who are going astray for lack of any call to morality and faith. I hear that every day they grow more dissipated. The work is no longer progressing. Every morning we come across men who are so drunk they can't keep to their feet."

He narrowed his eyes and brought his face close to the Franciscan's, who turned away under his breath.

"I believe that a still more terrible trade is spreading, one that touches the flesh," said Villegagnon.

He spoke these words in so loud and rumbling a voice that one of the Scots stuck his head in the door.

"Leave us!" shouted Villegagnon.

Then, seeing Just still standing near the entrance, he sent him packing sternly: "What are you still doing here? Get out, and don't breathe a word of what you've heard to anyone."

Just was just leaving when he heard Villegagnon turn back to the cosmographer and say, "Let us now examine together, Monsieur l'abbé, what measures we might take to pluck out these evil shoots."

CHAPTER 18

It was careless, of course. But there are pleasures one allows oneself to be drawn into because to refuse them would be to commit a crime against oneself. When Colombe saw herself surrounded by the Indian women, felt them caressing her and fussing over her in a babble that she understood without exactly catching the words, she didn't try to resist or correct them: she felt as though a burden had been lifted from her. A moment earlier she had still been indifferent to her male disguise, so watchful not to call herself a woman that she was no longer even sure of being one. Yet her body had changed during the crossing, and only the meager shipboard diet kept her from assuming an adult fullness. The island regimen had breached this dike, and the rags she wore could hardly hide her new roundness.

As soon as the Indian women drew her off, the soldiers saw what only habit had kept them from noticing earlier. The Balt and his cohorts watched with equal parts of pleasure and horror as her sad vest was unresistingly removed and Colombe's two firm breasts, no longer a child's in any way, were bared to the sight of all. Once more aware of the soldiers' presence and their stares, she advanced toward them without trying to cover herself and said cheekily:

"Now that you know my secret, be the cowards that you are and tell anyone you like! I will stay on here. It is perhaps the last of the admiral's orders that I will have the chance to carry out."

The Balt emitted a grunt and drew the others away. After they had eaten from the wooden bowls the Indians offered them, they set off once again on the trail of the heretics. Two Indian warriors volunteered to guide them.

Colombe was left alone, and the soldiers' departure filled the camp with what she registered as a great silence. It took her a moment to understand the cause of this strange calm. The Indians moved soundlessly. The village lay in the center of the forest and its humans made no more noise than the birds, snakes, or insects.

A few brazilwood fires burned without smoking. Removing the rest of Colombe's clothes, the women made gestures with their fingers to show their revulsion at her dirtiness. Even as she was stripped of her last garments, Colombe felt a sharp desire to be rid of the grime that coated her like an intimate lining. The Indian women drew her joyously after them toward a little stream flowing through the forest. Climbing up several basalt steps, they reached two tiny waterfalls that poured into a small pool. One of the women dove in first and showed Colombe that she needn't worry about losing her footing. Then Colombe climbed down in turn, and the Indian women gathered around and scrubbed her with handfuls of a mosslike plant that made white suds on her skin.

They returned to the village a little later, and Colombe, naked with the others, felt neither fear nor shame, even when their group passed in front of the men.

Twilight was falling. The women settled around the fires. Colombe shivered, unused to the evening cool, and the women smilingly threw a length of white cotton cloth over her shoulders.

It was at this moment, in the warmth of the coals and the shawl, that Colombe, rubbing her water-numbed feet, realized her full predicament.

The soldiers would return to the island within a week, and they would immediately denounce her to Villegagnon. If for some reason they didn't, she would be at the mercy of their blackmail and would have to confess the whole thing herself. She had betrayed the admiral's trust irremediably. Just would also suffer the consequences of having lied with her.

What would be their punishment? She had no idea, but she sensed that she and Just would be separated. An animal desire to nestle against Just overcame her, and she shivered. A feeling of injustice and unhappiness filled her eyes with tears. In this delicious moment of the revelation of her sex, she rejected all lies and illusion. She saw her life and its cruelty unadorned: the wandering, the abandonment, and now her exile.

The antidote to these poisons, her life's rampart, Just, whom she adored, was no longer a refuge for her love: when she appeared before him as a woman, she would be forever denied the natural tenderness they had shared as children—a tenderness that had already in recent times been disturbed by a subtle embarrassment.

She wanted to call for Emilienne. Then, as her tears flowed, she started to feel the severity of the forest, which was dark already while the sky was still blue. Two Indian women brought her a bowl of soup. A child ran toward her waving a small branch. An old woman carrying a wooden bowl full of red paste knelt in front of her and drew signs on her face, which she found soothing. A quarter moon, gliding through the jacarandas, was the last image she carried with her into sleep—her first as a woman.

• • •

"Protect yourself, you big jackass," shouted Villegagnon, lunging.

A fourth hit appeared on the leather plastron Just was wearing.

"It's just that at the same time . . ."

"Exactly," bawled the admiral. "It's *at the same time* that you are fighting that you must answer. Come now, engage and recite: 'When you see your neighbor suffer, why does your own soul not suffer also?'"

"'Because it is dead,' chapter 1."

"Good, stand straight! One foot back. There. And to whom must you not address yourself if you are to be reborn to a Christian life?"

"'To monks who are hateful and . . . irascible and too . . . swollen with . . .'"

"'. . . Self-regard.' Chapter 2. A touch, but that was better toward the end."

Just was drenched in sweat. His bare feet sank in the fine sand of the beach, and he had to leap strenuously to stay beyond the reach of this devil of an admiral. Some twenty colonists, seated on stumps, followed the lesson from afar and greeted each attack with shouts.

"*En garde*! Where then can we find salvation and our spiritual nourishment?"

" 'In divine law as it is revealed to us in sacred and profane literature,' chapter 4."

"Which is to say?"

" 'Saint Paul, Saint Augustine, Denis the Areopagite, Origen . . .' "

"And?"

" '. . . Plato.' "

"Well, about time too. Straighten up. Is man good?"

" 'Yes, since he is the work of God.' "

"Is man free?"

" 'Yes, since he is made in the image of God.' "

"Perfect! A touch! That will do for this morning."

Villegagnon walked up to Just and took back his sword and plastron. Linking his arm with Just's, he climbed with him back up to the straw huts. On the terraced area at the top of the island, the outlines of the fort were starting to appear.

"You have read Erasmus properly, and I am going to give you another work. But tell me . . ."

He stopped and stared at Just with his terrible eyes.

"Why does all this not interest you?"

"All what?"

"All that I am teaching you."

"It does interest me," said Just without much conviction.

The admiral held him by the arm and shook him: "Don't lie."

Just met the dark eyes boring into him with no attempt at evasion. He assumed a proud and challenging air.

"You don't look like your father," muttered Villegagnon, letting Just go and resuming his path. "But you're just like him all the same. The pride!"

Just felt his heart beat faster even than when he had been leaping about earlier with his sword. He had a burning desire to know, to push all scruples aside and ask the questions that obsessed him, but the word "pride". . .

"The last time I saw him," said the admiral pensively, "was in Venice, at the house of Paulus Manutius, the son of Aldus, who had taken over his father's printing press. It was in 1546, I was returning from Hungary where I had been fighting the Turks."

"And he?" asked Just, unable to contain himself.

"You see how curious you are, when the subject interests you," said Villegagnon, looking sideways at him. "He was on his way to Rome, where I followed him a short time later. But he was in the service of the Medicis, whereas I was bound to the Strozzis. We almost had to fight each other. There, that's the truth, do you understand?"

"Yes," said Just.

"No, you don't. You don't understand anything."

They had reached the edge of the coconut trees, and the rows of stumps rising from the gray sand suggested a cemetery filled with gigantic tombs. Villegagnon stopped.

"You can't know how much I admired the man . . ."

The giant still held clasped against him the swords and leather breast-shields.

"I arrived in Italy at the age of thirty, and believe me I was still steeped in the old traditions of our chivalry, according to which a man expends himself in vigils and prayers, is seamed with scars, and never takes any notice of himself. My first shock came in Florence, on seeing Michelangelo's *David* and Sansovino's *Baptism of Christ.* The principle of God still lived in man, then, despite Adam's betrayal. One had only to cultivate it. Man—the man, of ideal beauty, the masterwork of his creator, the man of parts who excelled in the arts of war and peace, the good man, the calm, elegant, and serene man, the master of himself—could become an ideal."

Following his thoughts, Villegagnon stared into the distance toward a far-off cloud, round and motionless in the sky.

"The second shock I received was when I met your father, for I had never met anyone who approached these perfections so nearly, to the point of almost attaining them."

He seemed suddenly to come to himself and cast a glance at Just.

"I say 'almost' because he wasn't without his faults, as events were to show. But that's another story. For the moment I simply want to tell you this: whatever you may think, I had nothing to do with your being shipped off to the New World."

In a few sentences, he told Just what he knew of the family machinations that had led to their being sent away from Clamorgan.

"And now, to answer the question you are so eager to ask me but are unable to because of pride, the simple truth is this: you won't find your father here because he isn't in America. He never has been and never will be."

"Why did you lie to us?" asked Just, erupting with rage on hearing his suspicions confirmed and turning it full on Villegagnon.

"Kindly retract that word!" the admiral thundered. "I was only waiting for the right moment to tell you the truth. Had I told you on the boat, you would have had only the sight of the sea to console you. Whereas now, take a look around you."

Villegagnon opened his arms wide, north and south, on the sumptuous expanse of the bay, with its luxuriant forests and majestic heights.

"Before you stands Antarctic France. All is yet to be built, all is yet to be conquered."

Then, inclining his long nose toward the young man, he added, "All is yours."

"Is he dead?" asked Just.

"Yes."

A sweltering heat was already rising off the jungle, stirred by the south wind. Terns wheeled in the air.

Just looked at the mainland. The mystery that had clung to these forested escarpments was gone, melted away like a vapor. The colors were sharper and cruder. There might be life in these expanses, but henceforth they represented solitude. Villegagnon had turned away so as not to witness Just's tears and perhaps also to hide his own. Then, after a gruff, clumsy embrace, he walked away.

"Go to your work, but stop by again this evening. I have a copy of Copernicus's *Commentariolus* for you."

Just watched the tall figure stride off, stooped and a little twisted. For a moment he remained dumbstruck, listening absurdly to the shushing song of the waves. Just was surprised to find that at the very moment he had been given so many new reasons to leave, he had lost all desire to do so.

•   •   •

There was not the slightest secrecy in Indian life. Each person lived naked, in a communal dwelling, and activities took place in the open space of the camp. Yet it would take a lengthy period of observation to understand what animated this human community, so motionless did it seem. Everything, from the expression of emotions to everyday gestures, from ordinary life to exceptional moments of celebration, seemed from the outside to wear a languid, muffled, and mysterious aspect.

Colombe naturally absorbed all of this. She took some time at first to efface herself. Her presence as a European, though she wanted to be calm and discreet, had a jarring effect on the harmony of Indian life. Verbal language was actually the easiest aspect. The women introduced her to conversational basics, which she soon picked up. But the language of the body was much more difficult. Her entire instinct for feeling human emotions was disrupted in this new universe. The Indians expressed themselves on a disconcerting scale. A muscle tremor, the position of a person's limbs, even subtle changes of tumescence in a man's penis all had meaning, a meaning that was at once obvious and hidden, as easily read as a book but also as mysterious, at least when the language was unknown.

Colombe also understood that the Tupi looked at her and saw signs and correspondences that fit in with their thought and beliefs. From the very first day, of course, they had noticed her eyes. The natural paleness of her eyelashes filled them with admiration. They called her "Sun-Eye." When she understood their language better, she learned that her face also reminded them of a forest raptor, one that they believed carried the spirits of the dead. When a warrior met this bird's gaze, the energy of all his dead ancestors returned to him and filled him with new strength. The men therefore took the habit of standing before Colombe so that she could look at them for a long moment before they set off on one of their constant expeditions into the forest to hunt or keep watch on their enemies.

The girls and women of the camp came for her every morning to take her bathing. Nothing seemed to give them greater pleasure than to steep themselves for long periods in water. The stream near camp was only a convenience. When they had the time, they preferred to go farther afield, to waterfalls on small branches of the river. They stayed there all through the hot part of the day, splashing themselves with water, combing their hair, and removing all their body hairs with small hardwood tweezers. Nothing was spared this treatment, neither eyebrows nor pubic hair. Sun-Eye, whose pubic thatch was only newly grown, saw it go with regret, but there was no avoiding the custom.

One day, the women set off early and made their way to the coast below the village, on the far side of the Butter Crock. It was a vast virgin beach facing onto the Atlantic, where enormous rollers crashed in plumes of spray. The wind was so strong that one's hair flew and one shivered from the cold. But the sand was baking hot under the sun. Colombe stood for a long time facing the jade-colored horizon. In her mind, improbable as it might be, she had the impression of seeing the coast of Europe and the gray moors of Normandy on the extreme edge of the round-backed sea. It was not nostalgia but rather an effort to bring her life's two shores face to face, the past and the present, without yet knowing on which side the die of the future would be cast.

But this deserted beach, called Copacabana by the Indians, was unsafe and the only place of those the women visited where they were always accompanied by several warriors. While the women bathed, the men maintained a silent watch, their eyes turned toward the forest.

Among the Indian women, Colombe quickly grew attached to one named Paraguaçu. She was a young girl of about her own age. She laughed more than the others and showed an almost farcical irony toward the group, which Colombe recognized as paralleling her own tendency to mockery. Paraguaçu made her a gift of two bracelets woven with shells and a crescent-shaped mother-of-pearl necklace. And in the morning it was she who took the wooden comb and dressed her friend Sun-Eye's hair.

The village's regular existence was occasionally troubled by incomprehensible alarms. Colombe worried about attacks from enemy tribes and imagined herself being captured and made a slave. But she soon understood that she need fear nothing of the kind in the neighborhood of the camp. The dangers that threatened the Indians were of a different order. Paraguaçu, who was grave and serious on this matter, made her understand that demons were the cause of these alarms. Imperceptible signs from the forest, a suspicious cry, the menacing shadow of an animal, were evidence of these hostile spirits. The Indians fetched gourds filled with shells from a small hut, and one of their number, the *caraíba*, or magician, made these maracas talk by shaking them. The rhythm, the sound, the mysterious rattling of these instruments told the natives what the spirits wanted from them. There then followed ceremonies for which everyone ritually painted themselves black with genipap, red with urucú, and white with a variety of pale earths. Then there were dances, nocturnal songs, an entire array of feasts, whose meaning Paraguaçu could not make intelligible despite her best efforts. The highly fermented *cahuin*, drawn from large earthenware caldrons, made the drinkers' heads spin. Big sticks of *petun*, or tobacco, passed their savory smoke from mouth to mouth. Colombe grew used to these intoxications and even, once calm returned, wished for their speedy return. Never had she known a sleep so full of visions and movement, though the forest that watched over that sleep remained a well of silence and darkness.

At night Colombe slept in the large communal house, where the shadows rippled with breathing, with cracking sounds, with murmurs. All the impressions of the day would flood back over her. Couples—sometimes quite close by—would grapple unembarrassedly to the accompaniment of moaning, panting, and heaving breath. In the morning, these unions were dissolved, but Colombe could never see the bodies of these men and women without thinking that the daylight hours, when they were disparate, was simply a detour on the way to their nighttime fusion, when they blended together.

Like the other unmarried girls, Paraguaçu took the liberty of giving herself to men of the tribe. She often slept with one of them, whom she seemed to hold in particular affection. His name was Karaya, and he was smaller than the other warriors. The stone piercing his lower lip was different and seemed to be a plug of clay. Around his neck he wore a necklace of white shells that were more rounded and more pearly than the shells the others wore. One festive night when the two girls had drunk *cahuin* and shared a fat roll of *petun*, they spoke of their desires and their hopes.

"Today I am having fun," said Paraguaçu, "and afterward I will marry my uncle."

"As for me," said Colombe, looking for words, "today I am being good. And afterward I will marry my brother."

They laughed at these confidences, as they laughed at a thousand things during the day. But when it came time to sleep, Colombe looked back with terror at her strange admission. The forest all around her had become familiar but exerted its oppressive influence on her all the more. It seemed as though its branches and roots now insinuated themselves deep into her mind and made demons appear there, as well as signs and desires that were alluring but rife with danger. She fell asleep, whimpering among lianas, and awoke twice, unable to breathe. She had shouted in her sleep, and an old woman came and touched her hand.

The next morning her terrors had ebbed away, but everything seemed very clear: she had to return to the island as quickly as possible. Whatever Villegagnon might say, she would confront his wrath. This long detour among the Indians—she could no longer even remember how many days she had been there—had certainly enriched her, but it had also made her nostalgic for her other life, the one featuring the opposite shore of the Atlantic, the admiral, the ships, Quintin, European dress, orderly thought, the freedom of a language clearly spoken, and, above all, Just.

When she told the Indians of her decision, they consulted their maracas and organized a great feast. The men spent two days adorning their backs, arms, and buttocks with feathers, which they glued to themselves with a kind of gum. Paraguaçu presented her friend with a newly woven hammock. In the morning, Colombe once more put on the clothes in which she had arrived, and which the women had carefully washed. She cut her hair short so that she might leave the valuable memento of her golden tresses with Paraguaçu.

Three men accompanied her to the stretch of coast facing the island. One of them was Karaya.

The way was long. Colombe, who could now make herself understood, chatted with the men. They talked about the other tribes, and about the Norman go-betweens, whom they seemed to fear more than anything. When they came to the beach, they sat down on the sand to eat and pass the time until they saw the boat that shuttled back and forth to the mainland.

At a certain point, one of the warriors said something to Karaya that Colombe did not understand. The young man laughed and started to untie the necklace around his neck. He slid one of the shells off the cord, knotted the necklace again, and tossed the pearl he had removed onto the sand.

"What are you doing?" asked Colombe.

"It's the full moon today," the boy answered casually, "and I must take a stone off my necklace."

"Karaya is a prisoner," said one of the warriors, laughing. "Every moon, one stone less. When no more stones, we eat him."

They all laughed together, and Colombe, horrified, was happy at that moment to see a boat nearing the shore.

CHAPTER 19

"Put your hands on your head, and don't make a move!"

The harquebus shot, echoing and re-echoing off the forest, had spattered the plume of a coconut tree with lead. It was hard to say whether the shot had been fired high deliberately or whether a wave had sent the shot wide as the trigger was being pulled. Colombe, walking confidently along the beach, stopped, petrified.

"Come on! Raise your arms and walk forward!"

The voice from the pinnace was one she had heard before. She hesitated for a moment, thinking she might possibly escape by running toward the forest. But the Indians would certainly have disappeared already, and it would be very hard for her to find their trail. There were six men in the boat, only one of whom was armed. But in the time Colombe took to consider, he had already reloaded and taken aim at her again.

I didn't think they would go so far, she thought to herself.

She fully expected Villegagnon to punish her after he learned of her lie, but not to have her shot down like a wild animal.

There was a long silence, while the waves whispered. Each of the parties, she on the beach and the oarsmen in the boat, eyed each other from a distance, trying to identify the adversary. Finally

Colombe heard a shout, delivered to the boat's crew by a man with his back to her.

"Stay, friends, hold your fire! I recognize him."

Colombe at that moment recognized the voice and called out, "Quintin!"

The little man jumped into the water and waded to the beach. Colombe rushed toward him, no longer fearing either harquebus or punishment, and threw her arms around his neck.

"My child!" he whimpered, holding his thin arms tightly against her. "You're alive! What joy! God is my witness that I never lost hope."

His thin tears followed the familiar runnel made in his cheeks over the years by earlier flows. The pinnace, meanwhile, bobbed a few cable lengths off. One of the rowers cupped his hands and called out:

"What are we to do?"

"Go fill the barrels at the landing stage and come pick us up on the way back."

The boat went off.

"Let me say a prayer," said Quintin quietly, turning toward Colombe.

He sank to his knees on the sand and muttered a thanksgiving prayer with his eyes uplifted toward his God. Colombe followed his gaze automatically. The sky, after the swarming presence of spirits in the forest, struck her as strangely empty and dead.

Quintin rose to his feet and took Colombe's hands.

"Where did you go? It's been more than a month . . . your brother has gone nearly mad."

"Didn't the soldiers tell you anything?"

Colombe could hardly think about them without getting angry. She still remembered the indignant look on the Balt's face when she took off her tunic.

"Tell us anything? Poor men! They were in no condition to speak when we found them."

"Meaning?"

"How is it possible that you know nothing about this? You were with them."

"No, they left me at an Indian village."

"Ah! I understand," said Quintin, and he managed, on the papier-mâché of his tear-softened face, to form the semblance of a smile. "What joy! What great good fortune!"

Colombe wondered whether the old man's insanity had not grown more pronounced.

But he resumed his accustomed seriousness and went on: "They died, my little friend. All of them. But you, you're here."

Again his tears flowed.

"Died! Where? How?"

"A horrible crime. When they were found on the beach, some distance from here," and Quintin pointed a thin finger in the direction of the Butter Crock, "they were . . . Oh! You are much too young to hear such things . . ."

"Say it."

"They had been decapitated, and their heads pierced ear to ear and strung on a rope, as though to form a hideous rosary."

"Who could have done such a thing?" said Colombe, ashamed of her vengeful thoughts as she said it.

"At first we thought it was the Indians. But on the sand next to the bodies, half erased, were scrawled the words: *Ad majorem dei gloriam.*"

A veritable fountain of tears now poured down Quintin's face.

"How . . . horrid!" he moaned, wringing his hands.

"The Anabaptists . . ." said Colombe, looking toward the forest.

"I never imagined they would be capable of such a thing . . ." sobbed Quintin.

Colombe could still see him imperturbable on shipboard, his hammock strung over a cannon, while the six Anabaptists slept around him.

"When did it happen?"

"A week ago. Since then, we've considered many things. Villegagnon wanted to mount an expedition to find them, and your poor brother was ready to die a thousand deaths to avenge you. Because we were sure those wretches had kept you . . . for their own despicable use."

Colombe thought back to her carefree days among the Indians, to her swims with Paraguaçu, to the nights of feasting, and she felt both a great remorse at having forgotten the rest of the world and a great nostalgia for the tranquility she had enjoyed.

Another ship's boat passed, headed for Fort Coligny. Quintin hailed it and they went aboard.

• • •

The island was unrecognizable. As her foot touched shore, Colombe had a moment of doubt: was this the same place where they had landed three months before? In place of the fronded palms was a sprawl of fallen trunks, and all the cedars were dead. The bunches of canes too had been hacked down, and even the reeds. The regular relief of the island had been planed into terraces and half-constructed walls. Two wooden redoubts had been completed on the rises to the north and south. Sentinels could be seen walking back and forth atop them.

The government house, toward which they went straight away, had also changed. A shingle roof covered the main rooms, in anticipation of the coming rains, and palm-rib partitions rising to manheight kept one from seeing in.

They found the admiral with Just in the main room, where the ebony cabinet presided in the midst of books. The noon light breaking in through the openwork screen blinded Colombe as she entered. Just rose so abruptly that his stool fell over backward. She saw him against the light, and his shadow seemed taller and wider than she remembered. Their desire to see each other again outstripped the means at their disposal to show it. They seemed to hesitate on the brink of a hug that would have been less telling than their quivering immobility. They were grateful to Villegagnon for quelling any outbreak of emotion by raising his hand.

"Where were you?" he said, in a voice whose loudness was meant to expel the heaviness in his throat.

"With the Indians, as you ordered."

Spangled with the light coming through the palm ribs, Colombe felt herself more than ever to be Sun-Eye.

Villegagnon blinked.

"Those Anabaptist dogs didn't hurt you?"

Colombe told how she had parted company with the soldiers.

"Why did you stay so long?"

She remembered her fears and suddenly realized that Villegagnon knew nothing of her secret. She instinctively buttoned her collar, which she had left open on the presumption that there was no longer any point in playing the part.

"I was learning the language," she said.

"And you speak it?"

"A little."

"Then it won't have been for nothing."

Just still looked at her intensely. He saw that she had changed, grown smooth and firm, that her breasts had developed and her beauty been released from its childhood limbo. He wondered in terror how it would still be possible to make Villegagnon believe she was his brother.

But the admiral had already turned to the contemplation of the great pictures that inhabited him. He examined them for a long moment in silence, then struck the table with his fist.

"Antarctic France is in danger!" he roared, rising to his feet. "Six of my soldiers have just died. We've had no news of the others, who left at the same time in the other direction. A band of miscreants is scouring the shore. And here, everything has given way to lust."

He glanced through the lattice of palms.

"Look at them! They get drunk. They fornicate. They go to the mainland at every opportunity, and I know very well why, by Saint Jack of Jerusalem! Those damned go-betweens offer them whores, and they can't resist. In the meantime, no work is getting done. The rains are on their way and nothing is roofed over. No defenses have been raised. If the Portuguese attack us, it will all be over!"

He collapsed into a straight-backed armchair.

His frightened gaze flitted about the room like a hunted animal looking for an escape. His eyes rested for a moment on the book-covered table, then moved to Colombe, back to Just, over to the ebony cabinet, and once again outside.

"All this," he growled, "is the fault of woman."

Colombe winced, but he was looking elsewhere.

"Woman corrupts everything," he went on lugubriously. "It's time you knew that. And your father, Clamorgan, would have done well to remember it."

Just and Colombe exchanged a questioning glance.

"Woman," said Villegagnon, straightening his upper body, "is the instrument of the Fall, the vehicle of Temptation and Evil. Always bear this in mind, and turn away from the flesh when it takes the form of licentiousness and contentment."

A group of workers were making their descent from the fort, singing as they walked toward their huts. An expression of disgust and horror crossed the knight's broad face. But as his gaze once more took in the room, it encountered the Titian painting, the Virgin's tender complexion and her protective gesture toward the Child.

"Fortunately," said Villegagnon brightly, "God ordained that this pit of sinfulness, this creature of pleasure and perdition, should also be . . ."

He smiled tenderly at the Virgin of the painting.

". . . the great path of salvation."

Colombe would have given anything to interrupt this soliloquy, take Just by the hand, and walk to the beach telling him how much she had missed him. But Villegagnon was astride his idea and planned to ride it to the end of the road. The strangest thing was that Just seemed to listen to him with respect and even to approve of him.

"The more I ponder it," the admiral declared, "the more I see that, in our situation, the principal sacrament is marriage. Only marriage can sanctify these unions and restore these excesses to order. Let them have women, let them go and take these savage women by force, pay them or rape them if they like, but let all this be consummated before God!"

An angelic expression stole over his beard-ravaged face. He seemed, as he contemplated the chevrons of palm, to be looking at the Holy Ghost.

"Then," he said in a piping celestial voice, "beautiful children will people Antarctic France and sing the king's glory. There will be no need for a laborious conversion of the natives since, by impregnating their wives, we'll be making little Christians."

For a moment he became lost in this vision, then he turned abruptly to Colombe.

"You say you speak the Indian tongue?"

"Yes."

"Then get ready to use it. I'm going to start after these damned go-betweens this very day. We've endured enough from Le Freux, who robs us and betrays us. Their example has corrupted everything here. From now on, I'll be the one making conditions. And if they resist, we'll know how to break them. Leave me now. I am going to draft a proclamation."

. . .

By the time Just and Colombe found themselves outside again, Quintin had gone. They walked side by side in the direction of the fort. The worksite was deserted at this time of the afternoon, except for the shanties where a few laborers stayed on. Colombe looked at the piles of stones and beams, feeling heartsick. She had only gone up to the fort to see the view she loved, toward the Sugarloaf and the bay. Just, for his part, viewed the cuts in the earth with the pride of someone who has paid in blood.

"Here will be the path round the battlements. The culverins will be like so, in the crenellations of the rampart, to cover every azimuth."

While he spoke, Colombe found her eyes searching the cover of the forest, already dark in the afternoon light, for the village where Paraguaçu lived.

"Anyway," she said, interrupting Just's explanations, "I missed you."

"You couldn't have. Otherwise you'd have come back sooner."

It was not a sincere reproach, but he did not want to seem behind-hand. He had certainly been very afraid of losing her, but he had not felt the pain of separation as strongly as she. Colombe made a note to herself that he now thought like a man.

"The chancelloress lied to us," he said in a dull voice. "Father is dead. De Griffes has stolen Clamorgan for himself."

Colombe started.

"I was sure of it! Who told you?"

"Villegagnon. He knew Father in Italy."

In point of fact, Colombe had resigned herself to the idea of never seeing her father again. Her memories of him were few, and she suffered less from losing him than from having at the same time to abandon any hope of knowing who she and Just were. Their origins, their blood relations even, would remain a mystery, affecting their future more than their past. The idea troubled her, and she thought again about the chancelloress.

"We shouldn't let her take everything from us," she said, furious.

"We can fight de Griffes, after all. We have rights. It may take ten years, but . . ."

She stopped. Just, silent, had shrugged his shoulders. She cast her gaze in the direction of his, beyond the shore, toward the west, daubed with pink splotches. With the rainy weather approaching, the sunsets on the bay were losing their molten purity. They were veined with striations and speckled with burrs, like fruitwood.

The bay's silence, broken by laughs and men's voices from the port, weighed on their hearts in a painful way. Colombe turned toward Just, moved his inert arms aside, and, mindless of any embarrassment he might feel, pressed herself against him to cry.

CHAPTER 20

It now rained several hours a day, a warm rain that splashed down
on one like a dog shaking itself. It left everyone feeling dull and list-
less. Then, for long hours, nothing would happen. The sun would
find a passage through the barrier of clouds. Like a lackey unwilling
to abandon his dying master, the sun would set about sponging up
the puddles through which the island's residents had to wade.

Every morning shortly after dawn, Villegagnon now held obligatory prayers in front of the government house. It was not a Mass, but
rather a short series of prayers, led with considerable bad grace by
Thevet. The cosmographer would arrive smoking a stick of *petun*.
Since the go-betweens introduced the plant to him, he had been
constantly exploring its medicinal virtues. He found it so beneficial
that he hardly passed an hour without taking a draft of its smoke.
But for all the good the treatment was doing his health, it had not
cured his melancholy. Other than his collection of curiosities, which
had now attained considerable size, the Franciscan showed great
repugnance toward everything that touched on his priesthood.
About one morning in two, he would not rise, and Villegagnon
would lead prayers alone. To give himself added solemnity, he had
enlisted the services of a village minstrel, assigned till now like everyone else to carry stones but who had a marvelous talent for playing

the sackbut. This clarion-like instrument, aside from sending super-natural, even celestial sounds into the still air of the bay, had the merit of persuading those who would otherwise have dozed at prayers that it was truly time to wake up.

Villegagnon was very proud of this newly instituted practice, pro-viding as it did a dawn reminder of the duty every man owed to God. He then watched with emotion as his company of laborers climbed together up to the walls of Fort Coligny. Few men were officially exempt from this slavery. The soldiers took part in the capacity of supervisors and sometimes lent a hand. The real slaves, some fifty Indians, proved incapable of initiative and came only to assist with the very hardest tasks. Villegagnon exempted only the indispensable artisans (the cooks, the butchers, a tailor, a hairdresser, and two bak-ers) from masonry work. As the fort rose, the project's ambitious scope became apparent, not to say its excessive size, given the mea-ger workforce on hand to build it.

The sand-filled panniers on the island's eastern shore, softened by the rains, formed skewed blocks between which it was possible to hide. It was there that Vittorio the Venetian came to skulk once prayers were over so as to escape the work detail. Anyone looking for him would know to find him there, seated on a rock counting his gold pieces or sharpening his chopping knife. He wasn't surprised that morning to see Egidio appear between the blocks.

"Greetings, countryman."

"Greetings."

"Le Freux wants to see you right away."

The go-between's orders were as readily obeyed on the island as Villegagnon's—more readily in fact, as Le Freux manipulated the double register of pleasure and fear, whereas the admiral vainly plucked at the slack cords of duty and idealism.

They rose and walked along the beach to the port for the ships' boats. At a sign from Vittorio, two oarsmen from the water detail got up from their places. Though he didn't show it, the Venetian was puffed up with pride: he was a person of importance in a place that hardly counted. But it was pleasant all the same to be feared and to be able to reward others. For he, Vittorio, was the man who rented out women, and through his traffic in these captives he enjoyed a paradoxical freedom.

When they reached the mainland, the two Venetians walked up to the Indian village that Villegagnon had visited on the first day. A path around it led to a small, isolated hut that served as Le Freux's lair. Weapons hung from the hut's wooden pillar. A few Indian women, crouching in a corner, their legs shackled, looked fearfully at the new arrivals. Le Freux was pacing, and a big boy with a flat nose swung in a hammock. Drawing near, Vittorio recognized Martin, who had left the island at the same time as Colombe.

"It can't go on like this!" burst out Le Freux, seeing that everyone was present now that the Italians had arrived.

He motioned them to take seats on blocks of brazilwood.

"Have you read Villegagnon's latest proclamation?" asked Le Freux.

"Yes," said Vittorio respectfully. "He wants the white men on the island to marry if they associate with the native women. He is crazy."

"Perfectly," said the go-between. "But that's only the start. As we might have known. The real news is even more incredible, and apparently you are still unaware of it."

Le Freux made a circuit, allowing his boots to strike against the muddy floor.

"This madman also wants *me* to marry."

For a moment dumbstruck, the two rogues burst into laughter, a bad laugh interspersed with coughing.

"The vice admiral of Brittany," went on the go-between, deciding to expose the full buffoonery of it, "governor of Antarctic France, summoned me, if you please, and said: 'Monsieur Le Freux, why do you not introduce me to your wife?'"

His parody of Villegagnon was good, capturing his military elegance, his rough but modulated voice.

"'My wife!'" Le Freux exclaimed innocently, imitating himself.

All the feathers on his doublet stuck up after this last startled jump. He held his cowhide helmet in his hand, like a fearful peasant in front of his lord.

"'But my lord,' I said to him, 'which one?'"

Renewed laughter.

Le Freux quelled it with the gravity of his imitation.

"At that point, he grabbed me by the collar, can you imagine? That lunatic grabbed me, *me*, by the collar and threatened me. 'Monsieur

Le Freux,' he said, 'I summon you to bring your wife here. I care little which one or of what race, on condition that there be only one
and of marriageable age, and to produce the proofs that you were
joined before God. If these are lacking, which I can understand,
Abbé Thevet, whom you see here'—the scoundrel was smoking a
stick of *petun* the size of a tree trunk—'will celebrate your wedding
in the approved form.'"

"And if you refuse?" asked Vittorio indignantly.

" 'If you refuse, Monsieur Le Freux, it will no longer be necessary
for you to appear on this island again, nor to send any of your friends
in your stead. We will do without your services.' The beggar! 'We will
do without your services.' "

"He has lost his mind," said Egidio.

"Clearly, he hasn't any idea," chimed in Vittorio. Then he asked,
"What will you do?"

Le Freux, standing in the scarlet yard before the hut, pointed at
one of the terrorized captives and said evenly, "I will take one of these
young ladies. We'll have a handsome white dress with a train sewn
for her, and I'll appear before the friar, where I will vow to love her
and forsake all others my whole life through."

"Are you serious?" asked Egidio, touched in spite of everything.

Le Freux opened his eyes as wide as gunports and leveled two
bombards at the little Venetian.

"Idiot!"

Catching up his sword, carved from heavy wood and hardly less
terrible than a metal weapon, the go-between wheeled about
dangerously.

"I'm going to strangle Villegagnon and his troop, that's what I'm
going to do! Starting tomorrow, we will stop supplying the island
with anything at all. No flour, no fish, no venison. Nothing. We'll
pour two sacks of Indian powder in the water they come to draw, and
when they realize it's poisoned, they won't go there again. I give that
admiral two weeks to come crawling back to me for pardon and
mercy. Then it will be my turn to marry him off as I see fit."

This impassioned tirade was met enthusiastically by the two
henchmen. They were sure, in any event, that they had already gotten just about everything that Villegagnon and the colonists had to
offer: the ships' holds were empty, and the men's savings nearly used

up buying *cahuin* and women. All that remained was the admiral's mysterious chest, which Villegagnon had never opened for them. The idea of showing their strength once and for all appealed to them.

"It all sounds good," said a voice from the hammock, "but I think you'd be making a mistake to do that."

Martin slowly extricated himself from his web. The others looked at him with some surprise, having almost forgotten his presence.

"Say your piece!" said Le Freux.

"Well, as you know," said Martin, raising himself painfully, "I have just returned from the Norman settlements on the other shore."

"Yes, and I'm wondering why you didn't stay there. I thought you intended to return to France."

"I still do. But I no longer intend to remain poor."

"Don't worry. When the admiral coughs up his ill-gotten gains, you'll get your share."

"I don't think so."

"Are you doubting my word?" asked Le Freux.

"No, but I doubt your method. I believe you'll give me my share, only it will be my share of nothing. Villegagnon won't cough up anything . . . unless we rip him open first."

"Don't you think I have the means to choke him off?"

"My dear Le Freux," said Martin, a note of irony in his voice, "you are the most powerful man on this shore of the bay, I grant. But there are other French traders, at the head of the bay, and they are not all your friends. If Villegagnon asks them for help, they won't say no."

"Hah! Then you imagine that he'll cross the bay to get water."

"It's the rainy season, and he will have finished building his cisterns."

Vittorio confirmed this unwillingly. Le Freux was shaken.

"So what would you do?"

"I'd attack."

"Attack six hundred men, including a troop of knights armed for war?" said Le Freux, sniggering.

Martin in turn leapt into the blood-red arena of the yard.

"Listen, Le Freux, you've been a beggar just as I have. But apparently you've forgotten the principles of our trade. The adversary is *always* stronger. Our weapons are surprise, speed, and cunning."

Massive in size and heavy fisted, the boy embodied these virtues effortlessly, being agile, quick, and permeated with an evil intelligence.

"We have one week to act."

"Because of my impending nuptials!" said Le Freux, guffawing.

"No, because of the ship."

"What ship?"

"The *Grande-Roberge*. It's full of brazilwood, and they are just putting aboard the last cages of sagoins and parrots. She sails in a week. Why let such a prize escape? As long as we're about it, let's take everything."

Le Freux remained silent for a moment. Then, raising his hand in brotherly greeting, he clasped Martin by the shoulder.

"Look at you, how you're dressed! It's fine for running about in the jungle, but I think one of my doublets would better suit a partner of mine."

They went inside the hut to settle the sartorial question and talk.

•   •   •

Vittorio and Egidio spent nearly two days going from group to group collecting on their accounts. There was moaning and groaning on all sides.

"Really, I owe you that much? Can't you give me credit a little longer?"

The Venetians sighed.

"My friend, we're just as sorry about this as you are. But talk to Villegagnon about it. He's the one who issued a proclamation forbidding *cahuin* and women."

Some, addicted to their pleasures, offered to pay higher prices. But the answer was always the same: "If you don't mind being hanged, that's your affair. But we prefer not to push this lunatic too far, since we think he might do what he says. And he's promised the noose to anyone who disobeys."

Among the sailors, artisans, jailbirds, and even soldiers who formed Le Freux's clientele, there arose an angry rumble of curses directed at Villegagnon. Vittorio assumed a modest air and even allowed himself the luxury of sometimes saying a few commiserating

words about the admiral. These would be met with hateful imprecations, a clear demonstration that if danger ever threatened, the
knight would not find many to fight at his side.

In the end, every man paid up. The islanders all had small savings
that they kept on their persons or hidden in holes. But one had to be
careful, on this island where new building sites were constantly being
excavated, not to leave one's treasure unwatched for too long. And it
was hard to dig without being seen. Hiding one's coins was almost a
daily chore.

Vittorio and Egidio collected their debts in a canvas sack. Those
who couldn't pay in ready coin were assigned debts in kind, according to their trade. The artisans received tasks in keeping with their
particular skills. A hatmaker was ordered to make four caps out of a
length of velvet the Venetians dug up for him. He acquitted himself
of his debt.

Each time, they took the opportunity of pouring more poison into
the minds of these unhappy men.

"To think that a man as skilled as you are should be made to break
rocks!" the Venetians would say insinuatingly whenever they saw an
artisan pounding at gravel. "What a shame! If this island weren't governed all wrong, you would long ago have become prosperous and the
others on the mainland would have made you rich."

All thoughts now turned to the coast, where the women, the
cahuin, and all hope had gone. The defense of the island was neglected
or even opposed.

"All the same," said Vittorio to his crony, on their way from one
debtor to another, "you have to admit that we're doing good work."

They had almost finished. Their list had left on it only a few scattered individuals who had to be dealt with one by one.

"Hey there! Quintin!" called out Vittorio, seeing one of the very
men they were looking for.

"What can I do for you, my brothers in Christ?" answered the
small dark man who disliked finding anyone antipathetic—he would
call himself to order by convincing himself that all men are brothers
no matter what.

Vittorio looked down his list, and Egidio helped him to the best
of his ability, though he could not read.

"Quintin!" said the bearded man. "Here we are! No *cahuin*, but four women three times a week."

Vittorio gave a lackey's flattering smile, and a tender expression crossed his face.

"Bravo," he said earnestly.

Quintin, stiff and gaunt as ever, didn't blink.

"That will be six pounds, one sol, and two deniers," said Egidio, who was the quicker at arithmetic.

"I don't see what you are talking about," said Quintin contemptuously, starting to move away.

But the two toughs barred his path and brought their faces close to his.

"The money," said Vittorio, jingling his bag.

"As far as those women go," said Quintin with dignity, "I was catechizing them."

"Fine, and we're just collecting the tithe," snickered Vittorio, making his crony howl with laughter.

"Have you not heard that salvation is freely given?"

"Nothing is freely given with us. We bring you women, you pay. That's it. 'Charity suffereth long . . .' if you want to play at quotations."

"Oh, I am quite sure," said Quintin, drawing in a great spiritual breath that carried his gaze toward the sky, "that these poor women have seen many trials. But they have now been introduced to the Gospel. I am the only one, do you hear, the only one on this island who has made an effort to bring the Word of God to the natives. Even that priest has not taken the trouble to make them attend his clownish masses."

The Venetians were growing impatient, but since Quintin was searching his pockets, they expected him to produce some coins.

"I moved those four unhappy women to tears with my recitation of Our Lord's passion. My method, in three brief words: God is love. They were penetrated by this truth in every way."

"Hee! Hee!" Egidio sniggered.

"Enough," shrieked Quintin, "you may not soil everything with your obscene minds!"

And with a definitive gesture, as though dropping the curtain on a tragedy, he pulled what he had been looking for from his pocket all along: a large checked handkerchief.

Vittorio, furious, leapt at Quintin and put his blade roughly to his neck.

"Now for the money."

"I'll bring my complaint to the government house," said Quintin.

"The money, I say!"

"Villegagnon will never tolerate this blackmail."

"Leave Villegagnon out of it, he won't be around much longer," said Egidio, on edge.

When he was angry, his rasping, high-pitched voice carried a good distance. A group of soldiers was passing not far off on their way to the southern redoubt, and one of them turned to look. Vittorio hid his dagger.

"I'll give you till dinnertime tomorrow," he hissed at Quintin.

"Six pounds, one sol, and two deniers," Egidio reminded.

"Otherwise . . ."

Vittorio made the gesture of cutting a sheep's throat. The two then went off. Quintin stood there for a moment immobile, dreaming, then ran after them, shouting, "If you see those young ladies before I do, tell them all to come back soon . . . And that I love them . . ."

The Venetians quickened their pace to get rid of him.

•   •   •

Storms compounded the threat that seemed to hang over the bay. Their shadow made the Sugarloaf black and icy. The forest, glistening with water, took on shades of crushed glass, and the amethyst-colored sea had a mineral stillness too precious to last.

Villegagnon was turning in circles in his government house, watching for leaks in the palm-leaf roof and moving books as drips appeared. Ever since delivering his ultimatum to the go-betweens, he had noticed a worrisome quiet come over the island. The work during the day had gone slack—slacker than before—the sound of sledges and hoes had almost stopped. Conversations were held in whispers. The boats no longer came and went. At night, the sound of voices from the camp never disturbed the air. The thunder that echoed off the headlands did less to break the silence than to emphasize it. Its rumbling from seaward heralded an imminent lightning strike, but whether it would come from heaven or from earth none could tell.

Villegagnon had given up on his fencing lessons with Just for the moment, as they had been too often interrupted by showers. Concerned for his books, he no longer wanted them taken from the room, where he could watch over them. Just and Colombe therefore had permission to read them in place. Their silent, attentive presence soothed the admiral somewhat, as he paced back and forth scanning the horizon.

The ultimatum to the go-betweens was set to expire in four days, when a curious little character stopped Just as he was climbing up to the fort one afternoon to survey the work. The man was leaning against a shovel, which he seemed not to have put to any other use since morning. Around him there was nothing to be seen but sodden mud and a jumble of rocks, which is what the fort had become since the rains had poured into it.

"My lord Clamorgan," the laborer called softly, as Just came up to him.

"Yes."

"Might I ask you humbly for a favor?"

The tone wasn't hypocritical, only commercial, in the manner of those who provide services to the great houses.

"My lord, I am a hatmaker by trade."

"And an honorable trade it is."

"Thank you, although, as you can see . . ."

He raised his arms to show his rags and the muddy lower reaches of his bare legs.

"In my spare time, I recently made four velvet caps. Those who commissioned them specifically commanded me to ask that you deliver the caps to them."

"Where are these men?"

"On the mainland."

The weather was momentarily exceptional. The sun, jostling the clouds aside, had returned to rummage in the bay, like a man out for a walk who momentarily returns home to look for an object he has left behind. A cloud of vapor rose from the neighborhood of the waterfalls, where the colonists filled their water barrels. The whistling of macaws grated against the silence.

"Who are these people?" asked Just.

"I don't know, it was only an order for caps."

It was clear that the man didn't know the whole story. What trap lay hidden behind this proposition? Venturing to the mainland alone was to court danger. But not going was perhaps to ignore an opportunity for negotiation. Villegagnon would not have accepted. But Just reflected that it was probably for that very reason that they had addressed themselves to him.

A watch was now kept over the ships' boats, and none could make the run to the mainland without an explicit reason and an escort of soldiers.

"Tonight," said the hatmaker, "at moonrise, a native pirogue will pass along the rocks under the western redoubt. It will take you across."

•   •   •

The conveyance, made of a long tree hollowed by fire, held ten people. Just settled in the middle without difficulty despite the darkness, as he'd been able to make his way along the edge of the rocks until he could enter the boat almost dry-shod. The paddlers, men and women, were naked but apparently felt no discomfort from the cool damp night. Lightning streaked the western sky.

Just thought about Villegagnon, to whom he'd simply said that he was going for a walk on the beach. Colombe had put up more resistance: she had sensed something abnormal. When he'd admitted what he was doing, Just had then had a hard time convincing her not to accompany him.

The reflection of the veiled moon coated the water with a veneer of gray, which the dipping of the paddles seemed intent on dissolving. Just had not been off the island since the first day when they had visited the Indian village. He was intimate with every detail of the building sites, knew Antarctic France's plans for the future, and even the boldest town- and kingdom-building projects that the Chevalier de Villegagnon harbored in his breast. Sitting in the hollowed trunk, in the formidable solitude of the bay, surrounded by silent savages naked as the first men, Just measured the strength of Villegagnon's will. So superhuman was the dream of this France-to-be that the admiral was either mad or entirely admirable. Using his weapons of war, Villegagnon attacked raw nature with the gusto of an artist addressing a freshly quarried block of marble for a *pietà*. In their long conversations about Italy, art, and the movement of ideas, in which they threw back the entire layer of old Gothic errors, Villegagnon had often used this comparison to Just. But it was the first time Just had fully understood it.

The pirogue glided along so fast that in a short time they heard the shushing of the waves on the beach. Just leaped into the water and waded to shore. He heard a whistle from the shadow of the trees. He walked in its direction until he suddenly felt a large hand clasp his own. Just had tucked a dagger into his belt. His fingers clenched around its handle.

"Easy! You have nothing to be afraid of."

Just recognized the childish, husky voice of Martin. He walked behind him until they reached a camp. It consisted of a small cabin, its doorway spilling yellow light. They sat on blocks of wood under an oil lamp. Martin offered him a choice of *cahuin* or fruit juice. He went to an earthenware jar and filled two bowls with a clear liquid that smelled of pineapples.

"We thought you were dead," said Just, glad to see Martin, but embarrassed in his presence.

"People are always too quick to bury me . . ."

"It's because of the soldiers who were killed, those who went in the other direction."

"Yes, I knew about that. But what an idea, to go haring off after those Anabaptists. We went quietly to the Norman trading counters. And my brave soldiers are happily there as we speak."

"So why did you come back?"

Martin paused for a brief moment, which was sufficient time for him to make a choice and invent a lie.

"Do you think I would abandon my friends?"

"What friends?"

Martin slapped his knees with his broad palms.

"What friends? Listen to him. There's my reward. I cross the whole damned forest to come get you, and you say, What friends?"

"You came back just to do that?"

Just felt a lingering mistrust of Martin. But believing eagerly in man's essential goodness, he never passed up a chance to further confirm it. Martin lowered his eyes. He took no pride in easy victories, especially when they murdered virtue.

"Where is your brother?"

"On the island."

"Good. Do you think he'll be able to join you tonight if I send the pirogue back for him?"

"But follow me where?"

"Don't you still want to return to France? I know the way to the trading posts now. You can both be free."

Just had a momentary vision of Clamorgan, of Normandy, of all the gardened expanse of France, the plains of Italy, the coastline of umbrella pines and olive trees.

"Answer me, what's it going to be?" Martin insisted. "We need to set off tonight, tomorrow at the latest. I've arranged passage for us on a ship that leaves ten days from now, and it takes at least eight days to get there."

Just started on hearing these words and suddenly understood what troubled him. He hadn't given up on returning to France, but he didn't want his departure to be an abandonment of the enterprise. He now felt enough confidence in Villegagnon to ask him straight out for passage back on one of the returning ships. If Colombe wanted, it could even be on the next one, which was loaded and ready to sail. But he wanted no part in a betrayal.

"We prefer to stay here," he said.

Martin's face twitched. The urge to take this bastard by the collar and knock his fine airs and hollow notions out of him was strong. He was tempted to blurt out that they had no choice, that if they refused to run away . . .

"You have until tomorrow night to think about it," he said angrily. "If you change your mind, take a lantern and flash it three times from the west end of the island."

"You're not going to come back to the island to make your report to Villegagnon?"

Astonished at the question's naiveté, Martin only shrugged, shook Just's hand, and accompanied him back to the edge of the beach.

When he returned to the cabin, he found Le Freux, who had come forward out of the dark.

"Too bad," said Le Freux soberly.

"After all," muttered Martin, as though talking to himself, "too bad for him. I've repaid my debt: I owed him for my freedom, not for my life."

CHAPTER 21

Rupert Melrose, Scots guard and bagpipe player, had devoted himself to Villegagnon for the past eight years. His devotion was the result of an extraordinary stroke of fortune, which he never remembered without tears in his eyes.

It was in the days when Mary Stuart, then six years old, had almost been married twice already. The king of England wanted to make her his wife in order to arrogate Scotland to himself. Henry II of France had chosen her for his son, the Dauphin, so as to save Scotland's Catholic party. The poor girl was sequestered with her mother in Dumbarton Castle, under blockade from her rebelling Protestant subjects.

Rupert, a poor Highlands lancer, was one of the loyal men who marched up and down the fortified banks of the Clyde. Like all the Catholic soldiers assigned to guard her, Rupert was in love with the little dark-haired princess. He watched her fondly during her morning walk along the ramparts. That a child could be the focus of so many plots and at the same time radiate such innocence struck him as a troubling mystery. In the warm month of May, the little girl sometimes appeared outdoors with her arms bare, though she still wore a farthingale. Rupert would have suffered a thousand deaths before he allowed anyone to sully such a treasure.

Alas, under the pressure of the Lutherans, the trap was closing in on the captives. Before another winter came, the fortress would undoubtedly fall. That spring, the last before the inevitable end, was sadder and more full of flowers than any that dour Scotland had ever seen.

Other than admiring little Mary, Rupert had only one passion: he played the bagpipe. The instrument had always satisfied him until then. He had learned his melodies watching his uncle's fingering, and nothing seemed more harmonious to him than a chaunter duet, sustained by the rounded line of the drones. He had been mortified to learn from his captain that the little queen disliked the sound of his bagpipe and even dreaded it as a fateful omen. Rupert therefore received orders not to play during his rare off-duty hours, unless he managed to walk out far enough along the rocks downwind of the castle to hurl his notes into the emptiness of the sea.

It was known, even among the soldiers, that the king of France had sent an armada to deliver the child and her mother, Marie de Guise. But the English were formidable on the high seas. Admiral Strozzi, who commanded the French fleet, was prevented from reaching Scotland, and short of engaging a battle against superior forces, he had no way of breaching the British blockade.

The French noblemen who surrounded the little queen spent their days gazing toward the southwest through their spyglasses. But Strozzi never appeared.

Clusters of blue wisteria drooped over house fronts, willow copses were silvery with new leaves, and the twig ends of the durmast oak formed green buds. Rupert, using his bagpipe's two chanters, rendered these joys against a tragic ground of bass notes. He played on the tip of a granite promontory lashed by the waves to the west of the fortress, from where he could barely be seen. It was there, one morning in mid-May, that he received the great shock which his remaining life was forever to echo.

Three slender galleys were racing across the water with all the speed of their oars. The sea was calm, and they were approaching rapidly. Rupert soon made out their colors: they were French. For a moment bewildered, he checked the orientation of the sun. There was no doubt about it: the ships, incredible as it might seem, were coming from the northwest.

Holding his instrument by the pipes as you would hold a hare by the ears, the Highlander ran to the castle to give the alarm. The children were playing on the dungeon terraces: Mary Stuart with her friends, the three Marys—Seton, Fleming, and Livingstone. They ran to the opposite rampart from the direction they had so often scanned in vain. The three galleys, whose drums could now be heard, were entering the estuary and slowing to land at the quay. Dumbfounded, and thinking it a trick, the French guard and the Scots had at first hastily aimed their harquebuses at the boats. But as they approached, a crowd of soldiers could be seen on the bridge waving their helmets and shaking their swords in a sign of joy. Hardly had it touched land than the first galley vomited a bawling flood of Frenchmen, who capered in celebration. At their head, where none would have thought to usurp his place, was a boisterous giant, his nose red with tears, a large Cross of Malta on his stomach, charging at the fortress. The gate was shut, and while waiting for it to open, the knight turned to face his men, made them kneel, and recited a prayer in Latin in a voice so loud that the rocks along the coast resonated with his orison. Little pink crabs edged out of their holes to see the soldiers' arrival. Finally the hinges creaked, the gate opened, and the queen regent was revealed, before whom Nicolas Durand de Villegagnon bellowed his name sobbingly and threw himself down on the ground in awkward idolatry.

From the top of the rampart, Rupert followed the scene. It was there that he saw for the first time the devil of a man who had led this expedition. Acting alone, he had convinced Leone Strozzi to let him attempt what none had succeeded in doing before the war: to skirt all of Scotland by the north, picking a route through the far northern islands to slip English surveillance. And with a poor map by Nicolas de Nicolay, stolen from the English by his spies, Villegagnon had managed to accomplish this prodigious feat.

The Scots court embarked that very night, and Villegagnon had the signal pleasure of tendering two of his thick fingers to the little queen that she might set foot without mishap on the *Réale*. A few days later she was safe in Morlaix.

This all happened in 1548. It was now 1556, and Rupert had not left Villegagnon's side in all that time. He belonged to his Scots guard, and within this elite corps to the handful of soldiers closest to the admiral who took turns guarding his door. No one could ever touch Villegagnon without Rupert first throwing his life into the battle.

Loyalty is a sentiment that is easily requited. One has only to tolerate it. As long as Rupert could follow his master, he was happy, in Brazil or elsewhere. His only regret was that the admiral, like Mary Stuart, had no liking for the bagpipe. He therefore went off alone to play his instrument.

As he was assigned that day to accompany the boat making the water run, he took his pipes with him. Barely two days were left before the admiral's ultimatum to Le Freux would expire. Things were quieter and stiller than ever. There was no one to be seen on shore.

Rupert was not an imaginative man. For him, quiet was quiet, and that was the full extent of it.

The sailors docked the pinnace at the landing near the waterfalls and started to unload the barrels. Rupert walked westward, for a time following the line of the coconut trees. He kept the boat in sight, thus not falling short of his responsibilities. But he allowed himself the little pleasure of going to the part of the beach where a whale had been stranded. The big animal had been there some time already. Its skin had dried in the sun and started to crack. It was easy to grab hold of the baleen plates and climb up on its head. Rupert liked to play there, on this species of black rock. He looked out at the bay and, so long as he avoided the too recognizable silhouette of the Sugarloaf, could almost believe he was in Scotland. At this time of year, the dark mists fairly imitated the summer in his native land. He started with an air from Aberdeen based on a little nursery rhyme from his childhood.

It took a long time to haul all the barrels to the little boat. Since the confrontation with the go-betweens, no one from the mainland helped with this task anymore. As the sailors started to fill the last barrel, night was falling.

Rupert was happy to have played to his heart's content. He let go of the mouthpiece and prepared to take his pipes apart when he was pulled over backward by two strong hands. Rupert's last sight was of the sky. Simultaneously, a practiced blade slit his throat.

Night had fallen when the men started whistling to the Scot to return to the boat. He did so at the last moment, his head closely wrapped in his tartan shawl. The moon had not yet risen, and the sailor at the tiller held a dark lantern. The Scot sat in the shadow at the far end of the boat. No one spoke on the return trip, as fatigue, worry, and the desperate certainty of never again enjoying the consoling company of *cahuin* or Indian women put a sullen expression on all faces.

The island was dark. The colonists had made too much use of candles during the first months, and life was now organized around what light the sky might willingly provide. On that stormy night, with neither stars nor, for the moment, any moon, each was reduced to a shadow and went to bed as soon as the sun went down. The sailors of the water detail retired to their hammocks, and the false Rupert—acting on good intelligence—made his way toward the guardroom. A water clock on a pillar allowed the sentinel at the admiral's door, who had a small lamp, to tell how much time was left in his watch. After turning the clock over twice, the man yawned, rose to his feet, and called "Rupert" from the guardroom. The changing of the guard took place in silence, as between men who are half-asleep and have nothing to fear.

Thus it was that, at one o'clock in the morning, as planned, Martin found himself dressed in the costume of a Highland piper at the door of Villegagnon's room. Looking out through the latticework screen onto the beach, Martin waited until the moon was bright enough, then, addressing a silent prayer to the god of thieves, in whom he firmly believed, he slowly opened the bedroom door.

The partisans' plan was simple: to isolate Villegagnon, then kill him. The first part of the program had already been accomplished. A vast majority of the immigrants were discouraged and irate about the degrading work they were forced to do. The blame was all heaped on Villegagnon, and more blame still for taking the one thing from them that could have made up for their misery. In the contest of wills between the admiral and the go-betweens, the immigrants' sympathy clearly went to the latter. They admired the go-betweens' freedom, and their access to pleasures, which in the unknown world of the tropics seemed in itself a unique and superior accomplishment. In the case of an attack, the settlers' neutrality could therefore be counted on, and perhaps even their help.

That left the soldiers. They too, for the most part, were sunk in despondency, except for the Scots guard, who never seemed to feel discouragement at anything. Yet from the most valiant to the most useless, they all followed the same military model: they needed orders. The attackers' first step was therefore to stop those orders at the source.

It fell to Martin to lead off the action by dealing a mortal blow to the supreme commander; everything was to follow from that. He now stood two steps away from the bed with his lantern. The curtains were closed. Martin could see, attached to one of the bedposts, the rope of the hammock Villegagnon had strung crosswise for himself. To strike through the curtain or to open it, the murderer's age-old dilemma, now confronted Martin. The girls of the port had often talked to him of the two kinds of men: those who keep the lamp lit when they make love, and those who prefer to put it out. He himself cared little either way: he took what was offered. The thought made him smile in the dark, and, as he liked being contrary, he told himself that for once he would choose: he flung the curtain open.

The hammock was empty.

He looked feverishly in the bed and underneath it, where the admiral's war treasure was kept, and which was not supposed to be taken until everything was over. But the chest was gone. Tearing away the plaid scarf that suddenly suffocated him, Martin raised his lantern to scan the darkness around him, his mind working as lucidly as at the most harrowing moments of an ambush. He could see no one in the room, yet he felt he'd walked into a trap. The moment had come to gather his courage, to call on his deepest reserves of instinct in the face of danger. The thief in him came to the aid of the conspirator. As though to mark the change by some outward gesture, Martin unthinkingly grabbed the gold frame of a miniature gleaming on the admiral's table. He stuffed the object in his pocket and, despairing of the larger treasure, went out. Alas, seeing him flourish his lamp at the door, his accomplices, hidden in the dark and frightened by the night sounds, thought that he was giving the agreed signal and launched their attack. A flaming brand was tossed into the Knights of Malta's straw hut and set the palm fronds ablaze. Le Freux, in command of the attackers' group, gave the order to fire through the flaming walls. Two harquebuses left with Martin by deserting soldiers and another stolen by Egidio made up the go-betweens' entire arsenal. But counting on their adversaries' surprise, they reckoned their artillery would be devastating. Effectively, unarmed and half-naked Scotsmen leapt from the guardroom, making easy targets.

The attackers thought they had gained a complete victory. But Martin felt that it was too quick, almost odd. No shouts were coming from the flaming barracks of the Knights of Malta. Other than the handful of Scots guards, no one had emerged from the huts.

It was eerily quiet, other than the crackling of the flames. Far in the east, a storm flickered, momentarily lighting up the menacing bulk of the Sugarloaf. Martin sensed a trap. He sniffed the air like a hound and suddenly, on pure instinct, doused his lamp. A harquebus shot from the fort rang out almost at the same moment. In the sudden dark, the gunner had missed.

Other shots followed, and cries of pain went up from the dark mass of the attackers.

Martin understood immediately that his plan had been known in advance, and that the admiral had in turn set an ambush for them. Safe in the fort with his knights, Villegagnon poured a heavy fire down on the attackers. Panic spread through their midst. There were sounds of flight, of falling. The Scotsmen took advantage of the diversion to wrap a length of cloth around their waists and, so prepared, threw themselves furiously into the fray. From the construction site at the fort, Villegagnon's troop ran down toward the beach, effectively barring the go-betweens' retreat. The admiral's voice thundered from the midst of the battle.

The only part of the plan of attack that proved accurate was that the artisans remained neutral. Deep in their cantonments, they watched everything without moving.

The pirogues that had brought Le Freux's men had landed at two places: at the southernmost point of the beach and, on the far side, among the rocks facing the bay. The fleeing men flung themselves heavily into the boats, threatening to overturn them, and the paddlers added their shouts to those of the combatants and the wounded.

Martin looked for another way out. Seeing that the game was up, he found himself entertaining a familiar ambition, one he had always satisfied up till now: leaving others to their fate while saving his own skin.

He went toward the boats, but the Scots guard had anticipated him and were guarding them strongly. His first idea was to swim away from the island. He had long practiced this exercise, in preparation for the many escapes of which he had dreamed. But the coast was too far away.

There remained one solution. He climbed back up to the government house, intending to go around it to cross between the fort and the redoubt. As he turned the corner, he saw a shadow draw up to him, sword drawn. In the light of the nearby inferno he recognized Just.

"Don't move," said Just calmly.

"Well, look at that!" said Martin. "Clamorgan. Threatening me with his sword, yet. All right, let me go. I tried to save you, don't forget."

"You tried to draw me away."

"And rightly so," said Martin, "as you fight like a lion for your new master, from what I see."

Just still held him at bay.

"You used to want a fair fight," said Martin, watching him closely. "That's hardly the situation here."

He had as usual put his finger on what was bothering Just. Martin saw his adversary glance around him quickly.

"Are you looking for a weapon for me?" he jeered.

Seeing Just flustered, he leapt to the side. Just lunged, missed, and turned around. The situation was the same, except that Martin no longer had his back to the palm-leaf wall but to the open darkness.

"You fence every morning with Villegagnon, they tell me. So even if I had a sword, we wouldn't be matched fairly . . . my lord."

Feigning a low bow, Martin allowed his arm to drag on the ground and now, with a sudden gesture, threw a fistful of fine sand in Just's eyes. Blinded, Just lowered his guard and brought his free hand to his face. Almost immediately he felt Martin's big fist hammer him in the stomach, and he collapsed.

Floating in and out of consciousness, he heard the admiral approach, clamoring loudly. Hands grabbed him; he thought he saw

Colombe. And someone, in this seeming dream, lamented that Martin had gotten away.

• • •

At dawn, shivering, they counted the number of dead and wounded and the captives. The dead were quickly counted: other than Rupert, who had gone missing, three soldiers had died. On the attackers' side, one was shot to death by a harquebus, and two drowned trying to get away. Two other soldiers were wounded, but only slightly. Finally, four captives were being held on the esplanade across from the government house in iron cuffs fetched from the ships. These were Le Freux, Vittorio, Egidio, and a fourth, his face seamed with scars, in a feathered jerkin like his master, toothless and looking like a buzzard.

Just had been carried to the admiral's four-poster bed, where Colombe watched over him while he regained consciousness.

It was the time for morning prayers. Villegagnon sent for Thevet, who was finally discovered in the corner of a cistern under the wall of the south redoubt where he had taken refuge. He was trembling all over and mumbled that he had never been so scared in all his life. Supposedly to calm himself, he was taking short, nervous draws on an enormous stick of *petun*, which he had always claimed to be keeping for great occasions.

"Will you or will you not lead prayers this morning?" asked Villegagnon.

"I have made up my mind," said Thevet with the red glare of a cornered field mouse. "I am returning to France."

Villegagnon reflected that the learned man had always been more of a burden than a blessing. He deplored losing the colony's only chaplain, but when had the poor cosmographer ever been much more than a man of science?

"Do you hear?" shrieked Thevet, finding sudden courage in his adversary's weakness. "I demand to return aboard the *Grande-Roberge.*"

The admiral smiled wanly and said, "You may embark today, Father. We will manage without you."

Then he turned to Just. The boy was standing and drinking a bowl of bean soup.

"Do you feel better?" asked the admiral.

Just nodded.

"Praise be to God! Allow me to say that you fought very well."

Colombe kissed her brother. Who would have thought that these coconut-fringed beaches would be their land of crusades? Just looked handsomer than ever with his eyes darkly ringed from the sleepless night, his skin again paler in this season of diminished sun, and his taciturn and noble carriage, which was now entirely that of a man.

As a final matter before taking his rest, Villegagnon strode out onto the esplanade and stood in front of the prisoners. He stopped in front of Le Freux.

"Your plan almost worked," said the admiral. "But the unexpected happens even with the best-laid schemes. Without the zany who came to me asking that I marry him to the four women you claimed to have sold him, I would never have known anything. By the way," said Villegagnon, turning to Dom Gonzagues, "the poor devil can be let out of his hiding place. These gentlemen will no longer trouble him."

Dom Gonzagues limped over to a cave inside the fort where Quintin had been hidden away.

The admiral, meanwhile, still standing in front of Le Freux, pronounced the sentence.

"You will be hanged," said the admiral, looking at Le Freux. "And you," he said, looking at the other feathered go-between, "you were seen goring a soldier with your cutlass. The rope for you as well!"

Everyone watched the condemned men to see which way they would fall: toward abjectness and prayers for pardon, or toward the pure hatred they usually gave out so freely. In a manner that would have been comical under other circumstances, the go-betweens exhibited, one after another, expressions of terror, contempt, despondency, and insolence. Finally, understanding that nothing would make Villegagnon relent, Le Freux loosed a stream of spittle at him, which fell short and landed in the sand. It was clear to all that, for those two, the end had come.

Then Villegagnon spun around toward the two others, who were bound back to back with Le Freux by the same rope.

"And these two," said Villegagnon, "who are they?"

"Innocent men, my lord," said Vittorio.

Both he and his crony were in tears.

Le Thoret, who was standing near the admiral, pointed to the Venetian and said, "This one is a reprieved convict."

"Are you then fated always to be in chains?"

Vittorio saw this as an opportunity to redeem himself. After all, he had listened carefully until the very moment they had gone to attack the island, but no one had said the word "Ribera" to him. He had fallen in with impostors, and there was no reason to stand by them as they went down.

"Ah, my lord!" he whimpered. "My downfall has always been to be drawn into the hands of wicked people who force me to act badly. These men blackmailed me in order to rope me in."

So saying, he jerked his head toward Le Freux behind him.

"You roped yourself in just fine all alone," sneered Le Freux, "until this morning anyway."

"Shut up, gibbet meat!" screeched Vittorio. "You corrupted me, when I came here to redeem myself."

Seeing an opening, Egidio leapt in and started leveling his own complaints at Le Freux. Villegagnon put an end to this barrage of invective with an impatient gesture.

"Were they seen to kill anyone?" he asked for all to hear.

No one stepped forward.

"Then let us give them a second chance. They will remain chained while they work until I decide otherwise."

The sun shone all that day—proof that the rains were coming to an end. The admiral decreed a generous siesta, which allowed everyone to forget the fears of the previous night. Even the sentinels nodded off. So it was that when Martin, who had swum out to the *Grande-Roberge*, slid into the water on a rope, as he had learned to do as a child, no one noticed the little splash he made. He swam silently through the clear water to the boats, untied one of them, towed it behind him a cable length from the island, then heaved himself in over the gunwale and rowed away as hard as he could.

A drowsy Scot noticed him just as he was reaching the mainland. By the time he had gotten a harquebus and loaded it, Martin had already leapt onto dry land and disappeared.

CHAPTER 22

There are victories that inspire despair, and Villegagnon's was one of those. He shut himself away to reflect on his failure. For two days he did not come out of the openwork room in which he normally worked, ate, and slept. Except that during those two days, he neither worked, ate, nor slept, being entirely engaged with pacing up and down groaning. From time to time he stopped and slammed his fist down on the oak surface of his table.

The work was good, by Saint Jack of Jerusalem! Bringing the succor of civilization to the lands of the cannibal was a just, glorious, and necessary enterprise. But on whom could he rely to accomplish this great idea? On cowards and caitiffs, freed prisoners and bad workmen. The very night the go-betweens were defeated, some thirty immigrants fled in four boats to the jungle. They preferred a life of luxury among the Indians to the honest life he offered them.

Villegagnon had given orders that the civilian camp be guarded day and night from now on. A sentinel also was to sleep at the port next to the boats. The external enemy had not—as yet—appeared: the fatal corruption had come from within and menaced the entire enterprise. Should he abandon the attempt? The very word horrified him, to say nothing of the idea. Before the walls of Algiers, in 1540, under a driving rain, when Charles V—whom he had accompanied at the behest of the Order of Malta—commanded the retreat, he, Villegagnon, alone of 22,000 men and 400 knights, had returned to plant his sword in the door of the city. He had earned a harquebus wound, a badly broken arm, and a quantity of sarcasm. But it hadn't mattered: he had shouted to the astonished Moors, who were aiming at him from the top of the walls, "We will return!" So, an enemy like Le Freux . . .

When he considered it, Villegagnon realized that his whole mistake had been to entrust the guidance of his depraved flock to Thevet. The Franciscan was useless as a pastor. He had no more than the robes of a priest, and those he generally forgot to button. He could hardly be blamed for his religious indifference. In this he mirrored the Church of France, which was turned entirely toward secular interests. His interests, at least, had been neither in women nor in revenues but only in science. For this he could be forgiven.

But the problem remained. The admiral had written the king and Coligny to ask for troop reinforcements, new colonists, and funds. The letters would leave in two days with the *Grande-Roberge* under Bois-le-Comte's command. But even if they sent him what he asked for—and he had no great illusions on that score—it still left the central issue: the spiritual leadership of these wastrels, the moral backbone of Antarctic France, the soul of Genèbre.

This was the name by which he called the colony at his tenderest and most private moments. "Genèbre" sounded like "Geneviève," and Geneviève was a girl of fifteen who, when he was twenty, had refused him. Genèbre, Geneviève, Geneva.

Calvin!

Villegagnon's fist crashed down on the oak table, and the pewter pitcher went flying.

Calvin! Geneva! Calvin, the Genevan reformer; Calvin, the great Christian thinker who called for a reformation of the faith. Calvin, the man of wit, so unlike the uncouth Luther who had loosed anarchy and vice on the Germans but who had fortunately been dead for ten years, damn his soul. Calvin, his friend!

Though their destinies afterward diverged, Calvin and Villegagnon had studied at the University of Orléans together, for the admiral had not always been destined to carry arms. His forebears in Provins had all served the law, and the same had been expected of him. After completing his legal studies, Villegagnon enrolled as a lawyer at the Paris parliament. He only chose his true course at the age of twenty-one. Perhaps because of the three swords stuck in the sand on his crest, perhaps because of his childhood reading, perhaps because of his body, which was already too big for the counsel's bench and apter for bold action than legal defense, or perhaps because of Geneviève, he had put on once and for all the crimson tunic with the white Cross of Malta.

Yet when he looked back over his life and considered all those whom he had met, his loud admiration went to men of learning, to artists and philosophers. Cicero, Plutarch, Justinian, and Alciati were gods to him. And Calvin, in publishing his *Institutes of the Christian Religion* twenty years before, had taken his place in their ranks.

His passion for Calvin was all the more intact for their never having met again in the intervening years. When he thought of Calvin, Villegagnon saw the pale schoolboy straining over his copybook, the thin, feverish young man whom a secret familial humiliation drove toward a spiritual revenge.

To think that the sumptuous Latin phrases of the *Institutes* had been born of his pen! It hardly mattered to Villegagnon that the work had provoked polemics and condemnation. They lived in a time of new and bold ideas. The admiral had no doubt at all that Calvin, who wanted a return to the simplicity of the early Church, was just the man to fortify his dispirited flock.

He lit a candle, for at that hour of night he already could see little, and wrote Calvin a handsome letter. He first reminded him of the days of their friendship, then he described the colony to him in favorable but by no means deceitful terms. He expounded at length on the future greatness of Antarctic France but did not hide from Calvin that he had need of spiritual help to put his routed troops back on course. How many pastors should he ask Calvin for? After thinking about it carefully and at first leaving the number blank, he decided that five ministers would adequately provide for the island's church and that he was most likely to get them by asking for double the number. He wrote "ten." He interrupted himself to think, then rushed back to his desk: as long as he was being bold . . . In a firm hand he wrote that a shipment of young, marriageable girls would also be of great utility to the colony. He had no doubt that the introduction of females into his sanctuary would make for complications, but concessions had to be made to reality. These brutal men would always get hold of what was forbidden them. It was better to establish proper morals with modest young girls of sound outlook. The first weddings would thus be celebrated with helpmeets from Geneva. The colonists who failed to get one could at least take inspiration from those who did and regulate their behavior with the savagesses accordingly. And if among the good citizens of Geneva Calvin should find skilled artisans, virtuous laborers, or men of any sort equipped with an abundance of courage and faith who wanted to lend their talents to the great Brazilian enterprise, he should straightaway send them along with the ministers and virgins.

At the moment of sealing the letter, Villegagnon had a last flicker of doubt. There was little enough chance that Calvin would respond favorably to this request. He had many other responsibilities and ambitions. And supposing he agreed, what would be the reaction in Paris? As a friend of the de Guises, a Knight of Malta, and the vice admiral of Brittany, would not Villegagnon be accused of treachery for calling on those whom the Church held in suspicion? Willy-nilly, and despite the moderation of his teachings, Calvin was regarded as a Huguenot and lumped together with the plague of Lutheranism.

Villegagnon went around in circles for a time. Then he brushed his objections aside with the back of his hand, as though they were of no more consequence than the moths flitting around his candle in the humid air. He remembered the court of Ferrara, where he had once stayed. Renée of France, daughter of Louis XII and the duke of Ferrara's wife, maintained a tolerant and cultivated circle where new ideas were freely debated. Bishops were received there, and yet Calvin was also held in the highest esteem. He was even said to be the duchess's confessor.

Villegagnon refrained from banging on the table again, as he did not want to lose his light. But that was the answer! That is what he wanted to make Genèbre into: a haven of peace where each would have his place, where bold forays of the mind would nurture a true faith in line with the simple frugality of primitive times, to which the very conditions of the colony would naturally contribute.

He placed the letter in the ebony secretary with the others that were to go on the *Grande-Roberge*. Then, to the accompaniment of a great groaning of tenons and mortises eaten by damp and worms, he threw himself into his hammock and was instantly snoring.

• • •

Bad news came in gouts during the days after the victory. First of all, in making the tally of those who had fled, the colony discovered that it had lost all the practitioners of certain crucial trades: all its carpenters, all its blacksmiths, and its sole apothecary. Next, the sailors were attacked while on a water run, and four were riddled with arrows. When the bodies were brought back, it was easy to recognize the long reed shafts used by the natives, whose points were made of bone or the tail of a venomous ray. Clearly they could no longer count on the goodwill of the Tupi, at least those along the near coast, who sided with the defeated go-betweens. The upshot was that fresh food would no longer reach them from the mainland. They would have to make do with the reserves of manioc flour and salt meat that Villegagnon had fortunately taken the precaution of laying up. It occurred to them that there were still several barrels of seed left in the ships' holds: rye, wheat, barley, turnip, cabbage, and leek. There was enough to plant an entire crop. But in designing the island's fortifications, Villegagnon had set aside no arable land outside the fort and the dwellings. It was late to remedy the situation now, and besides most of the seed proved on examination to have been spoiled by the damp and vermin. All hopes therefore rested on the *Grande-Roberge*. Well brokered, its cargo would allow them to be reprovisioned with necessities. If they had to wait six months in the meantime, the colonists could be sparing with their resources and, if need be, make a few purchases at the Norman trade counters at the head of the bay—a humiliation that Villegagnon hoped to avoid at all costs.

On the eve of the *Grande-Roberge*'s departure, the admiral summoned his senior officers, Thevet, and his two pages to a farewell dinner. To make up for the small cheer on plates and in glasses, the conversation had to be lively, and Villegagnon applied himself to making it so with considerable success. His massive and powerful body, so at home on the battlefield, had also learned in princely courts to become an instrument of charm and poetry. His big voice allowed him to declaim verses with such controlled power that he seemed to be expressing the immense forces of the soul in love. He excelled at depicting the tragic, the pathetic, and, suddenly exploding into laughter, the comic. When one adds that he also sang in a smooth and steady baritone, it will be understood that this accomplished courtier was able for the space of the evening to make his company forget the desperate straits in which they found themselves.

A bottle of wine that had miraculously escaped the mishaps of the crossing and the trials that followed it was brought to the table by the Scotsmen with the care usually given a holy relic. Villegagnon uncorked it and ordered crystal glasses brought forth from a chest for the occasion. No pewter mugs for this nectar. It had to be drunk in its entirety, which is to say, first with the eyes, while making the candlelight shimmer in its scarlet depths. Before declaring a toast, Villegagnon put down his glass and, looking at Just, pulled a sheet of paper from his pocket.

"Just de Clamorgan," he read. "In the name of my superior of the Order of Malta, whose powers I hold for the occasion, I declare . . ."

The whole assembly, their faces again serious, but with a tender smile on their lips, looked toward Just.

" . . . that during the battle of 12 February 1556 in the Bay of Genèbre, at Fort Coligny, you showed great courage in observing and tracking the enemy, as well as in charging and repulsing him. A perfidious adversary dealt you a wound that might have compromised your life. In consequence of which, I grant you the honor, in service to Our Lord Jesus Christ, to bear the arms of knighthood."

It was an unexpected and outdated ceremony that, under any other circumstances, would have appeared farcical. But Villegagnon gave it conviction, as only those who are determined to pass on a tradition they know already to be dead can do. And Just, without falling dupe to his own pleasure, meant to take advantage of time's suspension in these forgotten lands to believe the truth of this fable. He rose, then Villegagnon rested his sword on his shoulders and head, uttered a few approximate formulas, and ended the whole thing with a frank embrace.

This was followed by a general acclamation, and then they drank. The bitterness of the wine had a taste of regret and farewell. Each followed the wine's progress as far within himself as possible, as though by accompanying its fire into his depths he might revisit his beloved places and lost loves.

"Your turn will come," Villegagnon offered to Colombe. "As soon as your beard decides to grow."

Everyone laughed except Colombe, who showed some embarrassment.

"My children," said Villegagnon, "not to dwell on it, but your valor is no accident. It is a sign of good breeding. Your father was an accomplished man-at-arms."

Then he sat down, a sign that he was upset and thinking.

"As misfortune would have it, he began his career with a defeat. He was at Pavia when King Francis I was made prisoner. And he accompanied him into captivity. Perhaps it all stemmed from that . . ."

He turned gloomy, following a thought that he did not utter. Abruptly, he came to himself.

"Then," he said, "he took part in the League of Cambrai's campaigns, and His Majesty sent him to Rome to negotiate the marriage of Catherine de Medici to his son, our present king."

Just's eyes shone.

"It was thus that he became a man of the shadows, my children, a negotiator, a secret emissary, entrusted with complicated tasks, dangerous ones. Two of the king's agents were killed on the Po in 1544, when the country was at peace."

"So when he took us from town to town," said Colombe, "it wasn't because he was fighting?"

"Sometimes he fought with actual weapons. But he often wielded other, more secret ones; he prepared the way for peace—or war."

He coughed.

Just and Colombe looked at each other. The idea that their father might be anything other than a soldier bewildered them. And nothing surprised them more than to learn that he had been a manner of diplomat.

"I cannot tell you a great deal more," Villegagnon concluded, "because we did not see each other often."

"And his death?" asked Just, as though calling for the payment of a debt.

The admiral looked down at the ground and reflected. Around the table, Bois-le-Comte, who was to command the *Grande-Roberge*, sat stiffly and without expression; Thevet slept; and Dom Gonzagues was off searching for an impossible rhyme for "Marguerite." Only Le Thoret followed the discussion with interest.

"I know what is common knowledge," said Villegagnon testily. "He was killed in Siena, in Tuscany, the year before our departure."

"Tuscany . . . Doesn't it belong to Spain?" asked Just, who had learned a bit about Italy from his recent reading.

"Yes, but the town of Siena was in rebellion and had called on the French."

A strange discomfort kept Villegagnon from speaking freely. He exchanged a distrustful glance with Le Thoret.

"Well, we fought there. And your father died."

"I have heard," said Just, "that he was in disgrace with the king of France."

"It's true that he had earlier refused to join the troops defending the Piedmont."

"Why did the king send him to Siena if he had refused to fight in the Piedmont?"

"He didn't send him," exclaimed Villegagnon, but the same discomfort kept him from saying anything more.

Le Thoret still looked at him intensely, then directed his steely eyes at the Clamorgans.

"Is it because," said Just haltingly, "he was with the Spaniards?"

"It's all very confused," put in Villegagnon hastily, and he added in a loud voice, "and besides I wasn't there."

There was a long silence.

"And our mother, did you know her?" asked Colombe.

She had been waiting for the chance to ask this embarrassing question for some time. As the situation could hardly be made more uncomfortable, she went ahead with it.

There followed a silence so tense that Dom Gonzagues surfaced from his poetry and Thevet from his sleep.

"No!" said Villegagnon. And to sidestep any further probing, he jumped to his feet and proposed a toast to the new knight.

"And now, my children," he said hastily before they could ask any more sticky questions, "I have one last thing to tell you. You have served me loyally despite the irregular circumstances of your enlistment. My duty . . ."

On the threshold of completing his sentence, he stopped himself, and a nerve above his blackly whiskered chin twitched.

"My duty obliges me to tell you that you are free. If you wish to embark on the *Grande-Roberge*, although it carries no passengers outside Abbé Thevet, I will authorize you to do so."

Just and Colombe shivered and glanced at each other, reading in each other's eyes the same perplexity as to the meaning of their emotion.

"I do not ask you for an answer here and now. Confer with one another. The *Grande-Roberge* weighs anchor tomorrow afternoon. Until the gangplank is stowed, the decision is yours to make."

· · ·

Just said nothing when they went to bed. The next day he drew Colombe aside for a serious discussion. They took the little path between the northern wall of the fortress and the ragged line of rocks, which had already become a place of meditation for the melancholy and of plotting for the rebellious.

Just had prepared a long speech, which Colombe listened to as she walked slowly beside him. He laid out frankly all the reasons they had for returning—the theft of the Clamorgan inheritance, their future, Colombe's dignity—and as a point of honor he gave all these arguments pride of place. Then he drew a picture of the opposite side: Villegagnon's desperate position, the help they might bring him, and the greatness of Antarctic France.

Colombe smiled and let her eyes wander over the distant coast, toward the great island of the Maracajá far away. The sun exulted in its victory. The vanquished clouds crawled on the ground in the west, clinging to distant mountain chains. Gorged with an excess of green from the rains of the past weeks, nature had grown even more tender and seductive.

When Just finally came to a stop, Colombe turned her luminous eyes toward him, freshly saturated with the blue of the sea, and laughed.

"You needn't go to so much trouble, Just!" she said. "Do you think I haven't known for a long time what you wanted?"

"And what's that?" he asked, blushing.

She took his hand and, skipping in front of him, sat down at the foot of the embankment. The cobbles were already dry and radiated the warmth of the sun. A few remains of bushes, white with salt and dust, shivered in the breeze.

"We're going to stay," she said, "and I'm glad."

Just was perturbed by conflicting emotions. He disliked the idea that his thoughts could be so easily read. In his eyes, a man—and a knight all the more—should be as impenetrable as he is valiant. On the other hand, he was relieved to know that he would not have to express all that he felt but did not wish to name.

For if Just was resolved to do his duty toward Villegagnon in his hour of danger, it was because he now felt a sincere affection toward the knight. And the political opportunity of forming Antarctic France was only the chance aspect assumed by the idea of honor, glory, and sacrifice, whose roots delved into the most magnificent chimeras of his childhood.

With the *Grande-Roberge* gone, commanded by Bois-le-Comte, the only officers left to help Villegagnon would be Le Thoret and poor Dom Gonzagues, whose health made him every day more fit for verses and less for any other endeavor.

Just felt called to action and a position of command. With her smile, Colombe absolved him of the need to explain all the joy he felt at the prospect.

"What about you?" he asked, confirming that for him the issue was foregone.

She took a moment to answer. She was no less clear about what she wanted, but she didn't proceed as he did by deduction from abstract arguments. She tried to analyze what she felt clearly and saw that two emotions predominated. The first was the pleasure she took in sharing Just's happiness. She preferred not to speak of it and let him believe that she subscribed to the same dreams. Yet it was no longer entirely true. The fact was that she cared little about Antarctic France. She looked on these grand ideas with the same ironic glance that she gave to Villegagnon, who claimed to embody them. On the other hand, a second emotion had for several days been percolating in her.

"I want to return among the Indians," she said.

She wanted to learn the fate of Paraguaçu and her other friends, and of the prisoner who cast off his pearls. The young, the old, the children, the warriors—she missed the entire tribe.

"The Indians!" said Just. "That's out of the question. They are now at war with us."

"Those along the coast," she objected.

Just's reaction forced her to make an argument. In fact, she had no plan, no fixed intention. She knew only that she wanted once more to experience the great peace of the forest, to bathe in its torrents, and to shed her shadow of noise to the point of walking in nature without disturbing it.

"I know another tribe, in the interior, that might be able to help us."

She was improvising.

"And I am now the only one among us who speaks their language."

Just looked at his sister. He had never been so struck before by the oddity of her face, those eyes that seemed to look inward and at the same time to reflect the soul of the person they contemplated, that beauty which was more and more perfected, long and slender, Florentine, as the painters of that school had represented it in the last century.

What separated them, for the first time, was more apparent to him than all that had united them in childhood. And the confused attraction that arose from these differences filled him with turmoil.

"Yes," he said, trying to assume a political countenance, "you could certainly be useful to us as an interpreter, a go-between."

"And you could persuade Villegagnon of it," she added, not imagining that the new knight would seize on this suggestion and make it the basis for an agreement or, on his part, an oath.

He thought for a long moment.

"All right," he said finally, "I'll do it."

The two of them, surprised at the turn their fate was taking, walked back to the boats to watch the *Grande-Roberge* set sail.

CHAPTER 23

"Go on without me, I'm exhausted," whimpered Quintin, flopping down on a big root.

The ground rose and lacked firmness. It gave way underfoot. Trunks of sycamores and jacarandas lifted far above the ground the triforium of their first branches and the vault of their canopies. The sun, diffracted by leaves as if through vegetal stained-glass, completed the ordered, colossal, and cathedral-like aspect of the forest that put Quintin so ill at ease.

"Come on, this isn't the moment to give up," said Colombe testily.

In her hand was one of the ship's compasses that Villegagnon had been kind enough to lend her to find her way through the undergrowth.

"I thought you knew the way, knew how we might make contact with your friends . . ."

"All that," said Colombe, still examining the dark compass face, "was so the admiral would allow us to go."

"Godamercy!" whistled Quintin.

He was less terrified by the danger than despondent at the prospect of ending his life far from men and surrounded by capuchin monkeys.

"To think I might never see them again . . ."

"Them" referred to the four female companions he had been chattering to Colombe about since they had left the island three days earlier.

"I don't understand," Colombe muttered, indifferent to the preacher's jeremiads. "We are almost at the shoulder separating the bay from the other shore. And we haven't met up with anyone."

"Good Lord, who do you expect us to meet up with in a place like this?" asked Quintin. "It is only too apparent that no human being has ever ventured here."

The poor man knew nothing of the Indians beyond having rented four of them to lead them to paradise. But Colombe remembered having been through just such patches of jungle without disturbing their stillness. She knew that the Indians could leave unbroken the tomblike silence, which was occasionally shattered by the sonorous cries of invisible birds and howling monkeys. Not seeing any men since they entered the forest had at first reassured her, as she was afraid of the hostile tribes along the shore. But their isolation was now a source of alarm. She could see two possible explanations: either there was no one here and they were lost, or the animosity toward the colonists had spread to all the tribes, and they might expect to be attacked at any moment.

Her nose pressed to the magnetized needle, Colombe continued south, zigzagging between the trunks, when she suddenly let out a shriek.

"What is it?" asked Quintin, straightening up.

A moment later he stood beside her, looking around uncomprehendingly.

"There, on the ground," she mumbled, pointing.

A naked body lay on its back. It was an Indian of Paraguaçu's tribe, recognizable from his emerald lip plug. Death had softened his mouth, and the pierced lip had fallen over onto his nose, like the lid of a jug. The eyes were open. The corruption of the forest had begun, and a whitish halo of larvae swarmed around the corpse, having most likely infested its insides already. But the part of the body visible to the two Europeans was still intact. The skin, showing traces of ritual genipap paint on the thighs, was broken by no tear or wound. The man had not been killed in combat. Besides, it was rare for fallen warriors to remain on the battlefield. The Indians went to great pains to bury their dead. As to their enemies, they ate them on the very site of the battle, or so it was claimed. And this man had been tasted only by worms.

The gloom of the forest forestalled a thorough examination. But Quintin, stopping his nose, had the courage to kneel close by to verify a detail that had struck him.

"Look at these pustules," he said to Colombe, who showed no interest in the sight and tried to drag him away. "He has them all over his body. It looks like smallpox."

Macabre though the body was, it encouraged Colombe, as it showed they must be getting near the Indians.

"He must not have had time to reach the village," she said, continuing on the trail.

Quintin no longer thought about resting. He followed her, perplexed. An hour later they found another corpse with the same marks.

Despite everything, Colombe remained cheerful, because she was starting to remember her surroundings. They reached the wide entrance to the village where the trap lay hidden, whose mechanism she gleefully demonstrated to Quintin. They walked around it and saw the big hut in the distance. Colombe ran ahead joyfully, signaling her arrival with shouts.

But nothing broke the silence. The hut was empty, its roof partially caved in, and the jungle was hungrily nibbling at the clearing. Other than a few potsherds littering the ground, nothing remained of the village's past life. But there were no corpses either.

Colombe sat on a chunk of wood, lowered her head into her hands, and gave vent to her disappointment. Quintin, to whom these remains meant nothing, could see only that they had halted for the first time since their departure in a more or less proper place. He pulled his hammock from his pack, strung it between two posts, and climbed into it for a bit of sleep. The swinging made him remember that Le Freux was to be hung at this very hour, along with his unfortunate partner. It was one of the reasons Quintin had been happy at being chosen to accompany Colombe. But the thought made his mouth feel dry, and he sat up in his hammock with his hands to his neck. At that moment, he saw a man come out of the hut behind Colombe and silently try to reach the forest.

The man must have remained hidden while they were inspecting the inside of the hut. If he had been Indian, he would have slipped away into the trees effortlessly. But he was a white man, and despite his knowledge of the forest, he took too long in his precautions.

"Stop!" ordered Quintin.

He took advantage of being in shadow to make the man think he was armed. In his voice, two muskets were aimed at the man's back. But Quintin as usual had nothing to defend himself with.

Fortunately, the man did not appear hostile. Finding himself discovered, he spread his arms slightly, turned, and came to stand in the light of the clearing facing Colombe.

He had one of those ageless, deeply furrowed faces that the tropics have either aged before their time or conserved beyond their term—it is hard to tell which. A shock of blond hair on the top of his cranium suggested a place for him in Thevet's collection, among the pineapples. Like the go-betweens, he wore picturesque fabrics, but, unlike Le Freux and his cronies, he made no effort to mimic the dress of noblemen. His formless vest and long pants gave him a rough aspect similar to Colombe's, before whom he went and sat down.

"Hello!" he said peaceably in English.

"Are you French?" asked Colombe, surprised and almost reproachful, so much did she dislike finding a white man in this village where she had expected to be reunited with her friends.

"Everyone is French in these parts, so as not to be eaten." Then he added, his strong accent making his words almost incomprehensible, "Even I, who am English."

"And what are you doing in this village?" said Quintin in the same querulous voice he believed most likely to inspire fear and respect.

But the Englishman was so placid that the threatening tone seemed somewhat ridiculous.

"The same as you, I imagine, taking a walk."

"What happened to the Indians?" asked Colombe.

"And where do you come from that you don't know?" said the man, looking at her attentively.

Her strange and beautiful gaze fell upon him, but he showed no trace of fear.

"They left all together because of the epidemic," he said.

Quintin jumped down from his hammock, his curiosity winning
out over his mistrust, and he walked forward into the light.

"It was smallpox, wasn't it?"

"I don't know. There's no doctor here. But you know how the Indians are, they say it's an evil spirit and they've given it a name of their
own."

"Are they all dead?" asked Colombe.

"All, no. But many. Have you heard of Quoniambec?"

"No, who is that?"

"A valiant Indian who killed many enemies in battle and made
many prisoners. His people worshiped him like a king. The traders
at the stations had even taught him to fire a cannon. What he liked
to do was to put one on each shoulder and have the match lit while
he held them."

The Englishman rose and laughingly mimed firing two pieces
backward, turning his head to aim. Then he sat back down morosely.

"Well, the poor man died in just two days, covered in scabs."

Quintin shook his head. The loss of a man crazy for war hardly
left him inconsolable. But he was thinking about his four Indian
women, and he sniffed.

"Have you come from the trading stations?" the Englishman
asked.

"No, from the island. We are with Villegagnon," said Colombe a
little too readily, feeling confidence in the man.

"It's not possible!" he said, leaping to his feet.

She regretted her frankness and sensed Quintin backing away.

"If the Indians find you," the Englishman went on, "never admit
that you're from there. They are convinced that it was your colony
that brought the fevers."

"Who convinced them of that?"

"The go-betweens on the coast."

"Aren't you one of them? asked Quintin.

"Me!" said the Englishman, drawing back in indignation.

"I beg your pardon," said Quintin, "I thought that all the white
men along this coast were friends of Le Freux."

"Le Freux," said the Englishman contemptuously. "Yes, that is the
bandit you chose to deal with. And now you are reaping your
reward!"

"And so has he by this time," said Quintin, glad once he had said it that Le Freux was safely hanging from the gibbet.

There was an uneasy silence after these words.

"Have you never heard of Païe-Lo?" asked the Englishman.

Colombe and Quintin looked at each other in bewilderment.

"Is that you?"

"No," the Englishman exclaimed. "I am just Charles."

"Quintin."

"And I'm Colin."

These introductions out of the way, all three smiled with satisfaction. Colombe couldn't believe that the same setting where she had lived with the Indians now served as a backdrop for such different characters. The idea that a name could bring together two people and allow them to know who they were would have seemed laughable to the Tupi who had lived there.

"Païe-Lo is the most important man in all the bay," said the Englishman seriously.

"What tribe does he belong to?" asked Colombe.

Charles laughed, showing the horrible stumps of his teeth, which had survived many ocean crossings.

"The same tribe as we do. Or rather, the same as you. He is a white man, and he was a Frenchman before he became . . . what he is."

"And what's that?"

Quintin asked this somewhat sulkily, expecting to hear a new catalogue of war exploits, as with Quoniambec, or of villainies, as with Le Freux.

"A man of great wisdom and magnificent goodness."

"And where does this saint live?" asked Quintin, his voice brimming with irony.

He was hardly prepared to believe, from his knowledge of the country, that a man with these qualities could survive and find respect here.

"Two days' journey from this spot, in a forest the Indians call Tijuca."

"Why did you ask us if we knew him?" asked Colombe.

"You wanted to know if all the Europeans were followers of Le Freux. Well, I am trying to show you that there are many who fortunately do not recognize the authority of those brigands."

"And Païcom-Lo is in some sense their leader?"

"Hah!" the Englishman chuckled. "If he could hear you! Him, a leader? Maybe, when it comes to it, though I'd never thought of it in that light. In any case, he is a leader who gives no orders, punishes no one, and distributes no rewards."

This fond description of a man they didn't know left the new-comers more or less indifferent. Colombe in particular had gone back to her nostalgia for the Indians and would not be consoled.

"We knew some Indians from this village. Do you think there is any way to find them again?"

"It will be difficult," said the Englishman, shaking his head. "The Indians are used to going away like that, one fine night, because their maracas tell them they must in order to placate the spirits. Some have even gone as far as a great river to the west that crosses the forest of the Amazons."

With the tip of her foot, Colombe played in the dust with two little white periwinkle shells that had fallen from a necklace. For a moment she considered looking for such traces in order to follow the Indians in their flight. Then she realized the absurdity of it. She sighed.

"The only person who might know something," said Charles, "is Païcom-Lo."

"You described him to us as an old wise man, and I imagined him as a recluse."

"And so he is, but by some miracle he knows everything. I am quite certain, for instance, that he knows you."

"Us? You mean Villegagnon."

"All of you, and the two of you in particular, if you have had any relations with the Indians."

Quintin frowned and said, "And why did he never show himself, if he is so well informed and so good? Why did he leave us in the clutches of Le Freux until we almost came to grief?"

"Because Païcom-Lo knows how to wait."

"Then do you think he can help us find the Indians?" asked Colombe.

"Do you think," added Quintin, not waiting for an answer, "that he could also help the colony survive by supplying us with fresh food and water?"

"Paï-Lo," said the Englishman slowly and thoughtfully, "is not a trader. He has nothing to sell and wishes to buy nothing."

Quintin pouted in disappointment.

"But if your cause is just and if he wants to help you, he can do anything."

Colombe came to a decision, and when she turned toward Quintin, she saw that he was of the same mind.

"Would you be willing, Charles," she said, opening her eyes wide, "to lead us to this Paï-Lo, whom we would like to meet?"

The Englishman took her hands joyfully: "Oh, I'd be delighted to. Truly delighted. Whenever I can bring someone worthy of it to Paï-Lo, I feel as though I've accomplished . . . something useful."

His British reserve had cut short his lyric rapture, but the emotion in his voice was palpable even without words.

"Let's start out tonight, if you like," he said. "We are still too close to the coast for my taste. Le Freux may be dead, but it appears that a young brigand who arrived with you has managed to escape and now claims to be the leader of the traders on the coast."

Martin, thought Colombe.

"He is said to be more dangerous even than Le Freux."

Quintin went and folded his hammock. They ate two smoked fish each, drank a little water, and then set off.

Charles guided them through the forest. They crossed hills planted with large-leaved *pacos* and fragrant mastic bushes in the clearings. They found dark stands of tall trees and large dry expanses covered with flowering cassia.

Always climbing but detouring a thousand times around rocks and rushing streams, they looked back at times to the ever more distant bay. And one morning they entered among enormous cotton bushes, backed in the far distance by tall pines.

"Tijuca," said Charles, mopping his forehead. "We will soon see Paï-Lo."

III

Bodies and Souls

CHAPTER 24

A year had passed since the *Grande-Roberge* sailed for France. Winter had returned, with its damps, its puddles, its torrential storms. Then it had once again given way to the endless summer of the tropics. In this year of privations, when water was scarce and drawn from the bottom of cisterns, the merciless sun seemed bent on adding to the trials of the poor defenders of Fort Coligny: the heat stayed intense and desiccating for months. During the day the men no longer had the protection of shade as all the trees on the island had been felled. And all through the stifling nights, they were also denied the restorative of sleep: they groaned in their hammocks.

Everything proceeded at a slackened pace. Gaunt, exhausted, and in many cases suffering from fever, the colonists showed little aptitude for their work. The fort made no progress. Its ramparts at half height, far from being a sign of near completion, suggested to all that Villegagnon's ambition outstripped the forces at his disposal. The rainy season, soaking everything, had made some of the walls collapse. These setbacks undermined morale as much as the structure.

Since the return of hot weather, the lushly forested and shade-filled mainland had exerted a more powerful attraction than ever. Nine more men managed to flee despite extra guards and redoubled vigilance.

Just had entered a man's estate during this year, and it suited him. He had read all the books in the library brought over by Villegagnon and showed himself capable of reasoning on the great subjects of the day. The daily lessons in the use of weapons had made him a true man-at-arms. His strength at wielding the sword and harquebus was all the more remarkable as he was emaciated, like all the others, and plagued by scurf and sores. Already slender of body, these ailments seemed to attack his skin to the underlying warp, baring his skeletal frame. His two black eyes devoured his face; his beard, which he could not shave for lack of water, ate up the rest. Only his hair kept all its black vitality. Villegagnon had made him his right hand, equal in rank to Le Thoret, who led the knights.

Just held responsibility for the construction site. It was the most difficult duty, as he was in contact with the men and had to make them work. Their deprivations gave them an excuse for shirking. But the workers' real reason for stalling was their hatred of Villegagnon. Everything was laid at his door: their despair at being on the island, the cruelty of taking alcohol and women from them, and the surveillance to which they were now subjected. Just, who now espoused Villegagnon's ideas on Antarctic France, the value of chastity, and the redemptive beauty of sacrifice, met only with sarcasm and veiled hostility from the laborers. When he tried to persuade them of the need to finish the fort before the rains returned and especially when he evoked the threat of the Portuguese, he saw their eyes light up more with hope than fear. The men felt that anything was preferable to Villegagnon's hated dictatorship. If the Portuguese were to arrive, they would be hailed as liberators. A new rebellion was not out of the question. The knights and Just slept with their weapons and in a group, posting a watch. The pale beauty of the tropical dawn, the emerald sea, and the cloudless metallic sky hid so many terrors and hatreds that they came to be looked upon almost with horror, like so much grimacing face-paint derisively applied to the skin of a dying person.

On the mainland, Martin had assumed Le Freux's old authority and extended it through his own genius. To block the Normans on the far shore, who pushed their activities as far as Cabo Frio, he had started to weave a network of relations with the lands farther to the south, beyond Vases Bay, and very far to the north, as far as Bahia.

There was even talk that his emissaries were in contact with the Portuguese in São Salvador. His hatred for Villegagnon was as strong as ever, and he made it very difficult for the colonists to land on the mainland, ordering that their boats be attacked and forbidding the Indians to sell them anything at all. Yet his influence over the tribes was not undisputed. The majority of the Indians, except those along the coast in the direct line of Martin's fire, remained faithful to Paï-Lo, whom Colombe had met in Tijuca. Thanks to the agreement she had made with him, the island had continued to receive manioc flour, dried fish, and fruit. The boats traveled at night to the head of the bay, where a small group of Indians, protected by a rocky salient, managed to escape the authority of Martin and his go-betweens. Thus the admiral was never forced to apply to the Normans on the far shore in order to survive.

Following this diplomatic success, Colombe was assigned to travel regularly to Paï-Lo's country with Quintin. Just was still not comfortable with her venturing into the dangerous Indian lands, but he conceded the usefulness of it. Then too, he could but rejoice that his sister—alone of the immigrants—retained her bursting good health, which she sucked from the clear waters of the mountain, the gentle shade of the forest, and the fruits she picked from the trees.

She had been gone a month when, on a Sunday morning in March, the Scotsman standing watch over the island sounded the alarm with repeated shouts. Four ships had entered the channel and were sailing into the bay. They were not the first to be seen since the colonists arrived on the island. Each time there had been the same commotion. But up till now the ships had always traveled singly and set a course toward the trading stations. These four ships were heading directly for Fort Coligny. With a following wind pushing them along, their bows faced the island and their flags remained hidden.

There was a long moment of quiet anguish on the island. If this armada belonged to the Portuguese, defeat was inevitable. The alarm, far from prompting a show of force, had made patent to all the island's weakness. The unfinished walls would crumble at the first shot. The cannons, poorly maintained during the rains, would fire only if the powder were not too wet. And the soldiers were ragged, worn from privation. A good half of the island's so-called defenders were in any case likely to put their remaining energy into plunging a cutlass into the backs of the other half.

But if the ships were French, they were saved.

An hour passed without a single sign to identify the ships. The knights commended themselves to God, while the remainder prayed to the Devil to rid them of those same knights. It was suffocatingly hot, and a troop of mosquitoes, sallying from the little marsh where reeds had once grown, stung the islanders' shins like a traitorous vanguard.

Finally Villegagnon was able to make out a flag with his glass. It belonged to the king of France.

Hope is omnivorous: deny it the food that it expects, and it will happily feed on other meat, so long as it helps toward survival. All those who were hoping for Villegagnon's defeat and for the Portuguese to arrive cheered for the approaching French. True, the new arrivals would spare the admiral, but they would also save everyone else. On the island could be heard nothing but joyful shouts, the bone on bone of gaunt embraces, and the rubbing together of bearded muzzles. Villegagnon ordered two boats launched and took his place in one of them to pilot the ships between the reefs. He set off hatless in the full midday sun, with Just beside him in an open-necked shirt, standing on a pile of rope tossed into the boat in haste. When they arrived under the rampart of the first ship, its hull white with barnacles, they held a brief conversation with those on board. The leaders of the expedition wanted to disembark on the spot. The captain ordered a rope ladder lowered, and the two boats waited at its foot on the still sea. Three solemn figures climbed down over the side, one dressed as a nobleman and the other two all in black.

Introductions were made in the close quarters of the longboat. The three men were in excellent condition for having just finished a four-month voyage.

"Philippe de Corguilleray, Sieur du Pont," said the first, who wore a doublet of red velvet and breeches of the same color.

He embarked on the performance of a great terrestrial bow, but a sudden wave upended him into the arms of one of the oarsmen.

"Pierre Richier," said the first of the black-clad men, neither smiling nor departing from an air of worried seriousness.

He wore a short gray beard, trimmed to a point. His suit of thick cloth, black as crows' feathers, with its long sleeves and long trouser legs, was enlivened by no ornament. Showing that he was the leader and that no opinion would be heard except his own, he motioned briefly toward the other man in dark clothes and said, "Guillaume Chartier."

The next moment, a gust of wind moved across the bay and made the water around the boat shiver. But Villegagnon did not intend to be diverted by this sudden swell, though he waved his arms to keep his balance.

"Has the king of France sent you?" he asked, wanting to know to what great figure he should direct his tears of joy and prayers of thanksgiving.

"No," said Richier, a steadying hand on an oarsman's head. "Calvin. We are ministers from Geneva."

The waves had passed and the boat was again steady. It was surprise and the sudden commotion in his brain that sent Villegagnon reeling backward. He fell from his full height and nearly sent them all to the bottom.

• • •

Carried back unconscious to his bed, the admiral recovered his wits little by little. He gave Le Thoret and Just his instructions for billeting the new arrivals. Then, allowing himself a day in bed for the first time since his distant childhood, he plunged into the letter from Calvin that Sieur du Pont had brought him.

The four new ships meanwhile anchored next to the two others, their sails furled, forming a proud armada in the sunlight. A swarm of boats disgorged clutches of passengers onto the beach. This landing was very different from the one two years before when the first cargo of Frenchmen had set foot on the still-deserted island. The new arrivals, for one thing, were in good health. Without a Villegagnon on board to forbid them to attack other vessels, the ships had taken the time along the way to force a few prizes: solitary merchantmen, poorly protected convoys, and even men-of-war, when the advantage in numbers and in guns was on their side. Throughout their crossing they had consequently had all the provisions they needed, even palpably more. A carrack boarded shortly after their departure proved gratifyingly full of Madeira wine. Next they had

enjoyed the fresh provisions found aboard an English ship, which
had made such speed from Portsmouth that it had consumed almost
nothing. And shortly before reaching Cabo Frio, they had captured
a small Spanish ship carrying salt meat. Being so near their destination, they had allowed themselves the luxury of taking the Spaniard
in tow, after setting its crew adrift in two ship's boats. That was why,
though they had numbered three ships on leaving France, they
arrived at Guanabara four strong. Delighted at their pleasant crossing, cheered by their easy victories, plentifully nourished with food
and drink, the new arrivals clustered on the beach and stared with
horror at the silent troop of colonizers who had gone before them.

Emaciated, dirty, and harried, the island's residents were divided
between feelings of shame and unsavory pride—shame at being
reduced to the state of a savage tribe, pitifully secluded on a bit of
land they themselves had ravaged; and pride at having these innocent
victims delivered into their hands, whom they would have to instruct
in the harsh realities of the colony. They had endured much but now
had the bleak consolation of not being the endpoint of suffering:
there were others more unready than themselves to whom they could
pass it on. The newcomers were taken in hand immediately. Each of
the islanders, guided by a resemblance to his former self, approached
his counterpart: the soldiers went toward other soldiers, and the artisans, trade by trade, toward those who had just arrived.

Giving the newcomers a tour of the island, showing them where
they would sleep, which is to say, right on the ground under a palm-
leaf awning, and imparting the regulations governing work and the
daily schedule provided a first opportunity to establish ties. The new
arrivals' disappointment, their bewilderment, gave the islanders hope
of offering arrangements whose price could be negotiated.

Just was assigned to lead the most important members of the new
expedition to their lodgings: Du Pont, Richier, and ten Protestant
artisans, emulators of Calvin, dressed in priestly black and full of
their own importance. Villegagnon's orders had been to remove the
knights from their quarters and offer the vacated space to the dignitaries. These cabins, propped against the half-built wall of the fort,
were partially made of stone and roofed with shingles, and in the
general destitution these accommodations were viewed as practically
luxurious. Just presented these cells to the newcomers with the con-

sciousness of doing them a great honor. But when he opened the crude door to the first cubicle for Du Pont, the nobleman's only reaction was a gasp of indignation.

"Are we then to be lodged in this hole?" asked Du Pont.

He was about the same age as Villegagnon but, being of frailer constitution, seemed more worn and ill. Just, full of respect, did not know how to answer.

"This is . . . the best we have," he mumbled.

"What! In two years, with all these craftsmen, you have not been able to build better shelters?"

"That is, the admiral placed priority on our safety," said Just, embarrassed. "We built the fort . . ."

Du Pont lifted his nose toward the partially built ramparts, and the look of contempt he gave them made Just understand all at once how much remained to be done to make them imposing.

"I seem to remember noticing," said Richier in a reedy voice, vibrant like a taut spring, "that Monsieur de Villegagnon has arranged more honorable quarters where he was concerned. You found the time, it appears, to build a palace for him."

"No, not for him," said Just, maintaining his respectful tone. "We needed a government house that would reflect the king's authority over these lands."

"A government house!" said Du Pont condescendingly. "Perhaps, but what right has Sieur de Villegagnon to enjoy the sole use of it?"

On the brink of getting carried away, he received a tap on the arm and a meaningful glance from Richier, which told him that the time for settling the question was not yet ripe.

Du Pont regained control of himself, coughed, and, after taking a breath that would supply him with air for the duration of his visit, entered the first cell. In turn the others each took possession of their cells, with Richier having one to himself and the rest of the Protestants doubling up. After they deposited their effects and re-emerged, looking appalled, Just led them to the half-built fort.

"To avoid any disturbance, the admiral would like work to resume tomorrow. Would you order your men to proceed here immediately following the morning meal? We will assign them to different groups. I will await you here myself to show you your places."

"Our places!" said the new arrivals.

"Does Villegagnon imagine," said Du Pont, puffing out his chest, "that we are his laborers?"

"Not *his* laborers, your lordship," said Just gravely, "but those of Antarctic France. No one is exempted from this work. It is of the utmost importance that the fort should be completed before the rains. Till now we have been spared an attack from the Portuguese . . ."

"Young man," Du Pont started in, "your admiral no doubt excels at organization . . ."

He exchanged an ironic glance with Richier.

". . . but let me tell you that he has no understanding of politics at all. The Portuguese are less likely now than they have ever been to antagonize the French in America. Since the emperor's abdication . . ."

"What!" said Just. "Charles V has abdicated?"

"A year and a half ago. Can it be possible . . . that you had not heard?"

Just's astonishment showed plainly enough that he had not. The new arrivals glanced around them at the island with greater horror still. Its inhabitants were more utterly forsaken than castaways. They were certainly the last civilized men on earth not to have heard any reverberation from the fall of the world's greatest prince.

"Consequently," Du Pont continued, with the patience of a man educating a child, "Spain and the Holy Roman Empire are no longer united. Charles V was not able to bequeath all to his son Philip II, and his brother Ferdinand has taken the imperial crown. All the European powers have signed the peace. The Portuguese are unlikely to touch off a powder keg for . . . this island!"

The news was good, but the last few months of obedience and hard work had made Just a true soldier.

"Never mind," he said with a shake of his head. "As long as the admiral hasn't decided otherwise, we will continue with the fort. Tomorrow I will lead you to your places."

• • •

Night caught everyone in the disorder of late afternoon. Sea chests lay on the beach, and boats plied back and forth. As might have been predicted, ten of the islanders took the opportunity to run away to the mainland, a fact that was only noticed the next day.

But the newcomers were not accustomed to the curfew forced on the islanders by the scarcity of candles. They lit many lanterns and even torches in their rooms. Each of them brandished his lamp or his candle, and the entire island seemed to be celebrating.

While all the lamps were shining brightly, Richier came looking for Just, carrying a huge hurricane lantern, and plucked him by the sleeve.

"Now that it is dark," he whispered, "it is time to land the young ladies."

Just looked at him for a moment as though he had been asked to resume Le Freux's secret and reprehensible trade. But taking the pastor's austere aspect into consideration, he understood that it was just the opposite. Disembarking would entail straddlings and ladder descents that were hardly compatible with the dignity of pure Protestant virgins. Destined for honest marriages, they should not be seen beforehand in positions more suited to Circassian dancers.

"What have you prepared for them by way of quarters?" asked Richier.

As he had a suggestion of his own, he went on: "Couldn't we house them in the government house?"

Just was alarmed at the idea of a bedridden Villegagnon abruptly finding himself in the care of these creatures. But what else to propose? His mind cast desperately about and, leaping from dresses to kilts, arrived at a solution.

"The Scots guards' hut!" he said proudly.

The poor Caledonians had made worse sacrifices. They could all sleep in Villegagnon's antechamber, and the admiral's life would only be the safer.

The young ladies were waiting in one of the ships, closeted in the roundhouse with their governesses. Just accompanied Richier to fetch them. When they entered the room, the two men discovered five slender black figures standing and as many duennas sprawled on chairs. The closed space was suffocatingly hot. When Just entered, the ladies lowered their eyes and assumed modest expressions, while furtively examining the handsome young man who accompanied the pastor. The lights burned brightly aboard the ship as elsewhere, but Just gathered no very clear impression of the young ladies. What struck him in fact were neither their bodies nor their faces but the black sheaths, the ample sleeves, the smell of soap mixed with the acidulous scent of sweat that was not the sweat of men.

The ship was hardly comfortable. Yet Just was horrified at the idea of these delicate creatures being subjected to the rough conditions on the island. The fact that Colombe lived there with him effortlessly and that Indian women had peopled this land alongside Indian men since the earliest times never crossed his mind.

The first flutterings of emotion past, the room filled with cooing voices and the rustling of pleated fabrics, accompanied by the grumbling sighs of the governesses. Ten faces passed in front of Just, who remembered none of them, except the exceedingly crosshatched face of one of the ladies-in-waiting, which made him think of an iguana. He reproached himself for the thought and stared at his feet, red with embarrassment.

Meanwhile the young ladies, whipped by the cold wind, clung in disarray to the ladder down to the waist, emitting little cries.

"Help me carry the last one," said Richier, whom Just had forgotten.

Following in his wake, Just entered a cubby in the roundhouse separated from the main room by a hanging cloth.

"How is she?" the pastor asked the governess sitting by the bed.

"I think she'll need to be carried," she whispered. "Her fever hasn't gone down."

"With this one, who is unwell," said Richier wheedlingly, "it might be best to assign her a vacant cabin next to those you so kindly made available to us."

He made as if to bend over the dark alcove. But his frail body hardly seemed capable of lifting a person, even a girl. Just offered his help, and the pastor exchanged places with him. The patient was wrapped in a large cloak whose hood hid her face. Just reflected that anyone swaddled in such a heavy layer would have to be boiling. He reached his hands under the prone body and felt it flinch. Swiftly he scooped it up, surprised at its lightness.

"Be careful," said Richier.

To dispel any ambiguity, he added, "She is my niece."

Just was already at the door and stepping out onto the deck. A gust of wind swirling around the mast suddenly pushed the patient's hood back as two large lanterns hanging from the boom indiscreetly cast their light on the uncovered face. Framed by long black tresses, the feverish eyes seemed to smile, and the face struck Just as of such great beauty that he almost cried out. A slight tightening of her lips checked him, and he freed a hand to replace her hood, reflecting that one would design a mouth no differently if one wanted to convey the idea of a kiss. The girl did not emerge from the shadows again up to the point that he left her on the threshold of her cell.

CHAPTER 25

The year had been a happy one for Colombe. Unrestricted in her movements, she came and went freely between the island and the mainland. She lived with Just and felt a deep joy at having left childhood and entered adulthood without losing sight of him. She found him handsomer at every turn, laughed with him over a thousand memories, and considered that his new role as a valiant knight suited him well. He showed great energy in their difficult circumstances, and she admired him for that. He was severe without being hard, knew how to inspire men, and his eyes shone with idealism. Every-thing that had passed into excess and almost ridicule in his model, Villegagnon, retained a certain balance and modesty in him, which was a true sign of greatness. The admiral preached chastity, ever rehearsing his same imprecations against woman. Colombe could no longer hear his tirades without a feeling of disgust and rebellion. Just, for his part, adopted the ideal of chastity as a self-discipline yet maintained a definite gentleness toward women: he proved it again and again by his humane treatment of the Indian slave women on the worksite. Within this discipline, Colombe felt comfortable. The whole island had by now guessed that she was a girl. But as her trips to the mainland made her useful and as she was also well liked, no one denounced her to Villegagnon, who persisted in noticing nothing. Thus passed fraternal days during which Colombe and Just, while recognizing their difference in sex, agreed in some way to take no account of it. They gave their love the free and protective scope of a chaste friendship, a camaraderie based on action, a virile knightliness that might, in short, have suited Joan of Arc.

Colombe accepted it because she had no other choice and because it pleased Just. But she would have accepted it less readily if her long absences among the Indians had not filled her with another happiness.

The moment she had come face to face with Paï-Lo, she knew that she had once again found the world of the mainland, and that it was abiding and loyal, when she had thought it vanished and hostile. She retained an unforgettable memory of that first meeting. Following behind Charles, the Englishman, and Quintin, she had reached the wooded highlands overlooking the southern end of the bay. The Sugarloaf appeared tiny from up there, and the high peak that would later be called Corcovado hulked above it. The stifling air of the bay was replaced by a cool breeze from the sea, sharpened by altitude. No boundaries marked the confines of Paï-Lo's realm. One realized one was entering it because the wild tree species, brazil and pine, were gradually interspersed more and more thickly with useful, almost domestic trees: cashews heavy with fruit; copaibas, their trunks oozing a precious balsam; and dense thickets of cotton shrubs. No one knew whether they had been planted at some point or whether, perhaps sensing Paï-Lo's presence, they had advanced toward him, like Orient kings bearing gifts.

Traversing a cool pine wood rustling with dry needles, they came to the foot of a long stairway made of logs. For nearly an hour, they climbed hundreds of soft steps of wood and loose dirt that wound up a shaded hillside through a sumptuous forest. Along the path, groups of marmosets and parrots voiced their acclamations. Farther up, some thirty peacocks extended their colored pennons like directional arrows. The walkers crossed a tribe of Indians descending the stair— naked, as was only proper, and smiling.

Finally they saw the house. Charles had to point it out to them, or they wouldn't have noticed it. It was in fact an arabesque of leafy roofs supported by the trunks of living trees. The natural colonnade of the forest had in a sense been covered, and the house was no more than a set of wooden partitions extending between the boles, lifted by outgrowths, split, raised, and folded by the pressure of the plants to which the thin lattice walls were attached. Yet the whole was orderly. Although doorless, the house had an entrance, to which the stairs led. On the floor of this vestibule, Portuguese tiles had been set into the dirt, featuring an elegant basket of fruit in the center. Large, brightly enameled earthenware jars stood around the perimeter of the room. A jumble of canes, old fruit, and umbrellas was heaped there. Following behind Charles, they penetrated farther into the house. In its shadowy spaces, one forgot the great trees that formed its skeleton. Only a smell of fresh clay and resin reminded them that the structure was but a recess within nature, pacifically ceded to man. Its designer had shown great skill on the one hand in nestling it into the mountain so as to hide it, and on the other in opening it wide to the unobstructed space of the horizon. The view on the far side tumbled over the bluish waves of the forest to the distant bay, which was the color of pale lichens. The great convulsions of the coast, the sharp hills like the jawbone of a dog, seemed laughable from this height, no more than a child's tantrum. And to the west, the endless expanse of mountain crests showed the bay to be only a minute indentation on the margins of a vast continent.

The beauty of the view to some extent eclipsed the house's interior. But when one turned again to the half light of the rooms, one was no less struck with astonishment. They were furnished with objects that were at once familiar and surprising: an enormous grimacing effigy, ripped from the prow of a ship and draped in red and gold, leather chests with decorative bronze studs, French enamels, a service of silver plate. All this lay about almost pell-mell, a prey to disorder and familiar use by animals. Two parrots had taken possession of an open drawer, high on a bureau. A train of insects linked the worked wood to the dirt floor, where roots snaked and burrows gaped open. At dusk, toads started trilling rhythmically by the dozens in the half light, like so many little beating hearts torn from sacred breasts.

At the time of their first visit, Païve-Lo was ill. They were greeted by his wife, a grave, slender Indian woman, wrapped in a white cotton shawl that made her look like a Roman patrician. Many other women, both young and old, came and went about the house. They laughed and made no distinction between mistress and servant. Quintin's eyes shone at seeing so many potential converts. Colombe had to call him back, if not to reason, at least to caution. Martial-looking Tupi warriors arrived and departed. Sometimes admitted to the room where Païñ-Lo lay, they emerged afterward brooding on his advice. The house was so lightly built that despite the opacity of the partitions and the many objects in each room, one could hear every noise, as in a forest. The shouts of invisible children gave clear indication that Païñ-Lo's domain included many other huts tucked into the woods and a numerous household.

Quintin and Colombe's first encounter with the master occurred one morning. Charles, who had come to fetch the two, announced with a big grin that Païñ-Lo was feeling better. He was waiting for them on the log terrace that extended from the main room. Built without an awning, this simple wooden projection held out its open palm among the trunks of sycamores and pines against the sparkling background of the distant bay. Any person had the look of an apparition here, but Païñ-Lo was striking in the extreme. Everything about him was frail: his fragile body, his thin neck, his large hands. Yet like a stubborn assailant who shrugs off shot and arrows, he seemed capable of holding death at bay longer than his fate had ordained. Païñ-Lo was not simply old. He was the very image of Time. All that is revealed when the years have worn a life down to its heart and spirit was visible in his wrinkle-lined face. His features nestled in the calm cradle of a silky white beard. Two clear eyes shone happily from their puckered purse, seeming to have banished all reproach, all bitterness, and all hatred, to look outward with limpid curiosity.

After greeting the two new arrivals, Païñ-Lo turned toward Colombe and, placing his gaze in the fire of her blond eyes, said, "So, I am seeing 'Sun-Eye.'"

At the sound of these words, Colombe felt she had returned among the people she was seeking. Even Païñ-Lo's intonation was similar to Paraguaçu's, and she was convinced he must have learned her nickname from her friend.

But before entering on the subject of Indians, Païñ-Lo methodically answered Quintin's prepared questions, introducing himself and speaking to them of their mission.

They were immediately struck by the fact that he truly did know everything. From Villegagnon's landing on the island to his most recent wrangle with Le Freux and Martin, Paï-Lo was acquainted with every detail of the colony. He dispelled the mystery straight away:

"What can you expect," he said simply, "the Indians tell me everything. They know me. I am the oldest European in this land."

"You were shipwrecked, no doubt?" said Quintin.

"As extraordinary as it may seem to you, that is not the case. I came here of my own will, and I stayed here by choice."

"You were a merchant?"

Paï-Lo, so thin beside the gigantic trunks of the trees, rubbed his eyes to rid them of a veil of weariness.

"Not in the least," he said. "My name is Laurent de Mehun, and the Indians turned that into Paï-Lo, that is, 'Father Laurent.' My parents, as it happens, belonged to the minor nobility. They instructed me in the quadrivium, and I became a doctor in philosophy. I was fascinated by geography. It was in the company of Norman traders that I came here in the opening days of this century."

"But the Portuguese," said Quintin, "only arrived here in 1501!"

"Yes, and if you had arrived here even two years ago, you would have met one of the men they left here on that first visit. As you know, they landed a little higher up the coast, toward Bahia."

Paï-Lo gestured to the north, and with the vast view of the continent before them, it seemed that hundreds of leagues could be indicated by a slight spread of the fingers.

"Cabral, the leader of this first expedition, enlisted a large number of reprieved convicts, because no one else wanted to gamble his life on the adventure. When he landed in Brazil, he erected a cross on the beach and ordered two of his convicts to be left there. It was horrible. The poor wretches yelled and clung to the gunwales of the boats until the sailors struck their hands with the oars to make them let go. There they were alone and terrified on this unknown coast."

"And you were already here?"

"I had been here a year. I refused to return with the Normans. When the Indians found the two Portuguese, they brought them to me. One of them lived here until his death. The other went to São Salvador when the Portuguese founded that city."

"Then it was you," said Colombe, "who discovered Brazil!"

"That has strictly no meaning. Only the Europeans would have the presumption to believe that this continent was waiting for their arrival to exist."

Colombe hung her head. She was angry at herself for having used such a naive expression.

"As far as I'm concerned," said the old man kindly, "it was this country that discovered me."

Such was Paï-Lo, and in the course of subsequent long walks and conversations they learned to love him.

When they asked him why he had allowed Le Freux to extend his rotten influence over the island to the point of practically destroying it, he answered, "In these forests, evil fights evil. The weak species that manage to survive can only hope that their enemies will kill each other. Why should I have more sympathy for Villegagnon with his ideas of conquest than for the go-betweens of the coast, who are admittedly bandits?"

Yet when they visited him a second time two months later, Paï-Lo agreed to help them resupply the island. He had spoken to the Indians and arranged for a tribe on the bay to provide goods that they would come to pick up, taking care to avoid Martin's ambushes.

"I'm doing it for you, Sun-Eye," Paï-Lo said. "And for your brother, who treats the Indians humanely on your island. But he's the only one who does so."

The only request Paï-Lo had granted with good grace was to seek news of Paraguaçu and her kin. The tribe had passed that way on its flight at the beginning of the epidemic, but he did not know where it had gone afterward. And despite his every effort, he turned up no new information.

They were on their third visit to him, and the tribe had still not been found. Perhaps it had succumbed to fever. Perhaps it had fled unwarily into enemy territory. Farther south, the Maracajá, allies of the Portuguese, pitilessly attacked the Tupi who strayed into their territory.

On each visit, beyond the time they spent traveling, Colombe and Quintin stayed for long weeks with Paï-Lo. His house no longer kept any secrets from them. They knew its every corner, terrace, and tunnel. Its most bizarre furnishings had become familiar to them. Paï-Lo collected there everything that had been deposited along the coast by shipwrecks. Whenever a ship grounded on the reefs, the Indians loaded any chests it contained onto their backs, along with any papers, objects, and sculpted pieces, and made the climb up to the old man's house, in theory to make him an offering of these objects. If they discovered any survivors, they brought them along too. Païe-Lo supplied the Indians with everything they needed and, without giving them any orders, showed them his way of life. These men, now his loyal partisans, were then free to go wherever they wanted. Some stayed with him, as had the Flemish cook who prepared sausages and braised knuckles in the style of Antwerp. Others dispersed around the bay, forming so many points where Païe-Lo's gentle influence extended.

Aside from his present wife, the patriarch had had many female companions, always keeping to Indian customs and never departing from the rules the natives respected. He had raised a large number of children, and his kin were so numerous that everywhere along the bay were Tupi hunters who claimed descent from him. In the forest, he had left a trace of blue in the fierce eyes of naked warriors. Seeing them, the Europeans could never have imagined how full of their own blood these natives were.

When the ships carrying the Protestants arrived in the bay, Colombe was on her third visit to Païe-Lo's, again with Quintin. She had arrived almost four weeks earlier, and her stay was coming to an end. She was with the women one morning, learning to knot feathers into a fabric, when Païe-Lo had her summoned. She found the patriarch in the company of two Tupi warriors, their split lips distended by large plugs.

"My nephew, Avati," said Païe-Lo pointing to one of the Indians. "He has just climbed all the way here from Copacabana to tell me that a convoy of ships has arrived in the bay and is making its way toward the island."

"The Portuguese!" said Colombe, suddenly imagining that Just was in danger.

"Apparently not," said Païe-Lo, shaking his head. "There has been no cannon fire from these ships, and if there had been any sounds of battle, we would have heard them even from here. I believe it must be the reinforcements Villegagnon sent for."

Then, looking at his gnarled hand, he added, "Alas."

Quintin arrived at that moment, all out of breath.

"Still preaching the Gospel?" asked the patriarch laughingly. He knew all about the little man's missionary ardor and, like everyone else in the village, found it highly amusing.

"Perhaps you would rather stay here to see how matters turn out," he said. "You are free to do so."

But Colombe could hardly contain her impatience.

"If you would like to leave now, Avati will take you. The go-betweens are growing more and more dangerous along the coast. Follow his advice, and he will keep you from falling into their hands."

For the third time, Colombe and Quintin said good-bye to the old man and plunged down toward the sunny bay.

CHAPTER 26

Once recovered from his indisposition, Villegagnon sent word to the ministers and to Sieur du Pont that he would welcome them officially at the government house the following day. The admiral and the newcomers would then proceed together to the small square where prayers were held, to celebrate the Eucharist at long last.

Du Pont lent himself ill-humoredly to this meeting, wearing a blue doublet he had kept clean for the occasion. Villegagnon, in contrast to his usual untidiness, wore an impeccably washed tunic bearing the Cross of Malta. Just made a dignified lieutenant, squeezed into a velvet jerkin confected by the tailor the previous day. Richier and Chartier, the pastors, struck a dissonant note dressed all in black.

In truth, the newcomers' gravity repeatedly disconcerted Villegagnon. He had been kept from greeting them by his illness. But now that he was well again, he showed a manifest delight at their presence and was surprised not to see them share it.

"My dear friends," he cried out at the sight of his guests, "I pray you, be seated."

Du Pont drew back at these words as though bitten by a venomous insect. He pushed away the chair that was brought for him with all the energy he would have used to deflect a dagger from his throat. The conversation was conducted standing.

"How was your crossing?" asked Villegagnon, more and more surprised.

"It couldn't have been better," said Du Pont coldly.

Meanwhile he looked around him, noting all the things that could be counted luxuries in comparison to the accommodations given to him: the four-poster bed, the table and pitchers, the books ... Since the attempt on Villegagnon's life, a few improvements had been made to the government house, particularly with a view to making it safer. Its walls were of stone, with shutters of thick wood and a floor of palm trunks planed with a hoe, which felt soft underfoot.

"And in France, were you able to see Coligny?" the admiral asked.

"Admiral Coligny," said Du Pont with the same offended look that puzzled Villegagnon deeply, "is my neighbor. My estate, Corguilleray, lies near Châtillon, which is his property. He not only received us, he selected us to proceed on this mission."

Villegagnon saw nothing in this he might object to, saving the man's tone.

"I am pleased to learn," he said, "that new ideas are no longer persecuted in France."

"These past two years, the Church of the Truth has spread there actively," Richier interposed.

The unction he used in forming his words gave his arrogance a patina of gentleness.

"And it will grow even more hardily in Antarctic France!" said Villegagnon enthusiastically.

For a second, he was on the point of offering his guests a drink, but he remembered the forthcoming sacrament and was glad he had said nothing.

"What sort of France?" asked Du Pont, squinching his eyes.

"Antarctic. It was the idea of a cosmographer who was here, Abbé Thevet. He suggested 'equinoctial,' then settled on 'Antarctic.'"

"Thevet ..." said Du Pont. "Is that not the man who brought back the herb he causes to be smoked by all around him? He calls it 'angoumoisine,' being a native of Angoulême, and argues like a dog with Nicot, who claims to have gotten it from the Portuguese first."

This behavior hardly cast Thevet in a serious light, and Villegagnon regretted having mentioned his name.

"Has your lieutenant given you the news, about the emperor?" asked Du Pont, motioning toward Just.

"His abdication. Yes! A gift of God. Then you are quite certain that the Portuguese . . ."

"Will leave us in peace."

Villegagnon exchanged brief glances with the nobleman. Suddenly he realized why Du Pont's presence there seemed strange. If Coligny was not afraid for the colony, then why had he sent this man-at-war here and what promises had he made him? He felt a flood of suspicion, which he tried to dispel.

The truth never even crossed his mind. Far from being made to come by Coligny, Du Pont had in fact intrigued shamelessly to be chosen for the mission. Ambition was a factor, but nature had actually forced his hand. The poor captain was horribly afflicted by hemorrhoids, which left him no peace. To distract his mind from them, he was ready to take part in any battle as long as he did not have to reach it on horseback. As he said unsmilingly, it was his fondest hope to die standing.

"Father," said Villegagnon, turning toward Richier, "I have led prayers unassisted all this year. You might say that I have assumed the roles of Caesar and the pope. I willingly relinquish the latter to you."

This was his way of declaring unequivocally that he intended to retain the former.

"Now, if you like," he went on, "we will gladly follow you to celebrate the sacrament of the Lord's Supper."

Villegagnon knew enough, since the Zwingli affair and his stay in Ferrara, to banish the word "Mass" and use the modern term in its place. Richier nodded his agreement.

"You will see," said the admiral, "how well this island is suited to the practice of a pure religion, in keeping with the ancient customs of Our Lord's own day."

This apology for the island's simplicity, which the Reformers could only applaud, cut short the criticisms they had prepared about their primitive living conditions. Without a pause, Villegagnon lunged for the door, opened it to the sunlight, and, taking a deep breath of the light-filled air, dragged everyone with him outdoors.

On the square, the residents of the island were gathered for the ceremony. The old inhabitants and the new maintained their distance and looked at each other without friendliness. The gauntness, grime, and laxity of the former struck the new arrivals as scandalous, and they swore to never let themselves fall into such a state. Whereas the health, strength, and good hygiene of the newly landed group struck the old colonists as so grave an insult to their sufferings that they could not long endure it.

The service called on God to arbitrate these differences. And each was surprised to see Him answer the call. The ministers' black garb, their grave expressions, their unctuous manners suddenly found their use, becoming a miraculous lure for the Holy Ghost. Those who had been longest from home remembered their fervent last ceremony on the quays of Le Havre and wept. Since then, neither Thevet's distracted prayers nor the disciplinarian orisons, led like a charge by Villegagnon, had awakened the least sentiment of piety in them. In their hand-to-hand with Nature, it was she who had continually imposed her strength: they had become the playthings of her sun or her rains, her monsters, her vegetation, her salt tide. No God had come to take their side in this battle. And here, all of a sudden, by the grace of these pastors, He showed that He had not abandoned them. The men raised their heads and looked at the bay in a wholly new way. Its silent beaches, its stifling jungles, its sharp hills, and especially the Sugarloaf drew back in fear before the great quiet radiance of the Creator. The assembly looked around them now with an appetite for vengeance and a glimmer of pride in their eyes.

In the pastors' liturgy, the slowly recited prayers had a conversational tone: there was no need to raise one's voice as He was directly among them. Everything about the ceremony seemed both new and familiar. More texts from the Bible were used than in the Roman Catholic service. The Virgin and the saints no longer interposed their troubling shadows; thus the faithful could benefit directly from their divine host and His son.

When the time came for communion, it was performed simply and naturally, as though around a table. Yet the two elements that were its instrument had become so rare on the island—the white bread of the host and especially the wine—that the physical effect of consuming them convinced the men that a divinity had entered their bodies.

Villegagnon followed the whole ceremony in a welter of tears. The

joy, the shock, the sense of having triumphed and of owing it all to
this God of simplicity and delight—the feelings all melted together
to provoke in him the most pressing enthusiasm. He was grateful to
the pastors for not requiring any prosternations or other great physical demonstrations, as he would certainly have been incapable of
restraint and thrown himself at their feet sobbing. But at the sharing
of the Eucharist, he motioned all the same for a small cushion of
purple velvet to be placed on the ground, which Just had brought
from the government house on his orders. He received the bread and
wine kneeling on this square, less for the comfort it provided than to
interpose a screen between himself and the ground, to ward off any
evil spells of nature's and to allow himself to dwell, however low he
might be, in the pure and holy space of the heavens.

•   •   •

Little by little, the two populations mixed in the narrow space of the
island. The activity there was once again so intense that it seemed
overpopulated. And the differences between the two groups tended
to lessen: the newcomers, placed on a diet of manioc, started to
assume a gray complexion, while the older settlers, reinvigorated by
the wines the Protestant convoy had captured, walked less steadily,
perhaps, but with a new confidence.

Work on the fortress resumed, and the walls had almost reached
the prescribed height. It had only taken ten days or so to make this
progress, proving that much had been accomplished beforehand and
that only the colonists' despair had made them think the project
impossible.

The only breach in the regular fabric of daily life had been the
announced departure of some thirty of the newcomers. As one of
their ships was obliged to return immediately to fulfill its owners'
contract, these few recalcitrants had declared that nothing would
make them stay at Fort Coligny any longer. Villegagnon would have
dealt summarily with the matter, but Du Pont took the side of the
fractious group and they were allowed to leave. It set a bad example
for the others. Yet the newcomers had arrived so recently and the
older settlers so long ago that they were all either still unsusceptible
to or quite beyond nostalgia and regarded these defections with
indifference.

Everyone went back to work.

The presence of women marked a new era, and the first convoy's circumstances receded into prehistory. Those able to look back to the time when Le Freux had supplied the island with female captives could measure the full extent of the changes. The women from Geneva displayed none of the licentious nudity of those submissive bawds. They were serious and more than dressed. But therein precisely lay their charm. Toward the end of every afternoon, they emerged from their hut on the arms of their governesses, like chicks hatched out by the heat. A strict system, instituted by Villegagnon, ensured that the path was kept clear for their passage. The Indian slaves were inspected to see that no improper part of their anatomy had been left uncovered for the strolling ladies to see. The laborers were required to button their shirts. Even the little monkeys capering on the rubble heaps were chased away with stones so that they might expose their blue bottoms elsewhere.

Then the young ladies would appear. They wore black or gray dresses, and this simple nuance sufficed to make them distinctive. The colonists were accustomed to the violent colors of the bay. The blues of the sea, the greens of the jungle, the yellow of the parrots, and the red of the saturated mud were all aspects of the natural horror that held them in its grasp. The black and gray of the young ladies' dresses were pure human inventions and triggered in the colonists a vast appetite for civilization. None of these young ladies was positively pretty, according to strict canons of beauty. Shunning all artifice, they allowed their faces to be adorned with pimples rather than paint. Poor diets had made them either scrawny or plump. In short, none of these Venuses, individually considered, was without her faults. Yet their perfection leapt to the eye. For they were each of them—and collectively all the more so—the idea of woman, as Villegagnon would have said. And what is more, the Pure Idea of the Pure Woman. In this world where nature spared no one the sight of its corruption, where everything interpenetrated, raped, and impregnated everything else, they were virginity, the unique devotion of a being to purity, that is, women with whom love could become prayer.

Nothing exhausted the laborers so much as seeing the young ladies pass and not being able to throw themselves upon them.

It was unclear who had established the route of their walk. It would certainly have been difficult to provide them with a deserted area for strolling. But there was also no necessity to lead them along the narrow paths of the construction site, where they had to brush past the wretched laborers. The arrangement betrayed the contradictory intention of parading the young ladies' modesty before everyone, and at the same time signaling that they were for the taking. The reason for their presence on the island was still marriage. And so long as they remained without a mate, they had as little occupation as a mason without a trowel.

Not surprisingly, requests came flooding in to Villegagnon. He hastened to ratify two engagements on the very first day, with two young men from the first convoy who served as his lackeys. That would give him time to inspect the other candidacies, which were numerous and importunate. The situation gave the admiral the pleasant certainty that even the duennas, though brought on other business, would also find takers.

Yet of the six young ladies who had landed, one remained invisible. Since Just had carried her onto the longboat and brought her ashore, she had remained secluded in the straw hut assigned to her. This absence nagged at Villegagnon, for it threatened to remove one of the rare and precious occasions for marriage he had been granted. Just, for once, did not wait for the admiral's orders. After a few days, he suggested that they should perhaps seek news of her. His sincere concern struck him afterward as a ruse, when Villegagnon put the task of inquiring after the young lady into his hands.

The hut where she lived with her governess was the last in a long row, toward the western redoubt. A cluster of bamboos had once grown in this spot, and a few stray shoots still poked up around the walls. When he arrived, Just paused in indecision for a long moment outside. The cabin had a curtain instead of a door, and he was uncertain how to announce his presence. From inside he could hear the tiny plucked chords of a musical instrument.

Just coughed, and the noise that emerged from his throat overwhelmed the melody. There was silence in the hut, followed by whispering. Finally the lady-in-waiting drew back the curtain with a stern look on her face.

"I've come," Just mumbled, "to get some news of the young lady."

Then he added, as though brandishing a shield, "On behalf of the admiral."

"She is better," said the matron curtly before dropping the curtain and disappearing.

Just felt the awkwardness of this rebuff. He stood in place for a time, while the whispering started up again inside. Finally the doorway opened.

"If you would care to see her," said the duenna with an amiable grimace.

Just entered. The cabin's narrow space had been divided in two by a hanging cloth. In one corner was an open virginal, the sheets of a score fluttering above its narrow keyboard. A straw pallet, rolled up on a chest, was likely the duenna's. There was no trace, in this antechamber, of the young lady. But when the governess drew back the cloth partition after giving a last glance around to the other side, she was revealed in the midst of all her effects. Open chests, a table stacked with books beside the little window, a porcelain *nécessaire* for toiletries, a few dresses hanging from the rib of a palm frond that had been wedged between the stones of the wall to serve as a clothes rack—all this formed an agreeable decor that swept away the cabin's bareness. The girl was seated on the edge of the bed, her hands on her knees and her eyes cast down. She allowed Just the time to drink in her beauty freely and, this time, in full daylight. A harmony in black, reprising the designs on her dress, was provided by her pulled-back hair and slender eyebrows. Her white skin alternated with these dark keys, as on the keyboard of her instrument. He saw her regular nose, her delicate chin, and the sides of the forehead where, in a dark-haired woman, down traces a light shadow above the face. As though all this were not enough, the young lady raised her eyes and trained on him the two muzzles of her pupils.

"Thank you, sir," she said in a steady, rounded, almost deep voice, "for not abandoning us."

"The admiral," said Just—who had forgotten the very existence of the word "I"—" "is concerned about the state of your health."

The girl sighed and, extending her long hand toward the edge of the bed, gently smoothed a wrinkle in the fabric.

"My health is better, thank you. But . . ."

Just winced. It seemed to him that she was on the point of crying.

". . . But I don't yet feel well enough to go out."

"There is no hurry."

It might have been the idea of seeing her alone again, but Just had spoken the sentence without thinking.

"Ah, sir!" said the young lady, turning her eyes to him again, which he saw to be full of tears.

Just could think of no appropriate response.

"You look so kind," she said. "I believe one might talk to you."

"Certainly. If there is anything I can do . . ."

She shook her head, but gently, so as not to jar her features.

"You are not unaware, I suppose, of why they take us on walks or of what they plan to do with us," she said, proudly raising her head. "For all that I am the niece of a pastor, I am no exception. I will soon be put to auction with the rest."

"But why did you agree to come?" asked Just, who saw in her distress an echo of his own rebellion at having been tricked into coming. "Was the truth hidden from you?"

"No, sir, I was informed of it, but I had no choice. My parents died during the Protestant persecutions ten years ago. I was only spared the stake because of my uncle. And when he decided to come here, there was no question of my staying on alone without him."

Having roasted her admirer on one side, the young girl decided to attack the other. She changed her tone and her mood suddenly. With a gay demeanor and a lilting voice, yet with no lapse in her deportment, she continued: "But do forgive me! I have been going on about my own life . . . I am boring you, perhaps. And I have not even introduced myself. My name is Aude Maupin, from Lons-le-Saunier. My lady-in-waiting is Mademoiselle Chantal."

First one, then the other curtsied elegantly to him. Just responded awkwardly, as Villegagnon had taught him nothing on this subject. He gave his name.

"You were not able even to attend the Lord's Supper yesterday?" he suggested gently.

"I would very much have liked to attend, for I have great need of the sacrament. But if I made an exception for that appearance, I would be forfeit to all the others as well."

Just was as indignant as she. To think that this pure creature might be haggled over and paraded with the other lambs before men trying to decide whether to take them as wives.

"Perhaps we might exempt you from this practice," said Just. "I will speak to the admiral. He has excellent relations with your uncle, and perhaps . . ."

Aude made a face, and Just, afraid of displeasing her, stopped himself short.

"Excellent, in a manner of speaking," she said sharply. "But I am not so sure they will remain excellent for long."

"Because of your living conditions?" asked Just. "Oh! I know, but you must believe me that we will make every effort to improve them."

"It's not only that," said the young lady, her face growing more and more severe. Her dark eyes shone wonderfully when her expression hardened.

Just grew alarmed.

"Your admiral," she said gravely, "must mend his ways."

"Mend his ways? But how?"

"His conduct during the divine service was highly suspect, according to my uncle. There are remains of idolatry in him that must be plucked out immediately."

"Idolatry!"

"Did he not kneel on a square of velvet to receive communion?"

"Certainly. But what is the harm in that?"

Aude glared at him. But an instant later, she seemed to dispel these thoughts with a shrug of her shoulders.

"My uncle," she said, "will easily put an end to these outrages."

Just was on the point of responding, of arguing the point, but she was already smiling and passing on to other matters.

"I am touched, sir, by your kindness. It seems to me that, with your protection, I might feel safe enough to go out a bit. Do you know when the next service will be?"

"I believe that your uncle and the admiral are making arrangements for two wedding ceremonies, which will be celebrated together."

"Chantal, did you hear that?" said the young lady. "The Lord's Supper will be celebrated again soon. Oh, if you only knew, sir, how much comfort communion brings me, and how much I miss it."

"I will accompany you, if you like."

"Oh, thank you! Thank you!" she said, taking hold of Just's hands.

This burst of enthusiasm lasted only a brief second. Yet he felt the warm pressure of her slender palms on his hands for a long time. The rest of the day was spent in daydreams.

CHAPTER 27

Meanwhile the shock of new ideas was spreading from mind to mind across the island. The original colonists had at first seen nothing in the Genevans' arrival except material assistance and increased numbers. With proximity, this perception was gradually replaced by another: those who had just disembarked had not only the naiveté of men in good health, but also bizarre ideas and unusual beliefs. These were met during the chaotic enthusiasm of the first days with a mixture of deference and disregard. But one day the word "Huguenot" was spoken, and everyone started to look at them more closely.

Some of the men, former prisoners whom Villegagnon had freed, were already familiar with Protestant ideas. It was their seduction by Luther's writings that had cost them their freedom. But that first movement of the Reformation had been quashed twenty years before. The former prisoners of conscience, never having known anything but persecution and hiding, looked admiringly at the new Huguenots, who ruled in Geneva, organized reformed churches more or less everywhere in France, and came freely to the American continent with the recommendation of Henry II's closest ministers. The convicts quickly sided with the followers of the new religion.

But many of the others balked. They needed preaching, convincing. The pastors gathered groups everywhere on the island whom they instructed in the new doctrine. Bibles circulated. Texts were commentated. Fed up with the jungle, the sea, the Sugarloaf, the colonists threw themselves voluptuously into theological discussions, where they once more found the precious distinctions of human ideation and the very essence of civilization.

But this same proselytizing aroused the indignation of a third group: those who categorically refused to forswear the Catholic faith. Dom Gonzagues was the spokesman for this strict sect.

"Never," he said to Villegagnon, his little beard trembling, "will I abandon the Virgin Mary."

True, he did not like clergymen and found them to have many faults. But when all his Catherines and Marguerites had so unfairly spurned him, the Mother of God, for her part, had always looked on him compassionately, and he did not intend to prove ungrateful.

Villegagnon calmed him as best he could. To tell the truth, he too felt that it was at least tactless of the Huguenots to require a profession of faith from those who joined them. There was no need for conversion: the beliefs were so similar. Was not the Reformed Religion a return to early days? He had said it at the time of the first Lord's Supper, and the words had seemed to appease everyone.

The admiral in turn set madly to work to bolster this ecumenical doctrine. He deplored that his library was so limited and his memory so weak. But with what he had—and he knew thousands of pages by heart, or very nearly—he could assemble solid arguments against one side and the other, with a view to bringing them closer together.

He went at this debate with the same attitude he brought to armed combat. This was his way; he approached everything as an athlete. Just sometimes helped him far into the night, reading old texts by candlelight and recopying fragments. The admiral was delighted at this abrupt return of curiosity, of culture, of speculative thought. In the process, he neglected construction on the island completely.

It was Colombe's return, discreet as it was, that provoked the first crisis. By the time she had traveled back from Paï-Lo's, avoiding the ambushes along the coast set by Martin's henchmen and the tribes he controlled, the Huguenots were already well established. At first the new ships, the massive reinforcements to the island, and the travelers' good health made Colombe rejoice. Though she didn't share her brother's dreams for Antarctic France, she could only be pleased at seeing an end to privation and fear. But Quintin broke the spell, gripping her tightly as they set foot on the beach.

"No!" he cried out, suddenly pale. "It isn't possible. It can't be the same ones. Help! Save me!"

And he ran full tilt to hide behind the panniers of sand.

"What's happened to you?" asked Colombe when she caught up with him.

"Those men in black . . ." Quintin mumbled, his teeth chattering.

"Yes?"

Colombe had suspected that he was going to cry, as he had not given himself the pleasure at Païchi-Lo's for a long time. But she had not expected his noisy blubbering, his spasms of terror.

"I must get back to the mainland," he announced.

He was already walking toward the boats. Colombe stopped him.

"Tell me. If there's a danger, it's a danger for all of us."

Quintin seemed to come to himself. He sniffed, wiped his cheeks with the back of his hand, flecked as it was with grains of sand, and took a deep breath.

"It was the year before our departure," he began, "and I was in Lyons."

"But aren't you from Rouen?"

"Yes, but that year I was traveling. A small group of us had gathered around an extraordinary man. He was a Spanish physician, you can't imagine how good a man he was. He knew everything. His Latin was absolutely pure, and his books were marvels of intelligence. His name was Michael."

"Michael what?"

"Michael Servetus," said Quintin, no longer trying to stop his tears. "The French condemned his books. What could be more normal in a country that has no understanding of truth?"

"And the men in black?" asked Colombe, unwilling to prolong the situation.

"Poor Servetus thought he would find help in Geneva. I accompanied him to the gates of the city. That's where I saw them. All these pastors, these men in black."

"But you too, Quintin, you too are in black."

"No, it's not the same. These are the very ones I saw in Geneva. One of the oarsmen confirmed it."

He stuck his head around the sand basket. Richier stood at the entrance to the beach on a little wooden platform, preaching inaudibly.

"They burned him, Colombe."

"Who?"

"Servetus. Calvin disagreed with his views and treated him even more harshly than the French would have. He had him burned at the stake, do you realize?"

"I thought the Huguenots stood for liberty."

"Their own! But the terrible Théodore de Bère wrote a pamphlet the following year called *Of the Right to Punish Heretics*. Believe me, I have to go. I won't stay another moment on the same island as those men."

Colombe spent almost an hour bringing him to reason. She promised to arrange for him to leave soon on a new mission. In the end, he agreed to stay hidden rather than set out on a journey through the forest alone.

Looking around the island for Just, Colombe was surprised at what she saw. Work on the fort had progressed but now seemed to have stopped. Everywhere were knots of men animatedly discussing such inhabitual topics as the immortality of the soul, salvation through grace, and predestination. On the construction site, preachers held forth spontaneously. Solitary walkers along the shore now clutched a Bible under one arm. It seemed as if the whole colony had suddenly plunged into deep reflection.

But this reflection had nothing pacific or fraternal about it. Hostile glances shot back and forth between groups. The place where the pastors and Huguenots lived was separate and seemed to be under surveillance. Far from leading to harmony and optimism, this spiritual revival seemed to be aggravating feelings of animosity, isolation, and anxiety. When she finally found Just at the government house, she saw to her chagrin that Villegagnon and he were caught up in the same fever of reasoning.

The admiral greeted Colombe amiably and asked to hear the story of her stay with Paï-Lo. But the subject seemed to interest him little, whereas the things she had noticed since arriving back on the island seemed genuinely to open his eyes.

"Blood and wounds!" he said. "You're right, Colin. We are facing anarchy."

He seized a sheaf of papers he had blackened with notes and started to assemble them.

"It is all now clear to me," he announced. "Or almost. In any event we will gather all the pastors together tomorrow and debate the question. Enough of these quarrels. We must provide our men with certainties and start work again."

Colombe stayed for dinner at the government house with Just. She found him odd and changed. Physically he was the same, though perhaps more attentive to his appearance than before. Villegagnon had lent him razors a long time back, and he hadn't used them. But now his cheeks were smooth, while a neatly trimmed beard followed the line of his jaw in the Spanish style. And he hardly paid any attention to her.

She was used to his being taciturn and quiet. But this seemed a different quality of abstractedness, though she couldn't explain it. Her intuition told her that it wasn't reserve but that he was wholly absorbed by some other preoccupation, one she knew nothing about.

The solemn interview between Villegagnon, Du Pont, and the ministers was quickly organized, particularly as the Protestants had many grievances of their own to discuss. They arrived at the government house in the middle of the morning. The admiral had decided to receive them alone, as he feared an outburst from Dom Gonzagues on the subject of religion. Yet he asked Just to remain with him so that there would be a witness to the conversation.

From the moment the Huguenots entered, it was clear that the conversation would be a difficult one. They had not been back to the government house since the day of the first Lord's Supper. Du Pont, from the way he looked at the furnishings and decoration there, clearly nourished a ripe hatred for this pomp, from which he was debarred. Villegagnon, ignoring the nobleman's now-known disability, sat down in an armchair and invited the others to do likewise. The pastors complied, accustomed to leaving Du Pont to practice his self-discipline alone. He remained standing.

The admiral inquired first after their health and accommodations. His solicitude, interpreted as a provocation, met only with grunts.

"My dear brothers," the admiral went on with a grave air, "I would like to discuss what has been preoccupying me. In brief, the work is no longer progressing. I believe we need to re-establish order. There is too much arguing on this island. Theological ardor is a great thing, I grant. But it must not obstruct the demands of life, of survival. For without its fortress, Antarctic France remains at the mercy of its innumerable enemies."

Richier allowed his eyes to wander across the room, feigning indifference. But when he reached the Virgin by Titian, he started as though he had touched an electric eel, and his gaze, tottering, returned to Villegagnon.

"Among the diverse beliefs present on this island, I think there is more commonality than conflict. The crux is the marvelous goodwill that makes man a work of God. I believe in man, and so do you, I am certain. And as men are reasonable, we may give them reasons for their belief, by bringing out what forms the common basis in our beliefs. Thus may each man, without betraying himself, look with respect on others."

Met by hostile silence from his audience, Villegagnon left them the floor so as to learn their thoughts.

"We quite agree with the need to restore order here," said Du Pont in contemptuous tones. "That was our very first thought upon arriving. But we have not had an easy time of it. By making us perform donkey work from the start, you have tried to neutralize us. And you reserve the use of this government house for yourself alone, when it should be the symbol of a shared power. What do you expect from us?"

Villegagnon, pricked with indignation, opted to remain calm: "In the first place I believe that sermons should be limited. It seems to me that half an hour a day suffices to remind a man of his duties toward God. It also strikes me that the sermons should be moderate in content. So as not to offend certain men who remain attached to tradition, I believe we must ban insults aimed at the pope—for whom I have no fondness, as you know—and at the Church in general."

Du Pont tried to interrupt. The admiral indicated that he wished to finish.

"Finally, I sincerely believe that no abjurations or conversions are necessary. Better to unite all in Christ than create divisions between men who believe in Him."

"We bring together those who know and practice the truth of the Gospel," Richier objected severely. "I quite agree with you that we must suppress the spirit of reasoning and doubt on the island, because it obstructs the serene acceptance of the Word of God."

"I was certain," said Villegagnon with a rush of enthusiasm, "that we would agree on this point."

"The fact of it," said Richier, unmoved by the other's joviality, "is that by offering man the Bible, by giving him free access to the sacred texts, we have taken the risk of confronting him with his own nullity. And we did immediately see madmen who claimed to interpret the Word in their own way and who drew absurd conclusions. Some even claimed that if man cannot be saved by his works, it is useless for him to make the least effort to improve himself. Let man kill, steal, revel: only God can bestow His grace on man and redeem him, if He wants, from his lustfulness."

"I know those fanatics," said Villegagnon. "We had a band of Anabaptists on this very island."

"Where are they?" asked Du Pont sharply, as though ready to draw his sword.

"They are said to be living naked in the jungle and to have returned to the state of cannibalism."

His audience sat in horrified silence.

"That is why freedom is nothing without explanation," said Richier, relieved that the Anabaptists had so neatly prepared the way for his conclusion. "We cannot offer the Gospel without at the same time requiring a profession of faith to bring the believer within the safe confines of a Church that orders his faith and regulates his conduct."

"I readily concede the necessity for a Church," said Villegagnon. "But you must agree that in general—and even more pertinently on this small island—it is superfluous to have two."

Richier signaled his approval by an imperceptible nod.

"We should easily reach a compromise by examining each point," the admiral went on, reinvigorated by these first exchanges. "For instance, the celibacy of ministers: there is nothing in the Gospels to forbid the marriage of priests, and that is a decision on which we should reasonably find agreement . . ."

"Stop this blasphemy!" interrupted Du Pont.

From his tone, from his way of pacing the floor of the government house as though he owned it, it was clear that he was now confident of his power and that, in taking the Huguenots' side, he spoke in the name of a force that was numerous and impossible to withstand.

"Yes, stop talking to us about reason, about debate, about compromise," said Du Pont. "God is nothing to be haggled over. There can be no compromise with idolatry. Half of this island approximately has embraced the true faith. It has done so freely, that is, recognizing the truth of the tenets of our Reformed Church and agreeing to obey them. We are not going to trouble the quietude of those souls by reexamining what has been acknowledged as the truth."

"By your leave," said the admiral. "I am not one to practice idolatry, yet I object to certain of your practices."

"And which might those be?" asked Richier in glacial tones.

"Well, for instance," said Villegagnon, happy to be getting down to the real controversy, "let us consider the communion in two kinds. According to the writ of the Church Fathers, it is perfectly lawful. But Saint Clement, a disciple of the Apostles, supplies an added detail: the wine must be mixed with water. Yet yours is pure. This is a practice you must agree to alter, barring proof of its theological soundness."

He ended with the subtle smile of the rhetorician on his lips. But the Protestants seemed in their indignation to have been drained of blood.

"And who are you," Du Pont thundered suddenly, "to question our Church's rules of truth?"

"And who are you to impose them on me?" retorted the admiral. "Why should I believe this rather than that, if reason doesn't govern my choice? What is the use of having studied the great authors, who for centuries gave man the benefit of their minds?"

"None whatsoever," said Richier mournfully.

Villegagnon froze.

"The authors you refer to," said the pastor quietly, "did not know Christ. Their thought, steeped in darkness, cannot be of any help to us. One must believe, that is all."

"That is also what the priests and the pope say," said the admiral gloomily.

"Yes," said Richier, "but with the difference that they are wrong."

Villegagnon looked despondently at the little pile of papers he had prepared. He had forestalled every argument, found subtle parries to every foreseeable objection, built a synthesis acceptable to all. And now he was denied even the use of this wonderful liberty. The Reformation, which he had looked to for deliverance, was trapping him in a net of violence against which he struggled in vain. He rose and paced the room in his turn, stopping in front of the ebony secretary where, forgetting himself, he performed the familiar gesture of wrapping his arms around it. In moments of great confusion, it was there that he drew strength. The others looked at him in embarrassment. Against his stomach, the wood and ivory surface gave a majestic echo. They had scheduled the weddings for the next day, and only the pastors could perform them. Villegagnon sensed that he must once again sacrifice his feelings, swallow his indignation, and look only to the good of the colony. He turned back toward his guests smiling.

"Well then, so be it," he said, strenuously mastering himself, "let us set our differences aside for the moment and apply ourselves to putting the island back to work."

"You may count on us to combat idleness as assiduously as idolatry," said Du Pont.

There followed an interminable list of demands concerning their own exemption from labor, the right of the pastors to meet in the government house, and the establishment of a council to advise the admiral, led by Du Pont.

Villegagnon saw these measures not only as an attempt on his authority but also as reinforcements that would allow him to count on the Protestants' obedience. And, in the end, in return for an agreement to shorten and moderate the sermons, he consented to everything else.

CHAPTER 28

They were the most oafish, they had to be the most elegant. The first two grooms, freshly outfitted by the tailor, had been chosen in haste by Villegagnon. He had crowned these laureates himself, whose virtues he knew, if not their endowments. His choice had fallen on two not overly thievish lackeys, one from Picardy and the other from Provence, beef-witted louts from birth, but good workers and even-tempered. The young ladies felt some chagrin at their catches but took pride in being the first females to receive the marriage sacrament.

On the appointed day, the event took place on the usual esplanade. So that everyone might fully absorb the example—and wish to imitate it promptly—Villegagnon had arranged for the ceremony to be performed on a small, elevated stage constructed of coconut beams. Everyone was required to attend. The Indian slaves, both men and women, were convoked in particular. The admiral placed them in the front row. Thus nothing would impede their view of the spectacle, which was expected to have a profound effect on their minds. The young ladies made their entrance on the arms of two Protestants, chosen from among the oldest, who might have been their fathers. No change had been made to the severe black dress of the young

ladies, but their hair—perhaps in hidden revolt at their costume—
had been subjected to the boldest fantasies. That is, their braids were
coiled at their temples and pinned, despite any fears of a last-minute
admonition, with immodest ivory combs. Standing side by side with
their intendeds, the two girls blushed a natural and becoming red.
And as the two rascals, whose only vice had been to drink as often as
they could, turned pale, the boys and the girls stood before the moist-
eyed public with cheeks of almost identical color, closely matching
that of a ham knuckle.

But this harmony, raised onto the stage, hid anxious movements in
the audience and in the wings. A subtle play of glances brought three
people together who were otherwise separated. Aude stood primly
below the stage among the next set of females to be auctioned off.
She kept her eyes lowered, unlike the gooses on either side of her,
who were intoxicated by the stares of the starved colonists. But from
time to time, as she had located Just in the second row on the left,
she darted a single lightning look at him that was at once sorrowful,
modest, and lascivious. Just wavered between the noble attitude that
was natural to him, his gaze abstracted, considering the ideas that
Villegagnon had made him aware of, and a surreptitious, anxious,
and avid observation of the young woman who now filled his mind.
And he wondered by what bizarre weakness in his character he no
sooner obtained the answering glance he sought than an irrepressible
force made him turn away from it and toward the distressing spectacle of the virgin shepherdesses and their piglet grooms.

Colombe, across from them, could watch Just and the Protestant
girl simultaneously. She saw everything: Just's anxiety, the girl's interest in responding, and the effort both made to let nothing show. At
first she was amused by this little game. It was the first time she had
seen Just shed the chaste knightly reserve he preached by example.
But the Protestant girl's behavior displeased her. Her sly way of pretending she hadn't solicited any response, of looking innocent and
vaguely irritated when their glances crossed, made Colombe think
there was more deception here than passion. She sensed danger in the
duplicity and was irritated to think that Just had no suspicion of it.

Standing where he did, Just noticed Colombe's pale gaze resting
on him first. His surprise made Aude search on that side too and find

Colombe. From then on, the game changed, and each marked the greatest displeasure at sensing that they were being observed.

Meanwhile, a more considerable drama was being acted out just as discreetly near the stage. Villegagnon, in keeping with his rank, stood at the front of the gathering. As the Protestant liturgy recognized only the two sacraments mentioned in the Gospels, baptism and the Eucharist, the ceremony was quickly assuming a resemblance to the Lord's Supper. It was to end with Holy Communion. The admiral, standing on his pride, did not intend to concede the one point of doctrine he had raised with the pastor: he meant to drink his wine watered. As Richier had not agreed to the request, the difficulty was adroitly dealt with. Villegagnon took communion flanked by his steward. At the moment of seizing the chalice, his attendant added some water to make the liquid conform to the admiral's conception of the holy blood. This had been the focal point of all their quarrels earlier. The pastor, seeing the admiral determined, felt it was out of his hands. It was then that an unexpected yet perfectly foreseeable incident occurred. Villegagnon brought from his pocket a piece of embroidered velvet, spread it on the ground, and kneeled on it. The gesture was particularly appreciated by the Indians, who uttered cries of admiration.

But the pastor was pale with fury.

"Come," he whispered. "Get up."

He held the communion wafer in his hand, without giving it to the communicant.

"Never!" the admiral hissed back. "When my Lord appears, I bow before Him."

"What sort of example are you setting the Indians?" the pastor asked, still in a low voice. "It's pure idolatry."

"I worship the God who is here present."

"You worship a wafer of bread."

"What?" said Villegagnon, abruptly raising his voice. "But then ..."

Richier, his hand still holding tightly to the little white disk, cast about him like a drowning man. In this jungle- and rock-strewn landscape from the dawn of the world, no human landmark offered respite to the eye. They were alone. It was on their decisions, their failures, their errors, that the little group on this square depended.

Murmurs were already rippling dangerously through the assembly. Suddenly, in the blur of faces, Richier recognized Du Pont. The great politician blinked, a sign that the general interest called for a tactical retreat.

The pastor stuffed the wafer into Villegagnon's eager and ill-dentitioned mouth and moved on to the next worshipper.

As people milled around after the ceremony, they all agreed that it had been a success. These first weddings held out the hope of a new era, similar to the old days in Europe that everyone remembered nostalgically: households, legitimate children, the harmonious cooperation of man and woman, peace.

Colombe looked for Just in the bustle, not for any particular reason but just to be near him. Ever since her return, she had felt alien and alone, and she longed to feel the old sense of security in his company. She chanced on him while he was talking to Aude. It was too late to turn away.

Just was fumbling. His natural lordliness seemed captive to an invading timidity that made him awkward. And the young Protestant, far from pitying the victim of this unequal combat, held the weapon of her face, her eyes, and her scent at the young man's throat, while his eyes begged for mercy. Colombe's arrival increased her brother's embarrassment.

"I'd like to introduce . . ." Just stuttered, "my brother, Colin. Colin, Mademoiselle Aude Maupin, Pastor Richier's niece."

"Your . . . brother?" said Aude, speaking the word doubtfully. "Such a pleasure."

Aude trained her lancing gaze on Colombe, pierced the frail integument of her grimy clothes, searched her chest as though to lay it bare, and pricked her heart, drawing a first droplet of blood.

"He is an interpreter with the savages," Just put in, thus excusing Colombe's disreputable dress on this day of celebration.

She was wounded by this cowardice but would have said nothing had not Aude, attacking her in turn, taken the initiative in the duel.

"Among the Indians," she said, with heavy compassion. "Poor boy!"

"And why should I be pitied . . . Mademoiselle?" asked Colombe, her eyes locked with those of the young Protestant.

"Why, because they are savages!"

Her ironic tone implied, And living with them, one also becomes a savage.

"As far as I am concerned," said Colombe, angry at herself for finding nothing better to say, "they are human beings."

"You are right to hope that they will become humans," sighed Aude. "Fortunately, we are bringing them the faith."

"And they bring us fish and manioc flour."

There was a brief pause, and an exchange of murderous looks. Just could think of no way to end the clash.

"Lovely comparison!" said Aude, looking to press her advantage. "You equate faith with commodities. That is indeed how the Papists consider it, who make a commerce of spiritual acts and prayers. But alas, faith is not a matter of actions but of grace."

"Those you call savages are not so devoid of grace as you think," said Colombe.

The sudden remembrance of Paraguaçu, the waterfalls, and Paï-Lo's house made Colombe feel for the first time that she would find more solace there than by Just's side.

But Aude would leave nothing unresolved.

"That is not possible," she retorted. "Those who ignore Christ cannot attain to grace. My uncle says as much: these natives are without God."

"Without God!" said Colombe. "It seems to me on the contrary that they have many more than we do."

"Pah, idols!" said Aude, showing her disgust. "No, dear sir, these have nothing to do with the God of salvation. True grace cannot be imitated."

Colombe plunged the steel of her pale eyes into the open face of her unwary adversary.

"Ah, unlike virtue," she said.

Herself surprised at the vehemence of her attack and seeing the young Protestant turn pale, Colombe suddenly remembered that Just was standing beside her. Furious at him for his cowardice, she was also furious enough not to let him make things worse by taking sides against her or, worse yet, playing the part of the embarrassed arbiter. She turned abruptly on her heels and disappeared into the little crowd.

. . .

At random Colombe took the path by the sea, below the fortress. Since arriving on the island, she had always found it a place of solitude and meditation. But now the rampart towered above it, its sentinels pacing audibly back and forth. In places, the wall was breached by narrow openings through which water drained, just large enough for a man to crouch in. As she passed one of these, Colombe was startled to see Quintin suddenly leap out at her.

"I've found you! When do we leave?"

She had somewhat forgotten him.

"This morning I was almost enlisted for the construction site," he whined. "And a little while ago, one of those Protestant assassins plucked my sleeve while I was getting water and asked me if I believed in purgatory."

"And what did you say?"

"I almost said that hell is where they are, while paradise is everywhere else, but you don't joke about such things. When do we leave, Colombe?"

"As soon as possible," she said.

And it was what she was really thinking.

"I watched the port closely last night. The soldier who takes the third watch is a big tub of lard from Mecklenburg. I know him well: he can't keep from dropping off to sleep. We just have to climb into one of the boats . . ."

"But they are chained," Colombe objected. "And you know they have orders to shoot if they see anyone fleeing."

Quintin was aware of these obstacles and had no solution to them. They were both silent.

"Give me a day," said Colombe. "I'll see what I can do."

She thought she would go and speak to the admiral. But for the moment, she mostly wanted to be alone. She told Quintin to stay hidden and continued on her walk along the rocks.

Reaching the tip of the island, she encountered a group of Indian captives washing their laundry in the sea. Fresh water was too scarce on the island for them to use it for that purpose. Men and women had stripped naked to dunk their tunics in the water. Those who had finished waited for their clothing to dry, spread out on a rock in the sun. The admiral had authorized a little celebration near the port in the newlyweds' honor, and surveillance had consequently been relaxed. The slaves were for once alone. Colombe walked toward them and, as they showed signs of withdrawing in fear, reassured them in their own language.

She sat down next to a group of women and stayed silent. For a moment she imagined that she was back in the days of her walks with Paraguaçu, and she felt an urge to strip down like the others. But she remembered that she was on the island. And these captives were a far cry from her old companions. Bought back from their enemy captors by Le Freux, they had been working on the construction of the fortress since the beginning. Their pitiful, submissive appearance clearly showed in what fear they lived. There was also an air of sadness about them that nothing could dispel. They weren't mistreated. Villegagnon had so far not acted toward them with too much cruelty. But captivity, by removing them from their tribe and putting them on this island where all natural life had gradually vanished, had deprived them of the forest, of hunting, of feather ornaments—in short, of the spiritual framework of their lives. In some sense, they were already dead and accepted this supplementary existence as an unavoidable hell. In the uncomfortable silence caused by her presence, Colombe asked the Indians what they had thought of the morning's ceremony. No one seemed to want to answer. Finally, a wrinkled older woman said in Tupi, "Why do you not make more noise when you dance?"

Colombe asked for the question to be repeated and made queries of her own to try and understand what it meant. She finally gathered that the Indians, who had learned no French except the brief orders barked at them, had not fully understood the point of the ceremony. The dress and ornaments, the stage, the gestures of one person and another had been interpreted by them as a celebration, and they were mainly surprised at the extremely slow rhythm of the white men's dances.

"It wasn't a dance but a wedding," Colombe explained.

But the Tupi word evoked something entirely different for the Indians. Two or three of them shook their heads incredulously and somewhat reprovingly.

"And why do you dress your women in that way, if the ceremony is meant to give them children?" asked the old woman.

The brides' dress had been what most surprised the Indian women. Colombe realized that aside from herself, and she was dressed as a boy, they had never seen European women in their finery. Though glimpsed from afar after their landing, the Protestant ladies had not offered themselves to view before this, or at such close quarters.

"Well, they're dressed now," said Colombe, "and . . . they'll undress later."

This strained and relatively unnecessary explanation made her blush, and then she burst out laughing. The Indians, timidly at first, then with growing pleasure, joined in.

When silence returned, they stayed a moment looking at the water, which, licking the sides of the rocks, was turning pink in the late sun.

"So that's what they want from us!" said a woman, and the others nodded.

Colombe asked her what she meant. Hesitantly, she explained that for the past few days, the men of the island had been after them again. In Le Freux's time, they had been forced to submit to the islanders, then there had been a long period of restored calm. The Indian woman didn't know that this had been in response to the admiral's orders. Now that marriages were possible and even encouraged, the women were starting to be taken aside and forced.

Colombe was ashamed to hear of these brutal acts, and her thoughts flew to Just, who was unintentionally an accomplice in them.

"Then what they want to do with us," said a woman, "is to put us in black dresses like those others."

Colombe wanted to laugh at this leap of mind, but the truth behind it was so poignant and so serious that she restrained herself. Banished from living humanity, these Indian women still understood that there were levels of degradation. Though they were prisoners, they still kept their freedom over themselves, and though they were slaves to all, they could still dread becoming a slave to a single man who would be free to have his way with them.

"Have you never thought of running away?" asked Colombe in a low voice.

A shiver went through the Indians, who looked at each other in terror. Far off, in the direction of the port, the sound of the revelers could be heard. A glance around reassured them that no guard was watching them. A tall man with scars crosshatching his stomach detached himself from the group and approached Colombe. He spoke in a low voice: "You know our language, and your eyes say that you are not bad in spirit."

A shiver of joy traveled up Colombe's back, as freedom does when one has made up one's mind to accept it.

"You see that trunk over there," said the man, inclining his chin toward a long palm log stranded across one of the last rocks. "We have been hollowing it out quietly every night. The pirogue is ready."

"How many men can it carry?" Colombe whispered.

"Ten, but it's the women we want to save."

"Good!" said Colombe. "When are they leaving?"

The slave suddenly seemed uncomfortable. He looked at his feet and said mournfully, "Not yet."

"Why not?" asked Colombe indignantly. "Everything is ready. You mustn't wait."

"On the mainland," the captive finally admitted, "they will be even more dead than they are here."

"What do you mean? You know the forest. You can hide, run away."

"But where would we go? After all the many moons that we have been prisoners, how are we to find our own kin again? All the tribes along the coast are our enemies. We have no weapons."

Colombe thought of the Anabaptists, who had had no such fears and who had apparently survived knowing only a fraction as much about the jungle. But this was not to understand the Indian mind. Without spirits and omens to help them, without maracas or a *caraíba* to interpret the oracles, the Indians saw the forest as a place of evil curses and hostile forces against which they were powerless.

Colombe rose, walked a little way toward the fort, and looked from a distance at the hollowed trunk and at the bluish coast so close by on the other side of the strait. She remembered the Protestant girl's words. The hatred she felt and could not direct at her brother, together with this latest ignominy, suddenly burst inside her. She walked back toward the Tupi smiling.

The afternoon sun shone directly in her face, and the dazzling light brought a pearl of tears to wet her lashes. She felt herself more than ever to be Sun-Eye, and she summoned all the mysterious power of her gaze to ask them, "Will you help me if I help you?"

They didn't need to answer, as they plainly loved her already.

CHAPTER 29

The general will to end the theological anarchy paralyzing the island found expression in a minimal measure: sermons would henceforth be limited to one half hour, once a day, in a designated place. They no longer contained attacks on the pope or blasphemies about the Virgin Mary. This moderation restored a measure of calm. But at the same time, the new religion was no longer progressing, and the other, faithful to Catholic dogmas, was in a position to claim that it had won the day. Two mutually mistrustful camps were beginning to form, and their hostility threatened to explode at any moment.

A solution that would preserve unity was still urgently needed. Concern at the top replaced agitation in the lower ranks, where an end to the sermons had brought peace. For each man had his own conception of unity, which required the capitulation of the others. For Dom Gonzagues, reinvigorated by leading the Catholic faction, the newcomers would be pardoned when and if they recited the Creed. For the Protestants, only a full renunciation of idolatry would be acceptable. They went to work reinforcing their camp, teaching Calvin's principles to their new converts, and organizing an internal police to extirpate heresy wherever it might lurk. Du Pont was the temporal leader of this faction, and nothing was done among the island's Protestant half without his concurrence.

Villegagnon alone had not abandoned the idea of a reasonable compromise. In order to study the Genevan reformer's most recent pronouncements and see whether they could still be reconciled with the Roman religion, the admiral asked Richier to provide him with Calvin's most recent work, *The Ecclesiastical Ordinances*. This had been no easy task, as the pastor had only one copy and feared that Villegagnon planned to destroy it.

What the admiral discovered in this text horrified him. All the freedom, boldness, and molten lava of the spirit that flowed through the early Protestant texts had solidified in the *Ordinances*. Under the pretext of putting his ideas in order, Calvin was putting them to death. Reformation, under his pen, was becoming regulations, punishments, and police. Villegagnon chided himself for having unwittingly called on such a man. But the error had been made and had now to be dealt with. Night and day, taking no food or walks or rest, Villegagnon chopped all these ideas up fine, mixed them with aromatics from the Ancients, stuffed them with fragments of the Gospel, kneaded them, browned them, and seasoned them with the free hand of a man-at-arms. This theological cookery allowed him to assimilate the principle difficulties and reduce the central problem thoroughly. As his intuition had foretold, everything could in the end be arranged. The celibacy of priests was not discussed in the Gospel, and salvation without intercession was not seriously questioned by Dom Gonzagues's Catholic party: the clergy were too deeply distrusted to be credited with the power to save. And nothing prevented a person from having prayers said in return for hard coin—they might assist in salvation, though they could not assure it. The Virgin Mary was a more serious obstacle. But Dom Gonzagues's poetic soul provided the solution: the Catholics could be allowed to celebrate Mary, yet without any recognition of her divine nature. After all, it wouldn't be the first time a woman was imagined to have more powers than she in fact had. The Protestants could allow this show of affection without mistaking it for idolatry. As to the liturgy, communion in two kinds agreed with the spirit of primitive times; and as to the purity of the wine, each might decide to his liking.

Finally, the crux of the controversy, the very center of the debate, which might, depending on its resolution, divide the two parties for ever or bring them together as one, was the issue the admiral had glimpsed at the moment of the Lord's Supper: was Christ present in the wafer? It all hinged on this. If He was not in the wafer, then man had been abandoned. He might receive divine grace, perhaps, but all communication with the God of salvation was denied him. It was neither possible to address Him, nor to take nourishment from His Life. God had sent down His Son, then taken Him back, and all that was left to man was the Savior's word. On this island at the edge of the world, Villegagnon knew the meaning of solitude. If he had never suffered from it, it was because the narrow channel of communion allowed him at all times and in all places to be in the presence of his consoling God, the source of life and eternity.

If Christ was in the wafer, the believer was never alone, never lost, never starving. And on the Day of Judgment, the resurrection would apply not just to the spirit of the dead but to their flesh, made living by the actual absorption of the body of Christ. On this point, nothing was clear. The Catholics spoke of "transubstantiation": the bread and the wine became the true body and the true blood of Christ. Luther used the word "consubstantiation": the bread and the wine, while retaining their profane and substantial existence, *also* became the body and the blood of Christ. But what did Calvin say? He seemed to reject Catholic as well as Lutheran ideas on this point, denying the material presence of Christ. Yet he castigated those who, like Socinus and Zwingli, reduced communion to a symbolic act, empty of God, the pure, sad, and eternal commemoration of the lost Savior.

This was the crux of the debate. He would order the Calvinists to make their position plain. By pressing them on this point, the admiral hoped to make them come down finally on one side or the other: either they accepted (if only half-heartedly) Christ's real presence, and Villegagnon could then smooth away all the remaining differences they had with the Catholics, or they rejected it. Then this unapproachable God, this God who abandoned men to solitude and death, could be served by no one. The pastors were therefore impostors and the sacraments were so much mummery. The Huguenots would never survive this ridicule.

Villegagnon was convinced that the fruitless deliberations of the ignorant—fortunately now at an end—needed to be replaced by a joust at the very highest levels, under the brightest light possible. The Reformers had brushed aside his first attempts at a debate, but they would not be able to avoid this one, which would be clearly circumscribed, decisive, and, of course, mandatory. He called Maître Amberi to draft in due and proper form a summons to appear.

The following day, Du Pont received notice of the colloquium to which the admiral was inviting Richier, Chartier, and a few Protestants (ten at most) whose participation might be judged useful. The safety of the participants was strictly guaranteed, and no weapons would be allowed in the enclosure where the debate was to be held. Tempers were hot enough already, particularly on Dom Gonzagues's side, to make this precision necessary. Du Pont immediately sent back word he would attend.

●　●　●

On the practically finished curtain wall of the fort, large rectangular stones carved to form the merlons and crenels still needed to be set in place. Just oversaw this delicate operation. The subtle art of military fortification was now familiar to him. In Europe this knowledge, at least as it pertained to the sea, was entirely in the hands of the Knights of Malta. No seagirt fortification was built in Europe without their advice. They never consigned the secrets of their art to a book, where it might too easily be robbed. The art was only transmitted from master to student, and Villegagnon had never had a more attentive one than Just.

Despite all the colony's mishaps, the young knight felt a deep pride whenever he contemplated the fort. Every jog in the wall spoke to him: he understood its utility, admired the intelligence of its placement, and marveled at the way military thinking converted movement into geometry, foresaw the attack, its axes, its speed, and offered it a stationary resistance in the form of a well-built rampart. He didn't wish the Portuguese to try the correctness of his calculations. But if they did, he was confident the fortress would hold.

That morning he paced the edge of the curtain wall where a stone parapet was soon to be raised. The creaking of a hoist, a noise he loved, accompanied the slow rise of a stone block on the tower of a wooden crane. This rigorous work, which would effect an exact correspondence between the rigid masses of the carved materials, was a calming diversion from the difficulties of human intermingling. In those realms of the mind and, even more, of the heart—which Just disliked even thinking about—everything was always so unpredictable, so blurred, so fluid. Intentions veered, feelings were never very far from their opposites, agreements proved unstable, propitiation was always delicate. Nothing rivaled the simple goodness of one squared stone resting on another, swearing centuries of loyalty.

Just therefore found himself slightly irritated when, just as the block reached his height and began pivoting with two men pulling on it, he saw Colombe walking toward him along the curtain. He walked a few steps toward her so that their conversation, which he dreaded, would not be overheard by the workmen. She stopped in front of him. On this hot morning, in the clarity of the austral autumn, she looked different. He couldn't say how exactly. Perhaps her air of wrath, her anxious glance, which sought to avoid him, made him fear some angry or ironic remark. But she spoke softly and, uncharacteristically, without smiling.

"I'm leaving, Just. We have to say good-bye."

With his broad man-at-arms's frame, his sharpened face, his straight blade of a nose, his still-fleshy lips, now chapped by the salt wind, he looked so different from the rough-hewn adolescent who had landed there two and a half years earlier. He seemed to have been built along with the fort, and from the same solemn, polished, incorruptible matter. Colombe would have liked both to take her fill of this face one last time and not to have to look at it. She was afraid of provoking a painful ceremony of farewell.

"Where are you going?" asked Just.

It was like using the smallest tool possible to handle a substance that was delicate and perhaps dangerous.

"Among the Indians."

"Again!" he burst out.

Colombe resented his comparing her present decision to her earlier trips, which had been performed in another spirit entirely. But she immediately saw that by treating it as unremarkable, he saved her from having to confess that this time she did not intend to return.

"Yes," she said. "Again."

Just lowered his eyes. It wasn't all clear to him, but he felt the reproach implied in her decision. As he could not conceive of the Indian world as anything but savagery, the abominable opposite of civilization, Just realized how much criticism, and insult even, her action held. To love the forest was to look on the colony with pitiless eyes, to formulate the most radically negative judgment of it.

"Come, Colombe," he said, with a mixture of shyness and despondency. "Everything will work out here in the end."

Just's instincts pulled him in two directions at once, telling him that she was right, yet that she was mistaken.

"You'll see, we'll come through," he added.

And in that moment, she felt how incomparable are the attachments made in childhood. From their games at Clamorgan, from their brilliant hardship in Italy, to the dark days of their ocean crossing, full of fears and hopes, they had known how to convey great love and courage to each other with those words: we'll come through. And now the fate of this magic phrase was all the crueler when, little doubting that they would come through, she no longer wanted to.

"We'll come through to what, Just? To see the slave women raped, the island destroyed, and hatred everywhere? Are you blind?"

But the straight line of the battlements, the stone block now being lowered toward the parapet, the proud weapons, the ships at anchor, the whole bay awaiting the conquering thrust of a victorious Antarctic France answered on Just's behalf.

"I can't stand lying any more," she said, plucking at her shapeless shirt.

From the great lie of the colony she moved on to the tiny lie that concerned her, one on which they could at least agree.

"We could tell Villegagnon the truth," suggested Just.

But this was a false suggestion, and she knew him too well not to feel it. Given the delicate situation of the colony, Just had no intention of heaping this new problem on Villegagnon. And too many hazards beset Just at this tense moment when everything could turn to storm. She reflected that he was as courageous as ever under fire or while working, but that he still lacked the kind of strength that turns outer boldness into intimate courage. She remembered the looks he exchanged with Aude, and all her resentment returned.

"I won't be on hand for your wedding," she said, unable to keep her eyes from smiling and causing even more pain than her words.

"My wedding!" he said. "But what are you talking about? I've never . . ."

"Stop it," she interrupted, shrugging. "At least face the plain fact: you love her. Good for you."

She felt suddenly ashamed to have applied the iron of words to the sore of truth.

Thrown as if hit by a lance, Just sputtered. It was not so much what she had dared say to him as that he had been too cowardly to say it to himself. Whipsawed between his indignation and the evidence, he didn't know which way to turn. Colombe felt that her victory had been too easy and would have despised herself for leaving things there.

"Dear Just, be on guard against yourself."

Yet who was to say that she was not secretly pleased that Just's new passion was disrupting their tired routine of chastity and virile camaraderie? The tragedy was not that they had each finally dared to become what they were—a man and a woman—but that in losing their childhood bond they had been unable to forge another. For they were first and foremost, whatever doubts she might still have, brother and sister.

Breaking their embarrassed silence, a shout rang out behind them. The workmen had set down the stone block too violently, and it had cracked. Just ran over to the hoist.

Colombe took the opportunity to slip away without looking back.

• • •

The colloquium took place the very next day, the Huguenots having sent word that they were ready for the confrontation and needed no additional time to prepare.

The participants gathered in a new enclosure adjoining the government house. Villegagnon had had it built to accommodate the island's future council, whose establishment he had consented to. The two pastors with a half-dozen followers settled on the benches to one side while Du Pont stayed in the rear, standing for his comfort. Across from them, Dom Gonzagues led a small group of artisans in whom he had awoken a violent attachment to the Virgin Mary and an earnest hope of preferment.

Villegagnon took his place at the narrow end of the room, equidistant from both groups. Just and Le Thoret stood behind him on either side of the doors. And finally, the notary Amberi sat at a little desk between the two lines of adversaries, seemingly intended as the first victim in their exchange of fire. The room was filled with palpable hostility. In the preceding days, several of the new converts had gone back on their abjuration of Catholicism. They had been pressured, and threats had been made against them. A fight had broken out at the fort. Now each individual had to declare his allegiance to one camp or the other, though the exact differences between them were uncertain. No one knew quite why you became a Huguenot or a Papist, but once the choice was made, there was no question of changing sides. A stir of impatience was felt in the room. Through the hastily built palm-leaf panels, the white of the sand and the jade line of the water could be seen in the distance. A veil of mist, strange for the season, had dampened the suffocating heat. Several members of the assembly, uncomfortable and wondering whether they wouldn't be better off hopping over the trellis and running away, exuded a fumet of anxious underarms into the still air.

"Are you ready, Maître Amberi?" Villegagnon finally asked.

The notary's nod of assent marked the beginning of work.

"Sirs," began the admiral, employing his bard's voice, with its intimations of fraternity and joy, "we all believe in Our Lord Jesus Christ. We hold in our hands the light and the truth that will make of this abandoned land a garden for the king of France."

Dom Gonzagues sighed. The word "garden" always suggested poetry to him, for he liked to describe woman—her combed hair, her tint, and her eyes—in metaphoric terms, as straightly drawn alleys, flower beds, and limpid pools.

"But," shouted Villegagnon, yanking the old knight from his poetic torpor, "faced with the dangers that surround us, it is our duty to remain united and not trouble the minds of our men with unimportant differences."

These last words provoked indignation on all sides. Chests swelled, and several cleared their throats, as though preparing to draw swords.

Villegagnon, for all that he appeared to be at ease, was cautious. He had joyfully welcomed the Protestants, believing that the spirit of freedom and healthy controversy would flourish in the colony, but he had learned to his sorrow that the Reformers did not welcome debate. He must not allow the two sides to cross swords over trifles.

"We are going to limit ourselves to the essential," he said, "and the rest will proceed from it. I will therefore formulate the question directly: is Our Lord Jesus Christ personally present at Holy Communion, yes or no?"

Working from a single sheet of notes he had prepared beforehand, he exposed all the implications of Christ's presence for salvation and the impossibility, as he saw it, of founding a religion that did not acknowledge it. On this point, though by intention a centrist, he showed himself closer to the Catholics. Dom Gonzagues nodded his approval. Richier solemnly took the floor.

"Yes," he said quietly. "Christ is there during the Lord's Supper."

Villegagnon's tense face relaxed. Dom Gonzagues proudly raised the tip of his beard.

"As Calvin has written," said Richier, reading from his own notes, " 'our souls are sated with the substance of His body, so that in truth we will be made one with Him.' "

"Ah, brother!" said Villegagnon rising to his feet, "I embrace you."

But Richier, under the looming threat, promptly continued:

"Allow me to finish! The Christ is there, as I have said . . ."

Villegagnon sat down again, smiling with happiness.

". . . and he is also not there."

An "Oh!" of indignation shook the Catholic side, and the admiral turned pale with distress.

"He is not there," went on Richier, raising his hand for silence, "because Calvin has written: 'Here is only bread and wine. And they are not such things as can guarantee our souls' salvation; they are fallen meats, as Saint Paul says, intended for the stomach.' "

"By Saint Jack of Jerusalem!" thundered the admiral. "Make up your mind. Either he's there or he isn't. But it is not your prerogative to put him there or take him away."

"Actually, it is. Christ is there because we put him there," Richier explained.

A roar went up from the Catholic bench.

"It is the believer's faith," the pastor went on unperturbed, "that summons him in spirit, in his divine nature. But as to Christ personally, he is on the right hand of God, as far from the bread and wine as heaven is from earth."

"Then," shouted Villegagnon over the uproar from Dom Gonzagues's side, "man has been abandoned—man, whom God created in His own image, and who mirrors His perfection . . ."

"Stop!" shrieked Du Pont, who had until now remained in the background. "Yes, stop your prating, Admiral, on the goodness of man. Man is not good. He is lost, damned, and forever fated to desire evil and perform it."

"And his soiled body," the pastor added, his eyes full of disgust, "his paltry flesh, will take no part in the Resurrection on the Day of Judgment."

There was a long silence, of which Villegagnon was the source. Until now he had defended the Catholic tenets sincerely but with moderation, seeking to appease and find a middle ground. But suddenly, in what he had just heard, he had been touched to the quick in his faith as a humanist, his most closely held convictions. The blow was a grievous one. He rose in a mass and with such force that the whispering abruptly stopped.

He looked in turn at Du Pont and at Richier with unspeakable hatred. Of all the sins they might commit, they had succumbed to the one sin he could not forgive them: that of not loving their neighbor. He defended the idea that man might be saved because he, Villegagnon, was filled with the sense of man's beauty, greatness, and perfection, which made him always a mirror of God—even if a mirror that was shattered during the Fall. But as for these men, they hated themselves. He now understood how this religion of love could also produce the monstrous Anabaptists. If man is evil and can do nothing to save himself, then he may as well sin to his heart's content and revel in his own horror.

"Take note!" Villegagnon finally growled, pointing his finger toward Maître Amberi. "Take note of what separates these worthies from ourselves and what will always separate them."

He started drafting a declaration of disagreement, which Richier contested, until between the two of them they had drawn up veritable divorce papers. The notary's quill raced scratchily across the poor paper, while those assembled tried in appalled silence to calculate the consequences.

It was just at the moment of signing that the cries reached them. The least noise entered this unwalled room freely. This time, the cries did not come from a bird, and they were nearby. As they grew even louder, it was heard to be a woman's voice. The admiral signaled to Just, who opened one of the doors. A lady-in-waiting, her hair undone, her black dress torn and hanging on one breast, her eyes haggard, entered the conclave shrieking.

"Well, Chantal, what is it?" asked Richier.

"Mademoiselle Aude! Mademoiselle Aude!" the duenna howled.

"Come then, tell us."

Half swooning, and with one hand on the notary's head, the poor woman said, "The cannibals have eaten her," and fainted dead away.

CHAPTER 30

Two years of madness, yet nowhere was it written that he would give up. Monsignor Joaquim Coimbra had made the reconquest of Brazil a personal matter. He was the standard bearer of the faction, regrettably a minority, that believed Portugal should remain in America not solely to bring back gold and extract sugar. He saw it as the locus of a vast expansion of the faith, a new crusade. And if Dom Joaquim had any chance of wearing the papal tiara one day, it would be through the successful accomplishment of this plan, which had the twin advantages of weakening the French and serving Christianity.

But in the two years since Cadorim had informed him of the French expedition, so many obstacles had cropped up in his path that the prelate had begun to believe the cause was lost.

Racing back to Lisbon, as he had told the Venetian he would, but at the top speed of his all-too-slow team of horses, he had arrived after the abdication of Charles V. The news that greeted him on reaching the Tagus was that France and Spain had signed a truce. The Portuguese sovereign, as he feared, had wanted to take no action in the Americas that might disrupt this European concord. France, now at peace and freed of its main enemy, would have made him pay any aggression dearly.

Coimbra returned to Venice despondent. Fortunately, it was to discover that the peace was unlikely to last long. Italian affairs remained what they had always been—a powder keg—and the prelate, with a simple-hearted air, struck assiduously at his flint.

Those who expect the worst are always gratified sooner or later. For the bishop, gratification came in the blessed summer of 1556, with the arrival of two items of news. One was public: the arrival of François de Guise in Italy at the head of thirteen thousand men. The ambition of this great captain, whose burning desire was to be crowned king of Naples and put his brother on the throne of Peter, broke Europe's truce. The war between France and Spain would be resuming almost immediately. And a good thing, as it freed the Portuguese of all scruples in America!

The other item, more secret, he received from Cadorim. The Venetian had been sent abroad once more, much against his will. His orders had again taken him to France, where, living in Paris, he spied on the court. Coimbra had proved so generous to him that Cadorim still occasionally sent him dispatches. The last had contained an important piece of information: that Calvinist ministers were departing imminently for Rio, with the blessing—if such a word can be applied to heretics—of the king of France.

Armed with this precious news, Coimbra had leapt into his carriage, and, at the cost of fracturing three axles, a shaft, and his nerves, he had arrived in Lisbon alert despite everything and knowing what he needed to do.

Coordinating his attack with the king's confessor and his Jesuit entourage, the bishop mounted a second charge against the sovereign. This time, circumstances could not have been better. It was the beginning of 1557, and the break between France and Spain had been declared. There was war in Flanders. The road was clear. Furthermore, Joao III was extremely devout, and the entry of Huguenots into his territory of Brazil was unbearable in the highest degree. For the Normans to go there and sin was one thing—one could still turn a blind eye to it. But to preach to the cannibals of that country a religion that distorted the truth could be neither accepted nor justified.

The king named a new governor of Brazil, directing him to leave as soon as possible for Salvador de Bahia. His first task would be to put an end to the absurd passivity of the Portuguese colonists, who thought only of their sugar mills. There were poor Jesuits in the jungles struggling to spread the faith. It was time to bring them help, because Portugal's true mission lay with them. And as to Rio, the matter was simple: it had to be conquered and every last one of the diabolical seeds recently cast there pulled up. Villegagnon's days and those of his damned Frenchmen were numbered.

Dom Coimbra could return to Venice satisfied. Yet before he consigned his vertebrae to the torture of the poor roads again, he wanted to hold an interview with the new governor of Brazil. The warrior no sooner arrived in Lisbon from his native province than he responded to the prelate's invitation.

The meeting took place near the Church of San Francisco, in a quiet little cloister whose walls were covered to the height of six feet with glazed tiles. Mem de Sá, the governor designate, made an entry that was no less than magisterial. He was a small rickety man, so frail that he relied on his cuirass, which he never removed, to make up for the weakness of his skeleton and keep him from flopping to the ground like an unstaked plant. Belying his bodily debility, he carried his enormous head erect, with its protuberant eyes, fleshy lips, and bulbous nib. His face, exaggeratedly stamped with cruelty, violence, and appetite, was completed by a mass of thick and tightly curled black hair, of which his eyebrows and mustaches formed outlying and equally bristling archipelagos.

Bishop Coimbra greeted his visitor with a movement of mingled horror and satisfaction: it was impossible to imagine a more perfect exterminating angel to send the Huguenots.

"Ah!" he exclaimed, opting with prudence not to extend his ring toward the jaws of such a mastiff. "How pleased I am to see you, Governor!"

A grunt did the duty of a courteous reply with Mem de Sá. And as a bit of saliva ran onto his lip at the same time, he wiped it away with the back of his hand. Coimbra was delighted at the prospect of this gift to the French.

The bishop showed his guest to a leather armchair and started talking to him about Brazil. He recounted the entire story of Rio: the first Portuguese suspicions when rumors from Paris seemed to indicate a rival attempt at colonization; the information that had come from Venice; the departure of the Reformers. Dom Joaquim took satisfaction in noting that this word caused Mem de Sá to shed his immobility and make movements with his nose and ears indicative of the hunt and scenting quarry. Then, patiently, very simply, as one invites a foreigner to repeat a few words, Coimbra tried to coax from the governor an inkling of his plans. But the man-at-arms seemed not to hear the question marks clearly placed by the bishop both before and after his sentences. A certain malaise, an acrid smoke, entered the conversation and made the prelate cough. Finally, when Coimbra had in turn grown silent, discouraged almost to the point of panic, Mem de Sá opened his mouth, revealing strong teeth, pink as coral, and said, "We must make war, in Rio."

His voice had the deep and ligneous sound of a ventriloquist's cupboard.

So he did speak. He both spoke and thought. And what's more, he thought well. Color returned to the bishop's face. Heartened by the response, which showed he hadn't preached in vain, Coimbra began with suavity, humor, loquacity, and sincere joy to sketch in for the governor a thousand quick pictures of Brazil, the Jesuits, the cannibals, French perfidy, the Venetians' helpfulness, the execrable state of the roads, the sweetness of Douro wine, the king, the court, and himself. On reaching this subject, which was dear to him above all others, he finally sighed and was silent.

The bass bell in the clocktower struck twice, calling the faithful to Mass, and the sound resonated in silence of the cloister.

"We must make war, in Rio," said Mem de Sá again, in the same octave as the bell.

"Yes," said Dom Joaquim, lowering his head.

There are forces to which one must simply submit.

And to show that he intended to digest these nourishing words to their last shred, he folded his hands on his stomach and was silent for a long moment.

Mem de Sá continued to wait patiently. At times, his heavy eyelids swept their stiff lashes across the unpolished globes of his eyes. Coimbra reflected that he had little time to get to the crux of the matter, and dispensing with preliminaries, he made for it.

"Governor," he said, enunciating each syllable, "you have but few soldiers in Salvador de Bahia. As far as I know, the king has ordered no new troops to accompany you. Yet, as you have said so truly and foresightedly, we must make war in Rio . . ."

"Yes," Mem de Sá interrupted.

". . . Quite," Coimbra went on, sponging his forehead with a handkerchief. "Well then, allow me to inform you of a little arrangement we owe to our Venetian agent."

Swallows with forked tails swooped high in the pale sky. Mem de Sá lifted his eyes toward them and sniffed.

"An important arrangement," said Coimbra, raising his voice as his temper mounted. "May I tell you of it?"

But knowing how little store his interlocutor set by questions, he did not wait for an answer.

"You will have a man amongst the French," he said, leaning in.

In the simplest possible terms he gave an account of Vittorio's existence.

"The password for finding him is 'Ribera.' "

Nothing moved in the governor's face.

"Ri-be-ra," Coimbra repeated, sweat trickling down his forehead.

There was no reaction. He gave his explanation a second time. Mem de Sá, noticing the glass of port he had been served, stretched out his bony hand to it and greedily drank down a great gulp.

"Ribera," said Coimbra finally, with a smile that poorly masked his despair.

The hour tolled from another, more distant clocktower that was pitched to a higher note. Mem de Sá listened, seeming to count the strokes. At the last one he rose, adjusted his cuirass with a shimmy, and tugged on his sleeves.

The bishop accompanied him attentively to the little door by which he had arrived. There, Mem de Sá paused, looked at the prelate, and said in a voice that was suddenly clearer:

"We must make war, in Rio."

Then he stiffened and added, like a war cry, "Ribera!"

And with that he vanished through the postern.

CHAPTER 31

The crush of alarmed visitors found Aude lying on her bed under a woolen quilt whimpering. Her uncle and Du Pont came first, but Villegagnon and Just followed close behind. Around the cabin could be heard the buzzing of an indignant group that included sectarians of both parties.

Aude moaned, a proof of suffering she was obligated to give because of that idiot Chantal's errors of vocabulary. The lady-in-waiting, arriving with the visitors, sniffed as she tried to restore her modesty behind the tattered strips of her dress.

It was clear that she had misspoken. The cannibals had not, in the true sense, eaten Mademoiselle Aude. From the visitors' astonished and almost disappointed looks, Aude understood that they had thought her boiled and cut into chunks, when in fact she was still alive and able to explain herself. Richier asked her gravely to tell the whole story.

"It's too awful!" she sobbed, giving pathos to a scene that the spectators might otherwise have found too reassuring, when measured against their expectations.

"Come, child, you must tell us, for the sake of civil order," whispered Du Pont, taking Aude's trembling hand into the shelter of his two cupped paws.

"Very well," she said, mastering her frayed sensibilities. "It happened less than an hour ago. As on every afternoon, Chantal and I went out for a short walk behind the fort, along the rocks."

Aude nervously pressed a handkerchief to her cheeks. For though her eyes were dry, Aude intended the assembly to believe that she told her story in a puddle of tears.

"It was a place I always liked," she said dreamily, her use of past tense implying that she could never bring herself to go back again, "the sea there is so pretty."

"And it helps one's complexion," piped up Chantal.

All eyes turned to her, Aude's included, with the message not to intrude on the proceedings again with her inanities.

"Today," Aude went on, "we saw no one at first. I believe all the men on the island gathered together to learn the outcome of your conference. Is that not so, Uncle?"

Richier nodded, and Villegagnon, who was taller than everyone else in the room by a head, gave an embarrassed cough, for he had called the conference and feared it might somehow be responsible for the attack.

"Everything was quiet," said Aude, "and we decided to push on a little farther than usual, toward the tip of the island, which we find ravishing because you can see the whole circle of the bay and the forest in the distance. That's when the women attacked us."

"Which women?"

"Why, the Indian women," said Aude.

"Our slaves?" asked Villegagnon, under whose jurisdiction the slave group fell.

"Yes, the ones who help build the fort. Or rather, their wives, for the husbands seem to have kept their distance."

"And what did they do?" asked Richier.

Aude thought it would be a good moment to let out a sob, which she stifled with both hands. Her distress thus established, no one would think to find her account humorous.

"Well," she said with a look of disgust, "they stripped off their tunics all in a second. They were covered with horrible red and black daubings that made them look like demons."

"Just so!" said Villegagnon indignantly.

"They started to clap their hands and dance around us. You should have heard the horrible cries they gave, two of them especially, older ones, who looked exactly like witches."

The sound of Chantal's tearful hiccoughing permeated the room.

"The circle closed around us. We were speechless with fright. You can't imagine how awful they were to see—and to smell! Hell must not smell much different."

"But what did they want?" asked Richier.

"We could not understand. It was unclear even whether they had a plan and a leader, or whether they were just in the throes of some primitive madness."

"All the same," said Chantal, "there was that other one . . ."

"I was about to mention her," snapped Aude.

"What other one?" asked Richier.

The girl paused for effect and darted a quick glance into the assembly, hitting her target.

"There is one horrible detail I must mention, though I am loath to do so. Among these monsters from gehenna was one, the youngest, who belonged to our own civilized race."

"What! A white woman!" said Villegagnon, "but where could she have come from?"

"Oh, Admiral! You know her well."

An indignant murmur traveled in waves around the small room, and all eyes turned toward Villegagnon.

"She was daubed with the same paint as all the others, but she was still perfectly recognizable. She has those eyes as white as turnips that make her look like an idiot, which she is far from being, alas!"

Villegagnon turned incredulously toward Just, whose pallor was unmistakable.

"And a well-developed bust," Aude continued sharply, "which makes it surprising that she could have passed so long for a boy."

"Who is it?" asked Richier, who had never noticed Colombe.

Aude looked at Just.

"One of my pages, whom I was fond of," said Villegagnon proudly.

He wanted no one but himself to answer for what was his own responsibility. He would discuss the matter with Just at another time, and without witnesses.

"Dressed as a man?" asked Richier disgustedly.

"Apparently so," said Villegagnon. "I was unaware of it."

Many people on the island had known Colombe's sex, and the revelation of it was less surprising than that she had taken part in the attack.

"And what was this girl doing with the Indian women?" asked Du Pont.

"She was leading them. It was quite extraordinary, in fact, to hear her speak their language. The poor girl has become a savagess entirely."

"And what did she order them to do?" asked Richier.

"Oh, Uncle! Don't make me tell everything. It was already horrible enough to see that dance of the damned, in which they exposed their intimacies to me in bestial fashion. I don't want to become further soiled by offering a description of it."

The imagination, in this realm, can always be counted on to play its part. The skillful storyteller leaves the hearer to flesh out such scenes according to his or her age and desires. A breath of the obscene momentarily caressed this assembly of frustrated men, silencing them on the ridge between pleasure and indignation.

"And then?" asked Richier, painfully swallowing his saliva.

"What followed next was a complete outrage. The white woman gave an order and the others threw themselves upon us, ripped off our clothes, and gripped our limbs in their teeth."

"They wanted to devour you raw?"

This was the moment Aude had been dreading. Because at some point she would have to scale back the horror and allow something of the farce to appear. The teeth marks on her and Chantal's arms were not deep, and some of them had already disappeared. The whole scene enacted by the savagesses had been aimed at frightening them as much as possible, at raising the specter of cannibalism. But it was clear that the women had had no real intention of doing them injury. Of all their bites, the only serious one was the bite of ridicule.

And in displaying the love bites on her uncovered arms and shoulders, Aude inspired more pity than horror. The tragic summary offered by Chantal when she first gave the alarm stood in contrast to the present general feeling of relief and occasioned, alas, a few smiles.

"Did you not call out for help?" asked Du Pont. "Was no one able to come to your rescue?"

From his pleated brow, it was apparent that he sensed here the marks of some new negligence, perhaps a plot.

"We yelled for all we were worth," squeaked Chantal.

But Aude preferred not to dwell overmuch on the moment when, flat on her back, the mouths of her harpy tormentors latched to her skin, she uttered barnyard cries that seemed, if anything, to confirm her status as a comestible.

"All this lasted only a moment," she said, to bring this chapter to a close. "Hardly were we on the ground than they ran off, still under the orders of that Frenchwoman, who has reverted to savage customs."

Just felt Villegagnon seething next to him.

"And where did they go?" he growled, ready to follow them there on the instant and mete out the proper punishment.

"It was all planned in advance," said Aude, shaking her head. "A hollowed-out log was floating among the rocks. They rushed to it and fled to the mainland, paddles flying."

"And no one saw them, no one gave the alarm? No one shot at them?" shouted Villegagnon. "Where were all the sentinels on the redoubt?"

"I'm afraid," came a voice from near the door, "that just at that moment someone started throwing rocks at the ship's boats."

Le Thoret, as the chief officer of the sentinels, had spoken up in defense of his men. The admiral glared at him.

"And what of it?"

"Well, my soldiers concluded that someone was trying to steal the boats, so they rushed in that direction."

"And who had thrown the stones?"

"Some Indians were seen running toward the sand baskets."

"I understand," said Villegagnon. "A diversion while the others were running away. How many fled?"

"Nine Indian women," said Le Thoret, "and . . . her."

Even now that she was out of danger, he could not bring himself to denounce Colombe. The old soldier had known about her for a long time, but he had always tried to protect her. Twice he had spoken to his men to make them keep quiet about what they had learned or suspected. She was unaware of the deeds done on her behalf by this silent guardian angel.

It was too late. The culprits were already far away. In the room, Chantal sobbed audibly. Villegagnon gauged the situation for a moment, then strode toward the bed and said in a solemn, hollow voice, "My apologies, Mademoiselle. May God heal you and keep you."

Turning abruptly on his heels, he went out through a double hedge of grimacing faces, feeling hatred for all of them, without exception.

• • •

A fine rain, atypical for the season, filled the beach with a warm mist that did not wet the sand to any depth. As they jumped from the pirogue, Colombe and the Indians were still laughing at the fright they had given the two Huguenot ladies. Naked, glazed with a thin film of sweat, spray, and rainwater, Colombe was still elated by their recent action and its danger. She was happy to have won her freedom not only in the vast expanse of the world but also in the tiny place where it had been denied to her for so long. Furthermore, she was sharing her liberation with others. She watched with pleasure as the Indian women shed their submissive posture, rediscovered their woodlands wariness, touched living tree trunks, leaves, and roots, and re-entered the palpitating world of the jungle.

Quintin had gone ahead the day before, accompanying the water detail and staying ashore. He was waiting for them on the narrow promontory defended by the only tribe that had remained out of Le Freux's hands in the old days and out of Martin's today. It was this tribe that, at Païa-Lo's request, still consented to supply the island with water.

But though they showed themselves friendly to the French, these Tupi were still Indians, haunted by magical fears. When they saw the captive women approach, they took up their war clubs, whooped, and started toward them with the intention of killing them. Colombe saw a tragedy in the offing. She shielded the women behind her and threw herself at the leader.

"These women are innocent!" she cried.

"They are Tabajares," growled the Indian, not taking his eyes off them. "They are our enemies."

"Spare them," said Colombe. "Look at them: they are no longer Tabajares but poor slaves, half dead from overwork."

The miserable women huddled in a tight group. What they had dreaded was coming to pass. Yet their reaction did not appear to be one of terror. Perhaps they were relieved to find order again, albeit an implacable one.

"The Tabajares killed several of our warriors," the chief said stubbornly. "We cannot forgive them. It goes against our rules, and the spirits would hold it against us."

"Have pity on them," said Colombe.

But she felt how little meaning the word had in the present circumstances. Already the warriors were approaching to seize the women.

"One moment!" said Colombe, who had had a last-minute inspiration. "They are not yours."

The chief looked at her uncomprehendingly.

"You sold them to the white men," she said vehemently. "They are ours. If you touch them, you are stealing."

The French had put considerable effort into outfitting the Indians with a small array of moral ideas. The most clearly set forth, as well as the most foreign to Indian ideas, was respect for the property of others. The Tupis had nothing in their effects that their neighbor was not free to share without asking. The Indians' instinct was to act in the same way toward the white man, thus provoking the latter's indignation. Without quite grasping the grounds for it, the Indians had understood that "stealing" was the action the foreigners most abhorred. They secretly pitied these poor men, whose poverty no doubt drove them to place such a high value on inanimate objects. By way of proof, they pointed to the fact that these strangers came all the way to America for things as natural and abundant as wood.

At the mention of stealing, the Tupi chief appeared perturbed. He pondered, examined the captive women, and decided any profit he might get from them would be slight. According to the sound practice of anthropophagy, only men could be eaten. What could he do with these women? The more closely he looked at these work-weary wretches, the harder it was to envision consuming them.

"I'll let you have them," he finally said to Colombe, somewhat disgustedly, "but they can't stay on our land."

And so the band of runaways, carrying a large skin bag full of smoked game and root flour, set off at once toward the forest.

The summer mizzle coated the leaves in fresh varnish, intensifying the colors. Groups of anteaters and wild peccaries wandered in search of mudholes. The Indian women were radiant. Their feet no longer used to the varied and dangerous forest floor, they leapt from step to step with delicious fright, almost as if dancing. Quintin held two of them by the hand with the elated confidence of a man who knows the road to paradise.

They slept two nights along the way, sheltered by rocks. The rain stopped on the second day. Summer again took possession of the sky, like an adult reassuming a task after momentarily pretending to turn it over to children.

During the entire climb, Colombe felt perfectly happy. Not that she was proud of her pitiful attack. She had simply planned to scare Aude a bit and had followed the inspiration of the moment in playing at cannibalism. But she was happy above all to have dropped her mask and confirmed her freedom doubly: by unveiling her true identity and by showing that, although a woman, she was not forced to shut herself in the prisons of modesty, decency, and flounced dresses. At this moment, running among the copses of euphorbia and frangipani, her body hardened and caressed by ritual painting, young and springy like the turgescent leaves of the rubber shrub, she felt at the crossroads of all strength and gentleness, of all firmness and tenderness. No other place in the world, no era, could have given her this freedom, this power. As the pale blue of the water in the bay spread into the sky above the trees, she felt her soul take on the same shadeless color of happiness.

Colombe now knew the paths along the coast well. She took a longer but safer route that climbed in loops through black rock sprinkled with flowering yuccas. On the heights, they reached a columnar pine wood, easily recognizable on its promontory. All they had to do was to follow a wide valley carpeted with hibiscus and service trees to come within sight of Paï-Lo's house.

The old man was seated on a sort of throne made of twisted roots tied together with raffia. Two very young Indian girls combed his long hair and beard gently. From the scent he exuded of flowers and shells, he had clearly just emerged from his bath. He used an enormous jar made of baked clay and filled with water warmed over the fire, in which he liked to stay for several hours.

Colombe told him the whole story of their flight. When she came to the Tabajares women, he looked thoughtful.

"I know their tribe, it has moved away, and it's unlikely that they could reach it without falling into the hands of the Waitacas, who are as stubborn as mules and will on no account be stopped from cutting them to pieces."

The women had scattered into the wide expanse of trees and huts that made up Païlo's realm. The Indians had welcomed them with kindness and offered them food and drink.

"But if they like," said Païlo, "they can stay here. My family, and all who live with us, will allow them to go unharmed."

Colombe had settled at his feet with her head on his lap. She was silent a moment, while he caressed her blond curls.

"I've had news of your friend," said Païlo.

"Paraguaçu? Is she alive?"

"Yes, her tribe came back through these parts. They lost many of their number during the epidemic."

Colombe realized, for the first time, that she herself might unknowingly have brought the Indians illness and death.

"Can I go see her?" she asked.

"She says that she'd prefer to come visit you. I'll let her know that you are here."

Colombe laid her head down again. Two toucans, perched on a carved chest from Europe that had now set down roots among the ferns and bougainvilleas, looked on solemnly.

The dangers traversed, the long and weary trip, the exciting departure—all receded gradually in the quiet warmth of the forest. Her mind once more at rest, Colombe's thoughts returned to the island. The disgust that had so forcefully driven her away was giving way to a nostalgic mist from which the beloved figure of Just emerged. When she was preparing her flight from the island, she hadn't considered how thoroughly she was burning her bridges and making it impossible to see him again. Her elation at her freedom ebbed away altogether at the thought that, in order to be free and whole, she had amputated half of herself. And she found herself chained to the desire to be reunited with Just.

CHAPTER 32

Since the fatal day of the break with the Protestants, the attack on Aude, and Colombe's departure with the Indian women, Villegagnon had not been outside the government house once. A lackey served him food and drink without seeing him or addressing him. No one was admitted to his presence anymore, and Just was no exception.

The island was holding its breath. The work of construction ground forward at a slackened pace, and nothing was getting done. A heat spell, after the brief rain, imparted to the general idleness a heavy and languid character. Men slept in shady corners and dreamt on the rocks, their feet dangling in the water. They seemed to be awaiting some mysterious signal, a rumbling of the earth or the waters, that would tell them what to do and, more importantly, why they were there. Fort Coligny—handsome, imposing, in many respects admirable—rose before them like an enigma and seemed designed less to protect them from an improbable enemy than from the sun.

At night, the island became animated. It was a far cry from the bawdy celebrations of Le Freux's day. His corpse, which still hung with his accomplice's from the gibbet where Villegagnon had had them tortured, not only measured the time that had elapsed by the yardstick of its putrefaction, but also provided the symbol of those days of drunkenness and amorous oblivion—to the point that no one passed these specters under the western redoubt without doffing his hat and sniffing.

Since the divorce of the two parties, the nights no longer echoed with caresses but with plots, secret meetings, and sometimes fights. The Catholics, who were still the more numerous, gathered in the neighborhood of the government house, or on the port, or at the very entrance to the fort. They liked to see themselves in groups, as their only superiority was in numbers. But nothing was going well otherwise. Among the members of this faction were sincere believers who were well versed in church dogma and in papal decrees, nostalgic for Roman pomp, for the Mass, for the varied sacraments, and, among these great sinners, for confession. This was the rarest group. Others fought for the Virgin Mary or one or another patron saint to whom they attributed their survival. Many were simply there by happenstance—they would have been sorely pressed to explain their choice. Although the least fanatic, these were regarded as the most dangerous, for it was toward them that the propaganda of the opposite faction was directed. And to relax the suffocating vice of suspicion that encircled them, they loudly and clearly voiced a hatred they did not at first feel but which, after being repeated collectively, at last filled them.

More serious still was that the Catholics had no leader. Dom Gonzagues held the post by default. But he was starting to be laughed at and to cause serious concern. It needed only for the debate to go on a bit long, or for the evening to be less animated than usual to send him publicly into a dream of poetry, which soon turned into loud snores. And as a final blow to the Catholic faction, which yet believed itself to represent rightful order and kingly power, it had no doctrine. It was known that the pope had convened a great council at Trent, but it had been going on for ages and had not yet given the faithful of the Roman Church a clear message as to what they should think and do.

Violence was thus the only hope and binding element of this loutish faction. A description of the tortures and murders they would inflict on the Protestants was more effective than any prayer in maintaining enthusiasm. They employed their energies in spying on the enemy and in devising plans for killing them. These activities gave the business the reassuring simplicity of a military campaign.

The Protestants, less numerous though forming a strong contingent because of their recent conversions, had congregated on the far side of the fort. The island, measuring ten acres in area and two hundred paces from shore to shore, was divided by an invisible line that separated one camp from the other. And though Maître Amberi had not marked the line on his land registry, he had drawn up its birth record at the colloquy on the Eucharist. Among the Protestants, the leaders were strong: Sieur du Pont led in temporal matters, constantly giving orders and seeing to their execution, while Richier led in spiritual matters, armed with Calvin's doctrine. He had banished doubt, if not the devil, and was able to administer the sacraments and lead prayers.

Yet the Protestants had not wanted the break, even if their intransigeance had caused it. The crisis had checked the spread of their influence, and the Huguenots' numbers were limited. Villegagnon's seclusion and the uncertainty of the situation provoked long meditations on the part of the Protestants and sharp debates among their leaders. Richier favored an aggressive offense, perhaps because of the humiliation his niece had suffered. He was for resuming the sermons, for holding public prayers and inviting the undecided to take part, for demanding, for pushing, for provoking. A Jericho to his trumpet, the Catholic party would not be long in tumbling down. Du Pont counseled caution, though it was not in his nature. They needed to win over more men, to bring to a discreet conclusion certain conversions, already well under way, of moderates who had not yet chosen one camp or another. In the meantime, he proposed sending one of their ships back to ask for reinforcements from Geneva. They would attack only after receiving them.

Finally the two points of view agreed on a compromise. Chartier, the second pastor, would go to Geneva to solicit Calvin's advice on the crisis and recruit fresh troops. These would be as skilled at weapons as they were at prayers, so as to speak to the Catholics in the only language they understood, which is to say, force. But to satisfy Richier's thirst for action, it was also decided that the Protestants in the meantime would exploit their initiative in the one field where their superiority could not be doubted. As only they had women and pastors, the holy transaction of matrimony was theirs to conduct unopposed. Richier let it be known that in two weeks' time he would publicly celebrate two new marriages.

•   •   •

The loneliest person, in these days of bitterness and waiting, was incontestably Just. No one felt more keenly than he the sensation of having lost everything. Villegagnon had taken him aside after Aude's recital and asked him in icy tones to confirm on his honor the allegations made about Colombe. Just had done so with a heavy heart. The admiral did not ask for reasons why they had lied to him for so long, and Just gave no explanation. The Knight of Malta left with a terrifying expression on his face, one that combined detachment, indignation, and contempt. Just had been crushed by it.

Just also knew that Colombe had left for good. At their final meeting, he now understood, he had been given one last chance to keep her from leaving. He looked at the jungle surrounding the island with the same horror he had felt on the day the expedition landed. The same impression of swarming, invisible creatures, of monstrous life forms desperately trying to perpetuate themselves in the midst of dereliction and absurdity, tightened his chest and oppressed him. He now felt the additional remorse of having driven into the jungle the one being he cared for most in all the world. Colombe had made a desperate choice, in rash reaction to disappointment, and he saw himself as the sole cause of this tragedy.

Neither the Catholic faction, with the posturing Dom Gonzagues, nor the Protestant party, which he felt to be hostile, offered him any haven. Just wandered all day long on the ramparts, in the sole company of his abandoned construction site. This work of human hands, robbed of its meaning by men's quarrels, was the concentrated expression of his melancholy. And as such, it warmed his heart. At certain times of day, when the sun was high and the Sugarloaf and all the forests along the coast displayed their murderous interlacings, their chaos, Just felt pride in belonging to the only species capable of ordering nature according to its own ideas, of creating a pure, rectilinear, and balanced image of perfection in stone and wood. All the admiral's lessons—as much those on Plato as on military fortification—seemed to hold mankind's distinguishing characteristic on earth. But at other times, especially at night, when a great visor clapped its darkness over the blue of the water, Just was filled with disgust. He sadly contemplated the ramparts in the violet shadow of the last light of day, which picked out the walls' imperfections, the chisel marks, the uneven alignment of the stones, the off-square blocks. He and his like had no other capacity but to build walls, to separate, to divide, to constrain. They had started to build the fort immediately on their arrival, and then to stop defections, they had surrounded the island with sand-filled baskets and watchmen. Now the walls served as a border between two opposing factions. And tomorrow, the two sides might fight over those same walls.

He paced the curtain wall all night, listening to the cries, the soughing, carried across from the mainland on the moist wind. Was Colombe calling him? When the moon rose, the unfinished fort took on the look of a ruin. He thought of Clamorgan's dungeon, its ivy, its empty moats. And if he finally fell asleep, huddled against the parapet, it was to escape his bad dreams.

One afternoon as he paced the battlements on the north side, alone as usual, he heard clear voices floating up to him from below. More from idleness than curiosity, he leaned over to hear. On the path by the sea, the same solitary path where he had often wandered with Colombe, two women were walking. By the time he had recognized Aude and her governess it was too late, they had seen him.

Since the business of the attack, Just had not been to visit the young Protestant woman. Unable to analyze his feelings toward her, he had driven her from his mind. He was angry that she had provided the immediate cause for Colombe's departure, and perhaps the motive as well. Whenever he remembered their conversation after the wedding, he flushed with anger and shame. But what most kept him from seeing her again was Colombe's simple remark: "You love her." He rejected the idea all the more violently because he was not so certain it was unfounded.

Aude started when she saw Just's crown of black hair through the crenels. She squeezed Chantal's arm, and the two stopped. It was then that Just noticed the two soldiers walking ten paces behind them, soldiers who had defected to the Huguenots and served as Aude's bodyguards. The girl looked as though she were about to speak, but the two men would soon be upon her. Instead, she shot

Just a long look, expressing a reproach, a question, and a promise. Then she continued calmly with her walk.

That night, Just thought back to the encounter, and he was angry with himself for being troubled by it. After his dinner, which he took alone behind the government house, he managed to drive Aude from his thoughts, and congratulated himself on it. Melancholy, at least, calls for no decisions. It cradles its votaries, turns them into infants suckling voluptuously at its breast. But this consolation, apparently, was not to be his. Arriving at the fort, where he intended to sleep, he found one of the soldiers assigned to guard Aude waiting for him in the darkness, sitting on a carved block of stone.

The rampart formed the advanced line of both camps. Few people ever walked along it, but it was understood that the sectarians of one religion and the other could move freely there. The soldier consequently showed no fear.

"I have a message," he told Just.

He was an old campaigner from the Savoie, simple and good-natured. He got along with everyone except Villegagnon, who had treated him high-handedly—and Du Pont had adroitly exploited his bruised feelings.

"Pastor Richier wants to have a word with you. They say it's important. Will you follow me?"

As in Le Freux's time, this call from the enemy seemed both dangerous and seductive. But Just no longer wanted to save anyone. If he went, it was more from indifference than conviction.

Entering the Protestant area behind the soldier, Just was aware for the first time of how deep the distrust between the two communities had grown. The peaceful figures scattered here and there along the path, seemingly daydreaming or asleep, were in fact outlying sentinels, ready to give the alarm in case of an enemy incursion. A soldier challenged them and only let them pass on hearing the proper password. The Huguenot camp had formed behind the eastern redoubt. The men were gathered around mess fires, their weapons at their sides, as though at a battlefield encampment. Just, who was widely known as Villegagnon's right arm, drew threatening glances.

Now that construction on the fort had stopped, Du Pont set the laborers to work for him. They had erected cabins with solid walls and even built a large room that was to hold the leaders' assemblies.

Just indignantly noticed that several blocks of dressed stone intended for the fort had been transported there and incorporated into the hastily raised structure of this counter-government house. When the soldier reached this building, he passed around it and, continuing his path, arrived at a small, newly built structure against the fortress wall covered in freshly cut palm fronds. A terrace had been cleared between the entrance to this lodge and the sea. On it were a table and two benches. Alone in the light of a hurricane lamp set on the ground, Aude was waiting for him. She waved him to the seat across from her, and the soldier disappeared into the darkness.

Just took his seat and looked around him for a moment. The sea was close by. Water lapped against the rocks a few yards away. On the wall side, the new cabin was lit up and open: it was clearly empty. Toward the redoubt, a steady murmur of preaching and praying rose from the mass of Huguenots crowded around the fires. The place had been well chosen for a meeting of this kind. Modesty was satisfied, as the two were in the sight of all. But it was far enough away from the others that their words, as long as they were spoken in low tones, could be uttered freely and heard only by themselves.

"I am happy that you have come," said Aude. And to head off any objections she added, "It was my uncle who had you called. He thought it necessary that I see you."

Just felt uncomfortable answering. He reflected that his embarrassment was explainable by the circumstances, but the pure beauty of the face before him, splashed with bright light and deep shadow, played its part in the astonishment of his soul.

"I wanted to tell you . . ." Aude went on.

Then she paused, to reassure him that she too felt troubling emotions.

". . . how much I regretted the incident."

Just straightened up, prepared to express his regrets too, but she stopped him.

"Let us not speak of it any more," she said. "I was not alluding to the event but to its consequences: my forced seclusion, your silence, and the reproaches you perhaps endured. I simply want you to know that I consider you innocent, and that it has in no way altered my . . . esteem for you."

This speech, clearly prepared beforehand, was peppered with hes-

itations, as an actress might do when she knows her text perfectly but
wants the audience to believe she is inventing it. And the final words
had been chosen with the deliberation of a hand palping the offerings in a fruit bowl.

"I am honored," said Just finally, reassured by the protocol. "Please
believe that if I had been able to prevent this outrage . . ."

"The worst of it was not the outrage against our persons," Aude
interrupted. "I have told you before: it is forgotten. But this irre-
sponsible act caused a division between the men on this island.
Christianity, which we represent, is making a spectacle of its
divorce."

These were Just's thoughts exactly. He was angry at Colombe for
having seen nothing but her own feelings, her loves and her hatreds,
without holding them in check to the general interest.

"Brothers are at each other's throats," said Aude.

The break between a brother and a sister had often been painfully
present in Just's mind over the past days. But at these words, it was
eclipsed by a much more serious rupture in fraternity, namely, in the
brotherhood that held together the fragile community of all men.
With her buttoned dress, her severe but delicate lace collar, her dignified and mysterious attitude, the young Protestant was not unlike
the fortress, rigorously ordered, with its curtain walls, scalloped parapet, and elegant strength. She was the counterweight to the vicious
unrestraint of the lawless and cannibalistic forests to whose disorder-
liness Colombe had surrendered.

"There are not many people," Aude went on, "who understand or
who feel what we are discussing here. If there is ever a chance of
bringing together the Christians on this island, it will be by strength-
ening the bonds between men of goodwill. And you are one of
them."

With matters thus on a general level, Just felt free to agree with
Aude and even expand on her thoughts.

"Yes," he said, "how right you are! All is not lost as long as we fend
off the fanatics. Even the admiral, I'm certain, is just waiting to be
shown that the love between men is stronger than the quarrels tearing them apart."

"Love, exactly," said Aude, an expression of enthusiasm on her face
that made her eyes shine even brighter, "the love . . . of man for man."

At these words, Just was momentarily flustered. Then, in a sudden release, they both laughed with embarrassment.

"What we need," Aude went on, not giving Just the time to inquire too closely into his emotions, "is to pick the best from each side, so as to set the example."

And as her plan depended on a perception of urgency, even if it meant exaggerating, she hesitated ever so slightly, as though making up her mind to run into the flames, and burst out, "My uncle has decided to hold weddings no matter what. It would be a shame if they didn't serve to bring together what is most divided, that is, the two groups of Christians who are tearing each other apart, counter to Christ's commandment to love one another."

Just hadn't fully understood.

"Does your uncle already know who he will join together?"

"No," said Aude, "that's the point. He will celebrate the weddings as they are proposed to him. But for lack of any relations with . . . across the way . . . he will be forced to marry couples from within our own religion. And that will not help toward reconciliation."

"I understand," said Just approvingly. Then, contradicting his statement, he asked, "And what can I do to further what you propose?"

"Well, you might find boys in your group to marry our girls. And convince the admiral, or someone else with the proper authority, to allow these unions to proceed."

Just frowned. He had no access to Villegagnon, and he had trouble imagining Dom Gonzagues or his partisans agreeing to anything but an abduction.

"I fear my chances of success are poor."

"Does hatred so rule their hearts?"

Saying nothing, Just gave a slight acknowledgment.

Aude remained silent, as she had planned. Then, easily, almost with relief, she embarked on her conclusion.

"In that case," she said gravely, "each person must shoulder his own responsibilities. When speech is no longer lawful, then one must do as Christ did and preach by example."

The tune of Psalm 104, softly sung by men, rose from the direction of the fires.

"If on each side," said Aude, looking intensely at Just, "the hand-

somest person, the wisest, the boldest, the most filled with forgive-
ness and peace, should come forward, and if the will of the one and
the other should be to make a union that embodied peace, order,
morality, and love . . ."

Her mouth, as she pronounced this word, momentarily assumed
the shape Just remembered from the first night, when he had carried
her from the ship, when it had so strongly suggested a kiss. But she
grew flustered and brought her sentence quickly to a close, whispering, ". . . then I think the island could be saved."

Silent, the whispering of the sea and of muffled voices washing
over them, they looked at each other a long moment through the
clear halo of the lamp. Little moths circled the flame, like the impatient souls of children dancing in limbo.

Everything had been said, and what hadn't been said was not
meant to be. Aude rose and, as though unable to control the powerful emotions welling inside her, gave a brief farewell and set off at a
rapid pace toward the great room, where her uncle was most likely
waiting for her. Just, though falling all over himself, had time to take
in her narrow waist, the soft drapes of her ample dress, the delicate
flesh of her wrists under the lace of her sleeves. Indifferent to the
coarse nudity of the savages, which horrified him as much as the surrounding jungles, he felt a violent emotion at the sight of this well-
appointed woman. The genius of civilization lay precisely in making
sexuality blossom while keeping it hidden away, in revealing through
dissimulation, in moving the very soul through modesty and artifice.

Walking back to the Catholic side with the soldier who had
brought him, Just had the terrible feeling of returning to exile.

CHAPTER 33

Chartier had left for Europe in early June, taking advantage of the favorable winds. The ship that carried him was the smallest in the fleet. The Catholics, all too happy to see the opposite camp weakened, if only by a little, had agreed to supply him with water and food. Chanting psalms, the Protestants followed the boat with their eyes as far as the cloud-heavy horizon. All their hopes now rested on Calvin, whom the pastor was to consult as soon as he landed. The rains were no longer far off, with their cortege of mud, of shivering, and of miasmas. Richier, to stave off the discouragement that menaced his troops, made a point of taking the initiative. The date of the weddings was hastily set, and preparations for the ceremony were to be completed in a week.

From all indications, the point of the wedding celebration was not simply to join the two remaining young girls to the two artisans chosen for them by Du Pont. Although the brides who had preceded them were already with child and thus promised to swell the Protestant numbers, it was clear that this stratagem could not be used in the short term to overwhelm the adversary. The real value of the weddings was to provide an example. It was not a question now, as it had once been, of turning the colonists away from vice: the religious conflict had had the unintended merit of distracting them from it. The Huguenot leaders' ambition was to demonstrate to all—and especially to the other faction—that they alone were still able to call on God and guarantee salvation. It was important, therefore, not to hold the ceremony inside the Protestant cantonment: the standard of the true faith had to be raised in the sight of all. The only site capable of providing such a platform was the fort. A neutral presence whose mass dominated the two opposing territories, the heights of the fortress would make a good altar, as close as possible to heaven.

Two days before the ceremony, a guard who was bolder than the rest and had no enemies in the opposing camp was assigned by Du Pont to carry the news of the celebration to the government house. He delivered a letter to the Scots duty guard and reported on his return that he had been well received, though Villegagnon, from what he understood, was still in seclusion.

Du Pont was unsure how to interpret the admiral's disappearance from view. It confirmed that the opposition was leaderless, which in itself was cause for rejoicing. But the silence also weighed too heavily not to seem freighted with mystery—of just the sort the Papists liked. And to the persecuted, mystery always carries the suggestion of a trap.

Whatever lay behind Villegagnon's behavior, it was too late to turn back. A military response—deploying armed men along the boundary—was not practicable. By tacit agreement, the two factions left one another's soldiers unmolested in the fort, lest they trigger hostilities. The procession therefore advanced at daybreak as a jovial troop, with the pastor in front beside a bareheaded Du Pont, followed by the betrothed and the few civilians the Protestant camp could boast. On reaching the roof of the fortress, Richier had the satisfaction of seeing a crowd of onlookers gathered peaceably on the Catholic side. Some took their hats in their hands and gave the sign of the cross when they saw him, a good omen. The entire complement of Indian slaves, being always short of distractions, had taken their place among the curious.

Free to act according to their lights, the Huguenots gave the ceremony a simple and good-natured, while yet grave and reverential, character, which to them was the appropriate way to address a God and not an idol. The wedding couples stood around the pastor, and everyone was struck with their good and natural aspect, at least in comparison to those who had gone before them.

Aude was in the first row of the audience, sitting unaffectedly and as if by chance on the side that gave her a view over the port, the government house, and the whole Catholic camp. Her eyes followed with rapt tenderness the devolution of the little crowd around the celebrant, and she seemed not to notice the hungry stares fixed on her from all sides as the last remaining female to be married. True, there still remained the reserves, consisting of the governesses, but they generated less enthusiasm. Aude, modest and unperturbed, royally ignored the carnal thoughts she inspired. Her gaze often wandered off into the distance, and one would have been hard put to guess how specific was the object of her search and how desperate she was at nowhere seeing it.

The ceremony was already well underway before she finally had the satisfaction of seeing Just appear. He had stayed hidden by the southern redoubt a long time, looking toward the coast. It was as though he were waiting for some mysterious signal from the jungled slopes, some cry not from a heron or a monkey. But nothing, of course, came to offer a counterweight to his decision. Since his nighttime interview with Aude, he had been able to think of nothing else. His fascination had had the effect of lifting his melancholy, and his despair was gone. The girl's energy, along with what he could not bring himself to call his desire, filled him with new hope. He had been offered a solution. A horrible rift divided the men and undermined their works, but he and Aude could counter it through the grace of their union. Yet were there not other reasons for wanting this? What, in a word, did he feel toward her? He was resolved not to ask himself the question, instead putting the general and generous motives for his decision to the fore. He nonetheless sensed that under his reasoned arguments lay unclear and perhaps contradictory feelings. The young lady herself attracted him and filled him with fear. Of course, she was the first civilized woman he had had a chance to meet since becoming an adult. Everything about her was beautiful, just, and good, a reflection of the idea of man, which God—as Villegagnon said—had placed in woman so that she might, despite her vices, be the instrument of man's redemption. But just as the varnished surface of the forest, with its green hummocks, pure plumes of sycamores, spreading brazilwood umbrellas, hid within it the smell of death and loveless struggles, Aude's sweet, humble appearance intimated more troubled depths, a tenuous patience, and perhaps, quite simply, violence.

Yet on this desolate island at the edge of the world, balanced as it was on the brink of a fratricidal war, Just was not looking for tranquil happiness but for the force of an ideal, the thrust of an act. His was not the choice the bourgeois makes, of measuring his ease and spreading it harmoniously throughout the family. Aude might harbor frightening energy, but this did not entirely displease him. The truth was that on the very night of their conversation, he had made himself a vow: he would marry her. Only the thought of Colombe, the certainty that by this act he would lose her forever, caused him pain. But no sign had arrived to turn him from it.

With the rudiments of a courtesy he had learned from his sister— though she hardly practiced it herself—Just went and washed his face and pulled a currycomb through his hair. He changed his shirt for another, exhausting his wardrobe. The new shirt was collarless— he was baring his neck, he thought, like a man condemned to the gallows. It was at this point in his reflections that he was spotted by Aude as her prayerful gaze swept the horizon.

Just's plan was simple. And thinking of what he had to do was a good way to calm himself. He had calculated it to the last detail, even to the number of steps between one point and another. He would first take his place in the audience, follow the ceremony, then, at the last moment, before the pastor could dismiss the assemblage, he would walk forward and solemnly ask Richier for his niece's hand. If it was granted to him, he would then address both camps from the platform with a harangue calling for peace. He offered silent thanks to Villegagnon for having supplied him with cultivated references: by going from one quotation to another, as a traveler proceeds from inn to inn, he would be less likely to lose his path or be attacked along the way.

Just entered the fort silently, climbed the stairs to the ramparts, and took his place in the ceremony. His heart was thumping. He avoided looking at Aude. The precaution would prove useless, though he did not know it yet, for it had been ordained that danger would arrive on that day from an unexpected quarter and in an unforeseen shape.

The celebrant had decided to recite texts from the Gospel. Things were proceeding at a ceremonial pace, which is to say that a pleasant drowsiness was stealing over the assembly, a state helpful in assimilating the sacred and allowing one's soul to speak.

Large stationary clouds on the horizon, in violet robes and white hats, formed almost a second assembly, vaster than the first and surrounding it with a mute benevolence. Stirred by an impending storm, small flocks of parrots flew haltingly from one treetop to another. A big red and blue butterfly, which the inner child might well see as an angel, fluttered for a long time around the pastor. One of the couples, hard put to contain themselves, burst into giggles.

Richier read the parable of Lazarus, while shooting glances over toward the Catholics. Everyone understood what corpse it was that Christ might bring back to life. And more than one person reflected that the Catholics' lack of a priest had led to the spiritual death of many among them. A nostalgia for harmony and communion gently stole into all hearts. The pastor sensed it and fanned the feeling all the harder with his inspiration.

A sudden noise from the government house shocked the peace. First came sounds of raised voices, of rattling ironmongery, of doors opening and closing. Then a small group formed on the esplanade and soon advanced toward the fort.

Mainly visible in this detachment were the tall figures of the Scots. In full regalia, wearing kilts, bonneted, armed with halberds, the Caledonians marched in formation, yet their aspect, reassuringly, was more ceremonial than warlike. In their midst, toward the front, trotted Dom Gonzagues, his beard combed smooth, wearing the tunic of the Knights of Malta, his face a mask of anger, distorted further by the pain of his rheumatism. But upon reaching the foot of the ramparts, the group opened like the two halves of a walnut and disgorged by way of nutmeat Villegagnon's giant frame, which swept majestically into the fort. Though the pastor continued with his litany as though oblivious, no one was listening to him any longer. All eyes were trained toward the head of the stairs, where the admiral slowly emerged. He was a frightening sight. His long days of fasting had left him gaunt, practically skeletal. His skin, wherever it appeared under his brushy beard threaded with gray, was yellow and shining, stretched over points of bone that threatened to pierce it. The knight's eyes, set in a maelstrom of dark rings and wrinkles, sunken like a dying man's, cast a spray of sparks around him.

But most spectacular of all was his dress. Abandoning the uniform of Malta in which all were accustomed to see him, he had inserted himself into a new costume, made for him in great secret by the tailor during the preceding days. His doublet was sewn from blue cloth of gold that shone in the sun, while bright yellow breeches puffed around his hips, and his meager legs were encased in tammy stockings of apple-green. A blood-red cape and a white toque, made of sail canvas, completed the plumage of this monstrous parrot. But the long sword at his side silenced any impulse to laugh.

The ranks parted and the admiral, with the majesty natural to him, settled in the front row, face to face with Du Pont. Dom Gonzagues followed limpingly and took a position at his side. Then Villegagnon locked his terrifying eyes on the pastor and waited. Richier showed his courage by continuing to officiate as though nothing had happened, or almost nothing, but the hand holding his Bible trembled visibly. The silence had reinstated itself, churned by a moist wind, and the sacred words of the service drained from it as from a cracked cistern. Suddenly, rising above the droning tones of the celebrant, came Villegagnon's voice. The power of this instrument was familiar enough for all to know that he was still speaking quietly. Yet he was heard from one redoubt to the other.

"I don't understand," he said, leaning imperceptibly toward Dom Gonzagues, "where are the chasubles, the surplices, the monstrances?"

Richier, in black as ever, grew slightly flustered. He began to see what was to follow. The moment had arrived to join the brides and grooms. He advanced toward the first couple, took the right hand of each betrothed, and pronounced a few words.

"Ah!" said Villegagnon. "Gonzagues, the holy chrism, I pray you."

The old captain, prepared beforehand, pulled an earthenware vial from his pocket.

"Here!" said the admiral to Richier. "It was confected according to rule: one part salt, two of olive oil, and one of saliva."

So saying, he walked forward, holding the little vial. The pastor drew back with a show of horror.

"What!" said Villegagnon. "You don't anoint the bride and groom with holy chrism?"

He allowed a few seconds to elapse, holding out the vial, while the other shielded himself from it. Then with an ugly smile and a false air of courtesy, the admiral returned to his place.

"That's odd," he said to Gonzagues. "A wedding without holy unction. Well . . . let's see what happens next."

Du Pont was growing restless. The assembly, frozen with fear, could see the wagon of catastrophe hurtling down the fatal slope and waited for the explosion.

The couples were joined one after the other in the Protestant way as Villegagnon looked on, feigning surprise and disbelief. Then it was time for the Eucharist, and Richier, his mind racing as he officiated, calculated what he might do to avoid an incident. The wisest course would have been to stop the ceremony there and then. But a board had been laid across two trestles, and the bread and wine waited there too ostensibly to be neglected. With a mental effort of courage—for the knight's broad frame loomed in the front row—the pastor started to administer the sacrament.

"By the Virgin and all the saints!" said Villegagnon joyfully. "The body of Our Lord Jesus Christ!"

The pastor took up the bread, frankly trembling. The admiral walked toward the altar and planted himself in front of it, tall and threatening.

"Before I kneel," he said, looking at the pastor with eyes feverish from fasting, "do you affirm that He is truly there?"

Du Pont considered that the time had come to intervene. He leapt to Richier's side of the table and said firmly, "Stop this scandal, sir! Step back. Take your place again."

"My place is in the front row before God, when He has the grace to offer Himself to me."

"That grace is given you only in proportion to your humility," Du Pont retorted.

"Do you affirm that He is truly there?" Villegagnon repeated, dismissing everything but the pastor and the host that quivered in his fingers.

"He is there in substance," said Richier, attempting a last theological feint.

"In substance! How very excellent," said Villegagnon with terrifying joy, "for it's His substance that I want. I am hungry for Him, do you hear, I want to tear at His muscles and drink His blood, feed on His flesh and feel in my guts the warmth of His holy heart."

He had shouted these words, his bass voice thundering like a storm, and his strange costume, which was the color of the threatening sky, of blood, of lightning, had transformed him into a being from another world, set there to wreak incalculable vengeance on man.

Richier stepped back. Everything was about to collapse. At that point, Du Pont bounded forward, taking the celebrant's place, and standing directly in front of Villegagnon slowly pronounced the one word:

"Cannibal!"

The brilliant green of the water seemed to wrinkle under the shock. The very Sugarloaf doubled over at the blow, the walls of the fortress shook. Stupor alone prevented the crowd from running away. Villegagnon stiffened as though he had been pierced from end to end. His immobility was so terrifying that the violence, when it came, seemed almost reassuring.

In the general stupor only the Indians, on the Catholic side, voiced an admiring murmur. The ceremony seemed to them less static than the earlier ones and, if truth be told, more like their own idea of a celebration. Villegagnon fired them a look that effectively silenced them and abruptly drew his sword. Dom Gonzagues did likewise, and the Scotsmen raised their halberds.

Only the presence of the chalice and the host, whose sacred power was only now being acknowledged, kept Villegagnon from striking the man who stood behind them.

"I will stuff that word down your throat," Villegagnon shouted.

At the sound of shouting, the Huguenot soldiers ran to their weapons. Harquebuses were hastily loaded. On the Catholic side below there was an uproar as well. But Villegagnon remained stationary, sword in hand like a great heraldic bird. Then suddenly he pronounced his sentence, which put off the massacre until a later time.

"Be gone!" he shouted. "Impostors, heretics, assassins of the true God! I give you two weeks to leave this land, which you besoil with your presence, and never return."

Du Pont knew the disparity in arms too well to sound the battle call himself. He formed his face into an icy mask of indifference and contempt.

The admiral, his sword still unsheathed, turned brusquely and went out, accompanied by Dom Gonzagues and his guards. Once he had gone, the Protestants in turn trooped down the stairs.

Just had stood still and watched Aude pass in front of him, her eyes to the ground. He was unable to read anything in the brief flashing glance she sent him.

He remained alone on the fortress, stunned and distraught, knowing that he too must leave this site blasted by hatred and choose his camp. He thought for a moment of Colombe, of wanting to be near her, of playing once more their old games at Clamorgan. He looked for a long time toward the jungle, then he descended the stairs. And his steps, despite himself, led him to the government house.

IV

The Legacy of Siena

CHAPTER 34

Martin now ruled over an empire, but an empire of terror. The violence he used to subdue the coastal Indians was meted out by a band of lawless and godless miscreants whom he had to terrorize in turn. Five times during the preceding months he had escaped attempts at assassination. The most powerful man on the coast, he faced the same challenge he had faced in childhood as a street beggar: to survive, to save his skin, to roll in the muck of uncertain scuffles and treacherous ambushes. He slept only by day, in a hammock of thin cotton, through whose fabric he could, when awake, see threatening shadows approach. He kept a dagger in his right hand and a straight razor open against his side. The nights were spent in drinking. By making the *cahuin* flow like water and the women submit to the caprices of his henchmen, Martin demonstrated his power and prodigality as a leader. But ever the hunted bandit, he found it reassuring to see his rivals addled and vomiting. And when, in the depths of their drunkenness, they foolishly revealed their dark plots against him, he killed them.

The truth was that he could not get used to the dark solitude of the jungle. The hours of the night were periods of horrible anguish and disgust for him. He built his house at the highest point of the forest on the flanks of the Sugarloaf. This promontory reassured him because it escaped the terrifying blackness of the jungle's depths. Backed against the hard, smooth wall of the mountain, he was at least sure that he need fear nothing from that direction. And at dawn, in the other direction, he could clearly see the bay and the island from which the dog Villegagnon had driven him.

Designed by carpenters who had defected to him and built by Indian slaves, his house bore a resemblance to the houses of merchants in the port of Honfleur. Back in the old days, lying idly on the wharfs between one dark assignment and another, he had often dreamt of being a prosperous and well-respected bourgeois. He would live in a half-timbered house, wear gold-embroidered cloth, and receive the powerful. He would hear children running on the floor above and servants drawing water from the well in back. At present he was richer than the wealthy men of that Norman burg. At his feet lay the largest bay in the world, where the riches of a continent glistened. He could have bought ten houses on the inlets of Honfleur. But because he ruled in America, because he had only incompetents and primitives to work with, his palace was no more than a pale, ramshackle copy that threatened to collapse at every hard rain. He had had it decorated with the handsomest objects stolen from trading stations and ships, but the hodge-podge had neither style nor distinction. For the most part, he held his meetings in clearings along the coast, as Le Freux had once done.

He brought people to his house only to show them his power. At night, lit by dozens of torches, and with each room attended by three slaves dressed in blue livery, the rudimentary structure took on almost majestic airs. Martin would put three Indian women at his feet, chosen from among the prettiest, and seat himself in a large claw-footed Spanish armchair. With his deeply circled eyes, his big fists, his broken nose, he had the melancholy aspect of a cruel child. But the scene could work its illusion only on a stranger, and strangers rarely came. And so, when the news arrived one morning that the Greek was returning from Salvador with a Portuguese emissary, Martin prepared his favorite nighttime ceremony to receive them.

Night had fallen two hours before, black and starless, with lowering clouds in the sky overhead. But the rainy season was not quite upon them, and Martin hoped it would come as late as possible. His poorly built house leaked at every pore. It lost all its majesty in bad weather. Fortunately, the sound of the wind gusting in the jacarandas meant that the air was still hot and dry. The visitors entered through the great door, and an Indian in lackey's costume led them to the master.

The Greek still had the surly and begrimed face of a footpad. He was one of the convicts whose reprieve had been bought by Ville-gagnon, and he had fled on the very night Le Freux attacked the island. Martin trusted him to carry out the violent and distant missions he assigned him, but he did not expect him to show any admiration: the brute never noticed anything. The Portuguese stranger was likely to give him more satisfaction.

The man was small and unclean, in the way of one who has just lived several weeks as a savage, but evident behind this poor appearance were the reserve and gravity of a well-born personage. His youth—he could not have lived many more years than Martin—was weighted by a thick beard and short, almost frizzy hair. He had an extremely long, thin nose and prominent cheekbones, which gave him a fierce, proud aspect. Martin, who knew something about men and owed his survival to the knowledge, immediately caught a flash of intelligence in his visitor's eyes, a look of nobility and cunning, that made him most welcome.

"Agostino Alvarez de Cunha," said the man, bowing.

He showed respect for the lord of the land while carrying himself with a confidence that seemed to say, We belong to the same race of rulers. Martin liked that.

"I believe you have been looking for me, Dom Agostino?" said Martin, allowing one of his hands to drop down from his throne to the submissive hair of one of the slave girls.

"Are you not the most powerful man on this coast? Can anything be done here without you?" said Agostino with a courtier's seriousness, which yet admitted a smile of connivance.

Martin was not used to such airs and graces, though he had done all he could to teach them to the miscreants he led. He looked with lordly ease toward the four or five acolytes sprawled on stools around the room.

"And what do you intend in these parts, sir?" asked Martin, in the same courteous tone he would have liked his cutthroats to adopt.

"The same as yourself, most illustrious lord."

This expression, a literal translation from the Portuguese, was somewhat excessive. Martin glanced at his knaves angrily. The louts would certainly make fun of him for this title at their next orgy.

"My name is Martin," he said.

"I know it, most illustrious Lord Martin," replied this stubborn man with his exaggerated sense of protocol.

"And what is it," went on Martin, leaving the question of titles behind, "that you have come to do 'like us'? Are you also here to trade for wood and fruit?"

He had spoken this with the nasty expression of a merchant addressing a rival. But he didn't believe it. The Greek, in requesting to bring Agostino to him, had hinted that the man's business might prove very lucrative to Martin and his band.

"No," said Dom Alvarez, "we have no intention of hampering your activities in that field. Our aim is purely political; we would like to capture Fort Coligny and kill Villegagnon."

In certain circles, milieus where violence is commonplace, the announcement of a crime may be met with the same deep and heart-felt gratitude a person more usually shows at receiving a birthday present. Martin rose on hearing these words, walked toward Dom Alvarez, and took his hands in his.

"Splendid!" he said, pressing his hands warmly. "An excellent idea."

"This country," went on the emissary, "belongs by ancient and incontestable title to Portugal. All who farm it or who trade here are welcome."

He nodded amiably toward Martin, who responded in kind.

"But those who come armed to defy our king, who pillage the land and, what's more, pervert it with a false and violent religion, those we will drive out."

Martin returned to his seat and ordered chairs brought up for the Greek and Dom Alvarez. *Cahuin* was served, and a large tray of fruit. Martin suddenly saw his efforts paying off. Lord knows how many lessons it had taken to introduce a semblance of civility to the jungle. He had even had to strangle with his own hands an Indian who obstinately kept reaching into the most indiscreet part of his livery while serving drinks. Now, owing to this educated Portuguese noble-man, it was all making sense for the first time.

"Our king," said Dom Alvarez after they had drunk several toasts, "has just sent a new governor to Bahia, His Excellency Mem de Sá. I had the honor of accompanying him. We arrived in Salvador three months ago. He has asked me to extend his greetings to you, in the name of the Crown."

Martin was bursting with pleasure. He had crossed the Atlantic in the bottom of the hold, conquered an empire with steel and blood, eaten human flesh with the Indians, made native women pregnant, amassed gold, killed more men than he could count—and now a king of Europe was extending his greetings to him.

"Please be so kind, Dom Alvarez, as to extend him mine in return," Martin simpered. "Tell him, pray, that there is nothing he could ask me to do that I would not perform on the spot, if it should lie within my power."

"Quite so."

Martin started nervously. Now they were coming to the crux of it.

"His Excellency Mem de Sá is a man of faith," went on the Portuguese. "He is unwilling to continue merely defending the planters and merchants as his predecessors did. We are not on the American continent for sugar and cotton, but for honor and the true faith. He is determined to launch an expedition into the Bay of Rio de Janeiro to annihilate Villegagnon, replace his usurping rule with one loyal to our king, and, in time, bring a powerful army of Jesuits to spread the faith throughout this country. Your help, most illustrious sir, will be decisive to our efforts."

They were now beyond protocol and playacting. Martin rose to his feet in order to think fast and well.

"You may count on my help," he said, "but what exactly can I do?"

"Our colony's forces are still limited. We must guard against two dangers. First, that of sending too weak an expedition and having that dog of a Frenchman hold us off. We must have the capacity to destroy him despite his defenses. And the second danger is to send too many troops and needlessly weaken our settlement in Salvador de Bahia for the duration of the campaign. Consequently, we need precise information on the enemy's strength."

"That's not impossible," said Martin. "We could put sentinels on the beach to observe, count the cannons, and draw a plan of the island."

"Very good," said Dom Alvarez. "But that is not enough for us."
He leaned forward.

"We want to know his forces from the inside," he said in a lower voice. "And even, if you catch my meaning, prevent the enemy from making full use of them."

Martin looked steadily at him.

"I understand. A betrayal . . ."

The Portuguese nodded in assent.

"That will be hard," Martin grumbled, frowning. "The island is under constant watch, and I can't imagine how to land anyone there. Unless we manage to bribe one of the men who come to the mainland. But they always come in groups now, accompanied by a guard."

"Don't trouble yourself," said Agostino proudly. "We already have this intelligence."

Martin's face showed surprise.

"Yes," said the Portuguese, "we have a man on the island. All we ask is that you make contact with him, bring him anything he needs, and relay his information back to us."

This was unexpected news, almost inconceivable. Martin asked what the spy looked like. Dom Alvarez described Vittorio the Venetian to him. That wretch? thought Martin, but he kept it to himself.

"He answers to only one signal," said Agostino. "You have to say 'Ribera' to him."

"Ribera!" said Martin sniggering, for he was thinking of Vittorio and couldn't help admiring his duplicity.

"Give us your price for contacting him," said Agostino.

The Greek gave Martin a greedy look. This was just what he had predicted. There was much money to be made in this business. A chance at a fortune, which Martin would surely make the most of. But the young leader reflected. From the moment he had heard Dom Alvarez's proposal, Martin had been measuring the strength of his position: without him, the Portuguese would be taking a great risk, and Villegagnon's military skill could prove their undoing. Rio de Janeiro's future was in his hands. Money was no longer the issue. Being powerful in a country with nothing in it no longer sufficed him. Already his riches outstripped what could be bought. What he really wanted was to be someone when this land was something. He thought for a long time in silence, then said:

"I accept the assignment, but here is my condition."

Dom Alvarez made no motion. He was waiting for a figure and knew what he could pay.

"I want letters patent for this land in which we find ourselves. I conquered it on behalf of the interpreters of the coast, whom I lead. It belongs to us. Your king must recognize this . . . and make me a duke."

A chill wind, which had risen with the full moon, came in from the terrace. Dom Alvarez, feeling the cold, shivered all over his body. The words disconcerted him, coming on top of the *cahuin*. He asked to be excused to consider his answer.

· · ·

Since emerging from his long seclusion, Villegagnon had not been still for a moment. The altercation with the Protestants had acted as a declaration of war. The admiral strode through his camp as though giving final orders for a battle. The neglect of the past weeks of leaderlessness had had a terrible effect on discipline, dress, and provisions. Villegagnon distributed rebukes and punishments with no sign of the gruff humanity he had once shown. Passing under the gibbet where Le Freux hung in a final state of decomposition, he felt a sudden urge to suspend new fruit from the structure. When a colonist was caught during a water detail polluting himself with a native woman, he was summarily hanged. Until the last moment, no one believed the punishment would actually be carried out, not even the hapless sinner, who approached the rope smiling. But the admiral himself kicked the barrel out from under the man's feet. As he struggled at the end of his hemp noose, the condemned man's expression registered more surprise than pain.

The Indians were the next victims of Villegagnon's new cruelty. One of them was sentenced to a whipping, ostensibly for falling asleep at work but more likely because he had laughed out loud during the wedding ceremony. Finding the executioner too lenient, the admiral took the strap from him and beat the prisoner himself, so long and hard that the Indian collapsed on the ground unconscious.

All standing orders had been harshened. Anyone on the beach at night without leave was to be shot on sight, even if nowhere near the ship's boats. All contact with the Protestants was considered an act of

high treason, and Villegagnon himself would administer whatever
sentence he considered appropriate. This was understood to mean
that death would be too light a punishment and that the admiral
would preface it with other torments. Obligatory prayer meetings
were now held morning and night. As there was no consecrated offi-
ciant, Villegagnon led the reading of the Word and the orison. He
had designed a series of ceremonial outfits, and the tailors worked
night and day to finish them. He went so far as to take down the
hangings in the government house to make stoles and chasubles. He
had vestments made for him of nankeen and raw silk, of sailcloth, of
camlet, even of upholstering leather. He no longer appeared except
in these brightly colored tunics and billowing capes, capped by
flounced toques, broad hats, and bonnets pricked with feathers.

A sackbut player accompanied him everywhere, announcing his
arrival with a resounding flourish. A clogmaker, blond and porcine,
was chosen to act the part of his page. He followed the admiral when
he went to prayers, holding Titian's Virgin to his stomach.

When Just returned to the Catholic camp, he had at first been a
quiet witness to these developments. But on the second day, Villegagnon summoned him to the government house. He received him
alone in the large audience hall. Just was surprised to find the admiral in a simple cambric shirt. The ceremonial clothes in which he had
paraded that very morning hung from a wooden mannequin.

"Come in!" ordered the admiral. "Sit down."

Just waited a long moment while the admiral, who seemed to be
listening to voices from the heavens, remained silent.

"You lied to me," the admiral thundered, coming back to earth.

Just was afraid he too would be put to death by way of example.
In fact, he was so mortified he would not have objected.

"It proves that you're no better than the others," Villegagnon went
on in the same stentorian tones.

But suddenly his expression softened, and he settled at the far end
of the table, resting on one elbow.

"But you're not the worst either, not by any means."

He wiped his big hand across his tired eyes.

"At least you're brave and intelligent. All men commit sins. I was
wrong to believe you were an exception to the general law."

Just didn't know how to behave: as a condemned man or a penitent. He kept his two hands resting on his knees and his eyes on the ground.

"I forgive you," said Villegagnon summarily. "I forgive you and I invest you with my confidence once more. Or rather, I'll extend it to you on loan, because this time, believe me, I'll be watching you. You will command half my army."

This last sentence made no sense. Just raised his eyebrows surprisedly.

"We are at war, did you not know?"

Just shook his head.

"There are no longer soldiers and colonists here, nor slaves and workers. There is only an army. It consists of two parts: the knights and old campaigners on one side, and on the other all those who worked for you building the fortress and whom you will now lead in war."

"But those who worked for me know nothing about fighting," Just ventured.

"You'll teach them discipline and the basics of combat. They can fire the cannons and wield wooden cudgels. I have ordered the forge to make a cutlass for each of them."

Villegagnon gave a further host of details as to what he expected of his new troops and their leader. The day had grown hot. It was the middle of the afternoon, made stifling by the giant hand of a distant storm. Villegagnon showed less energy than at the beginning of the interview. At a certain point, his tone became unguarded and wandering, no longer giving orders but taking the sinuous path of confidences.

"I taught you that man is good," he said, not waiting for an answer. "It was my great mistake to have believed it. These Protestants saved me, in their way."

He looked at the painting of the Virgin, which the clogmaker had hung back up askew.

"The truth is that man is a fallen creature, besmeared with sin to varying degrees. Some men are still perfectible, while others are beyond redemption. They embody evil, and that's all. To perfect humankind, we must educate those who are susceptible to education . . . and eliminate the rest."

Villegagnon finished his peroration practically in a whisper. But suddenly he awoke and leapt to his feet.

"I have seen my mistake," he shouted. "It is *useless*, you see, to call on reason to justify faith. To believe, by Saint Jack of Jerusalem, is to submit. Men don't go to God, they *render themselves* unto Him. In other words, they capitulate before his omnipotence."

He stood in front of his yellow and blue suit, which was perched on the wooden frame like a parrot.

"Only through might can we serve God. Ornaments, music, the most ponderous art—that crushes men under the sense of their own insignificance—this is how God can triumph. Otherwise, it is those vipers, those accursed . . ."

So saying, he raised his nose like a mastiff in the direction of the fort and beyond it to the Protestant camp, thirsting for vengeance.

"I'll only rest when those pigs have left," he growled.

Then, turning back toward Just, he calmed down and resumed his earlier practical tone.

"You will see that they are taken over to the coast in ten days. I want no delays, no weakness, and no naiveté either: they'll be dangerous to the very end."

"But where will they live on the mainland?" Just dared to ask.

"Where?" snickered Villegagnon. "Why don't they rely on the providence of their false God to tell them where! Let Him provide caves for those swine, and abysses, let Him hurl them into gehenna and roast them! Unless He'd rather have wild animals swallow them up."

Just left the admiral still fired up with ideas of vengeance and engaged in feverish prayer.

He had next gone to the knights' headquarters, where military preparations were underway. A terrible melancholy overtook him. He was no doubt happy that Villegagnon had forgiven him. But he shared neither the admiral's excitement nor his hatred. When it had been a question of building Antarctic France, the knight's ardor had won him, and he had felt the same desire to give his life to defend an idea and build a lasting work.

In a young mind, teaching only plucks strings that are already strung and ready to be played. When the admiral had presented the humanists' ideas to him, Just had recognized his own palette in their clear colors: their azure blues, light ochers, and mauves, which he had perhaps picked up in his forgotten years in Italy. Whereas today, his whole being rebelled against the dark philosophy the admiral professed. Even the idea of assuming one of the main commands on the island left him indifferent, almost ashamed. Flight was forbidden him, ardor inaccessible. He hardly dared think even of Colombe, so strong was his shame at seeing himself through her eyes.

CHAPTER 35

Colombe now lived naked. She had made the decision when she returned to Païz-Lo's. Her early distress after leaving the island had been replaced by a dull rage against everything that came from there. Since that world had rejected her, she would reject it in turn. Nothing could seem more grotesque and criminal than this laughable attempt at colonization. She saw Villegagnon as a monster drunk on his own power. His hatred of women was simply an expression of his terror in the face of life, of nature, and of love. In place of these joys, he cultivated war, destruction, and hatred. Little by little, to assuage the loss she felt at Just's absence, Colombe came to include her brother in the dark picture she painted of the island and its residents. If he had so readily accepted the stamp of authority to the point of becoming its instrument, it was no doubt because Just was made of a softer, baser metal than she had thought. Rather than continue to suffer, waiting for news of him that never came, she preferred to bury him in the mass of grievances she held against the colony.

And so she came to believe that by driving her from that hell, fate had done her a good turn. Her misfortune was in fact an opportunity, provided she found the boldness to follow its implications to their logical end. First, she should never return to the European world. Second, she was forced to recognize that she now belonged to

America's forests. She must abandon herself to their simplicity and peace. Paï-Lo's was only a stage on her way. Eventually she would join a tribe and live among other Indians. In the meantime she had to combat everything in herself that tended to separate her from this natural life, everything that the old world had left her in the way of hateful prejudices and needs. Going unclad had been the first step in this new direction.

Paï-Lo's women pursued their lives in a variety of costumes, and nudity was only one of a number of ways of being. They accepted Colombe's decision simply: they cut her hair in the Indian style, painted urucú tattoos on her skin. The first time he saw her in this guise, Paï-Lo showed no surprise or disapproval. He said simply, by way of a fond and respectful compliment, that if he weren't old and inert, he would marry her. He gave her a present of bracelets of periwinkle and mother-of-pearl.

Only Quintin showed some uneasiness before the Indian Colombe—he who had been the first to teach her of the pious simplicity of the body was now scared to see it naked beside him, perhaps because of its whiteness. As it was, the poor man was presently undergoing a crisis of conscience. He had entered Paï-Lo's woman-rich precincts with a strong missionary ambition and had at first converted a half-dozen women of the household to his religion of love. He embraced them one after the other, lavishing caresses on them, spicing his performance with readings from the Bible. But he quickly realized that it was largely a game for the women. They always arranged for one or another of them to walk in on the lesson in progress. The woman being proselytized would run off giggling with her friend, and Quintin would be left at a loss.

And then one day, one of these women had shown herself to be more serious. She was a big Indian with heavy features, and her name was Ygat. Her flat, square face registered expressions slowly. She wasn't, like her friends, quick to laugh and mock. When he introduced the Gospel to her, he hadn't felt the somewhat frivolous excitement that ordinarily overtook the women he tried to convert. This one neither submitted nor imposed: she answered his actions with actions of her own, marked by gravity and tenderness. He lost himself in her the first day, thinking less of the Gospels, for once, than of the smile of ecstasy he had brought to her thick lips.

When a preacher finds a willing ear, he inevitably wants to repeat himself. Quintin ended up devoting the major portion of his time and energy to Ygat's education. More seriously, he no longer felt the inclination to carry his teaching elsewhere. This state of affairs cast him into gloom. He spoke to Païe-Lo of his problems.

"And what exactly makes you so unhappy about all this?" the old man asked.

"Don't you understand? I have devoted my whole life to spreading the Gospel of Love, and now I don't have the strength to carry out my apostolic mission."

Païe-Lo stroked his beard with his bony hand.

"Might you not also introduce me to your teaching?" he asked ingenuously.

"Never!" said Quintin indignantly. "I preach the free expression of desire. And my desire leads me only toward women."

"That's not what I meant," said Païe-Lo. "Couldn't you simply explain to me how this love that you find hidden in Christ's message is manifested?"

"Well," said Quintin gravely, "it is a language, and the body is its alphabet. It is articulated through caresses, through tender gestures. And it concludes with that communion which frees men and women from their individual limits and allows them a glimpse of eternal life."

Païe-Lo pondered for a long time. Then, as a little red squirrel hopped nearby, he absently held out his hand and said to Quintin, "I'm going to provoke you a little, all right? But it seems to me that the Protestants are right in wanting to burn you."

"And why is that?" asked Quintin.

"Because they deny salvation through works, whereas you practice it."

"I don't understand a word you're saying."

The squirrel had climbed onto Païe-Lo's fingers, and he lifted him up. The animal's round eye examined Quintin mistrustfully.

"You give too much importance to gestures, my friend!" said Païe-Lo. "To prove the existence of love, which I believe as you do to be divine, you think it is enough to practice its rites. But, if I may say so, you never get beyond appearances."

Quintin lowered his eyes.

"You give caresses the way others trade in relics or sell indulgences for getting into heaven."

"And what else can I do, since those are our desires?" Quintin retorted.

"Oh, I have no advice to give you," said Paï-Lo mildly. "I simply believe that what is happening to you is a great opportunity."

"An opportunity! No longer to be able to spread love?"

"No longer to spread it, perhaps . . ." said Paï-Lo.

And looking at Quintin with a disarming smile, full of light and goodness, he added gently, "But to know it."

•   •   •

One day, finally, Paraguaçu arrived. Her tribe was in the neighborhood, and she came over on foot and alone to see her friend. Colombe was at the waterfalls that morning with the other women. Paraguaçu found them there, and the reunion took place in the clear water with tears, shouts, mock fights with branches, and crowns of flowers.

"How you've changed, Sun-Eye!"

"Changed in dress?" laughed Colombe.

"No, changed in body. When I knew you, you were a little skinned cat, and look at the beautiful woman you've become. Have you taken a man yet?"

Colombe pouted. The Indian women's lack of inhibition on this subject didn't embarrass her. She would have liked to copy them and speak freely of her desires and loves. But for all that she now dressed as they did, she hadn't yet abandoned the heavy modesty whose weight, in Europe, chafes against the soul's wounds.

"No," she confessed.

Paraguaçu laughed and so did Colombe.

"And . . . your brother?" asked the Indian girl, who remembered their shared confidences back in the village.

"He died," said Colombe quickly.

Then she blushed, but as Paraguaçu seemed deeply moved by the news and was caressing her cheek, she added:

"For me."

This avowal surprised even her, but she was unwilling to probe any deeper. The subject troubled her too much to pursue it. She drew her confidante in another direction by asking what she had been doing all this time.

"The great punishment of the spirits fell on my family," said Paraguaçu. "They raged against us. They killed my uncle, my father, my mother, all my cousins. We had to flee in order to placate them. But despite all our sacrifices, our offerings, the *caraíbas* were not able to calm the demons' fury. Now there are only six of us left."

Colombe remembered the corpses she had found in the forest and the deserted village. She took Paraguaçu in her arms and cried helplessly for a long moment.

She didn't dare ask about Karaya, the young captive with whom Paraguaçu used to share her nights. Colombe was afraid to learn that he too had died, devoured by the sickness or by men.

They spoke no more on these topics but returned to their games and to their happiness at being together. Now, because of Paraguaçu, Colombe could hope to enter the Indian world completely. She felt that she was ready, and she wanted to. When her friend returned to her tribe, Colombe would offer to accompany her.

That night, Paï-Lo organized a great dinner for Paraguaçu. Despite the lowering clouds, it was still hot, and the day had been a beautiful one. The meal was served on the terraces, under the light of hurricane lamps and chandeliers. Plates of venison, seasoned with spices and accompanied by manioc, arrived from the kitchen. These dishes were prepared on brazilwood fires in Indian pots, served on silver chargers bearing the royal crest of England (salvaged from the wreck of a warship), and eaten by the guests with their fingers.

In the jumble of sea chests and chests of drawers heaped around the house, Colombe had discovered a finely wrought flute of Austrian manufacture, intact in its taffeta-lined rosewood box. She played a few pieces after dinner. Paï-Lo closed his eyes, overtaken by nostalgia. The Indians remained quiet. More sensitive to rhythm than to melody, their expressions varied with the instrument's register. At times the flute calmed them with soft trills, at others it alarmed them with low, threatening arpeggios. Colombe afterward passed the flute around among the Indians, who examined it inside and out and finally convinced themselves it was a simple metal tube. They looked at Sun-Eye with even greater respect. They saw clearly that the mysterious bird whom the spirits of the dead visited (and whose semblance they detected in her face) resided in her. They did not doubt that what they had just heard was this bird's song.

In the concert's wake came a sweet torpor. Païi-Lo had wanted the dinner to be accompanied by Madeira wine. Barrels of it had newly washed up near Cabo Frio and had been carried up on the backs of men. Unlike *cahuin*, which excited the Indians' spirits, wine brought them to a silent, dream-filled state. The forest around them echoed with animal sounds: cackling, whimpering, devouring. But from another direction there also came the sounds of a celebration, the dull percussion of drums, the rattling of maracas, and loud laughter.

When Colombe asked Païi-Lo about these noises, he answered simply: "The Indians have recovered their strength since the epidemic. Now that the storms are coming, they are in a hurry to celebrate their sacrifices."

"Their sacrifices . . . ?"

"Human sacrifices."

Colombe was overcome by an unexpected horror. Strangely, she had envisaged her Indian life as a surrender to gentleness and nature. The sinister term "cannibal" was part and parcel of the hatred and ignorance Villegagnon showed when he spoke of the natives. In the end she had denied to herself the very existence of these practices. Païi-Lo sat quietly smoking a stick of *petun*. She eyed him with sudden mistrust.

"Then you believe it too?"

"What's that?"

"That they are cannibals."

He blinked slowly, perhaps to drive away the smoke that surrounded his face.

"There's no call to believe or not to believe. It's a fact."

"They eat their own kind."

"Yes."

"You've seen it?"

"Of course."

Paraguaçu, sitting next to Colombe, tilted her head sideways onto her shoulder, staring at the moths around the lamp. She did not understand French but liked being lulled by its soft intonations.

"Why do they do that?" asked Colombe, suddenly feeling vulnerable in her nakedness and shivering.

"Why?" he said dreamily. "Who knows exactly? Certainly not to feed themselves, as our friends on the island believe . . ."

He started to smile but, seeing Colombe's pained expression, he became serious again, and his voice assumed a gentle tone.

"The Indians," he said, "live in the forest where everything dies and is reborn, where forces are constantly shifting from the point of death to the point of birth. When they eat their enemies, and only their enemies are ever eaten, it's to assimilate their power. In fact, they start by making their prisoners live a long time in their midst."

"But why don't the poor prisoners run away?"

"Because they share the same beliefs. If they managed to return home, they'd be treated as cowards and put to death anyway."

Colombe looked at the sleeping Paraguaçu and thought again of her friend's old lover. She would never be able to ask about him for fear of what her friend would say.

"Then," she said with seeming casualness, "they let themselves be slaughtered like animals?"

"No," said Paï-Lo after a long moment's thought, "I wouldn't say so. They are resigned to their fate but show great courage. The first thing done in preparation for their sacrifice is to tie them by the waist to a tree for eight or ten days. They have their hands free to throw anything they can reach at the villagers who are going to eat them. They insult their murderers to the very end and vow that their families will avenge their deaths—and they are often right."

Colombe had gone beyond disgust. Fascinated, she wanted to know everything.

"And how are they put to death?"

"How?" said Paï-Lo, surprised. "Well, the *caraíbas* organize a whole ritual with dances and the oracle of the maracas. Then the executioner steps forward, carrying a club decorated with red cross-hatching where it will strike the forehead . . ."

"And they eat . . . everything?" asked Colombe, pale but determined to know.

"Absolutely everything. Each piece of the corpse is ritually assigned to one group or another."

At the old man's confident answers and easy tone, Colombe felt a sudden suspicion.

"You speak of it so freely," she said. "Have you ever . . . ?"

"Taken part in the ceremonies? Yes, of course. I've lived here so many years. But as to eating human flesh, I have never consented to it. Never," he repeated firmly.

She might not have loved him any the less if he had admitted the opposite, but his answer relieved her.

"I am entirely against putting men to death. The Indians know this, and those who live here have agreed to give up those practices."

"Perhaps they have," said Colombe, "but what about those others, the ones we hear now?"

The sound of the banquet was so close that the wind sometimes carried—along with the revolting smell of grease—the psalmody of a magician who seemed nearby.

"But what if we go to them," Colombe exploded, "what if we intervene, if we shout?"

She had almost done so, and a sleepy Paraguaçu raised her head.

"Well, they'll look at you as though you were threatening the group's life, which they hope to protect and defend by incorporating the dead man's strength into it. And you're the one who runs the risk of being killed."

"It seems to me that in just such cases as these, the use of force . . ."

Paï-Lo laughed silently, but in long spasms that Colombe found hateful.

"You are following right in the track of the Jesuits of São Vicente, who burn cannibal villages on the principle that Indians must be killed to keep them from killing!"

Colombe said nothing, but her chin trembled involuntarily. She had the sudden desire to flee. But where can you go when the world you come from has rejected you, and what dress can you remove when you live naked?

"I understand your revolt," said Paï-Lo gently, "and you must preserve it intact. I'd like you to know that my own has lost none of its vigor despite the passing years. Yet I truly believe that if we want to change the Indians, we first have to make ourselves recognize that . . . they are right."

He seemed to weigh this word in an invisible balance.

"You and I were both born, Colombe, in a world where it is normal to destroy one's enemy. The Indians incorporate their enemy into themselves. They have the admirable faculty of feeding on what is opposite. Toss out four musical notes, and they will absorb them into their melodies. Put your hat down on a stool, and they'll make it into a festival ornament. They have learned it from the forest, where everything interpenetrates and cross-fertilizes, and where what isn't devoured devours. Nothing is more foreign to them than our agricultural outlook, where we suppress every species but the one we find useful. And what they forbid themselves to do with plants, they don't do with humans either."

Paï-Lo reached out and stroked Colombe's forehead. Cold and bony as his hand was, the contact of flesh on flesh calmed her.

Paraguaçu reached toward a dish of food and started kneading a ball of manioc.

"We must allow them to change us, if we want to change them in turn," said Paï-Lo.

It was late for him, and with these words he rose painfully to his feet. A woman supported him as he retired into the darkness of his house.

Colombe went on dreaming for a long time in the forest where, after the sacrifices, peace gradually returned.

CHAPTER 36

Wars of religion are always a great boon to criminals. Violence suddenly appears holy, and as long as he can mimic piety, at least in words, the criminal is granted license by God to perform all the acts of infamy he has long dreamed of. Vittorio had not failed to notice the profit he might draw from the struggle between the island's two factions. When Dom Gonzagues took the leadership of the Catholic party during Villegagnon's long seclusion, Vittorio had thrown himself at his feet and begged to be allowed to chain himself to the Madonna's cause. It required only that his other chains be removed, the iron ones Villegagnon had ordered clapped to his ankles when he pardoned him after Le Freux's conspiracy. Dom Gonzagues had readily agreed to this request, and the Venetian had shown himself worthy of the confidence placed in him.

His slight build and his particular experience with weapons, which made him more apt to use them when his adversary had none, hardly prepared Vittorio for a position among the regular troops. But as a spy he did very well. He was one of the rare people who could roam anywhere, even among the Protestants, convincing them that he was angry at Villegagnon for having unfairly sentenced him. Everything he learned made its way back to Dom Gonzagues, who thus knew the enemy's plans and might forestall them.

Once the break between the two factions occurred, following the disastrous wedding ceremony, Vittorio had little to do, as the Protestants no longer allowed foreigners among them. The admiral, in recognition of Vittorio's services and to put his talents to good use, assigned him another task, more dangerous but also more profitable.

Villegagnon was shrewd. The moment he drove the Protestants from the island he knew he would face a new danger: that they would form an alliance with the interpreters of the coast against him. Despite his repugnance for the go-betweens, the admiral needed to develop closer ties with them. He had had the presence of mind in the throes of his anger during the wedding ceremony to allow himself some time to do this when he gave the Protestants two weeks to pack up and go.

In the meantime, he quickly sent an emissary to this fellow Martin, who reportedly ruled over the ruffians on the mainland. On Dom Gonzagues's recommendation, he chose Vittorio for the task. The risk, clearly, was that the Venetian jailbird would use the mission as an opportunity to run away. To prevent this, Villegagnon hinted at a substantial reward if things went well.

And so it was that, alighting from a boat that had gone one day to fetch water at the head of the bay, Vittorio wandered off and did not return, as though he had gotten lost. He was reported to Villegagnon as missing when the boat returned that night, and the admiral pretended to find the news irksome.

The supposed deserter walked for a long time along the beach under the meager covering of the coconut trees, waiting for a signal from the jungle to tell him he had been seen. This was the method generally favored by those who ran away. The Indians along the shore had orders to capture them quietly and bring them to Martin, who would then decide whether they were a sufficiently bad lot to join his elite band. And at first light a clutch of Indians surrounded Vittorio, who had gone to sleep peacefully on the beach, his head on a sand hill that he had covered with his cloth vest. They led him wordlessly and as gently as you could expect from such pierce-lipped primitives through the jungle to a straw hut where Martin was waiting to question him.

"How about that!" said the prince of the go-betweens. "You!"

"Ah, Martin!" answered Vittorio, with the sincere sob of a man rejoining humanity after a period in hell. "What a wonderful surprise!"

Falling into a habit he had taken up again with Dom Gonzagues and that harked back to the old country, he fell to his knees and blessed the Virgin Mary. But Martin's surprise outlasted even these invocations. The former beggar was looking at Vittorio with a stupefaction that could be read as hostility.

"Did you think I was hanged with Le Freux?" asked the Venetian, ready to dispel any suspicions and explain himself.

"No," said Martin, still staring fixedly at him.

Suddenly, he signaled to the others lounging about the hut to retire out of earshot.

"We have to talk," he said.

For the first time since leaving the island, Vittorio started to be afraid. When they were alone, Martin sat down across from the putative escapee.

"How did you know that we were looking for you?" he asked.

"You were looking for me?" said the Venetian, surprised. "I didn't know."

Martin probed him with his gaze, but it was impossible to read anything in this assassin's face except a blank bewilderment that suggested sincerity. Vittorio was growing alarmed. The plan the admiral had drawn up for him depended on his gaining Martin's confidence and returning to the island with his permission. This might prove difficult, given the suspicion he apparently was arousing.

"I have been beating my brains for a full week," said Martin, "to find a way to contact you."

"Me?" said Vittorio, now thoroughly concerned. His experience taught him that only bad could come of anyone looking for him.

"Yes, you," said Martin.

Looking at Vittorio through narrowed eyes, he added, "Can't you think why?"

Vittorio searched back through all his evil deeds for the one that might have given umbrage to the go-betweens. He could think of none. He then reviewed his good deeds, a shorter task. It was at that moment, with the forest around him moist from the first rains, all bark and leaves, that a word reached the Venetian's ear that conjured up the memory of a luminous facade in Le Havre-de-Grâce, of sparkling ships, and of Cadorim's soft voice.

"Ribera," Martin had said.

"What?" whispered Vittorio, lost in his dream.

"Ribera," said Martin again, looking at him unblinkingly.

Tears started silently down the Venetian's beard-encumbered cheeks.

"Finally!" he said.

Martin looked at him in surprise, feeling a wave of genuine admiration. So this thief, whom he'd ignored, a man so unprepossessing he looked fit for only the humblest tasks of larceny, was the person on whom the most powerful nations in Europe had founded their policy. He was the agent of princes, of bishops, of the governor—a fact he had skillfully kept hidden. He surely knew more than he was letting on. His providential arrival was proof of the superior influence that still guided him, though his modesty and caution instructed him to deny it.

"Where are they?" asked Vittorio, coming to himself.

"Who?"

"The Portuguese."

"They won't be long now," said Martin, his eyes shining, for he now expected as much from their arrival as "Ribera" did.

The two communed in silence for a moment, thinking of this liberation with its chances for glory and gold.

"You'll have to go back to the island," said Martin, speaking now in his practical commander's voice.

Vittorio was a little startled. He had always imagined that on the day he heard the magic word, he would be carried up to the sky, toward freedom. But since his new mission coincided—though for other reasons—with the instructions given him by Villegagnon, he agreed.

"I was just going to say the same thing," he said.

And in this prescience, Martin saw a further mystery, further increasing his respect.

"You'll have to arrange for Villegagnon to send you back here often."

"One thing that will make it easier," said Vittorio, "is that he sent me to you particularly on a mission."

He outlined the quarrel with the Protestants and their forthcoming expulsion to the mainland. Martin promised to make no alliance with them, a show of goodwill that cost him little since it disguised the fact that the real attack would come from the Portuguese.

"Give him my word," said Martin, with an emphasis reflecting the future duke.

"I will, but . . ."

"What? Is it not enough?"

"Yes, of course," said Vittorio quickly. "But I will have to prove to him that I have gained your trust."

"Well then, bring Villegagnon this," said Martin, drawing a medallion from his pocket.

It was a little miniature framed in a simple round molding. It showed a woman with a serious face and a lace coif over her hair.

"I took it from his table the night of the attack. A good-luck charm. When things go badly, I steal."

"With me," said Vittorio, "it's when things go well."

"You'll be the link between us from now on. At least that's what he'll think and the reason he'll send you here. But in fact you'll be doing a service to the other side. The Portuguese want to know everything there is to know about the island's defenses."

He listed the first items of information they wanted.

"I'll need to take refuge here before the attack," said Vittorio impatiently. "You'll have to warn me."

"Yes. But you'll have to stay over there until the end. If you do the job right, there won't even be a battle."

Vittorio frowned. Everything about the plan suited him except the ending. But he reflected that there was all the time in the world to come to a decision.

The conversation went on a long time. Vittorio gave a first report on what he already knew. At nightfall, Martin led him to his house on the heights to impress him with his power. He suggested that Vittorio bring back a flattering description of his headquarters to Villegagnon, though without giving details as to its location.

The next day in the middle of the afternoon, a report came from watchers posted by Martin on the beach that another boat was passing, this one returning with provisions. Vittorio went down to the water and shouted and made signals. The sails came in toward shore, recognized him, and took him on board. Martin, hidden behind a tuft of euphorbia, watched the dark figure wade out into the clear water and haul himself into the boat by the oarlocks. There was a certain poignancy in reflecting that the destiny of several nations, for a portion of their history at least, was bound up in so modest, yet so valorous, a person.

• • •

The day before the Protestants were to leave the island, the first storms erupted with unexpected force. It rained all night, and dawn was barely perceptible the next morning, so dark and thick were the clouds in the sky. The ground was sodden; the rain-gorged roofs of the straw huts dripped water in cold streams. Just half hoped that Villegagnon would postpone the expulsion. But there was no question of it. The admiral was unwilling to lighten his sentence by a single day, and the good news brought back by Vittorio gave him no incentive for caution.

Early that morning, Le Thoret posted heavily armed soldiers at various points around the fort and on the beach. A row of loaded harquebuses on forked supports lined the path the Reformers would take from their huts to the boats.

Just was assigned to bring Du Pont confirmation of the decision and to help organize the Protestant procession toward their second exile. The body search proved a prickly issue, but on that point the admiral was adamant: no weapon was to leave the island. Each of the banished Protestants was to be inspected in turn before being allowed to embark.

Du Pont was infuriated and called for a parlay, insisting that only the soldiers be subjected to a search. Just made the round trip to the government house only to bring back the news that Villegagnon would not budge. The Protestants asked for a delay. Just returned an hour later to find the problem oddly smoothed over.

"So be it," said Richier. "We will submit to a search."

Just breathed more easily.

"But on the sole condition," said the pastor, "that it be you and no one else who performs it."

Just was tempted to accept this accommodation without a quibble when he suddenly thought of the women. Would he really have to be the one to make the women undergo such a shameful process? He asked this of Richier.

"Judge for yourself whether you are free to exempt them from it," the pastor answered with contempt.

Alas, Villegagnon had given strict orders: no one, of whatever sex, was to escape the requisite vigilance. Just hesitated. Then he told himself that as long as the outrage was to be committed, he might as well be the one to do it: at least he would try to preserve every decency and perhaps even find a way to avoid it at the last moment.

Mighty rumblings ricocheted lugubriously off the mountains, then the rain started again, warm and heavy. The Protestants were crowded at the entrance to their huts, their baggage at their feet. The bundles and bags, already swollen with water, were shapeless and heavy. Just began by examining the soldiers one by one, after which they would wade off through the mud in the direction of the port. Du Pont had decided to set off with them so as to land on the mainland first and prepare a safe camp for those who would follow later.

The rain fell without letup and so noisily that it filled with disquiet the heavy silence of the group awaiting expulsion. Just felt their looks of hatred on him and was almost relieved. He was as unsparing toward himself and viewed himself with thorough contempt for having accepted the task.

After the first contingent shipped out, a bawled signal from the Catholic side recalled him back to his sinister examination. At least it kept his mind busy on something other than his shame and his doubts. A new group of men advanced toward him with their arms upraised. He felt them over from top to bottom, a task made easier by the rain, which glued their clothing to their skin and made it hard to conceal anything.

His anxiety made him thirsty. Inwardly he found himself smiling at his absurd punishment: to be parched in the midst of so much water.

Finally only Richier and the women were left.

The pastor argued that female dignity forbade the public exploration of their persons. The women were still hidden in the dark recesses of their huts. Just knocked on the first door. Inside he found one of the brides standing beside her husband, who was even more terrified than she. He hastily and almost without touching them

checked that they were carrying no weapons. Then he waited silently
for a decent time to elapse, so that those outside could see he hadn't
rushed his inspection. He then went on to the second hut. In the
third he found the two duennas of the brides, their hands upraised,
their eyes rolled skyward as though taking God to witness that resistance was to no avail. When they realized that Just meant only to
wave his hands over them, they received this mark of respect without
gratitude. In the next cabins, he found the two more recent brides
waiting without their husbands, proof perhaps that the violent inter-
ruption of the ceremony had left Richier unconvinced as to its valid-
ity. To his surprise, he found three ladies-in-waiting in the next hut:
those of the two brides and Chantal. In the latter's smile he read an
enigmatic and disconcerting message.

When he re-emerged, the storm was stronger than ever and turning to hail. A little carpet of white balls stretched over the sodden
earth. Mist rose off the warm ground and crept along the base of the
walls. Just hesitated for a moment. He had just counted the women
in the previous huts and deduced with some trepidation that Aude
awaited him alone in the last.

There are moments of finality when consciousness dilates like an
arch to include all those whom the heart has nourished and who,
because of some external violence, are about to perish. Just felt that
he had entered into one such interminable moment, where the emotions crowd together before an equal number of opposing thoughts
armed to destroy them.

Aude was standing quite near the entrance, so that when Just
entered the shadowy room he found himself abruptly before her,
almost touching her. She wore a black dress whose rounded collar
plunged toward the top of her breasts. From a high window with the
curtain pulled back, a pale glow penetrated from outside, barely
reaching her face and giving faint form to the ashes in the fireplace.
Only her wide-open eyes shone, and it seemed impossible in this
dank obscurity for them to be lit so brightly from outside.

Just felt the girl's feverish breath on his face, and a violent desire
made him sway. He stood unmoving, speechless, so filled with disgust for himself, with a violent sensation of nothingness and non-
presence, that he was suddenly tempted to leave his body there like a
husk. But almost at the same moment, he felt against his lips the

warm delight of an unknown chasm. For a moment he failed to understand that a mouth had pressed against his mouth. Then, as when a fruit is hardly tasted than it is devoured, he answered the kiss with all his being.

The hail on the palm trees drummed down around them. The air's wet warmth precipitated onto the embrace of their bodies, like an acid that suddenly makes the colorless substance it has been poured into visible.

Then, with an imperceptible push of her slender fingers, she drew away:

"Save us," she whispered.

Just was still drowning in the well of sweetness over whose edge he had just leaned. His mind was bumping against its walls. He couldn't form a coherent idea. A jumble of images came crowding to him instead. He saw himself with her along the shore, with her on a boat, with her on a sunny day in Italy. He yearned to enfold her again.

"Quick," she said.

The word abruptly brought back all the darkness and the storm, all the danger and the despair.

"What can I do?" he asked, resolved to carry out whatever she had conceived.

His hands holding her body felt a sudden and invisible stiffening. It was as though the alarm came from her.

"Kill him."

He looked at her without moving, though his eyes widened slightly, giving the impression that he was dreaming.

"Save us," she said. "Kill him!"

"Who?"

From having stiffened, she was now clenched. It was she who now held him, both hands clasped to the collar of his sopping shirt.

"Him!" she said.

And as if the hatred suddenly expressed in her eyes were not enough, she shook him. Then she spoke the execrated name, her lips as harsh and contemptuous as they had earlier been tender and surrendering.

"Villegagnon!"

Just let go of her.

"Villegagnon," she said again, in a loud voice that echoed the clapping of the storm. "Kill him and I am yours."

"No," Just cried out.

A space, immeasurable, but holding all the distance between love and hate, separated them.

"Never," he said, with the firmness of a person discovering his irrevocable will.

Everything had come back. The slight cold that dankness slips into the air, the weight of the objects and the walls, the nausea.

"A curse on the Catholics!" she said.

Then, as suddenly as he had felt the unexpected warmth of her kiss, he felt a sharp pain bite at his side and an unexpected humor warmly mix with the revolting rag of his soaked shirt. He put his hand to his side.

Aude had already stepped around him and leapt outside. Just turned and was on the threshold. He watched her walk away under the veil of water, noting that the hail had again turned to rain. The group of other women with Richier had already gathered and set off on the path to the beach. Aude joined them. They passed in front of the harquebuses. Capes thrown over the weapons made them look like odd wading birds, the barrels shining like beaks.

Just made no gesture to stop them, and his immobility, seen at a distance by the soldiers, was interpreted as consent. As the last boat drew off, Just looked at his hand, saw the blood, and understood. He held still as long as he could, and when the bark had disappeared into the mist, he let go of his wound and fell full length in the mud.

CHAPTER 37

Villegagnon, leaning on the backrest of his chair, watched the three men working on their ladders. On the ground floor of the fort, behind the great vaulted entrance, a high room with palm-beamed ceilings now served as a meeting hall and, during the rains, as a chapel for services. It was there, on one of the windowless walls, that the enormous wood panel had been erected. The cabinetmakers had worked for several days to saw the sycamore trunks lengthwise and assemble the boards. Then the monumental surface had been plastered with a mixture of pulverized bone and hide glue, and polished using the little pumice stones that littered the ground. Now the admiral had the satisfaction of seeing the colors applied.

The three painters were construction workers, for lack of true artists. But they knew how to draw more or less and were only being asked to produce a copy. On a small easel was the little Titian canvas of the Madonna, whose enlargement was to figure on the gigantic panel. The Venetian master's tropical disciples squinted continually at the original and reproduced its shapes in charcoal on the wall. The Virgin laboriously assumed her new dimensions. With each section of the future altarpiece under the care of a different master, the proportions agreed poorly. The Madonna's face was too small, her chest enormous, and the Baby Jesus disappeared in the welter of mammaries. It all had to be redone three times from top to bottom. Finally everything harmonized more or less, and against a crimson madder background appeared the monumental figure of the Mother of God, with which Villegagnon hoped to shake men's souls. One good effect of the Protestants' presence was that the admiral had at least come to a thorough understanding of what he needed to do. He wouldn't have had to whip the Indians or even be so harsh with the colonists if he had placed himself earlier under the protection of such fearsome and winning images as the one now taking shape before him.

As soon as the rainy season was over, he would start excavating the foundations for a church next to the fort. In the meantime, he continued to lead the service each morning alone, and he would soon be doing so under the protection of the gigantic Madonna, whose gentle, holy gaze would keep the assembly in abeyance.

Regrettably, as long as the painting and the church were still unfinished, they would have to continue with their strong-arm methods. Ever since the resumption of relations with Martin and the go-betweens, boats had been plying back and forth again to the nearby settlements on the coast. Vigilance was once more the order of the day, owing to the men's deplorable tendencies. The admiral had erected a pillory, and anyone found drunk was put in the stocks under the rain. For *cahuin* was finding its way back to the island along with other merchandise. And those who ferried goods over were again tempted to find pleasure with the Indian women. But it was difficult to catch them in the act. The dogs acted in a pack and covered for each other with ready lies. At the least suspicion, Villegagnon now pursued the question thoroughly. He was very proud of the little room the blacksmiths had fitted out for him with hooks, rings, and tongs. More and more often, he had the comfort of hearing shrieks emerge from that cellar as he sat working by the window of the government house. It made him smile with pleasure, sounding to his ears like the marching song of Truth. He could hardly be indifferent to the noisy efforts a man made when, helped by others, he sought to mend his ways. The method brought to light many guilty parties who would otherwise have remained tragically alone with their sins. Varying shades of punishment were applied, from the bastinado to dunking, and included public flogging and many other corrections. Only hanging was not performed for the time being: the weather was still too wet for the ropes to run properly.

The thought of discipline brought the admiral back to himself. The painters had been laboriously applying coats of pink to the sainted flesh of the canvas. He encouraged them according to his new method, that is, promising to gouge out their eyes if they didn't copy the Titian correctly. Then he went out. The rainy season had now fallen into a pattern: mornings were clear and cool, then clouds began to collect toward midday like curious passers-by. By nightfall they had penetrated everywhere, and the heat was stifling. Finally the storm would burst. Villegagnon was proud of his new boots of armadillo hide, made for him by an old cobbler on the island. With these he could walk through the puddles without getting his feet wet. This mattered little for his comfort, but a great deal for his dignity. He didn't want to be seen scurrying. Majesty was now a component of his system of government, along with cruelty and faith.

From the fort, the admiral strode to the back of the government house, entering the first of several rooms with outside doors. In it lay Just on a straw pallet, while two somber-faced men stood discussing his case.

"Well, sirs," said the admiral, "and how is our patient?"

With their mud-spattered clothes and calloused hands, the two men looked rather like ditch diggers. And they had in fact been manning shovels until the apothecary absconded and left the colony without a medical authority. One of them had volunteered that he had once clerked at a pharmacy. The other, whose brother was coachman to a doctor, put himself forward on these prestigious grounds as someone who knew a bit about healing. Neither could be accused of imposture since, while frequenting medical men, they had acquired the doctor's greatest secret: to wear an air of importance and to use learned Latin phrases, which kept illness in abeyance and the patient even more so.

"We have reapplied earth of vitriol to the wound," said one of the putative doctors. "No more blood is being drawn from it."

"And the vulnerary is operating well: we imbibed the dressing with tincture of aloe, for want of aristolochia."

"Ah yes," whined the other, and he repeated in sorrowful tones, "for want of aristolochia."

"Aside from that," said Villegagnon, who respected science but believed it a narrow field wedged between religion and the art of war, "how is he feeling?"

"He has a headache," said one of the consultants.

"We are discussing the advisability of a cucupha," said the other sententiously.

"Saint Jack of Jerusalem!" said Villegagnon. "Has it come to that?"

The two supposed doctors assumed stiff and contemptuous expressions.

"A cucupha!" said the admiral solemnly.

Then realizing that he was terrified by the mere word, he adopted a humble tone to ask:

"And what might that be, a cucupha?"

"A cucupha," said the first physician haughtily, "is a double-lined cap containing cephalic powder. It is applied to the patient's head when he suffers from migraines."

"And this powder, what does it consist of?"

"An herbal decoction."

"We recommend," the other chimed in, "that it contain benjamin, cinnamon, and iris exclusively."

"Well, what are you waiting for? Give him a cucupha if it will provide him relief."

"But we are missing some of the ingredients."

"Which ones?"

"Benjamin," said the first medical man.

"Cinnamon," said the other.

"And the irises," said the first ill-humoredly, looking at the ground.

"I see," growled Villegagnon.

And he showed them the door.

Just was still weak. His eyes remained closed. The admiral approached his pallet and rested a buttock on its edge, nearly bringing the whole contraption down and the patient with it. Just opened his eyes.

"Are you eating properly?" grumbled the admiral.

The sight of his wounded protégé pained and therefore embarrassed him.

"You have lost a lot of blood," he went on.

"I am fine, Admiral, just recovering my strength."

"Wonderful! You are going to need your strength, believe me. We are going to do great things. And first we'll avenge you."

Just shook his head.

"What!" said the admiral. "You still deny the evidence. Who is going to believe that you wounded yourself, as you claim? The blood-stained dagger we found lying near you was not yours, so far as I know."

The wounded man raised his right hand and made a gesture as though erasing a useless inscription.

"Sooner or later you are going to tell us exactly who struck you. My only concern is to see the criminal punished, by way of example, as is only fitting with so heinous an act. I know all about it in any case. Du Pont is the culprit, along with his whole band of heretics. That's what matters."

This was inevitably followed by a litany of thanks to God for making the blade slide along the ribs. Though the skin of Just's side was swollen and black from internal bleeding, his vital organs had not been touched. Villegagnon knew from battlefield experience that no wound is benign. Only once it has closed and the patient is back on his feet are there any grounds for reassurance. All the same, it could have been worse.

If Villegagnon prolonged his visit, Just quickly drifted off to sleep. The admiral would then pull out the medallion Martin had returned to him and peer at the beloved face of his departed mother. He prayed for her soul. Sometimes, while the sleeping patient breathed regularly and drowsiness came over him, he remembered himself at Just's age watching at the bedside of his sick mother, very much as today. It had seemed to him at the time that the brave woman was setting off to encounter God and hastening toward the moment of judgment. And in subsequent years, by way of imitation, he had continually hurled himself into battle, without ever feeling that his combats matched hers in bravery.

When Just, encouraged by the admiral's silence, went back to sleep, his visitor slipped out noiselessly. He walked slowly to the government house thinking of the decisions to be made. The Protestants' departure was only the first step. He wanted to be rid of them once and for all, either by having them die on the mainland or by getting them shipped back to Geneva. In any case, Villegagnon had never felt more confident about the colony's future. Its spiritual redressment was in progress, and the fort's completion would protect it from external attack. As to the alliance with Martin, though it was still admittedly limited, it would allow them to know more about the go-betweens for the day when, having gotten rid of the Protestants, the colony could turn its attention to them. The admiral had given Vittorio precise instructions on this point, and the spy always brought back invaluable details on Martin's forces and tactics.

His train of thought having put him in a good mood, Villegagnon was irritated to find Le Thoret waiting for him by the entrance to the government house.

"What do you want?" Villegagnon grunted.

He knew perfectly well. The captain was in disfavor. Villegagnon had ordered him punished, and ever since the announcement of the sentence Le Thoret had been trying to make him change his mind.

"I want an interview," said the old soldier grimly.

A veteran of the wars in the Piedmont, wounded at the battles of Ceresole and Cassel, Le Thoret had the right to see the admiral whenever he chose. If he asked for an audience, it was to emphasize the personal and exceptional nature of his business.

Villegagnon entered, leaving the door open for the other to follow. When they were alone in the audience hall, the taciturn captain waited, hat in hand, to be questioned.

The admiral took off his azure blue doublet and yellow cape, sat down, and at last addressed his subordinate.

"What is it you want now, Le Thoret? From the look on your face I can tell you don't want to talk about the only things that interest me: the island's defenses and the destruction of the Reformers."

"No," Le Thoret agreed, "that's not what I came to talk to you about."

As the admiral's longstanding companion in arms, he had the rare privilege of using the familiar form of address.

"For the last time, Admiral, I ask for justice."

Long and thin, Le Thoret had a narrow face that was further elongated by the escutcheon of beard hanging from his chin.

"Justice has been done," said Villegagnon, pouring himself to drink.

"Not true justice, Admiral."

He had a bass voice that emerged strangely from his skinny neck, where a large Adam's apple seemed to be performing on the trapeze.

"You well know," he said gravely, "that I didn't wrong La Faucille."

This was the commander of the fort. In theory he acted under Le Thoret's orders, but the hierarchy was somewhat blurred where the two were concerned. Le Thoret had ordered him to perform some task or other, and La Faucille had arrogantly refused. The old captain had then called him a knave, and the two would have settled the question with drawn swords had their men not separated them. The business had been brought to the admiral. In itself, it had no importance, but it revealed a corrosive climate of violence, suspicion, and jealousy. Referring to a code for armies on campaign dating from Charles VIII, a dubious exegesis of *The Gallic Wars*, and his own mood at the moment, Villegagnon had come to a judgment.

"You were determined to be the guilty party," said the admiral crisply, "and you'll take your punishment, which strikes me in any case as light."

Ignoring the underlying threat, Le Thoret looked deep into the eyes of his leader and brother-in-arms.

"For the last time," he said solemnly, "will you or will you not reverse this miscarriage of justice?"

For several months, Le Thoret had been growing more withdrawn and gloomy. His obedience seemed worn, like a carpet trampled by too many careless feet. He had served kings, marched with troops on campaign, confronted formidable adversaries, and it sat ill with him to oversee the forced labor of a band of unarmed artisans. The deplorable eviction of the Huguenots had further disgusted him. Yet he would have said nothing had not the fuse of injustice been lit in the powder keg of his despair.

"No," answered Villegagnon.

The two men locked eyes for a moment. Their gaze, knowing no rank, title, or precedence, hardened with no sign of wavering on either side.

"I will assemble the colony in two days to witness the execution of the sentence," said Villegagnon. "You will, as ordered, make honorable amends, hat in hand, on bended knee, and be suspended of your command for three weeks."

"As you wish," said Le Thoret, screwing his cap on his head.

The following day, after prayer service, Villegagnon was urgently called out to examine suspicious footprints and a case of weapons discovered in a rocky cove on the west tip of the island. Taking advantage of the diversion, which he had organized himself, Le Thoret calmly ordered his soldiers to bring around one of the boats in the port. He boarded it, and four harquebus men who had been with him since Italy took up the oars. They pulled away from the island without attracting any attention.

• • •

On reaching the mainland after their expulsion, the Huguenots gathered under the cover of the first trees. But the rain, though it tapered off at the end of the afternoon, had made everything wet: their clothing, the ground, and the foliage. The water pooled on the big varnished leaves and fell in thin streams, as though poured from little funnels. The first night had been horrible, and endless. The poor refugees shivered from cold and fever, huddling with their knees pressed against their chests to preserve some remnants of body heat. Du Pont stayed standing because of his infirmity until the middle of the night, finally dropping from weariness and lying full length in the sodden sand.

Aude confided her failed attempt to her uncle. Though Richier had avoided learning of his niece's intended methods, he had approved her plan unreservedly. She showed a courage he reproached Du Pont for lacking. He could hardly look at the old nobleman without a feeling of irritation. If he had only followed Richier's advice and gone on the offensive, they would long ago have gotten rid of Villegagnon, and his poor niece would not have had to sacrifice herself for their honor.

When Aude also confessed to having stabbed Clamorgan, her uncle only felt the more solicitous toward her. He had given her a dagger for self-defense, and he wholeheartedly believed she had only used it in the last extremity, to preserve her maidenhood. But the likely consequences mattered more than the circumstances. The attempt on Just's life would further infuriate Villegagnon. Not only were they trapped empty-handed with their backs against the hostile jungle, but also they could expect to be pursued like the Hebrews by a Pharaoh who was unlikely to be stopped by an arm of the sea.

In the morning, to their relief, they saw no sign of hostile preparations on the island, which they spied on from afar. This called for
a new round of prayers. Richier had never so congratulated himself
on knowing a great number of psalms by heart. He had sustained his
companions with them all night, and at dawn still had some left over.
God's clemency, which they had hardly seen until then, gratified
them all morning with a hot sun that dried out their clothing. But
clouds were gathering as usual, and they would certainly burst before
day's end. The exiles had to find a shelter quickly or else build one.

By further good fortune on this decidedly auspicious day, they saw
men emerge from the forest led by a young white man. Though they
had had little opportunity to visit the mainland, the Huguenots knew
of the go-betweens on the coast. Only one aspect of their reputation
was familiar to them: that they were Villegagnon's enemies. Hence
there was a chance of persuading the go-betweens not to be theirs.

In fact, the young rogue who introduced himself as Martin greeted
them amiably, though with a haughtiness that was totally out of
place. They had seen the ways of this miserable country enough to
know that impertinence was endemic to its residents, and they took
no offense.

"My lord," said Du Pont, addressing Martin in like manner, "you
see a band of innocents before you whom an unjust hand has struck.
The guilty party is no friend of yours, we know. Perhaps you would
agree to become ours."

Martin enjoyed respectful treatment from a nobleman, even if the
man had turned himself into a sugared doughnut by rolling in the
wet sand all night.

"Rest assured, sir," he said loftily, "that no harm will come to you
while you are on my lands. You may count on my protection."

A murmur of relief went through the shivering band of outcasts.

"We in turn would like to assure you," said Du Pont, exalted at
their reception, "that our forces—as soon as they have again been
recruited—will loyally join yours to fight this usurper, this tyrant, this
monster."

But Martin had no intention of going so far. His putative arrangement with Villegagnon kept him from taking any hostile action
against him until the Portuguese arrived in the bay. For the moment,
it was important that Vittorio be able to pass back and forth between

the two sides, bringing his precious information. Martin had no use for these Huguenots, in point of fact, and he could as easily have driven them back into the sea. Yet his sense of his own interest told him to spare them. In the first place, he expected to make some profit from protecting them, for such folk never failed to preserve some ready coin, even in the worst adversity. And he had to provide insurance for the future. If the Portuguese plan should fail, unlikely as that might be, it was as well not to be wholly unprotected from Ville-gagnon. And these ragged allies, with their powerful supporters in Europe, could in that case prove invaluable.

"Come, friends," said Martin, looking at the bedraggled refugees, "it would be a hard man who would enlist you in a fight today. It is enough for now that you should survive and regain your strength. Follow me, we'll find a place for you."

Knowing through Vittorio of their imminent arrival, Martin had had the Indian village on the edge of the forest evacuated the previous day. He led the Protestants there and showed them the palm-leaf huts. Though they were even cruder than the ones they had inhabited on the island, they seemed inconceivably luxurious and comfortable.

They spread out their belongings to dry and attacked the meal the Indians had prepared for them.

When the storm burst in the late afternoon, they were dry and under cover. It no longer seemed impossible to wait there quietly for Chartier to arrive with reinforcements from Geneva. Then would the hour of judgment toll for Villegagnon.

CHAPTER 38

Few of the Europeans who drank *cahuin* knew how this alcoholic drink was prepared. Or rather, they knew but preferred not to think about it or see it done. In this they were encouraged by the Indians, who firmly believed that good *cahuin* could be confected only in the absence of males. Ideally, it was virgins who prepared it. Married women could join in as long as they practiced strict abstinence during all the days the operation lasted. A few old women, restored to chastity by their great age, were also allowed as long as they had teeth.

Colombe liked the process of preparing *cahuin*. It was one of the most serene moments in the peaceful Indian life she loved. She had somewhat forgotten her alarm over anthropophagy, and the nightly noise of feasts was no more than a distant and habitual sign of celebrations.

Sitting cross-legged at the fire, she chewed on a manioc root softened by parboiling. The other girls around her and Paraguaçu at her side did likewise. They masticated slowly and methodically, trying to collect as much saliva as possible. This deliberate chewing differed from the reflex chewing of a person eating, just as feeding oneself, which is a selfish pleasure, differs from cooking, which addresses another's wants. When the root was juicy, soft, and glutinous, one had to get to one's feet. An earthenware vat as tall as a child of ten simmered over a low fire. The chewed root was carefully spat into it, with as long a train of spittle as possible. As the day wore on, the container filled to the brim with a mixture of juices and vegetable matter, and fermentation was promoted by the fire's heat. The precious beverage was then poured into flasks. The women kept the secret of *cahuin*'s entry into the world to themselves, along with many other fabrication secrets. It was presented to the men all clean and finished in pretty flagons shaped like half-liter Burgundy bottles.

During the process of manduction, the women could talk. The practice was even encouraged, as it relaxed the jaw and helped saliva flow.

After joking with Colombe a great deal that morning, Paraguaçu made an unexpected announcement.

"Tomorrow I am going back to my tribe," she said.

Colombe, her cheeks filled with manioc, remained silent.

"Already!" she mumbled.

Then she went to spit out her root, though it hadn't reached the ideal softness. Despite speaking Tupi fluently, she found it hard to make the proper intonations with her mouth full.

"I'll go with you!" she said.

Colombe had been waiting for this moment a long time. Her stay with Paï-Lo was only a stage along the way. She was therefore surprised to see her friend shake her head.

"That isn't possible," said the Indian girl forcefully.

"But I'll be discreet," said Colombe. "I'll respect your laws. I'll work."

Paraguaçu cast Colombe a dark look that made her blood run cold. Since their reunion, they had enjoyed a sincere complicity. During their long conversations in the evening, the Indian girl had questioned Colombe about France, about her life, about the Europeans' concept of love. Paraguaçu was surprised at the sentiment, not that the Indians ignored it but that they made a different use of it. To them, love was a multiple, exploded aptitude that was not satisfied by a single being. You loved your children, you loved your parents, you loved your tribe, you loved the sun and beneficial trees, you loved the water passing over the falls and the warm breeze on the beach, you loved the earth that supplies human wants, you loved the night and the day, fire and salt, the rhea and the tapir. And in this closely woven fabric of love and fear, the thought that a single being could hoard all the love for himself never occurred to them. Furthermore, with something as intimately tied to the order of the world as the choice of a husband and of a father for your children, the individual's preference didn't count and could even be considered criminal. You had to submit to laws of the tribe. Yet, in the thousand questions Paraguaçu asked, it was clear she found the picture of love Colombe painted for her seductive.

The intimacy of these conversations made her brutal refusal of her friend's offer all the more incomprehensible. Colombe pressed her a bit further. But each new attempt rekindled the same anger in Paraguaçu's eyes, and a fear that bordered on terror.

"Might I accompany you . . . another time?" asked Colombe.

"Yes, Sun-Eye!" said Paraguaçu, relieved at the idea. "Another time, and as many times as you like. But not now."

As strange as this compromise was, Colombe accepted it, and when they finished chewing manioc, she accompanied her friend back to the house. Apparently Paraguaçu had waited till the last moment to announce her departure, as her little traveling pack was ready and waiting. She left on the spot without a backward glance.

Colombe had no time to brood over Paraguaçu's abrupt disappearance, for Païlo-Lo fell gravely ill following the terrible storm of the previous week when everything had been flooded. The forest assumed a new life during the rainy season, with vegetation surging, moss greening at the base of tree trunks, and the wall of palm fronds growing denser in the humid air. Sounds were muffled, and the resulting hush, joined to the anxious silence kept in the house so as not to disturb the patriarch, created a climate of waiting and worry. All life seemed tense, armed, and on guard, as though death stalked and must be kept from entering.

Colombe was allowed to keep watch over Païlo-Lo, alternating with the other women. It was important to keep the sick man from being alone, to tend to his needs and wishes, and never to leave him face to face with the evil spirits who were trying to take him away.

The old man lay in his great hammock, which was spread at both ends by a wooden crosspiece. His room, whose floor was overrun with naked roots, was filled with a variety of objects, all of them dear to him. Yellowing maps hung on the walls, interspersed with Indian trophies. Decorated calabashes stood next to Delft vases. A large bamboo and feather frame contained a small European landscape showing a village under snow. A whole family of leather-bound books nestled on a plank; the humidity had warped them, and the pages had swollen like buds threatening to open.

Païe-Lo had difficulty breathing, and he was racked by an exhausting cough. But his mind was intact, and he liked to hold conversations, even though he sometimes had trouble forming his words. He continued to collect information from all who passed through. Thus he was able to tell Colombe of the Protestants' expulsion from the island. But it was often old memories that surfaced, and his talk mixed the most deeply buried past with the most recent events.

"My life changed," he said one night to Colombe, "when I read Pomponazzi. I would never have come here had it not been for his great book."

At his request, Colombe had gone to the shelf and found the volume. It was a small tome with worn pages, its margins crowded with Païe-Lo's notations.

"He was a disciple of Averroës," said the old man, leafing through the book sadly. "The only one who resisted Plato's influence."

His dim eyes could no longer see the writing, but he knew the text so well that the pages only served to prod his memory.

"For him, God is everywhere. He cannot be separated from the things of this world. He is in each being, and in each object. Nothing happens that is not the sign of His will."

He sighed and rested the book on his stomach.

"The biggest mistake of all was to put God in Heaven and enjoin Him never to leave it. A single God is not very many, and furthermore He is absent; we will only be reunited with Him after death. How sad!"

Suddenly raising himself painfully in his fabric bed, he adopted a tone of invective that Colombe had never heard him use before.

"Look at them tearing each other apart over whether God is still in the wafer or nowhere at all . . . They have driven Him out of creation and now quibble over whether to allot Him even a small place in it."

Excited by this effort, he let his head fall back and sighed.

"Stay calm, Païi-Lo," said Colombe, taking his hand.

At her touch, he subsided for a moment, and when he spoke again, his voice was more serene.

"When I met the Indians, I felt I was finally discovering a world that was free of this madness, a world that was respected."

His eyes stayed open on the empty shadows.

"Everything is sacred to them, the flowers, the rocks, the water flowing in the mountains. Innumerable spirits inhabit and protect objects, places, and living beings. You can't touch anything that doesn't free up these forces and limit the evil one can do to the world."

An Indian woman entered silently, carrying a basket of fruit. She remained standing near the door, and Païi-Lo, who had sensed her added presence without looking at her, smiled.

"But the others . . ." he murmured, bitterness rising in him again. "By stripping nature of the sacred, they have left it unprotected, vulnerable to man's murderous will. You only have to look at what they have done to their island. Nothing grows there anymore, and now they are ripping each other apart. If they are ever masters of this land, they will make it a field of death."

After a pause, he added:

"It wasn't man who was driven from the earthly paradise, but God. And man seized creation in order to destroy it."

The days passed and Païi-Lo's condition remained unchanged. He floated in limbo, no longer entirely a part of life, yet his dreams were thronged with memories and colors, happiness and regrets. His existence came back to him, making these hours before death a voluptuous distillation of his entire life.

One evening, two warriors climbed up from the coast to announce that a lieutenant of Villegagnon's had fled and was asking to come to Païi-Lo's, along with four soldiers. The two Tupis were suspicious of a trap, but the patriarch told them to let the fugitives come. And thus Le Thoret was led to Païi-Lo.

The old soldier was every bit himself: stiff, austere, and taciturn. Only the branch of his submission to Villegagnon had snapped in two. He appeared before Païi-Lo with the fierce dignity of a prisoner of war who has fought well. His sole request was that he and his men might be allowed to return to France as soon as possible on one of the merchant ships that visited the bay.

"Why don't you stay?" asked Paï-Lo. "The Indians need a man like you to teach them to fight the Europeans. A day will come when they will need to defend themselves not against brigands but armies."

Le Thoret rejected this proposal in the clearest way. It wasn't that he despised the Indians: he had no opinion about them. But he was trained to obey and had never wanted to be a leader over others.

He said again that he wanted to take the first ship back to France. Paï-Lo didn't insist. He knew the Normans at the trading posts well enough to send Le Thoret to them with a personal recommendation. According to his information, several small caravels came and went regularly at this time of year. He suggested that the old soldier rest a while with him before setting out for the far shore of the bay. Le Thoret demurred. He asked to leave as soon as an Indian guide could be found for him. His departure was set for two days from then.

Colombe came across Le Thoret that night, returning from the waterfalls. The sight of that dignified knight, associated in her mind with Villegagnon, standing in the great hall of Paï-Lo's house, with its baroque chaos and parrot droppings, surprised her like the unexpected meeting of two worlds. He was no less troubled to see her approach naked, covered in shells and Indian daubs, with an unconcern that struck him as the height of immodesty. Yet, overcoming his embarrassment and putting more sternness than usual in his expression so as to banish any ambiguity, Le Thoret expressed a wish to see her privately. Colombe suggested that they take dinner together. She rejoined him a little later in a room next to the kitchens, having wrapped a shawl around herself that covered most of what might make the veteran uncomfortable. But this still left her eyes, which she was not in the habit of veiling, and whose pale glow she settled on him.

Le Thoret began with news of Just. Colombe, who had thought herself detached and serene, was flooded with worry on learning of Just's wound. She plied Le Thoret with anxious questions.

"Don't be worried," said the grizzled soldier. "He is in no danger. In a few days he will be as sturdy as ever."

Then he added, with a thin smile, "And as handsome."

Since the expedition had left Le Havre, Le Thoret had never shown any open interest in Just or Colombe. In fact, he wasn't warm toward anyone. Yet from several small gestures of protection he had made toward them, Colombe had always felt that they could count on him. When Just had started taking lessons from Villegagnon, Le Thoret had not shown any mistrust or jealousy. He had helped him loyally. And Colombe had always felt that the day she fled with the Indian women, he could easily have stopped her. She had seen him in the distance on the beach, armed with a harquebus. But he had not fired his weapon.

While Le Thoret nattered on with inconsequential news of the island, the Huguenots, and the fort, Colombe sensed that he had something else to say. This retiring man, who would never allow himself the slightest breach of discipline, no doubt felt that the burden of silence had been lifted from him. He clearly wanted to talk to Colombe. It might even be his reason for having come to Paï-Lo's; for the detour, useful as it was, could hardly be considered indispensable. He might well have fled directly to the stations at the head of the bay. The risk that the traders would greet him with hostility was slight.

Colombe tried to help him say his piece with much patience and more Madeira wine. Finally, when they had exhausted every available topic, and when fat raindrops from a storm had started to stroke the palm fronds of the roof, producing that incomparable relaxation of the senses that rain gives those who are sheltered from it, Le Thoret decided to come to the matter at hand.

"I served under Clamorgan," he said, "in Italy."

The mention of the name made Colombe shiver. Since her flight, she had sworn always to call herself Sun-Eye. Thinking of herself as no one's daughter allowed her to dream that she had been born among the Indians she loved.

"I was with him for eight years," Le Thoret went on, as though this fact gave him the authority to speak.

Colombe understood with growing clarity that he had not come simply to air his memories, but that there lay in the midst of them some crucial fact that he was trying to reveal.

"What you were told about him is true," he said.

This was a reference to the leader he no longer served, to Villegagnon, whose very name he wanted to forget.

"But the man who spoke to you of Clamorgan could not do so as fully as I, for he never served under him."

In his soldier's language, this meant he never loved him.

"But it seems to me that now, given . . . what you have become, there are certain facts you should know."

Colombe said nothing but only waited. Le Thoret paused while he chose a breach through which to press his attack.

"The battle of Ceresole had just ended," he finally said. "Clamorgan led the footsoldiers, and I fought under him with my company of harquebus men."

He stopped for a moment, proud of his start and gathering his courage.

"All was confusion. The Imperials had been defeated, but many of them still roamed the area in bands. On our side were mercenary companies not directly under anyone's command who were exacting payment from the peasants. Columns of smoke rose all over the countryside: Piedmontese villages had been set on fire by these looters."

A big red and beige butterfly, driven toward the house by the storm, flew heavily above them.

"Clamorgan did what he liked with the orders. He followed his own genius, which was more than ample. We had all seen this at Ceresole. A good general would tell him that we needed a victory. That was enough. But when he saw the looting and was ordered to look the other way, he acted as though he hadn't heard. And he sent us to stop those bandits."

Colombe couldn't understand where this was going. She had never liked battle stories, and now less than ever.

"I was at his side," went on Le Thoret. "Victory had been ours a long time already, yet he was still risking his life in confrontations with the looters. These irregulars went on the rampage, they didn't want to give up their booty. We were fired on. We suffered several casualties. Each time we tried to protect a village, it would take the population a while to understand who was on their side. Sometimes the peasants greeted us with drawn pitchforks, or even set traps for us."

Remembering the battle was making the old soldier talkative. It was these regular campaigns, even with their uncertain outcomes, that he missed more than anything since coming to America. But noticing Colombe's silence, he quieted down.

"One morning," he went on in a lower voice, "we arrived in a little deserted hamlet that we'd been told the mercenaries had overrun. It was pretty high in the Piedmont; you could see the snowy peaks of the mountains in the distance. The entire village consisted of four stone houses with their stables. The animals were bellowing, from neglect. We posted soldiers all around and called out to the inhabitants, but no one appeared. Then, very cautiously, we went into the houses."

At this point, Le Thoret lowered his eyes. Valiant though he was, he had a secret horror of blood. He liked fighting because war puts you up against health, courage, and skill. But as soon as he was faced with the wounded, with prisoners, and with civilians, he lost all eagerness and became almost cowardly.

"What we found was horrible . . . All the peasants had been massacred in their beds before dawn . . . Their furniture had been overturned . . . everything had been searched . . . whatever poverty had left them had been stolen . . ."

His eyes were full of sights he did not describe, which left blanks between his sentences.

"We were going to leave when one of our soldiers shouted out. He had seen something move in one of the sheds. Clamorgan came up and saw . . . two children hidden in a hay wagon."

He looked at Colombe.

"One of them was a little girl with curly hair. The other was a boy."

"Just!" she said.

The lamps cast their yellow glow out into the darkness, where a parrot strutted.

"No," said Le Thoret gravely.

The room was silent except for the bird's scrabbling on the scrolled board that served as his perch.

"Clamorgan came out of the barn with a child in each arm, and we saw your eyes shine in the sun. All the soldiers gathered to look at you."

Colombe was moved almost to tears, but the riddle of this other child beside her provided a shield for her emotions.

"Who was it?" she asked.

"A little peasant, like you, but certainly not your brother because he didn't look like you. You were about two years old, both of you. In a neighboring village looted a few days earlier, they were short of hands, but they wanted only boys. And we left him there."

In the Indian night filled with unknown presences, Colombe watched this fragment of the past emerge, like an animal one has never seen but whose cry is familiar.

"Afterward, there was never any question of giving you away to anyone. Clamorgan lifted you onto his horse, and he proudly brought you everywhere with him. You could see he already loved you."

"And Just?" she persisted, glimpsing what Le Thoret had to tell her but wanting the details.

"You have to imagine," said the soldier, deciding to attack in a different direction, "what our life was like on these Italian campaigns. Of course there were battles, and more often skirmishes. But there were also long periods of idleness, and we were garrisoned in the towns. Clamorgan had made friends all over northern Italy."

Colombe couldn't make out exactly where this digression was leading. But she let Le Thoret continue for fear that he might grow impatient with her interruptions.

"Before this last campaign, the one where Clamorgan found you, we had had a long respite, and your father had traveled all over the country. What he loved most was the region around Milan, which he had entered fifteen years earlier with Francis I and which we had afterward lost. All this is very complicated, I know."

It was clearly not the moment to fill Colombe's head with political explanations.

"The important thing is that he had known a woman there, a relative of the Sforzas, though not a close one—a great family in any case but its name is irrelevant. I saw a portrait of her. She was a young woman with jet black hair, a very long but slender nose, and that's really the only remarkable thing I can remember about her beauty, which was perfect. Clamorgan had had a child with her and had left it with its mother when he went off to fight in the Piedmont."

"Was that Just?" she asked.

But Le Thoret wanted her to know everything.

"After Ceresole, Clamorgan left you in our care, in the garrison. And he rode to Milan. Of course it was wartime and he was a soldier. But you shouldn't imagine that the borders were closed. A lone man could go anywhere, especially if he had friends. When he arrived in Milan, I don't know what happened exactly. I wasn't there. Had the young woman died? Had she married another man? At all events Clamorgan brought his son back with him to the Piedmont. And it is from that time on that you and Just have been together."

The old soldier had been wise to compress his tale: Colombe's emotions were the less inflamed. It left a simple fact, but an overwhelming one, richer in consequences than she could properly measure at the moment.

The light shed by this revelation spilled over her entire life. As to its effect on her emotions, there was still confusion. Did she feel joy or displeasure? Did knowing that Just was not her brother make it easier to be objective, to judge him and perhaps hate him? Or, on the contrary, did it remove the last obstacle to loving him fully? She would have been hard put to say. What she felt at that instant was the cold night air, chilled by the storm. She rose to find a cotton blanket and wrapped it around her.

"Have you already spoken to Just?" she asked.

"No," he said, "I wasn't able to."

Just had in fact been wounded at about the time Le Thoret left the island.

"So he knows nothing of all this?"

"Well, when he arrived from Milan," said Le Thoret, shaking his head, "he was two years older than you, and I'm sure he understood the situation."

A wave of tenderness came over her. She thought of Clamorgan, who had wanted with all his might that they should be raised as brother and sister.

Yet Le Thoret, relieved of his confession, signaled that he had still many things to say. She questioned him until dawn about this father whom she seemed at once to be losing and, for the first time, finding.

CHAPTER 39

Three months had passed since the Protestants' arrival on the mainland. Their life had fallen into a regular pattern, alternating between prayers and guard duty along the beach and forest perimeters in case of an attack from Villegagnon. But no attack came. Their main enemy was boredom, which consigned the once-more stifling days to unending torpor. Several members of the little community fell ill to fever and tossed deliriously in their hammocks, seemingly the only ones to have found a distraction during the siesta.

A few of the women also found avenues of activity and showed some enthusiasm: three of the brides were pregnant, and all the ladies-in-waiting were busy readying cribs and diapers. Aude viewed all this with scorn. Since her attempt on Just's life, she had maintained a haughty silence and rejected several offers of marriage. The community was leaderless. Du Pont, exhausted by his trials, seemed to have lost the energy to resist or fight, and a nasty ulcer on his shoulder kept Pastor Richier weak and indisposed. Little by little Aude gained influence over the group, the influence that a fierce virgin may exercise over men—especially when they know she is capable of murder. She now dealt on an equal footing with Martin, taking advantage of the fact that the brigand feared and probably desired her. She gave clear indications that where he was concerned, she was not prey to the same susceptibilities. This asymmetry endowed her with a power over Martin that none of the other exiles wielded. And everything depended on him. The attempts made by certain of the Protestants, on Richier's orders, to reach out to the Indians and make alliances with them all ended in failure. One of the artisans, Jean de Léry by name, had visited the forest villages to observe Tupi customs. He had looked in vain for a trapdoor into their souls through which the true faith might be introduced. One day he met an Indian named Pindahousou who claimed to have been converted by Thevet, and this briefly gave him hope. Pindahousou wore a cotton robe that mimicked the Franciscan habit, recited the Lord's Prayer, and performed no action without first making the sign of the cross. But when Léry learned more of the Tupi language, he quickly realized that Pindahousou performed the gestures simplemindedly without any understanding of their meaning. He hadn't the least knowledge of God. He aped the forms of Christianity in admiration of Thevet, who had cured his sick daughter with European medicines. Any lingering doubts were dispelled when Léry found proof that Pindahousou, despite his so-called Christianity, was still a cannibal.

The idea that the Indians were incapable of redemption gradually grew in the Protestants' minds. Only the Papists, who were satisfied with outward gestures, could mistake mimicry for conversion, and playacting for a manifestation of grace.

Abandoning all plans to turn the savages into men and save them, the Reformers were content to observe their customs, as one observes the ways of animals or plants. And the respect they paid the Indians was only the obverse of their total indifference toward them, as they had cast them out of humankind. One doesn't bother to introduce antelopes or buffaloes to Jesus Christ, though one may take some interest in their social forms.

As the weeks passed, the Huguenots understood that they could expect no help except what might come to them from Geneva. Martin supplied them with just enough water and food to survive, and even then Aude had to haggle to the last inch to get sufficient rations. Inactivity and deprivation gradually weakened the religionists. Their morale was at an ebb. The least incident could plunge them into despair. Curiously, the anticipated crisis came neither from

Villegagnon nor from the go-betweens. This only made it more terrifying.

One evening, two artisans who had gone collecting plants in the jungle failed to return. They were thought to be lost. When they didn't reappear the following day, Aude sent word to Martin to look for them. He hedged and stalled. Only by ordering him point-blank and fixing her terrifying black eyes on him did Aude force him to agree. The bodies were eventually found hanging from a cedar branch. The poor men had been horribly mutilated, eviscerated by two machete strokes tracing a bloody cross on their stomachs. No Indian would have behaved in this way, besides which the Indians in the region were too afraid of Martin to take such liberties.

The crime remained a mystery until it was followed by another, even more horrible one committed not far from the Protestants' village. It was one of the brides this time, who had gone a short way off to answer a call of nature. She was found crucified against the trunk of a sycamore with her abdomen sliced open and the child ripped out and partially eaten.

This time Martin was obliged to reveal what he knew.

"It's the Anabaptists," he told Aude, who was questioning him.

She had heard of the sect, like everyone else. But Richier had never said much on the subject so as not to cause panic.

"They live in the area?" asked Aude, surprised. She had never really believed in their existence.

"No one knows. It seems as though they are constantly on the move."

"I thought you were the master of these lands," said Aude scornfully.

"The Indians are afraid of them, and I can't do anything about it," said Martin defensively. "They're convinced the Anabaptists are spirits, and they run away as soon as they see them."

"And your 'partners'?"

"The truth is," said Martin with a shrug, "that no one is equipped to fight such monsters. The devils run around naked. They set traps, ambushes, and besides . . ."

Aude waited, a fearful expression on her face. She had a nose for weakness, and she sensed it here.

". . . Besides, they don't do us any harm."

"You mean to say that they're your allies?"

"Not at all!" said Martin. "But they are only dangerous when attacked. And since we can't defeat them, we avoid provoking them."

"And what about us," retorted Aude, "have we attacked them?"

"It would seem so."

She was too young to know the blood-filled history of the Protestants. She had been born after the terrible period when Luther threw the cold water of the Bible on minds seething with medieval frustrations, to produce an explosion of sects that vengefully abused their newfound freedom. When she questioned him that night, Richier told her of the horrible fate of the Anabaptists and of their rage to perpetrate the most extreme evil. For the first time he also admitted the extraordinary tortures the poor fervent wretches had been subjected to throughout Europe.

Despite the story's pathos, Aude was not one to expend much pity on men who were threatening her. She organized the community for survival, posted guards around the village, and gave orders that no one was to leave the village alone and without good reason. Unfortunately, while these measures protected the exiles from any further depredations, it had a disastrous effect on their morale. After the first period of mobilization, which brought a welcome alternative to the encroaching torpor, the community fell into a deep trough of despondency. No longer able to enjoy walks, the poor outcasts paced within the narrow confines of their huts. Differences grew into quarrels. A brawl broke out between one of the husbands and a soldier who had looked at his wife.

Finally one night Aude went to visit her uncle. The canker devouring his arm was growing deeper and deeper. The pastor's face was twisted with pain.

"Uncle, tell me the truth," she said. "Do you believe that we will get help from Geneva?"

Richier thought for a long time.

"Calvin won't abandon us. Of that, I am sure. But . . ."

Aude sensed his reluctance to speak any further.

"Don't be afraid to tell me," she said.

The pastor had known since the attempt on Just's life that his niece possessed a strength of character uncommon even among the Reformers, who tended to the heroic anyway. The same fear that made the community obey the decrees of this very young woman made Richier unable to resist her will. Though he had sworn never to do it, he now voiced a criticism of his spiritual master.

"Calvin," he wheezed, "is a difficult man. By which I mean he is demanding. He doesn't like failure. If our case was not well presented to him, he might be angry at us for not having been able to neutralize Villegagnon. The plain truth is, I'm afraid he'll do nothing beyond send us a fine letter of recrimination and advice."

"He might abandon us?"

"Not at all," said Richier, already reproaching himself for having besmirched the Reformationist's perfect image. "And besides, Calvin has nothing to do with this. It's a plain matter of politics: either Geneva is still on good terms with France, in which case we'll simply be told to work out a compromise with Villegagnon, or the wars of religion have reignited hostilities between the two powers."

"And in that case?"

"In that case, it will be impossible to send us a convoy. The king of France will never agree to allow us free use of his ports."

"So we are lost either way."

Richier thought for a moment.

"My mistake was not to have gone there myself," he said, and the admission clearly relieved his soul of a painful and constant preoccupation. "Chartier is loyal, he is a good pastor and a brave man, but he is no diplomat. I know Calvin better. I would have been able to convince him, to demonstrate the importance of this colony and of the wrongs done by Villegagnon. And even if France had raised difficulties, I would have found help in Holland or England."

"Maybe it's not too late. Go! We'll wait for you."

"And what would I tell him now? When Chartier set off, we were still on the island, and everything was still possible. Today, I would have to admit to Calvin that his Church is now confined to three straw huts, and that we crossed the Atlantic for the sole purpose of being persecuted by a band of Anabaptists who have reverted to a life of savagery."

"In that case," said Aude, "we must all go back."

The pastor objected, but only weakly. He took pride in what he knew to be his niece's courage and authority, even if these qualities served a conclusion he was loath to draw. Giving up in this way did not please Aude, but at least it made the situation clear. She knew what she still had to do.

She asked for an audience with Martin the next day. The Protestants' decision relieved him. He was a little tired of the trouble this band of idlers was causing him. And he derived no profit from them at all. They no longer even had the wherewithal to pay for the supplies he gave them. And they further threatened to disrupt his provisional alliance with Villegagnon. Vittorio insisted at every visit that the admiral had no plans for a hostile incursion onto the mainland, but that he was growing more impatient every day to see the Reformers leave Guanabara. Their departure would make everyone happy.

Martin arranged passage for them on an old Breton carrack that was trading in the bay. The ship was in poor shape. It was meant to go into drydock on its return to Lorient. The captain had intended to take on a load of wood, but such a cargo was too heavy for the worm-eaten timbers of the hull. He agreed to embark the passengers in return for payment on arrival. The advantage of this cargo was that it could always be lightened in the event of a mishap by tossing a few people overboard.

In less than a week the surviving Protestants were ferried out to the ship by pirogue. After the toll paid to fever, the Anabaptists' murders, and a few natural deaths, the mournful convoy now consisted of twenty-two persons. Adding to their misery on boarding the old hulk, which they found uncomfortable and dilapidated, was the fact that it was named the *Sainte-Marie*. The captain ordered them to make their quarters in the hold, which was still strewn with spilled oil, rotten fruit, and monkey droppings. He resembled his boat perfectly: crude and unclean. He always went bare-chested— exhibiting fat, disgusting breasts—and had hair on his shoulders and back. Aude tried training her black eyes on him, but at her third complaint about the cleanliness of the hold, he dealt her a slap in the face, forehand and backhand, that settled the hierarchy on board for the rest of the trip. The whole crew was of the same stamp.

From the moment they weighed anchor, it was clear that the greatest danger on the voyage would not come from the captain. To say the sails were worn would be an understatement. Only a discerning eye could have told which among the square patches they consisted of survived from the original material. The mast was guyed down like a bow, and the creaking of the hull seemed to convey a violent quarrel between the timbers and the crosspieces to determine which would give up the ghost first.

The ship, which set out from the head of the bay, gave Fort Coligny a wide berth in case Villegagnon should take a notion to fire a cannonade in their direction. Despite the uncertainties of the crossing before them, the Protestants were happy to see the coast, which had been the site of much suffering, recede. The Sugarloaf watched them pass with the stupid indifference of nature toward the misfortunes of man—a provocation to which man responds with redoubled efforts to subdue and subjugate it. The weather was beautiful, inflicting one of the two cruelties of which it was ever capable: a fierce sun, following on the heels of a ferocious storm.

Before long the swell piled up, marking the mouth of the bay. The hulk groaned and screeched under the force of the open sea. An incident then occurred, somewhat earlier than expected, that confirmed the captain's fears. A plank in the bow broke at the waterline, and the ocean flooded in. Everyone was called to stand aft to ease the stress and lift the gaping hole out of the water. A makeshift repair was made and the hole sealed, at least for the moment.

The captain decided, after a consultation with the carpenter, that they needed to lighten the load. Several barrels of water and flour were thrown overboard. To further lighten the load and reduce the number of mouths to feed, given the quantity of stores remaining, the Huguenots were invited to choose eight of their number to return to land. As the ship had no boat, they were to crowd onto a raft for the trip back to shore. After protestations, lamentations, and the promise of a larger payment on arrival, the captain agreed to sacrifice four monkeys to replace two of the men. But they would still have to find six men to return. Five artisans and a soldier agreed to board the raft.

The ship resumed its course, and a chorus of heart-rending farewells went out to the six men, who crouched tearfully on all fours on the raft's deck.

The coast was still near, and the current entering the bay pushed the raft inside the harbor. The castaways saw the Sugarloaf reappear, as indifferent as ever. Unable to steer their makeshift craft, they let it drift toward land on the currents. Night came. As they entered far-ther into the bay, the current weakened, and the raft spun like a cork. The night being moonless, they had no idea where they would touch land. Finally, toward the middle of the night, a gentle shock alerted them that they had struck a reef. The raft advanced a bit more, then came to a standstill in a little cove rimmed with rocks. A man walked to shore over the sharp reefs just beneath the surface of the water. He came back shortly to report that they had in fact reached land, and all six disembarked. Only at dawn, discovering a wall rising above them, did they know that they had arrived on the island of Fort Coligny.

· · ·

"Did he confess?"

"Everything, Admiral," answered the torturer, proudly holding a sheet of parchment flecked with blood.

Villegagnon glanced at the man hanging from the wall, his wrists held by iron cuffs. Pieces of flesh had been cleanly ripped from his chest by heated metal pincers, whose jaws still smoldered with burn-ing skin. His whole body was lacerated from the lashes of a whip. His neck bore the red marks of a garrote, which had been tightened just until he lost consciousness.

Without hatred, suffering is a savorless spectacle, just as drink holds no pleasure unless it quenches a true thirst. From the pleasure the admiral felt at seeing this Protestant ripped to pieces, he could gauge the progress that his disgust for mankind was making in him. It gratified him as a sign of recovery after many years of inane indul-gence. One had only to look carefully to find the evil in one's neigh-bor. Villegagnon reproached himself bitterly for not having understood this earlier and examined men with more sagacity. This one, for example, the torture victim: in the past he would surely have believed the man's claims to being a simple castaway who had drifted onto the island by chance. Today he was no longer satisfied with such illusions—he searched more thoroughly. And he therefore found. The truth he might so easily have missed was written on this parchment.

"'I admit,'" read the admiral in tones of satisfaction, "'that I have tried to enter Fort Coligny in order to sow chaos and betrayal there.

My friends returned to Geneva to hasten the arrival of reinforcements that will allow them to gain control of the colony. My mission
was to prepare the ground for their return by assassinating Admiral
Villegagnon and secretly spreading calumnies about Rome and the
Catholic clergy.'"

Spread-eagled on the wall, the man had lost consciousness.

Villegagnon stuffed the confession in his pocket.

"Wonderful," he said to the executioner. "They all agree. The ones
you dealt with yesterday signed exactly the same declaration."

The torturer smiled graciously and, after wiping his blood-covered
hands on his apron, performed a little bow.

"Which just goes to show that there is only one truth," said the
admiral.

As he started to leave, he stopped and said, "Put him in with the
others. Oh, and try to get him looking as presentable as possible for
the trial tomorrow."

· · ·

The esplanade outside the government house had been decorated
specially so the court could convene with all necessary pomp. As it
was the dry season, the giant copy of Titian's Madonna had been
raised there facing the port and the jungle on the coast. To mark the
occasion, Villegagnon proudly wore a pelisse lined with gray squirrel
that the tailor had just finished making for him. He took his place on
a sort of scaffold beside Dom Gonzagues, who was growing increasingly crippled and doddering. Useless for anything else, he did splendid duty as a judicial sphinx, lost in a poetic reverie that could be
mistaken for bloody ruminations on punishment. The third man was
the dean of the artisans, who served as the people's representative in
the courtroom.

The six Protestants who had fetched up on the island in their raft
were judged individually. The court, unsurprisingly, condemned
them all to death, a sentence the executioner had already partly
administered. As the colonists were not only to be edified by this
judgment but entertained by it as well, several forms of execution
were decided on. Two would be hanged, two beheaded, and two
drowned. This last sentence was the most prized by the public. The

victims, a short chain weighting their necks, were thrown off the rocks. Their final agony could be followed through the clear water of the bay as from behind a pane of glass. The greatest enthusiasts of the spectacle waited afterward by the water to see the morays arrive.

Never had Villegagnon been more popular.

CHAPTER 40

Just recovered from his wound quite quickly. Nonetheless, he continued in bed, inert and sapped of will, well past his physical convalescence. An unhealthy languor replaced his bodily affliction, as though Aude had stabbed him in the heart after all.

In his melancholy state, fleeting images of his life paraded before him, but he now revisited his past emotions without feeling them. His dreams, as if diaphanous bubbles the murderous dagger had pricked, were gone. The Clamorgan estate, chivalry, his father's heroic battles in Italy, the grandiose visions of Antarctic France—all seemed so much mist to which he had absurdly lent solid form. Now that his eyes were truly open, not one of these illusions could still fool him. Yet in their absence, the prosaic world of appearances had not returned, for appearances too had been transpierced. The surface of those around him had gaped wide to reveal disgusting recesses. Aude, loved for what she was not, had shown how easily hate can wear the disguise of love, darkness that of beauty, corruption that of chastity, and how an outward show of tenderness can hide murderous intentions. Then, Villegagnon had revealed himself to be different from what Just had imagined. The chevalier came to visit him every day during his convalescence. By way of reassurance, Villegagnon told him of his actions and plans and, intending to cheer him up, gave harrowing descriptions of his cruelties, his tricks, and the hatred that now openly governed his deeds. How could Just have admired such a man? How could he have believed for so long in his goodness? He did not know which of them had changed. But Villegagnon could not spill such a great quantity of black bile and malice unless it had been forming in him for a long time, even if he had earlier kept it to himself. The admiral now aroused repugnance in Just, and what Villegagnon took for bodily exhaustion was in fact the revolt of a mind that could neither talk nor remain silent.

There was no one on the island whose secret and repulsive face Just did not henceforth have cause to ponder. Appearances seemed to have been reversed like a garment to reveal their dirty, swarming insides. Even he was not exempt from this transformation. His whole life reeked of cowardice, indecision, and error. Under the posture of nobility and elegance he had always resorted to the grossest compromises and upheld his own lies, pretending to believe them.

Colombe alone withstood this breaking wave of nausea. Just thought of her clear gaze, which was no longer trained on him, and felt that his new lucidity was a way of finally seeing through her eyes. How had he not understood her better? Why had he been too cowardly to accept what she had tried to tell him? She saw before he did the dark downward spiral in which this bloody and destructive colony was caught. She had come to warn him that she was leaving, and he had not heard. And she had read the treachery in the seeming love of the woman who later stabbed him.

He had met these surges of truth with nothing but lies. The lie of her dressing as a man, which he had accepted on her behalf and which she had cast off in a desperate action. The lie of a bid for glory in which he did not believe. And above all the lie of their being related, which had protected him from his true feelings for her. When they were children, making her believe she was his sister had been a way of saying he loved her. But perpetuating this myth had had, if not the aim, then the effect of keeping their love from growing and becoming adult as they themselves did.

In making these walls of illusion and error crumble, Aude had at least done one good turn. Below the husk, the skin, the pulp, she had caused the one solid kernel in Just to appear: his love for Colombe.

By an unhappy fate, he had discovered it too late to plant it in earth and make it grow, too late to express it or to live by it.

Little by little Just got back on his feet. He dressed, went out to walk on the beach, making a wide circle around the gibbets and places of torture. In fact he avoided looking at the island as much as possible. Even the fort, of which he had once been so proud, was now a painful sight to him. He looked only at the sea. In its green ripples, where the blue gleam of the water varyingly dissolved the yellow light of the sun, Just seemed to read the fluid and enigmatic message of his own feelings. The landscape of his soul, slack and liquid, stretched out between a future as white as the sky and the violet depths of his painful past.

It was there that Villegagnon came to find him one day, shortly after the castaways' execution, to announce his decision. Seeing the admiral approach along the water's edge, Just had the immediate and uncomfortable sensation of being pursued into the intimacy of his daydreams. On that morning, however, Villegagnon seemed less tormented by hate than usual. Walking along the rocks, he too had apparently been affected by the tranquility of the sea. His brightly colored costume trimmed with gold thread was less outlandish in the majestic precincts of the bay than in the fussy setting of his ebony chest and his Oriental carpets. He spoke in low tones, as though for himself. Just felt that, since being wounded, he had become indispensable to Villegagnon. By his daily visits the admiral had managed to protect a little patch of true affection in the clatter of violence that was carrying him away. Unfortunately, the object of this affection found him odious and he no longer felt able to return the sentiment.

"I've thought long and hard," said Villegagnon. "We've reached a dead end."

This admission of failure was highly unlike him. In point of fact, it was again the prelude to action. Raising his head proudly and looking toward the horizon, he announced, "I am returning to France."

Just still had trouble showing any interest, despite the singularity of the assertion.

"The fort has been completed," the admiral went on. "The Portuguese clearly missed their chance to attack us while we were weak. The colony's safety is now assured. We must go forward, harvest great quantities of wood, penetrate the depths of this continent, and discover the gold that exists here in abundance. Now that the Protestants have left, it is time to attack the go-betweens and rid the coast of them permanently. What I have learned of their strength, unfortunately, suggests that we will need a real army to conquer them, new means, and money to buy information. We can expect to find nothing of that here. I must go to Paris for it and plead the case for our promising colony before the king."

Just was afraid he would start again on the greatness of Antarctic France, and he hadn't the strength to hear it. But Villegagnon suddenly veered in a new direction.

"I knew Cortés well, when we captured Algiers," he confided. "I never saw so pitiful a man."

Just had already heard the admiral compare his work in Brazil to the conquest of Mexico, and Hernán Cortés's name was often on his lips. But this was the first time he had directly spoken of meeting him.

"He was a little crooked fellow, black as a crow and riddled with tics. Yet he gave more kingdoms to Charles V than any captain could ever dream of conquering. He defeated the emperor of the Mexicans all by himself and inundated Spain with the gold of America. When I knew him, he was already in disgrace and desperately bidding for his sovereign's notice."

At the admiral's approach, a few artisans strolling by the water pretended suddenly to be busy and took off. But Villegagnon paid no attention to them, absorbed in his description of the conquistador.

"They slandered him," he went on, "while he was risking his life to subjugate the New World. Spiteful courtiers represented him as a traitor, and Charles V was weak enough to believe them. When Cortés arrived back in Europe, the emperor treated him like a wretch. The old soldier looked for any opportunity to return to court. When Charles organized a sort of crusade against Algiers so as to rid the Mediterranean of that nest of pirates, Cortés jumped at the opportunity.

"When we landed at Algiers a horrible storm kept us from attacking. The expedition was poorly prepared and poorly handled. Everyone could see that it didn't have a prayer—even I, though I made a brave show of it. But Cortés wanted to redeem himself at any price. There he stood in the rain, wet to his last hair (and God knows he had hair), saying over and over, 'Onward! We must go onward!' And the emperor could not have looked at him with more scorn if he'd been a buffoon, a madman. It was pathetic."

The admiral looked at the sea, shaking his great head.

"Cortés ended in poverty. They say that at the end he would cling to the emperor's carriage and beg for help. Well, I don't want a similar misfortune to happen to me."

This was the first time Just had heard him speak of failure and loneliness.

"No, by Saint Jack of Jerusalem! I won't let cowards undermine me. Of course I wanted the Huguenots to disappear, but now that they've found a way back to Europe, I must be doubly on my guard, don't you see? Our interrogation of the castaways proves it: they are determined to ruin me. They are going to lampoon my work. I know their breed: they scribble tracts the way a monkey scratches fleas. They will spread libel about me. And there will always be good counselors to tell the king of France that 'where there's smoke, there must be fire.' Then anything could happen: He could disown me. Or he could decide to send me an army but put another Du Pont at its head, who would land here and immediately announce that he is taking my place."

While the admiral was giving these explanations, they arrived at the eastern redoubt. Villegagnon stood and faced the mouth of the bay, looking toward the open sea.

"That is why," he concluded, "I must make my defense in person. We still have a ship. I have had it readied. Within a week, I will be gone."

No longer in the habit of thinking practically, Just was uncertain what decision he should make for himself: accompany the admiral to France, or devise another solution?

He expected a choice and he received an order.

"In my absence," Villegagnon declared solemnly, "you will take command of the colony."

This decision hit Just like a crossbow quarrel in the forehead. Yet on consideration it seemed logical, even inevitable. Le Thoret had deserted, Bois-le-Comte had stayed in Normandy, Dom Gonzagues had spent his last strength in the religious strife. The other officers were good soldiers but with no aptitude for leadership. Villegagnon had educated Just as his heir apparent and given him all the qualities he would need to succeed him. All he lacked was the desire. The admiral, despite his insensitivity, had noticed this, but he believed that will could be summoned externally, by an order or, better yet, by a vow.

"Swear to me," he said, pointing his peccary-gloved finger at Just's heart, "on the memory of your father that you will watch over this land until my return. Swear to me that you will defend its interests against all those who might threaten it, and that you will allow your throat to be slit before you turn it over to them."

As with all his official pronouncements, Villegagnon had given these words an emphasis that bordered on the ridiculous. But at the same time, his strength, his size, and the pained but menacing expression with which he spoke prompted no humor or evasiveness.

"I swear!" said Just in spite of himself.

And so he became governor of Antarctic France.

• • •

Païi-Lo was growing weaker. Despite the returning sunshine, the dry air, he continued to cough and stay off his feet. He was carried onto the terrace, where he remained for hours in his hammock so still that squirrels sometimes came in twos and threes to sit on his body. Weak though he was, he continued to hear the news that was brought to him. He learned that Le Thoret, well escorted, had arrived at the trading stations and been able to embark for France. A few days later, some warriors on the coast had come to tell him that the last ship anchored near the island had sailed. According to rumor, Villegagnon was on board.

Colombe wondered whether Just had left with him. Since Le Thoret's revelations, the idea that their fates were separate and even at odds had grown in her. Her primary concern now was to imagine her life among the Indians, to find her true place there, and, starting from her newly recast past, to forge a future that would make her happy. Since Paraguaçu's departure she had been spending less time with the women. She wanted to share the life of the warriors who journeyed through the forest. When she asked them, they had been somewhat embarrassed. The Indians' rule was that a woman could take no part in such battles and adventures. But on Païi-Lo's urging, the men had finally agreed to make an exception for Colombe. Two of the patriarch's sons took her under their protection. They taught her to shoot the big bow and the arts of making arrows, tracking game, and imitating the calls of the forest. Then, during a ceremony conducted by the *caraíbas* and featuring a great quantity of *cahuin* and good omens from the maracas, they drew new figures on her body with genipap paint that were intended to make the spirits of the animals and of the forest merciful toward her. Finally they stuck little yellow and green feathers on her shoulders and hips. Despite the unpleasant sensation of having them attached to one's body, they had the twin advantage of making one invulnerable and hiding one's sex.

Colombe made her first expedition with a group of ten men. It was pure joy for her. They would start walking at first light and go to the far ends of the tribe's lands. Silent, alert to the faintest calls, they crossed bare passes, entered undergrowth choked with wild orchid and cineraria bushes. They slept at the foot of tall black cliffs and walked up streams so clear they sometimes took the backs of large stationary fish for rocks and fell into the water laughing.

The nearness of danger, evident in the abrupt way the lead-off man sometimes called for a stop and froze, ready to fight, made the safety of the group still more delicious to Colombe. She had never before in these empty expanses felt such a sense of confidence and protection. At night they made a small fire and without a word ate the dried meats they had brought in skin bags. One afternoon they killed a deer, cut it up, and carried with them the quarters they hadn't eaten.

During these endless marches, Colombe looked at her companions, smelled the odor of their bodies in the heat, admired their lithe muscles dancing under their glistening skin. She asked herself at length whether she could ever be the wife of one of them. Yet for all her attraction to their beauty, their gentleness, and their strength, she felt a mysterious obstacle in the way of this notion. Perhaps it was that Indian beauty seemed to belong to another order, to untamed nature. Wasn't the scent of their skin, different though it was, related to the scent of thyme growing on steep slopes, of marjoram, of lentisks? And this litheness, this agility, this beautiful musculature, wasn't it the human variety of the savage strength of leopards and antelopes? Yet she had no sooner framed this argument than she rejected it. She felt too close to the earth she walked on with bare feet, too much in harmony with the rocks and the beasts to feel the slightest difference with these men that would have kept her from mating one of them.

Sometimes she told herself that the obstacle lay precisely in having to choose one of them when her friendship was with the whole group. Would they still see her as one of their own if she showed a preference for a particular one among them? But this did not convince her either. She drove the thoughts from her head, kept the mystery to herself, and returned to the unbridled enjoyment of the present moment.

When they arrived back at Paï-Lo's at the end of one of these forays, they would rediscover the sounds of the household with pleasure, the loud laughter, the festivities. Colombe looked at everything more fondly, with a new closeness that she noted and cherished all the more for the distance she had traveled.

In the next few weeks she went on several long expeditions with different groups of hunters, which filled her with more joy than she would have thought possible. Paï-Lo complimented her on her courage and told her of the warriors' admiration for her behavior, her stamina, and her deftness, an admiration they could not voice to her directly.

Yet the old man was growing so weak that Colombe, despite his urgings, decided to put a temporary end to her traveling and stay by his side.

Nothing seems so immortal as those who have been weak and vulnerable for as long as one has known them. To Colombe, Paï-Lo was an ageless man and therefore not threatened with his end, as though he had already come through death and spoke to her from the far shore. But the recent transformation in him, the extreme thinness of his neck and arms, his shortness of breath, the long moments of absence with his mouth open and his eyes half-closed, had begun to intimate that he would soon breathe his last.

Everyone in the house did what they could to make his end gentle and peaceful, and no one could have predicted that it would be as tumultuous as it was. The alarm came one morning with the sound

of running in the forest and the shouts of pursuers. By the time
Colombe had risen from her hammock and gone to the door, two
panting shadows had already erupted into the room. In the forest,
where the dawn is slow, shreds of purple night still darkened the
rooms of the house though the sky was already light. At first
Colombe did not recognize the two intruders. They held hands, one
taller than the other, and their naked silhouettes announced them as
Indians. Paï-Lo was lying in the next room. His door was always
open, and a lamp burned night and day at his bedside. The shouts
outside were growing closer, and the two runaways ducked into the
room where the old man lay. When the lamp revealed their faces,
Colombe let out a yelp. She had recognized Paraguaçu. The man
beside her was the young captive, Karaya, about whom Colombe had
not dared to ask for news, believing he was dead.

At the same moment, a half-dozen warriors carrying clubs rushed
into the house. They took a moment to get used to the darkness, then
they caught sight of the runaways and leapt toward them brandishing their weapons. But when they saw, lying across their path, the
supine body of the patriarch, they stopped and a great silence fell.
Colombe slipped into the room after them.

"Save us, Paï-Lo!" cried Paraguaçu, falling to her knees.

Karaya, still standing, backed away until he came up against the
woven partition.

"What is happening?" asked Paï-Lo slowly.

His voice was low, and he was making an evident effort to keep his
hand upraised, with which he had checked the pursuers' weapons.

One of the warriors walked forward to the hammock and spoke in
a respectful voice, his breathing still labored from the chase.

"This man is a Maracajá. He was to be sacrificed this night."

Karaya looked at the ground. All sensed that he was resigned to
his death. But Paraguaçu had taken his side, and he stood under her
frail protection.

"Save us!" she repeated, her eyes flashing.

Paï-Lo lowered his hand, slowly closed and reopened his eyelids,
and called for Colombe.

"Help me to sit up," he asked her softly.

She supported him so that he was sitting in the hammock. The
effort made him wince. His handsome head, raised in the bed, moved

slowly from the imploring runaways to the warriors who wanted their death.

"You wanted to eat him, is that right?"

"It's the law," said the leader of the Indians.

Païl-Lo nodded to show that he approved.

"You are right," he said.

Paraguaçu cried out, but with a weary gesture of his hand the old man signaled that he was not yet finished.

"How long has he been a prisoner?" he asked.

"Twenty moons," the leader answered.

Païl-Lo nodded gravely. Then he waited. His mouth moved in a chewing motion that Colombe had never noticed before.

"What would you say," Païl-Lo finally asked, "if I proposed that you eat me?"

The Indian opened his eyes wide in surprise.

"Yes, me," said the patriarch, with a visible effort, "would you agree to eat my body?"

So saying, he motioned with his beard at his stomach and legs, which hardly made a bulge under the covers.

"Païl-Lo!" said the Indian, with true indignation.

"That's just what I thought," said the old man with strange alacrity, "you wouldn't want to. But do you at least know why? Oh, don't tell me that it's because I'm too thin—that doesn't matter to you. No, no, there's another reason."

From the room next door came the whispering of the inhabitants of the house, who were pushing up close to see what was happening.

"In that case," said Païl-Lo in a hoarse voice, "I'll tell you. You don't want to eat me because you have already done so."

The Indian's hairless face, plucked even to the eyelashes, registered pained astonishment and horror.

"I have been here more than fifty years," said Païl-Lo. "Think of it: hundreds of moons."

He shook his head with a desolate expression.

"And during all that time, there hasn't been a day when you have not devoured me. There isn't an atom of me that I have not turned over to you. You have eaten my heart, my arms, my mind, my eyes, my genitals, my stomach. Everything, you have chewed everything, swallowed everything, digested everything."

After uttering this long sentence, Païlo swayed a bit from tired-
ness. His mouth still worked fitfully, as though he were inwardly
making ritual incantations.

"That one too," he said, motioning toward Karaya with his chin,
"in twenty moons you have had plenty of time to eat him. He is now
part of you. You have taken his strength and his spirit. He is one of
yours. The law has been fulfilled."

The warrior who spoke for the others was shaken. His respect for
Païlo, combined with the great effort the old man had made to
speak and the goodness in his eyes, raised a barrier to his formulat-
ing objections.

"The spirits will take revenge," the Indian finally said, but in a
subdued voice with more fear in it than menace.

"No," said Païlo.

He was clearly at the end of his strength. His head was nodding,
and he was making an effort to hold it up.

"No," he repeated. "For I will soon be among the spirits. I will be
one of them. And I will tell them what I have just told you. They will
understand."

The patriarch's back bent as though crushed under the weight of
death itself. It was death and not he who formed the words, and
whereas one might refuse something to a living man, it was impossible to resist this voice that no longer belonged to the world.

"What is your name?" asked Païlo, turning his veiled eyes
toward Paraguaçu's companion.

"Karaya," said the boy in a trembling voice.

"Well then, Karaya, I am taking you with me. It won't be you who
stays here. It will be another. Henceforth he will be known as
Angathù, and no one will take revenge on him."

With these words, he let his head rest and closed his eyes.

Those in the room fell to their knees. Heads were lowered. A long
moment passed, during which the sound of the dying man's breathing grew fainter and fainter. Then there was silence. And while death
carried Païlo away, along with the soul of the man he had just
bought back, the room filled with a sound of wind or wings, no one
knew exactly.

When the assembly lifted their heads, they saw only Colombe's
eyes shining by the dead man. Her despair at losing Païlo was

mixed with the unforgettable bitterness of his final lesson. She suddenly understood what kept her, despite her attachment to the Indian world, from melting into it completely. Païma-Lo could never have saved Karaya if he had not kept his sovereign independence, which had made him respected. The Indians had certainly eaten him, but, a faithful student of their anthropophagic philosophy, he had also eaten them, to the point that he was able to impose a clemency on them that they saw as contrary to their laws.

The Indians, recognizing in Colombe's eyes the gaze of the great sacred bird that holds the souls of the dead, knew that Païma-Lo had survived in her.

CHAPTER 41

With Villegagnon gone, Just was left in charge—but of nothing.
It took little time to realize that the admiral's energy, his whims, his
cruelty, unbearable as they had been, had at least brought activity to
the island. In his absence, daily life fell into a trough of tranquillity,
which the colonists finally acknowledged by its true name: boredom.
Work on the fort had been completed. Its low rooms had been
smeared with daub and whitewashed; a large door had been set
across its entrance; cannons had been placed along the ramparts. It
was impossible to think of anything else to add to it. The chapel,
intended to house the monumental painting of the Madonna, took
the men little time to build, used as they were to the hard earthworks
of the fortress. And all possible improvements had been made to the
government house where Just lived.

The only thing left to occupy their time was regulating the constant dance of the sentinels. But whatever menace the jungles and the
hills held, it had become clear over time that one could (alas!) rely on
their clemency. The slovenly patrols that kept watch at the fort most
often neglected to load their harquebuses. From their mute contemplation of the sea, from the familiar cry of parrots and black monkeys, the souls of those on the island filled with a languor that was
equal in its violence to any assault.

Just's authority wore itself out against this weakening energy. His qualities were well known; he now began to reveal his faults. In the first place, he proved incapable of diverting the exiles by administering punishments. The instruments in the torture chamber grew rusty; the gibbets no longer bore fruit; and those who were tempted to disobey were discouraged beforehand by his clemency. Nor was Just able to reproduce the great spectacle of the prayer services, where Villegagnon appeared in brightly colored costumes with ever more preposterous headgear. The admiral had bequeathed a collection of hats to Just before leaving, ranging from simple caps to veritable tiaras, yet if Just had worn such crowns inlaid with beryl and topaz, he would have provoked more laughter than obedience.

For a time he considered harvesting brazilwood on the mainland again. The wood was hard, the logs were heavy, and the trees grew in isolated locations. Once in France, however, the wood, ground to sawdust and steeped in water to make a brilliant red dye, would constitute a valuable commodity. But Martin—to whom Vittorio transmitted the request—was against it, concerned that it would result in too many colonists moving around off the island. And then again, Villegagnon had taken the last ship with him: there was no way to export the logs.

They had to resign themselves to waiting and doing nothing. At first, this new regimen was welcome, after the immense effort of the pioneering years. An amiable civility reappeared among the men. They played cards and dice, recouped their strength, sang. But nothing is so wearing as a holiday that goes on too long. With no work, no prayers, no punishment, no Protestants to eviscerate, no admiral to fear or Portuguese to combat, the hapless men finally offered up their bodies to the distraction of illness. A few set the example by declaring that they felt under the weather. The others, visiting them, started to follow their lead and vied for unusualness. Each cultivated his own infirmity, whether it was a headache, or vertigo, or a slackening of the stomach. In the end, a real epidemic descended on this population that was so ready to receive it, making their complaints truly serious. The bedridden assumed uniform symptoms. It all began with red blotches on the skin, followed by fever, vomiting, and extreme torpor, which led in the most extreme cases to coma and death. The square of graves behind the eastern redoubt exhibited a rash of freshly turned mounds. Five deaths occurred in the first week. For all its cruelty, the epidemic had the kindness to carry off in the first wave the two charlatans who served as healers. If the disease inflicted its torments on the colonists, at least they were spared those of medicine.

Just was bedridden for two days, but because he had never, owing to his duties, succumbed to the general languor, he recovered quickly and without aftereffects. Yet he looked on powerlessly as the sickness devastated the ranks of the island's defenders. All the Indians died. Among the French, one out of two was affected, and rare were those who, once stricken, found the energy to recover. Several dozen bodies were buried in the red sand. Dom Gonzagues was one of the few whom the illness never touched: in the poetic world he now permanently inhabited, the miasmas of contagion no doubt found the air too pure.

When after several weeks the illness went away, sated, the colony's ranks were dangerously depleted. No longer were there enough men to defend the fort on all sides. The cannons now outnumbered the men on hand to service them.

Just knew the peril the island ran from being so incompletely defended and put his energy into reconstituting the colony's defensive strength. Of all the imaginable means, he chose two: the first was to make contact with the Norman trading establishments. The admiral had never consented to it, but Just had less pride. The traders at the head of the bay, from what he knew, were few in number and averse to war. But they might supply him with Indians to supplement his troops. Just's second action would be to inform Villegagnon of the new situation, so that he could send reinforcements posthaste.

Both courses depended on intercepting trading vessels entering or leaving the bay. According to their destination, he would give them one of the two letters he had prepared, for the traders or for the admiral.

He therefore set a watchman to look for sails in the straits. A boat was kept ready at all hours to fly in pursuit of the first ship that passed. The weather was calm, and it took two weeks before one was spied, arriving from the sea and sailing under the Sugarloaf. Just stood in the boat's stern encouraging the oarsmen, and in less than an hour they had pulled alongside the ship.

It was an old galliass, powered by a few small sails and oars. Just was invited aboard to speak to the captain. The deck was indescribably chaotic, almost entirely covered with a jumble of messily coiled ropes, baskets, greasy casks, and nets. Exhausted men were sprawled along the guardrails. An ammoniac fug drifted up from the hold, and the smell—so out of place at sea—awoke confused memories in Just. The captain, disturbed from his siesta, emerged from the master's cabin rubbing his eyes. Before Just had a chance to introduce himself, the man asked him, "Where are we?"

"Why . . . in Guanabara Bay."

"And you appear to be French!" said the sailor, recovering some hope.

"That I am," said Just.

"Then, we need not fear the Portuguese in this inlet?"

"No."

"God be praised," said the captain.

To celebrate the good news, the captain invited Just to join him in the roundhouse. He showed him a seat and apologized for having nothing to offer him by way of drink. Fortunately, out of precaution and to earn the favor of those he was visiting, Just had had a small cask of Madeira from the admiral's dwindling stock put in the boat. It was hoisted on board, and the captain, drawing two unwashed goblets from an old chest, was soon raising his in a perfunctory toast and tossing its contents down the hatch.

"Lord but that's good!" he said. "I'd almost forgotten the taste of it."

He was a small man with a flat face. Formerly stout, the crossing had wrung him down several sizes. His flesh hung about him like the ill-fitting clothes of a convalescent.

"Have you exhausted your stores, then?" asked Just.

"Every last bit," the man said, "and a long time ago at that. We were supposed to fetch land three months ago. We were going to the Antilles."

"But you've arrived in Brazil!"

"I know," said the captain disconsolately. "We met with storms when we reached the tropics and were driven to the equator."

"Why didn't you correct your course?"

The seaman emptied a third gobletful before answering.

"When we spotted land, my pilot—who died of fever last week—

said it was the coast of São Salvador. We swung around toward the north but found the wind blowing from dead ahead. With this old tub, we didn't make much way. That was when the Portuguese came bearing down on us."

"Merchant ships?"

"No, a squadron armed for war. An enormous fleet, maybe fifty ships."

Just turned pale.

"And where were they coming from?"

"They were sailing out of All Saints Bay and heading out to sea. And we were downwind of this armada! We had to get around them, on the other tack. You can imagine the panic!"

The blood had drained from Just's face, but the captain, absorbed in his adventure, garrulously continued his recital.

"Luckily for us, there were a lot of them. Some of the bunch were slow, and as they were traveling in convoy, the large ships didn't carry all the sail they might. So I decided to run downwind again. We fled until they lost track of us. When I saw the entrance to this bay, which at first I took for the mouth of a river, I thought we could hide in it. And here we are!"

"But where were the Portuguese headed?" asked Just, who was starting to understand.

"The Portuguese? Directly south."

"Which means . . ."

"I searched through my pilot's papers," the captain interrupted proudly, "and from what I found there, I learned that Portugal has another colony farther to the south, which they call Crablice Land."

It was highly unlikely that a war squadron would sail peaceably to São Vicente.

"No," said Just, who could see the disaster coming, "we're the ones they're after."

He gave a rapid history of the colony to the captain, who grew pale in turn.

"Then, this bay is not safe for us," the captain said, "if they're on their way to conquer it."

"I'm afraid that's true."

"Which means we'll have to set off again," wailed the seaman, "with nothing to eat or drink."

Then an idea came to him.

"Listen," he said, gripping Just's forearm, "couldn't you quickly supply us with food and water. In exchange, I'll give you what's left of my cargo. It's just weighing us down, and we won't be able to find a buyer for it anyway."

"What are you carrying?"

"Horses, for the plantations on Santo Domingo. Three quarters of them have died. And the others won't hold out much longer."

That explained the strange odor coming from the cargo area: it was the smell of horse manure, familiar from Clamorgan.

"What do you want us to do with them?" asked Just, a bit disappointed. "Our island is tiny and nothing grows on it."

"I beg you to take these animals off our hands," said the captain. "They are going stir-crazy down there. The men won't go into their stalls anymore. The horses bite and kick them. And when they die, it's even worse. We've been eating that monkey meat for two full months, and just the thought of it makes me vomit."

"How many do you still have?"

"Five."

Liking horses, Just took pity on them. He thought he might give them to the Indians on the coast who were still friendly. When the colony grew stronger, after Villegagnon's return, they could always make use of them.

"How much time do you think you gained on the Portuguese?" he asked the captain, whom the news and the wine had plunged into a terrified torpor.

"At the rate they're going," the captain answered, "I don't think they'll be here for a week."

Just pondered for a moment. All the languor of the long days of inactivity had left him. Hypotheses crowded into his mind, and he suddenly saw what he had to do.

"Sail on as far as that promontory that you see farther up the bay," he said. "I'll send a message to the Indians. They'll take your animals and supply you in return with water and manioc. After that, you can go where you like."

Having no time to lose, Just climbed down into the boat without waiting for thanks and returned to the island. He immediately sent two sailors to alert the Indians and called together the important

men of the colony. News of the Portuguese attack, coming just when
the fort's garrison had been devastated by disease, provoked a panic.
Some spoke of a plot, of poisoning. Everyone looked around them
with distrust, as though the enemy were not a formidable outside
force but were hidden in their midst and could be eliminated with a
dagger thrust.

Just brought them back to reality. His calmness under the circumstances had a wonderful effect. He gave firm and precise orders,
which reassured everyone. The general surprise, therefore, was all the
greater when he announced that he was leaving that very night. The
colony's dignitaries, who had always been skeptical toward Villegagnon's choice of a successor, recoiled—as though Just had revealed
himself to be the traitor they were looking for.

But all was so clear and so well organized in Just's mind now that
he easily found the words to explain himself and convince the others. His plan's boldness overcame all hesitation, despite its risks. He
scored heavily by challenging his detractors to suggest an alternative.
In the end, everyone fell in behind him. Boarding one of the boats,
Just was even convinced that his absence was the ultimate sign of his
authority. No longer responsible for the island, he could now concentrate on the last card he had to play.

• • •

The next morning at the Indian settlement, Just helped unload the
first horses. The Tupis had agreed to Just's request, but they were terrified of the strange beasts pawing at the sand on the beach with
their hooves. Three of them were big palfreys, so thin their ribs pro-
truded. Just had forage of capim prepared for them, along with a
ration of manioc flour. They ate it greedily. The two others were bay
stallions, covered with bite marks on their shoulders and withers. Just
showed the Indians how to catch them safely with a halter and had
them tethered in the shade of a jacaranda on the shore.

The Indian leader gave Just two warriors to serve as guides and
confirmed that he had sent a runner off the day before to give
advance warning of his coming. The group set off almost
immediately.

Just had rarely had occasion to visit the mainland, and he had
always stayed near the coast. Penetrating into the interior, he redis-

covered the forgotten pleasures of nature and the woods. Yet despite the pleasant sensation of being in the shade of the canopy, he could not shake off a sensation of fear and disgust, whose source he understood poorly. Perhaps it came from the idea that in these shadowy regions there were men devouring each other. Owing to Ville-gagnon's influence, the idea of cannibalism continued to govern Just's opinion of the primitive world. He slept uneasily in the forest, disturbed by dreams.

They walked another day and camped another night, this one cooler, at altitude. On the evening of the succeeding day his guides showed him the distant and already dark mass of the forest of Tijuca.

CHAPTER 42

A great serpent of light illuminated the forest. Its glow lit up the base of the big pine trees. On drawing closer, Just saw that little wicks had been floated in oil and placed on the log steps, where they burned in dried coconut shells. Two by two, and palely glowing, they traced the entire rise of the long wooden stair as it wound up the final slope of the mountain. Just's Indian guides were terrified to see the forest pricked with small flames. If the darkness held hidden spirits, then the unaccustomed light could only excite their malevolent appetites. Sensing their fear, Just walked in the lead. From a distance he saw two torches curling their flame around a set of doorposts. When he crossed the threshold and set his foot on the tiled floor of the entry, he was struck to see the reflection of porcelain plate and silver hilts shining in the dark.

The house was quiet, yet he was not afraid of it. The objects deposited in great disorder about the rooms were familiar, making the darkness around them less threatening. Small lamps projected their light onto this backdrop, flattening it, as though the narrow spaces were lined with strange works of champlevé, mixing glittering enamel and dark, engraved ground.

He advanced cautiously and stepped into a room of vaster proportions, at whose center stood Colombe.

The day before, when the runner from the coast brought her advanced notice, she had rummaged through all the trunks stashed in Paï-Lo's house. Some contained clothing no one had thought to unpack since the shipwreck that first brought them to Brazil. There she had discovered the long, blue velvet, English-style dress she was wearing. Its oval neckline, embroidered with pearls, suggested the court of Henry VIII. It was meant to be worn with a large diamond necklace, but as she didn't have one, she wound a double row of mother-of-pearl shells around her throat.

Her blond hair had been braided and cunningly coiled in the Florentine style. Two chandeliers lit her from the side, but without particular effect, as she was incapable of striking a pose and holding still. Just arrived as she was rounding the room impatiently, waiting for him.

Intent on his urgent errand, he had made no preparation for such a meeting. He still wore the velvet waistcoat Villegagnon had ordered for him when the Protestants first arrived. But his tousled black hair, his dancing veins swollen by the long climb, and his slender features, further hollowed by his nights of watchfulness, gave him an unaffected grace reminiscent of childhood.

They smiled at each other, but the awkwardness of being reunited, which was both wished for and unexpected, at first kept them silent.

Practicalities come to the rescue of the emotions. Colombe asked Just in an unsteady voice whether he was tired or thirsty. Not waiting for an answer, she picked up a crystal carafe with unsteady hands and filled two glasses with a sparkling liquid.

They drank, less to slake their thirst than to give their lips an excuse for not forming words immediately.

Then Just put down his glass and looked around with amused astonishment at the heterogeneous decor of the room.

"I thought you were among the Indians . . . ," he said.

She laughed, and when her eyes turned toward the triple flame of the torches, he recognized their familiar and mysterious paleness, so characteristic and unusual.

"I couldn't be more so," she said, laughing again at Just's astonishment.

"It's a beautiful house," he said, aggrieved at finding nothing better to say.

"I'm glad you like it. Come, I'll show you the rest of it, if you want."

She pulled him after her, and the movement, breaking their awkward immobility, relieved them both somewhat.

Outside, on the terrace, two shuttered lamps faintly lit the planks of the floor while leaving the eye free to pierce the darkness as far as the sea, which shone milkily under the moon. They looked at it for a moment, then entered another room.

"This was Paï-Lo's bedroom," said Colombe.

"Whose?"

"The master of this house. I'm sorry you never knew him. He died last month."

Since then, the life of the household hadn't altered, but everything reminded them of the patriarch's absence. Colombe had stayed on, and in consequence of an unspoken will, it was to her that the warriors now brought their news, and from her that they sought advice.

Paï-Lo's room had remained intact, its hammock empty. They passed next into other rooms and came back toward the great hall. Suddenly, at the moment they were entering it, Just cried out. Colombe turned to find him struggling with a shadowy figure sinking its nails into his shirt.

She leapt toward him, arms outstretched, and gathered the hairy assailant to her. What had clamped itself so frighteningly to the young knight's shoulders was an animal the size of a monkey.

"Oh! the *haüt* likes you," she said, laughing.

"The *haüt*?" said Just, rubbing the spot by his neck that the animal had clawed.

The animal Colombe held in her arms at that moment gave a deep, heart-rending sigh.

"You don't know the *haüt*?" said Colombe, surprised. "This one has lived in the house for years."

She put it down on a sideboard. With its four evenly sized limbs, its melancholy face, and long claws, the animal looked like nothing Just had ever seen. It slowly took hold of a corner of the buffet and seemed to fall asleep.

"The Indians call it the animal that feeds on wind," said Colombe. "You never see it eat or drink. Paï-Lo used to say it was the god of laziness."

They laughed. The incident, by capturing their attention fully, had swept the last awkwardness from their manner. They went and sat at the end of the big table lit by the chandeliers.

"How is your wound?" asked Colombe.

Just was disconcerted to find she knew about it, and he blushed, thinking back to the circumstances.

"Fine," he said. "I don't feel it anymore."

In reminding him of the accident and Aude, Colombe also put him in mind of the apology he had meant to offer her. But in so beautiful a setting, and finding her in such resplendent form, he decided that the subject was inappropriate and that, when it came down to it, nothing more need be said on that score.

Colombe pushed a large pewter salad bowl toward him filled with prepared yams. All around, arrayed in no particular order, were plates of meat in sauce and fruit.

"You're hungry, I imagine?"

But Just's throat was still constricted from his initial emotion. He took another long swallow of his drink and refused anything else.

"The runner told me you wanted to see me urgently," said Colombe.

She looked fixedly at Just. He could not have said whether there was irony in her look, or anger, or simply that same firmness he had found it so difficult to contend with before. He summoned all his courage and, ignoring his fears as to how she might answer, launched into the little speech he had mentally prepared.

"The Portuguese are on their way, Colombe. They will be here in four or five days, with a full squadron. Since Villegagnon's departure, I have been in charge of the island. My men have been dying of fever for the past few weeks. We are in no condition to mount a resistance."

She listened, immobile.

"I came to ask you to save us."

"Save you? How?"

She continued to look at him with an enigmatic smile.

"You know the Indians. You could persuade them to come fight alongside us."

As Colombe said nothing, Just added, more pressingly, "I know that we didn't behave well toward you. But I'm alone now. And I very much want you to return."

Was Just still talking about the Portuguese threat? Or was there another signal being given? Colombe delayed her answer long enough so that he might ask himself that question.

"Save you . . ." she said pensively.

She turned her gaze toward the gleam of the shining crystal on the table.

"Save what, Just? Antarctic France?"

She spoke these last words clumsily and with an effort, as one handles a borrowed tool.

"Listen, Colombe," he said, "I have weighed the situation carefully these past few days. Whichever way I look, I see nothing but death. In Europe, there is fanaticism everywhere, and different factions tear each other to bits over God. And here, there is cannibalism with all its horrors."

Colombe ran her long fingers abstractedly along the hem of the tablecloth.

"I don't know," she said softly. "Everything you say may be true, but I have no opinion in these abstract matters. I only know that I am happy here and want to stay."

"Then we agree entirely. I am asking you to help me protect a place where we will be free . . . and happy."

"The island?"

"Yes."

Colombe looked at the ground. She allowed a long moment to pass in silence, and Just started to hope she would agree. He felt a certain disappointment in hearing her say, in a voice that left off the question mark, "Villegagnon is going to return, isn't he?"

"It's true that he plans to," said Just grudgingly.

"And I imagine he will bring fresh troops?"

"Yes."

She turned her gaze back toward Just. He was no longer cheerful or sure of himself, but distraught and unhappy.

"And what difference do you see between the admiral and the Portuguese?"

Never having asked himself the question, Just offered a very simple answer, which even surprised him.

"The admiral," he said, "is France."

He knew that this assertion only raised further questions, and that at the end of these interlocking reasons there was something that did not entirely satisfy him.

"I swore to defend this land," he said. "I swore in Father's name that I would fight, as he did, for France."

Reaching her hand toward a basket of fruit, Colombe plucked two black grapes and carried them to her mouth.

"Le Thoret came by here before taking ship," she said.

Just was alarmed at this unexpected diversion.

"He spoke to me about Ceresole."

He started.

"And of a two-year-old girl found in a hay barn," she went on.

Her hand trembled slightly. She reached for her glass but didn't drink from it.

"You knew about this?"

"Yes," he said.

The shadowy space around them, littered with moldy chests and shipwrecked memories, could have been the keep at Clamorgan. They were back in the time of their intimacy, yet with large adult bodies, which were themselves full of shadows and quivering desires.

"He spoke to me of his death, in Siena," she continued.

"The death of . . . Father."

She nodded. Seeing Just wait inquiringly, she realized he knew nothing about the matter.

"Italy was at peace," she went on, relieved at having a clear idea to formulate when everything else was still so murky. "But the king of France wanted to resume the war and sent *agents provocateurs* into Tuscany. Clamorgan did everything he could to undermine them."

Just started at the name "Clamorgan," though it was natural enough for her no longer to use the term "Father."

"He knew that by inciting Siena to revolt, the French were only looking for an excuse to return to Italy. But they had no way of protecting the city. In fact, they were drawing it toward its own destruction."

Just was starting to see the truth. He breathed with difficulty. Not a muscle of his face moved.

"Clamorgan," she went on, "truly loved Italy. He went there to fight, but what he discovered there won him over. He loved the beauty of its landscapes and paintings, and the classical world that was being reborn in its present works. He loved its gardens, its music, its freedom."

Colombe spoke without turning her eyes from Just, but for once her eyes' brilliance seemed to be clouded, as though she were looking at an inner vision and not at what was before her. At last, she came back to herself and, in a voice suddenly turned cold, came to her horrifying conclusion:

"When the king learned that Clamorgan was going to foil his plans," she said, "he had him assassinated."

A violent emotion gripped Just, simultaneously pushing him to tears and holding him back. The core of his soul, which he believed to be loyalty, was splitting into two opposing parts. While he had stood with his country—only it had been a false view of his country—Colombe had stood against him and with their father—and it had been a true view of their father. He now understood that she had chosen the better part.

Clamorgan's heritage was neither an estate, nor a country, nor a name, but a love of freedom that admitted neither dogma nor boundary, neither injustice nor submission.

Colombe rose and walked out onto the terrace. When she came back toward him, Just looked at her from top to bottom, in her velvet dress. She was in and of herself all of blue Italy, the spring at which its artists drank, kin through her braided hair to those Roman beauties whose shimmering splendor only marble can render.

He rose in turn and they stood facing each other less than a foot apart. For the first time, Just's restraint, his fear and reserve, dissolved under the effects of a force that made him smile. With this creature who conformed so closely to his desire, whom he had known for so long and yet was still discovering, he had the sensation of having always been at one. And it was less to bring himself closer than to reconstitute their natural unity that he reached a hand toward her.

He grazed her neck, her shoulder, her naked arm. Not moving, she closed her eyes, rapt with the pleasure of this longed-for moment, so often dreamt of that it was mysteriously familiar and yet, however often it recurred in the future, would never again have the same incomparable taste as this first time.

Finally she came near, pressed against him, rested her head in the hollow of his neck. Just smelled the blond odor of her skin. Around his mouth floated the silky down at the nape of her neck. He felt Colombe's arms encircle his waist and her hands run over his back. She drew back slightly and her half-open mouth rose toward Just's hungry lips. Their whole lives, the Brazilian night around them, and their conquered fears were swallowed up in this long reunion of their faces, in the incomparable sweetness of intimacy, which cancels and crowns love by giving it not two bodies but one.

This barrier crossed, the open ground of pleasure lay before them, which they ventured onto eagerly. They squeezed each other, caressed, kissed feverishly. Just slowly undid the tie at her neck that held up the velvet dress. But at the sight of Colombe's breasts, he started abruptly. Her soft white skin had been freshly painted with red and black war paint, representing stars and lightning bolts.

Before Just's eyes swam the horrible memory of the cannibals. The dream of Italy was spattered with blood. He drew away.

Colombe had expected this, and even wanted it. She felt great pleasure at seeing this handsome face she loved tear itself away from her. At least she could gaze at it one last time. With a quick shrug, she made her dress drop to the ground. This was how she wanted him to see her and love her. They might be suffused with Italy, but they were elsewhere.

"Come," she said, drawing near, "don't be afraid . . . Let yourself . . . be eaten . . ."

Just hesitated, then his inner representations of the perfect elegance of Europe and the powerful beauty of the Indians melded into one. He smiled, drew toward her, and took her in his arms again. Before immersing himself in pleasure, he looked at Colombe's eye and saw a reversed picture of the world: a sun in which shone a great blue sky.

No longer afraid, he dove into it.

CHAPTER 43

Never had the Portuguese had such a feeling of power. In Europe they were too small a people to challenge anyone, and in America they had always occupied deserted or near-deserted coasts. But this time they were going to fight.

The hundred or so vessels in the squadron gave a proud appearance, at least from a distance. In fact, for every warship there were two commercial vessels hastily rigged with cannons. In addition, there were some thirty fishing boats, sailing along as they could and holding everyone up.

So as to avoid seeing this ragtag and bobtail, Mem de Sá stayed at the prow of the lead ship and looked straight ahead. Gloomy in nature, he was afraid of the sun and kept a wide-brimmed hat jammed on his head, which dripped with sweat. A page held a parasol over him. And finally, to ensure that no ray of sun might touch him, the governor of Brazil had ordered a cloth awning erected, under which he remained seated.

The Atlantic, under his implacable will, remained as still as a prostrated slave. The steep bluffs in the distance stood straight and motionless as though on parade.

While the other ships echoed with songs and drinking, the governor's was filled with silent pride. A line of military flunkeys stood at a respectful distance from the supreme commander, ready to leap into action at the first grunt he might utter. A surpliced priest, a few black-robed Jesuits, and an unruly knot of young monks and choir-boys huddled on the forward deck, at the foot of the great cross of timbers erected there by the carpenters.

The plan had been to sail south past Guanabara Bay as far as the Honest Islands. There the main armada from Bahia would join forces with reinforcements sent up from São Vicente and the Bay of Kings. With felicitous precision, the meeting occurred on the stated day, in a cove with wonderfully clear water and a pink gravel bottom.

Swelled with reinforcements, the squadron was heading north once more toward the bay of Rio. There were doubts as to the wisdom of having all the ships enter the mouth of the bay at once. Though it was wide enough, it lay within cannon shot of Fort Coligny. If the French greeted them with a sustained cannonade, there was a considerable chance that the best ships might be hit before coming into position to return fire. But the governor cut through his strategists' hesitations with one of the striking sayings that were his specialty.

"We must frighten them," he said.

Consequently, he was the first to enter the bay, surrounded by the largest ships. The smaller craft followed pell-mell.

Thus, on February 25, with the air clear and the sun shining brightly, a giant cross swayed on the water at the entrance to Guanabara. Twenty ships sailed in terrifying convoy, their canvas bellying in the light sea breeze, into the calm waters of the bay.

Mem de Sá had not taken off his hat, for he feared sunstroke even more than he did war. He stood straight at the foot of his caravel's mainmast, casting a predatory glance on the lands it was his duty to subjugate.

Nothing moved in the direction of Fort Coligny. Only the usurpers' white flag pricked with fleurs-de-lys floated insultingly over the island. This would be addressed soon enough.

As a concession to caution, the attackers gave the Frenchmen's island a wide berth. They hugged the north shore of the bay, sailed up to its head, then came back down the bay and anchored in the shelter of a headland, protected from any cannon shot that the French could direct at them. From here they would prepare their assault.

As night fell on that first day, a dozen pirogues drew off from shore and came alongside the governor's ship. At the agreed signal, a delegation of go-betweens was brought on board, led majestically by none other than Martin.

The former beggar had more manners than his predecessor, the unfortunate Le Freux. He was not so stupid as to present himself in a grotesque costume made of feathers. Besides, his trading operation was going well, and he had access to an abundance of costly cloth. He appeared before Mem de Sá in what he believed to be the required tenue for a dignitary of the rank he expected soon to assume. In accordance with his idea of a duke, he wore a doublet of sky blue silk with gold brocade, breeches of violet taffeta, and a small slashed toque. The only feather he allowed himself was an ostrich feather, stuck into his hat. He was highly satisfied to discover that he was by far the most elegant personage on the ship. With a little imagination, and nature had given him his share, he could read in the staring eyes of the crew a sign of sincere admiration.

When Martin was led up to Mem de Sá, he was a little disappointed to find the great man so poorly dressed. A long and silent examination, characterized by astonishment on both sides, marked the first contact between these two men. At last one of the Jesuits, Father Anchiéta, who had been lost in prayer since entering the bay, arrived to serve as interpreter, for he spoke French.

Martin delivered himself of a long peroration welcoming the liberators. He cunningly inserted words of scorn for the mutineers at Fort Coligny and a touching profession of faith in which he claimed to describe the Indians' eagerness to be preserved from heresy. He ended with a favorable description of his own influence on the lands that he now swore to administer solely for the glory of the Portuguese crown.

Mem de Sá answered by blowing his nose noisily on his sleeve.

A little disconcerted by this reception, but ready to interpret it as the caution of a seasoned politico, Martin asked in conspiratorial tones whether he might not speak to the governor privately. He had recently received new information on the enemy's strength and his ordnance.

With a jerk of his head, Mem de Sá ordered the assembled crowd to back away, which they did, all except Father Anchiéta.

The hooting of monkeys from the woods along the coast irritated Martin, making him wish for silent palaces where high diplomacy could be performed to the sole murmur of discreet jets of water.

"Here it is, Your Excellency," he began, "the precise state of the fort's defenses according to the latest intelligence from our agent Ribera."

Mem de Sá raised an eyebrow. To Martin, a keen observer, this mark of interest seemed extremely valuable.

"Seventy-two men, and perhaps even fewer, as Ribera mentioned on his last visit that a number were sick. Thirty-one cannons, four of them rusted, and five culverins that are too ancient to inflict much damage. Little ammunition, and their match all wetted from the rains."

Mem de Sá raised his second eyebrow.

"Fresh water for three months at most. And provisions for four."

Reporting on these last figures, Martin showed some confusion.

"I did everything I could, Your Excellency, to keep them from reprovisioning. But they found a way to get around me, thanks to some natives who will have to be punished."

The governor, at these words, stuffed his right hand into the opening of his shirt and scratched his armpit. Martin interpreted this as perplexity and undertook straightaway to clear it up.

"But you can be sure," he said, "that these stores will be of no use to them. Agent Ribera will not give them time to prepare for a siege, hee! hee!"

He gave a nasty laugh, and Mem de Sá, as a sign that he joined in with it, uncovered his teeth.

"Allow me, Your Excellency, to lay out the plan I consider apt for a glorious but economical victory. Agent Ribera has been informed of it and has agreed to perform his part. Now, on the first day you send a hail of shot raining down around their ears." Here, Martin looked around him like a conspirator before continuing: "That night, they go to earth, dizzy from the barrage of fire. You land your troops on the island under cover of darkness. A little before dawn, Ribera slips to the gate and opens it. The fort is yours before the sun has completely risen!"

Martin stopped, filled with satisfaction. This was worth a duchy and he knew it. He stepped back a little, out of modesty, waiting for the governor's judgment.

"Must sleep," grunted Mem de Sá.

Father Anchiéta showed a certain embarrassment in translating this. He allowed himself to add that the governor customarily retired shortly after the sun. Twelve hours of sleep barely sufficed to repair the damage caused to his brain by incessant thought.

"I understand," said Martin, in turn overcome with admiration.

He took his leave with all the dignity possible, as unsteady and confused as after a *cahuin* orgy. As he climbed down into the pirogue, he spoke three enigmatic words to his concerned lieutenants:

"What a leader!"

●   ●   ●

It took two days to make all the necessary preparations for the attack. Each vessel received exact orders as to the position it should occupy and its role. Only the best-armed ships would take part in cannonading the fort. One tactical detail, however, had required extensive precautions. Given the small size of the island, it was important that the Portuguese ships encircling it not bombard each other over the fort. The pilots calculated with precision the distance that should separate the ships. At last, everything was ready.

On the morning of the third day, the first attacker slowly edged his bowsprit out past the cover of the headland. A dozen large sail followed after him, making obliquely toward the fort, always keeping the island off their beam, their gunports open, and their cannons at the ready. When the wall of boats had securely taken its place around the island, Mem de Sá brought down a torch with his big hand and touched off the powder of the first cannon. Aimed too low, the gun dropped its ball into the water. The signal, however, prompted all the other ships to open fire. Exploding with smoke, the ships' hulls seemed to be the targets of the cannon fire, when they were in fact its point of departure. By contrast, at the distant point where the balls fell on the fort, there was nothing to be seen. Only the dull sound of the shot's impact against the thick walls echoed in the still air. After the terrible opening salvos, the Portuguese slackened their fire somewhat on orders from the flagship. The cannonade assumed a measure of regularity, one broadside succeeding another so as to keep the defenders under constant threat.

The tension Mem de Sá's men had felt before the assault all but disappeared. Despite their guns, the French had not fired a single answering shot. They were either truly terrified or cowardly in the extreme. Their reputation gone, all that still held fast on the island were the curtain walls of the fortress. These were admittedly well built, and their angles made any assault on them delicate. It was perfectly possible that the defenders had decided to wait until the attackers landed in order to massacre them.

These uncertainties did not prevent the crews, once their ships rode at anchor for the night in their positions, from drinking toasts to their probable and highly imminent victory. No one had been informed of the next stage of the plan, other than the footsoldiers who were made to board the ships' boats in the middle of the night. The Portuguese, a seafaring people, had less battle experience than other, more terrestrial combatants. Consequently Mem de Sá assigned to the landing troops all the continentals and mercenaries on the expedition: strays from Switzerland, German adventurers, five Dutch captives, and even some thirty Indian slaves kindly offered by Martin. In all, five rowboats approached the dark flanks of the island and spewed forth 120 soldiers determined to give no quarter. Crouched on the warm sand of the beaches, they waited for the first streaks of dawn. The sky yawned widely in the east, revealing a pink throat. The morning breeze arose at the soldiers' back as they muttered their prayers in the sand, making them shiver. Finally, when the light grew strong enough to see the door of the fort, the attackers found to their incredulity that it was wide open. Their ensign gave the order and they charged, uttering horrible cries intended less to terrify others than to reassure themselves. And they swarmed into the fort.

The assailants' clatter echoed in the vaulted passage leading to the fort's courtyard. The men jostled each other in the darkness. They could be heard stumbling, turning in circles, and swearing in a variety of languages. A small contingent climbed onto the ramparts and ran out along the battlements. Even in the brief time of the invasion, the pale daylight had started to tinge the walls and corridors with mauve. The gathering light had a soothing effect. The combatants walked calmly, whispered to each other. No shot had yet been fired. Surprised at their rapid conquest, the men assembled in the courtyard of the fort and waited. The ensign in command went out and made his way to the beach, where he waved his arms toward the ships to indicate that all was over.

Mem de Sá landed shortly after at the head of an escort. He carried an enormous pistol in his belt, leaving both hands free to wave his orders and prospect his nostrils.

The ensign who had led the first assault came up to make his report, his style direct except for its encrustations of Portuguese etiquette.

"Everything is in our hands, O Most Illustrious Lord Governor."

Then, stiffening with pride, he added, "We have taken a prisoner."

A murmur of admiration ran through Mem de Sá's escort. A single prisoner meant that all the others were dead. The artillerymen had done good work.

"May I lead you to him, Most Illustrious Lord Governor?"

Mem de Sá assented by wrinkling his nose. The ensign led the way and the entire troop entered the gallery, passing through the walls into the courtyard.

The prisoner, who was being held by four guards, showed no inclination to flee or to attempt hostile action. His hirsute face, at the sight of the governor, broke into a broad smile. When Mem de Sá stopped before him and motioned for him to be released, the captive fell to his knees and cried out in a tear-choked voice:

"Mercy, my Lord, O greatest captain of all times, new Caesar of the American continents, liberator of this fort . . ."

He wanted to continue, but Mem de Sá turned away from this negligible capture and looked around him. He was surprised to find neither corpses, nor prisoners, nor cannons in the fort's crenels.

"We have found three dead," said the ensign, anticipating the question.

The governor followed him to a staircase and climbed up to the battlements. There he saw the mortal remains of an ancient knight of Malta, his chest caved in by a cannon ball. The man was frozen in an attitude of dignity and prayer, his little pointed beard raised toward the sky. In his right hand he held a sheet of paper. Mem de Sá took it and handed it to Father Anchiéta, who had come along to serve as an interpreter with the prisoners. The Jesuit read the short and hastily scribbled text.

"It's a poem," he said, blushing. "Addressed to a certain Marguerite."

"The other two are below, in the great hall," said the ensign. "Apparently they took their lives with poison."

Surprise and the stirrings of anger were painted in bold strokes on the governor's dark face. He looked at the gun carriages along the ramparts, all empty of cannons except for two heavy bombards, which were rusted up. Livid, he climbed back down the stairs. The Jesuit, trotting behind him, understood that an explanation of these mysteries would have to be extracted from the prisoner.

When he saw Mem de Sá's band return toward him, the prisoner realized that he would finally have a chance to explain himself. He addressed the Jesuit, who spoke his language, and picked a title for him that would stimulate his forbearance.

"Mercy, Cardinal, have mercy!" he begged.

Sobbing, he added:

"I am Ribera."

That this little man, so obviously simpleminded, should be the agent Ribera, the man on whom so many powers had relied, seemed as incredible to Father Anchiéta as it did to Mem de Sá, who for once needed no translation.

"You? Ribera?" said the Jesuit.

"Yes," sniffed Vittorio, at once dejected and proud, like a combatant whose victory has left him in rags.

"Supposing it to be true," the Jesuit conceded wrathfully, "you can then explain things to us. You told us that there were seventy-two men to defend this fort. Where are they hiding? Where are the cannons? and the harquebuses? and all the other weapons?"

Vittorio saw that his case was improving. Already they believed him. He had now only to justify himself. The one difficulty was that he would have to stick to the truth for once, an exercise that always required his strict attention.

"Ah, Cardinal! It's terrible, terrible!" he whimpered.

"What?" asked Father Anchiéta impatiently. "What is terrible? Will you explain yourself?"

Vittorio hesitated on the question of whether he should fall to his knees again or whether it was more prudent to save this gesture for later. He remained standing, but he trembled.

"I was locked in here with the others . . ." said Vittorio imploringly. "I wasn't able to get a message out to Martin when it all started."

"When all what started?"

With the desperation of a Scheherazade, Vittorio threw himself into his story, certain that his life was safe while it lasted.

"First," he began with a sigh, "there was the epidemic, which killed off three quarters of the garrison within a week."

"And the rest, where are they?" asked the Jesuit, thus translating Mem de Sá's grunts.

Vittorio signaled that he was getting to this point. His audience's impatience was a happy sign of their interest.

"It was two days before your entry into the bay. An old tub carrying broken-down jades warned us of your arrival. That's when the young leader whom Villegagnon left here went off to the Indians."

Father Anchiéta translated each sentence as it was uttered. Vittorio now had his audience's complete attention.

"He came back three days later. I didn't personally hear his orders. I only understood what was happening when I saw the cannons being taken down. All the artillery pieces were gathered right here in this courtyard. Next, young Clamorgan, may he be damned in hell forever and his family too, by our blessed Lady and her Son our Lord, called us all together in the great hall you see yonder. He offered anyone who wanted to a chance to follow him to the mainland. Dom Gonzagues, a sainted man, may his soul rest in peace, refused to betray his promise to the admiral. Only two men chose not to flee and defend the fort with him. They were two old soldiers from Malta, and at the last moment the two fanatics chose to poison themselves rather than fall into your hands. As for me, what could I do, Cardinal? If I left, I would be in no position to open the fortress door for you; and if I stayed, I ran the risk of having you treat me as a traitor."

Vittorio had seen enough commedia dell'arte to know that at the moment of driving his point home, it was not amiss for the leading man to fall to his knees. Accordingly, he knelt with a thud and joined his hands in supplication.

"Have mercy!" he cried, coloring his voice with the fine sincerity of a man broken by a tragic destiny.

On hearing this news Mem de Sá filled with anger—an anger very much in his style, that is, violent and unspoken. He had conquered a deserted island, then! The army of the French dogs was still intact. He had stripped Bahia of its defenses for nothing, and any number of enemies might be attacking it at this very moment. His hand was already on the broad pommel of his pistol, prepared to shoot this grotesque prisoner, the bearer of bad news. But at the moment of striking down this pitiful prey, he felt a sudden disgust that drained the act of all pleasure beforehand.

At least he was in possession of the fort. The consoling sight of its well-made walls, the idea of the effort they must have cost the enemy, and the gratification of acquiring the place for Portugal all filled his heart—if not his face—with a satisfaction that allowed everything else to be somewhat forgotten. Ribera had done what was expected of him, after all. Mem de Sá looked at the rogue and, shrugging his shoulders, gave the signal to release him.

Followed by his retinue, the governor then set out to visit the different parts of the fortification and climbed up to the battlements again. At this moment a bustle of footsteps was heard below, disrupting the peace that had been achieved without war: Martin was arriving, followed by three more go-betweens, still tricked out as a gentleman. He climbed the stairs rapidly and presented his face squarely before the governor—the face of a thug under a thin glaze of courtesy.

"Magnificent, Your Lordship!" exclaimed Martin. "What a victory! What a triumph!"

Mem de Sá glared at him, but the other took this hostile look as the fierce modesty of a man accustomed to victory.

"All of this henceforth belongs to your king," Martin went on, embracing the whole bay with his arms.

The silence of the fine clear day vibrated on the rocks of the Sugarloaf and the yellow stems of the reeds by the swamp. Two herons uttered a brief squawk to signal their pleasure at being once again subjects of the Portuguese king. Martin, still smiling in contentment, drew a roll of paper tied with a ribbon from his pocket.

"Your Excellency," he said proudly, "I have drawn up a grant of property for the lands you have just liberated, lands that I will administer loyally in the name of your sovereign."

At the translation of this request, spoken in neutral tones by Father Anchiéta, Mem de Sá stiffened, caught between the anvil of contempt and the hammer of indignation.

"The great favor I ask of you," the go-between continued, "is to grant me on this very spot what you have been kind enough to promise me. A title conferred on the field of battle is the greatest glory to which a man can aspire."

Martin was sincere. But he also considered this speech extremely clever. It allowed him to press for a decision that would seem all the more natural in the heat of a victory. If he waited, there would be intrigues and delays, obstacles, possibly even a retraction.

"Duke of Guanabara," he announced gravely. "This strikes me as the aptest title."

Father Anchiéta translated. He added a word or two in undertones to remind the governor of the conversation he had had two days earlier with the go-between. Mem de Sá seemed in fact to have no conception of what the man was talking about. When he finally grasped the situation, he smiled evilly. All the rage he felt at having let the French escape concentrated on this individual, who was after all one of them and perhaps even served them as a double agent.

"On your knees," he said.

Father Anchiéta translated the response.

Martin, his heart filled with triumph, fell to one knee in knightly style and doffed his cap to receive the honor awaiting him. In his mind the duke had already taken full possession. He, who had never disarmed himself before anyone, who was ever on his guard and had evaded the most sinister plots, saw his mistake at the last moment. In renouncing the beggar he had once been, he had also laid aside the vigilance that had always kept him alive. By the time he raised his eyes and felt the cornered animal in him leap up, the barrel of the pistol was against his head and Mem de Sá had blown his brains out.

The report echoed off the walls and a great silence followed. It was the only shot fired during taking of the fort. Martin's corpse, in its agonal spasms, lay disjointedly on the stones of the curtain wall.

Mem de Sá, still holding the smoking pistol, raised his head and froze in an attitude of worry. He seemed to be listening to a distant sound, and those around him cocked an ear. From the still bay arose the ordinary whisper of hot breezes ruffling the foliage. The detonation had stilled the calls of animals, removing the only high-pitched sounds to normally trouble the silence. It was among the deep sounds, then, that something unexpected must be lurking. And there, behind the susurrus in the branches, the muffled lapping of the waves, a regular sound could be heard, a rubbing noise, coming from different parts of the coast. It had a distinctive rhythm, such as only humans could impart, a slow rhythm that tended to grow faster. The zizzing arose from two, three, ten separate localities. It soon seemed that the forests beat with the pulse of a gigantic heart of sand.

"The maracas," breathed Vittorio, who alone knew the sacred gourds that the *caraíbas* brandished.

The voice of these deafening oracles now arose from all the tribes in the bay.

Suddenly, the straining ears of the victors were split by the crack of the first explosion.

• • •

It was a miracle that they had been able to transport everything in two nights. Hoisting the cannons into boats and bringing them to the mainland had not been the hardest part. The guns then had to be dragged over the sand to where the Indians in Paï-Lo's camp could put them under shelter. Without the horses brought by Just, this would never have been accomplished. But the animals, fitted out hastily with wooden collars, had performed wonders. The artillery pieces had been dragged along the beach, and all of them had reached their destination by the dawn of the first night.

Next Just showed the Indians how to set up the guns at strategic locations. A dozen culverins had been strapped to men's backs and carried onto the high ground dominating the bay. Indian warriors, summoned by messengers Colombe had sent out into the tribes, trickled down toward the shore.

Quintin had agreed to fire one of the batteries, despite his repugnance for weapons, on condition that it be aimed at the water. To him was given the honor of firing the first shot. As soon as the ball was ejected, he threw himself into the arms of Ygat, the companion on whom he now lavished all his drive to convert. He cried in her big arms, uncertain whether it was out of fear, or gratitude, or happiness.

Paraguaçu and Karaya, perched on a hillock near the Sugarloaf, each laughed as they touched off one of the two culverins under their command. Ten other guns thundered afterward.

None struck the island, for Just did not mean to launch an offensive. He simply meant to show the Portuguese that though they had gained possession of the fort, the bay was not theirs. From the skillful placement of the batteries, they were to understand that they faced an organized force and a formidable one that would not leave them in peace. This was obviously still a great exaggeration. Yet Just was convinced that before long he could provide the Indians with the know-how to engage their would-be subjugators on an equal footing.

The cannons' voice, which spoke the Europeans' language, was complemented by the voice of the warriors, who filtered down toward the coast from all the tribes in response to Colombe's call and the maracas' oracle. Some twenty of the warriors had already learned to fire the harquebus. At a signal from one of Paï-Lo's sons, they directed a volley of lead toward the ships, striking down a few spars and sowing panic on the decks.

Just and Colombe looked on side by side at this feigned assault, applauding every stroke. They were near the island, under the cover of the coconut trees, each seated bareback on a horse. From their vantage, the fort seemed tiny, vulnerable, laughable. The horses rubbed their necks against each other, and when they drew close, the riders' legs touched. The devastated island seemed but a small and unimportant sore on the vast body of the bay, which, in the happy health of its full colors, shone with majesty and peace.

Colombe reached toward Just and grabbed his hair. He bent down to kiss her. When silence returned after the cannonade, they pricked their mounts and rode onto the beach. Giving the island a final wave, they raced over the sand at a gallop and rejoined the Indians.

Their happiness from then on belonged to this land, a land they would always defend but never seek to possess.

EPILOGUE

The Chevalier de Villegagnon arrived back in France at the time of the incident known to history as the "Conspiracy of Amboise." The retaliation that followed this Protestant plot was bloody, and the former master of Fort Coligny distinguished himself there by his ferocity. The hanging, beheading, and drowning of the Huguenots took a frenzied month of activity. "The streets of Amboise," wrote Régnier de la Planche, "flowed with blood and were carpeted in every part with bodies: so that one could not stay in the town by reason of the stench and pestilence."

By his cruelties Villegagnon became "the Guises' man for all seasons" and divided his time between savage acts against the Huguenots and pamphlet writing, intended to justify his actions in Brazil. But France, now joined in alliance with Spain to quell the Protestant threat, gave little thought to preserving its conquests in South America. Villegagnon obtained only letters of marque against Portugal, and eventually negotiated a settlement with Lisbon for 30,000 ecus whereby he renounced all claims to Guanabara.

When the Wars of Religion broke out in France, Villegagnon found himself in his element, particularly as those wars followed the same successive stages as their dress rehearsal in Brazil. As a reward for his brutality, Villegagnon received a commandery of the Knights

of Malta in Beauvais. And there he lived out his days in peace—
though his hatred never cooled—bequeathing his property to the
poor of Paris.

Richier, Du Pont, and the Protestants who fled Rio reached
France after a nightmare ocean crossing. Food was in such short supply that the passengers resorted to eating even the parrots brought
back as curiosities. Aude returned to Geneva, married a pastor there,
and never left the city again.

But many Protestants who survived the adventure were tried
severely during the Wars of Religion. Jean de Léry became the
chronicler, twenty years later, of this terrible "voyage to the land of
Brazil." Despite his expressed horror of cannibalism, he was to witness his co-religionists eating human flesh during the siege of
Sancerre.

In Guanabara, the Portuguese maintained their foothold and built
the city of Rio. The go-betweens on the coast continued to operate
after Martin's death. But certain of them returned to France, and it
was one of these that Montaigne hired as his secretary. To him is due
the inspiration for "Of Cannibals," the famous Chapter XXXI of
Montaigne's *Essays*, where the myth of the noble savage, which was
to have such a profound influence on the Enlightenment philosophers, originated.

But in all the rest of Guanabara Bay, the Indians maintained a
strong resistance. Owing to the military techniques taught them by
the French and a few Englishmen, they harassed the Portuguese
colonists for many years. The Indian blockade of Cabo Frio at the
start of the seventeenth century was the last act of this resistance. It
had lasted more than a half century. Afterward, the Tupis were
driven back toward the interior and the north, where their French
supporters accompanied them. When the Portuguese founded the
city of Natal, on Christmas Day 1597, they counted fifty French harquebus men among the ranks of the Indian tribes.

A number of these Europeans subsequently melted into the
Brazilian crucible; others preferred to take to the sea. They became
pirates and corsairs, looting convoys and creating a reign of terror on
the Atlantic sea routes.

The Tupis of the coast have disappeared today. All that is known
of them comes to us from contemporary accounts composed by trav-

elers on their return to Europe. They provide detailed descriptions of Tupi customs and myths. The most well attested of these myths tells of a flood that the great god Toupan sent down on men after they angered him. All humankind died in the flood except for a brother and a sister. From their union came the new race of man.

This legend is difficult to interpret. Ethnologists are divided as to its meaning. But we, who know this story, may have our own ideas on this. And no one can keep us from seeing in the two mythical heroes traces of two characters we have loved, all that is left of Just and Colombe.

ON THE SOURCES OF
Brazil Red

The most surprising aspect of this story is that it is true. Not that it appears unlikely: the Renaissance is rich in adventures more extraordinary than this by far. What is strange is that this episode in the history of France has been almost completely forgotten. How could such events have left practically no trace on the collective memory? Though of a lesser glory than Christopher Columbus or Marco Polo, the names of Jacques Cartier, of Cavelier de La Salle, of Argo, of Dupleix awaken some echo in our minds, if only because of the streets and squares named after them. Louisiana, the St. Lawrence colonies, Indochina, Pondicherry are places that still reverberate with the one-time presence of the French, but Brazil suggests nothing of the kind, and the name of Villegagnon has fallen into complete neglect.

The idea for this book dates back ten years to when I was living in Brazil, and more specifically to the day I visited a little museum in downtown Rio named the Paço Real. This building, built during the Portuguese colonial period, is today choked off by highways and skyscrapers. It takes a strong effort of imagination to picture it in its original environment. To help visitors shake the grip of contemporary Rio, the museum was exhibiting large paintings showing the bay at the time of its discovery. In place of cement blocks along Copacabana, one saw bleached swamps patrolled by wading birds, and the shantytowns were replaced by intact jungle around the shore. Only Rio's famous heights including the Sugarloaf—the sole wild features left in all the bay—were recognizable.

The poetic evocation of these early times attracted me irresistibly. I recognized in it the theme that obsesses me above all others: the moment of discovery, which contains in germ all the passions and all the misunderstandings to come. Within this unique and ephemeral instant is hidden a distinctive emotion: for though it applies to societies, it is related to the rush of romantic love that two people may feel on first coming into each other's presence.

Unfortunately these founding moments are buried, in Europe especially, under the constructions—and the ruins—of history, and rare are the sites where they still reach the surface. One such is Ethiopia, a country that has provided the setting for two of my books. Another is Central Asia, where the encounter of civilizations seems to produce nothing durable and the process repeats itself regularly with all the appearance of novelty. But nowhere as in Latin America does one find so fresh, so alive, and so nearly visible a trace in the coastal landscape of this first and fateful contact whereby one civilization takes root in another. In Central America and the Andes, this encounter took the form of bloody confrontations between complex and already developed societies that were in many ways comparable. In Brazil the situation was very different: the Indian world was dispersed, archaic, and weak. The Europeans disembarked into what might well have seemed to be untouched nature. This was the direction I first followed, expecting our society to enter a dead end of sorts in the emptiness of these new lands and be obliged to confront itself.

But this emptiness, as my research progressed, proved on the contrary to be well filled.

Filled with events, in the first place. I had thought and feared that the isolated colony was static, poor in developments, marked by torpor and doubt. On the contrary, I was to discover that this historical episode was extraordinarily rich in character. All its main figures are heroic and romantic, incredibly alive in the way of sixteenth-century lives, with their freedom, their charm, and their originality. And what might have appeared a distant adventure, cut off from the rest of the world, quickly suggested itself to me as a run-through overseas of fundamental historical issues. Inserted into the continental rivalry between France and the Holy Roman Empire, this attempted colonization of Brazil was also a general rehearsal for the Wars of Religion. And through Montaigne, it was the source of such philosophical concepts as the noble savage and the state of nature.

And filled with texts as well. If this moment in history is forgotten, it is because of a refusal to cultivate its memory and not for any lack of documents. Several contemporary texts are available, written more or less early on by the protagonists themselves. Most have been republished in our own time. The two main works are *Histoire d'un voyage faict en la terre du Brésil* (1578) by Jean de Léry, one of the Protestants on Villegagnon's expedition, and *Les singularitez de la France Antarctique, autrement nommée Amérique* (1557) by André Thevet, cosmographer royal to Henry II, and the author of *Cosmographie universelle* (1575).[1] There are also indirect accounts, such as the one by Hans Staden, who was a prisoner of cannibal Indians for several years and managed to escape: *The Captivity of Hans Stade of Hesse in A.D. 1547–1555 among the Wild Tribes of Eastern Brazil* (1557).[2] But beyond these readily available sources there exists a vast contemporaneous literature that can be consulted in archival collections: the many memoirs and pamphlets written by Villegagnon himself; Pastor Richier's refutation (whose very title betrays its tone: *A Refutation of the Mad Imaginings, Execrable Blasphemies, Errors, and Lies of Nicolas Durand, who styles himself Villegagnon*), the correspondence of the Portuguese Jesuits, and so on.

Setting aside the early accounts of the enterprise, there are any number of modern historical and anthropological studies. Among

---

1. Léry's account has been well rendered into English as *History of a Voyage to the Land of Brazil,* translated by Janet Whatley (Berkeley: University of California Press, 1990). Thevet's description exists as *The New Found Worlde or Antarctike: wherein is contained wonderful and strange things, as well of humaine creatures, as beastes, fishes . . . : garnished with many learned authorities* (London: 1568).

2. The English version, edited by Richard F. Burton and translated from the German by Albert Tootal, was published in London by the Hakluyt Society, 1874.

these I would cite, from the nineteenth century, Arthur Heulhard's *Villegagnon*[3] and the works of Ch.-A. Julien on the colonization of the Americas,[4] and, from more recent times, the works of Jean-Paul Duviols[5] and Philippe Bonnichon.[6] Jean-Marie Touratier, for his part, has gone beyond the limits of fiction in his wonderful novel *Bois-rouge,*[7] at the same time as he hews closely to historical and ethnographic sources (notably in the Tupi-language dialogues).

Where the literary and the historical intersect, a special place must be reserved for the exceptional work of the French historian Frank Lestringant. A specialist of the literature of the sixteenth century, Lestringant has applied his extraordinary erudition to the difficult subject of religious debate in the New World. His *Le huguenot et le sauvage: L'Amérique et la controverse coloniale, en France, aux temps des guerres de religion,*[8] *Une sainte horreur ou le voyage en Eucharistie, XVIè–XVIIIè,*[9] and *Le cannibale, grandeur et décadence*[10] are indispensable texts for anyone wishing to understand the thinking of this complex and fertile period. Lestringant juxtaposes, compares, and explains in a luminous and innovative fashion. The character of Villegagnon has, thanks to his work, gained in complexity and truth. Far from being, as the militants of the two camps would have had it, either a renegade Protestant or a victim of the Huguenots, Villegagnon was a mediator for whom reform was primarily an ideal close

3. *Villegagnon, roi d'Amérique* (Paris: Presses Universitaires de France, 1948).

4. *Les Voyages de découverte et les premiers établissements* (Paris: Presses Universitaires de France, 1948) and *Les Français en Amérique pendant la première moitié du XVIe siècle* (Paris: Presses Universitaires de France, 1946).

5. *Voyageurs français en Amérique: colonies espagnoles et portugaises* (Paris: Ed. Bordas, 1978).

6. *Des Cannibales aux castors: les découvertes françaises de l'Amérique, 1503–1788* (Paris: Ed. France-Empire, 1994).

7. Paris: Galilée, 1993.

8. Paris: Aux amateurs de livres, Diffusion Klincksieck, 1990.

9. Paris: Presses Universitaires de France, 1996.

10. Paris: Ed. Perrin, 1994. Published in English as *Cannibals: The Discovery and Representation of the Cannibal from Columbus to Jules Verne,* translated by Rosemary Morris (Berkeley: University of California Press, 1997).

to humanism, a return to the simple faith of early times. And it was in him that there appeared the fracture that was later to break the whole of France and the whole of the century and pit two irreconcilable clerical factions against each other. I should also say that to the joys of understanding, Frank Lestringant adds the pleasures of reading, for his works, while conforming to the rigorous discipline of scientific writing, are all magnificently written.

The great abundance of works on these subjects had a frustrating and paralyzing effect on me: Frustrating because none of the approaches, despite their quality, corresponded to how I had represented these events in my imagination. None fulfilled my desire to tell the story in my own way, resonating with my own life, ideas, and dreams, and weaving in the necessary links to the present day. And paralyzing because such a profusion of events, heroes, and books soon proved more of a hindrance than a help. What for the historian is an end in itself—the description of facts—is for the novelist only the beginning: he must move from the theme to the plot, from general events to particular actions. For that he needs air, space, and, in short, a bit of the unknown. And, above all, some emotion.

In this story filled with politics, adventure, and theology, and peopled with warriors, fanatics, and smugglers, I despaired of ever finding the shiver of an affect, and for a long time I set it aside. One should always impose such a period of reflection on oneself, after which one sees more clearly. It was after a hiatus of several years that I once again opened Léry's account and came across these lines: "In the other ship, called *Rosée*, from the name of its captain, there were about ninety people, including six young boys, whom we took along to learn the language of the savages."

These six children, torn from their orphanage to serve as interpreters in the midst of Indian tribes, suddenly transported me from the aseptic precincts of history and the abstractions of politics and religion. They brought in life—their own, of course, but also mine and that of every human being—for what great drama awaits childhood's end if not the forced embarkation toward a terrifying world whose language one is called upon to learn?

Just and Colombe were born, and with them *Brazil Red*.

The inspiration for their name, Clamorgan, came to me from Emmanuelle de Boysson, whom I thank. In her book *Le cardinal et l'hindouiste,*[11] she brings this illustrious family to life in the person of Madeleine de Clamorgan, her great-grandmother, who founded the Sainte-Marie schools. Her family has little connection to the facts related in this story, clearly, yet the now-rare and beautiful name struck me as wonderfully evocative of the tradition of these families, illustrious since the Middle Ages, that threw themselves passionately into the wars of Italy, and whose traces appear and disappear in the founding of the societies of the New World.

Finally, for their attentive reading of the manuscript and their advice, I would like to thank my son Maurice, Mme Paule Lapeyre, Jean-Marie Milou, and Willard Wood.

J.-Ch. R.

11. Paris: Albin Michel, 1999.